Edge of the Precipice

Book 1 of the Precipice Series

Edge of the Precipice

Book 1 of the Precipice Series

Charlie Mike Adkins

Edge of the Precipice

Book 1 of the Precipice Series

by Charlie Mike Adkins

Copyright © 2024 Charlie Mike Adkins

ISBN 978-1-956904-37-6

Printed in the United States of America

Published by Blacksmith Publishing LLC
Fayetteville, North Carolina

www.BlacksmithPublishing.com

Direct inquiries and/or orders to the above web address.

Acknowledgements

First, I want to thank all those who read the first edition. Your feedback helped me buff out the scratches, leading to this re-release.

My daughters, Michaela and Kinley Shae, provide me with motivation, inspiration and constant challenges.

My friends Shawn Robertson and Shawn Christian provided input, conversation and comic relief. They kept pushing me and helped me wargame ideas, ultimately influencing numerous aspects of the book. They are both big parts of my life and are always there to be a friend, talk trash and send me stupid memes.

Dolores Adkins joined the team for the re-release as the final editor. Her attention to detail is amazing and I can't overstate how much her input helped me. The book is better because of her efforts. More importantly, my life is better because she's in it.

I would also like to thank my friend Jeremy Drake. Jeremy consistently offered sage counsel on the content of the book and the development of the cover. One of his ideas led to the title of the book and ultimately, the series.

Thanks to Dr. Charley "Chuck" Maxwell. He's my longtime friend, teammate, fellow Green Beret, confidant and my brother who fought side by side with me in Afghanistan. His insight, and reviews of medical scenarios were invaluable in maintaining accuracy and realism.

To Green Berets, Drew Souby, and Paul LeFavor. They've both been an inspiration to me at dramatically different times in my life. However, they both left an indelible, positive mark on my life, and I'm proud to count them as my friends. Not to mention, they've provided me with some great material for my characters!

My Robin Sage Family has been a huge part of my life for many years now. It's hard to explain to those who haven't experienced it, but at Robin Sage, we became a family. I hope that these pages bring back as many good memories for you as they have for me.

The cover art was created by Rochelle Bolima.

This book is intended as entertainment. However, I hope that some part of this book or one of the following books in the series will help you in some way. We live in uncertain times. I've found the daily headlines are often more unbelievable than works of fiction. Plan accordingly.

Contents

1

What's Cookin, Good Lookin'?

Morning, May 19th, 2022

Charles and Edna Michaels' farm, Lawrence County, KY

The year was 2022. Inflation was rising at a rate never seen in American history. The United States government was creating money from thin air. A war was raging in Ukraine. Fossil fuel production in the United States had been dramatically decreased due to recent policy changes by the current administration. Americans were experiencing unprecedented interruptions in the supply chain. The average citizen was becoming accustomed to finding things out of stock. In the past, Americans were blessed with an abundance of products and resources readily available at their fingertips. Now, it was not uncommon for the average citizen to be unable to find certain products, foods, or supplies that had been readily available just a couple of years ago.

"Can you believe that gas is four and a half dollars a gallon right now?" Edna Michaels said to her husband of over thirty-nine years. Charles Michaels was just returning from working in the barn. "I know sweetheart, diesel is over five bucks right now. I just dumped five gallons into the old tractor, and I couldn't help but think of the cost as I did it. I can remember when I could fill that tractor *up* for five bucks."

"I know Honey, but what can we do about it?" replied Edna.

"I heard that there are hundreds or maybe even thousands of container ships stuck out in the ocean, waiting to deliver imports from all over the world, and I've been seeing empty shelves in the grocery store," commented Edna. "It's not like the store is empty, but certain products will be out of stock for an unusually long time. I was trying to find that Breakfast Blend coffee that you like. I checked two or three different times at the store in Blaine, and it was always out of stock. I was finally able to find some up at the Walmart on 23. But normally I don't have to go that far. It's just little things like that. It's just not normal," she added.

"Oh, believe me, I know," he responded. "I've been trying to get a part for the brush hog for over four months now. Finally, I just went down to the machine shop in Ashland and had them fabricate the part for me. That only took two days. Apparently, I should have just done that to begin with. They even painted it green to match the tractor!" he added with a smile.

Restrictions had been put in place in response to the worldwide outbreak of COVID-19 that had a cascading effect, including the restriction of shipments coming into the United States from other countries. This problem was compounded by the labor shortage as many Americans chose to receive a government check rather than return to work. The resulting effect was a backup of container ships waiting to enter ports all around the United States. This backup was compounded by the increase in fuel prices in the country, causing an increase in the delivery fees of everything from diapers to vehicles. The president had initially stated that the inflation was transitory and would not last. However, as the inflation continued to rise, the average citizen could not help but notice that the US dollar was worth less and less every day. Americans from all walks of life, in different economic classes, were feeling the squeeze of the weakening dollar. Two years ago, a dozen eggs could often be found for $0.79. Now, a dozen eggs cost over two dollars. A new avian flu, called H5N1, suspected of originating in China, was affecting the bird population in the country. Commercial chicken farmers were being forced to exterminate millions of chickens, turkeys, and ducks in an effort to prevent the spread of this new virus strain. This reduction of poultry resulted in an increase in the price of chicken and eggs countrywide.

As this was occurring, wild birds were picking up the virus and spreading it across the country. The United States Department of Agriculture and other organizations were scrambling to find a solution, but the virus continued to spread.

The cost of beef and pork was climbing as well. During the COVID-19 lockdowns of 2020 and 2021 many meat processing plants were forced to shut down. This left many farmers with nowhere to send their cattle or pigs for processing. The simultaneous labor shortage compounded the problem, resulting in many farmers choosing to cull their herds to reduce the cost of maintaining the animals. Additionally, they were unsure of the future of the meat market. These factors combined to create an imbalance of supply and demand. This imbalance led to continually rising prices of meat in the grocery stores, with a corresponding reduction in variety and quantity.

Charles pulled his weathered John Deere hat off his head and mopped his forehead with a battered old red handkerchief. He had accidentally splashed a little battery acid on this handkerchief a couple years ago resulting in several holes in the cotton fabric, but it was soft, and it was still one of his favorite handkerchiefs to carry. "But don't you worry, Honey. We'll be fine. We'll just have to figure out how to cut a few corners here and there. We have our crops, we have our animals, and we have each other." He paused as he returned the handkerchief to his pocket. "We'll be fine," he repeated.

Edna reached into the cabinet and pulled out a Mason jar with a handle on it. She sat it on the counter and retrieved a full ice tray from the freezer. She dropped three ice cubes into the jar and returned the ice tray to the freezer. Charles liked three ice cubes in his tea. Not two, not four, three. As she began to pour iced tea from an old Tupperware pitcher with a red top on it, she spoke again. "I know we'll be fine. But I worry about everyone else. At this point, I'm worried about the whole country. I worry about Paul and Scott. I'm just scared in general. I don't see how it's going to get any better." She handed Charles the Mason jar of sweet tea.

Two years earlier, Charles had been in a local farmer's market and a mother and daughter were selling handmade crafts next to the fresh fruit and vegetables. Charles had spotted a small, hand painted sign with a depiction of a Mason jar below the words "Everything is better in a Mason Jar." That little sign now hung from a piece of twine next to the cabinet.

Charles dragged the cold jar across his forehead before taking a sip and sitting it on the table. He pulled out his handkerchief again to wipe his forehead. "Honestly Honey, I don't expect it will get better. We just have to play it smart. Maybe we can hold back a little more of the crops this year than normal to can for ourselves. I'll bet we're in better shape than 90% of this country. Our cellar and pantry stay full, our little orchard produces fruit every year, and you do one heck of a job with your canning. Not to mention all the backup canned goods we have. Plus, I'll bet we have 500 pounds of rice sealed up and probably nearly the same of dried beans. Even if things get tight, we aren't going to be hungry."

He paused as he took a sip from the Mason jar. "As long as I continue to keep my chickens protected, they should be safe from that new bird flu, so we'll have chicken & eggs. I added a chicken wire roof to the yard in front of the chicken house. That should keep out any other birds that might spread the infection to them. Now that means that they can't free roam the yard like they normally do, and I'll have to supplement their food a little to make up for it. But that's fine."

She chimed in. "Don't forget the rabbits."

"Oh yeah," he agreed. "The rabbits are producing meat faster than the chickens, and if things get too tough, we can always eat Billie and Bucky."

Edna snatched the dishtowel off her shoulder and slapped Charles across the back with it. "You will not talk about eating my goats, Mister!"

Charles acted as if he had been hit with a baseball bat. "Okay, okay. We won't eat our all-natural lawnmowers. But don't worry Sugar, I won't let you go hungry."

"Oh, you won't let *me* go hungry, huh? If it weren't for me, you'd starve to death." She turned her back to her husband and moved back to the sink where she was running warm water for the dishes. She mumbled under her breath "You won't let *me* go hungry? You can't even boil water."

"What's that, Honey?" Charles asked.

"I just said that there is more tea in the fridge if you want some, Dear," she responded with a grin as she picked up her sponge and began washing the dishes in the sink. "Oh, by the way, the pantry is getting low on black eyed peas."

"Okay, I'll grab a case from the bunker and fill it back up for you."

Their two sons had started referring to the cellar as a "bunker" years ago because teenage boys are amused by such things. It eventually became the accepted moniker for the cellar.

Their house was not big, but it did have a good floorplan. The outside was traditional white siding and ten years ago, they had sprung for a new hunter green steel roof. Charles had opted to go ahead and install new aluminum gutters at the time as well. On one corner of the house, the gutter directed the water through a simple screen filter and into a rain collection barrel. The barrel was molded plastic and designed to resemble an old whiskey barrel. It had an overflow pipe running discretely out the back so that if it got too full, the excess would flow out a pipe to be diffused into the yard. At the bottom was a simple spigot to access the water. Edna used the water for watering her small flower bed that lined the side of the house facing the road.

Inside the house, it was a mixture of the original construction from 1976 and various improvements that they had done over the years. The floor in most of the house was the original narrow plank oak. The old hardwood showed its age and Edna had hidden some of the worse areas with the strategic use of tasteful rugs. The kitchen and bathroom floors had originally been a horrific green linoleum in the typical pattern of the 1970's. Charles and Edna had moved into the single story in 1988 and the linoleum already had several tears and holes in it. The first major improvement Charles had done was a new kitchen and bathroom floor of off-white ceramic tiles. Decades later, the tile was still there, although there were a couple tiles with cracks in them from abuse. At one point, Edna had dropped a large cast iron skillet after washing it. It struck the tile in front of the sink, cracking the tile and creating a noticeable chip. Now, a thick "anti-fatigue" mat covered the damage, hiding it from visitors.

The original pantry in the house didn't hold a lot, and it was full of other items that didn't necessarily belong in a pantry. Oftentimes, when Edna couldn't find a good place to store something, the pantry had become its new home.

Edna canned and her jars of canned food always occupied a significant portion of the pantry. Of course, they also used plenty of store-bought food, but in the past, they hadn't kept much of it on hand. When they got low on something, they would buy it on the next grocery run. That always seemed to be sufficient, but that was before their son had convinced them that it wasn't.

Several years ago, their oldest son, Paul, was explaining the need to prepare for emergencies. He had made a list for them of things that they should stock up on. At first, they just thanked him, and Edna put the list in a drawer. "I'll read it later," she had thought to herself, but she never got around to it. Then, in early 2020, when Charles and Edna started noticing changes in the country, their opinions changed. That's when COVID started to affect the global supply chain. Edna had gone back to the drawer to look for the list, but she couldn't find it. *It must have gotten thrown away*, she thought to herself, although she didn't specifically remember throwing it away.

That night, Edna had called her son and asked him if he would resend the list. He was working out of town on some security thing, but he had his computer with him, and he'd emailed her another copy. Edna didn't really like reading things on the computer, so she had opened the document and just hit "Print."

She was surprised when she went to the printer and found that the document was ten pages long. He had definitely updated this list since he had given them the first one. She remembered that the first one he had given her was only three or four pages. She took the stack of papers to the kitchen table, sat down, and started looking over it. The document had a few paragraphs dedicated to different areas of preparation. The first section was called "Financial." This section was short. It was really just a list of general statements:

FINANCIAL

Eliminate unsecured debt. For most Americans this is credit card bills.

Minimize secure debt. This is your home and vehicles.
Diversify your savings, if possible
Keep some cash on hand; a mixture of bills.
In the initial part of any emergency, cash will still have value as long as others believe it does.
Maintain miscellaneous gold and silver. If nothing ever goes wrong, precious metals are easily redeemed and are simply part of your diversified savings/retirement portfolio.
Gold advantages: You can carry a lot of value in a small package. Universally recognized value
Gold disadvantages: Due to the high value, it's a higher investment to acquire. Additionally, it's difficult to use as currency or barter except for other high value items.
Silver advantages: Lower value makes it more suitable for general-use currency or as a barter item. This also makes it easier to start stocking up on.
Silver disadvantage: Requires more volume of silver for high value items.
Additional note on silver: Junk silver (Pre-65 coins) may be more recognizable to the less informed and is an inexpensive investment.

The next paragraph was titled "SECURITY." It talked about "Hardening your home" and having a plan for defending your position. Edna wasn't even sure what hardening your home meant and she didn't ever expect to need to defend the farm, so she skimmed the pages, looking at the other section headings, which were in bold letters.

FIREARMS & AMMUNITION, MEDICAL, COMMUNICATIONS, FOOD, WATER, HYGIENE AND SANITATION, EXPENDABLES, POWER, and SUMMARY

She went back to the section titled FOOD. This was the largest section of the document. The FOOD section was divided into three additional subsections: Short Term, Long Term and Sustainable Food. The first paragraph read:

SHORT TERM

The short-term food prep is probably the easiest, so this is usually how most preppers get started. The idea here is to have enough food to weather your average 30-day emergency or supply chain issue. Figure out how much of your shelf stable food you go through in a month and keep at least that much on hand. If you know your family typically eats 5 cans of green beans per month, then 5 cans should be the minimum in your cabinet. When you get down to 5 cans, you need to buy more. Rotate your stock. When you buy new cans, put them behind the older ones on the shelf and it creates a natural rotation without much effort.

She had read that paragraph thinking that it was similar to what she and Charles were already doing, but it was a more organized approach. She took a few minutes to read the rest of the section on food preps. The section labeled "**LONG TERM**" discussed shelf-life considerations, rice, beans, prepackaged survival food, and even had a couple sentences on the military "Meal, Ready to Eat" or M.R.E.s. Of course Paul was going to put that in there, considering his background.

The last section was "**SUSTAINABLE FOOD.**" Oddly enough, they were already doing most of the stuff outlined in this part. They lived on a functioning farm. They had crops, livestock, and they canned their own harvest. Edna smiled as she read. *He learned this part from us,* she had thought.

The only part she saw in the food section that she wasn't familiar with was the reference to a home freeze dryer. She knew that Paul had invested in a home freeze dryer, but she simply didn't see the need in it. It was way too expensive.

Besides, she knew how to can most of the things they grew, so why would she even consider such an expense?

Paul had given them a box of freeze-dried meals for Christmas last year. He had freeze dried and packaged the meals himself. It all looked very professional to Edna. Paul had packaged the meals in these packets that looked like aluminum foil, but he called them something else, she couldn't remember what it was called. Each packet was two servings, enough for her and Charles in one pouch. On the outside of the packet was a neatly printed label describing the contents and exactly how much hot water to use to reconstitute it.

The labels showed contents like "Spaghetti with Meat Sauce" and "Breakfast scramble with sausage." Other items were simpler, like "Eggs, Scrambled & Cooked" and "Hamburger, Beef, Cooked." Edna had smiled when she read the military-style descriptions on the bags.

She had glanced over some of the other sections as well, but she didn't see the need for most of this other stuff. The section on "COMMUNICATION" didn't really seem necessary. Radios and secure email accounts? No, she wasn't interested in that stuff. Besides, weren't all email accounts secure? However, the food storage made sense to her. She had decided that day that she was going to get more serious about stocking up on food for an emergency. If nothing else, it would lessen the impacts of these "Supply Chain Issues" that she kept hearing about.

That next morning at breakfast, she had brought up the subject with Charles.

"Honey, Paul sent us another copy of that prepping list he made, and he's updated it quite a bit."

"Oh, is that right?" Charles responded and took a sip of his coffee.

"Yeah. I read some of it last night. I kinda like the idea of stocking up on some extra stuff. I'm not talking about anything crazy, but it would just make me feel better if we had more of a buffer. You know, just for emergencies."

Charles was putting a bite of sausage in his mouth. He nodded his head slowly as he chewed. He swallowed and dabbed the corner of his mouth with a paper napkin before he spoke. "I don't have a problem with that, Babe. What are you thinking?"

"Well," she began. "First things first, you're going to need to straighten up the bunker," she said with a slight smile, looking at him over her coffee cup.

He sat his fork on the table and put his hand on his chest in mock insult. "What do you mean? That bunker is a well-oiled machine!"

"That place is a cluttered mess. Half the time you can't find what you're looking for and you should be ashamed of that sorry excuse for a shelf. You know you wouldn't accept something like that in your precious barn."

Charles smiled back at her and picked up his coffee cup. "OK, that's fair. I tell you what, this week, I'll make it a point to get in there and clear things out. Plus, I wouldn't mind having a good set of shelves in there. How much room are you thinking that you'll need? "

"I don't know. I think maybe I'd like to at least have a case of every kind of vegetable that we like. Plus, it would be nice if we had some mouse-proof storage down there too. I could use that for the stuff that's not in cans, like pasta or beans or rice" she replied. "Oh, and maybe some flour and sugar." She paused for a moment and thought about that last statement. "Actually, I think I want to put the flour and sugar in the house, but I'd still like to have some dry, mouse-proof storage in the cellar."

"Hmm. I think I could do that. I tell you what," he said as he leaned in closer to his wife. "How about I pick up some of those big black and yellow totes like I have in the barn? I'll measure them and build the shelves to fit those."

"Oh, you know what else I'd like to stock up on?" She continued, without waiting for her husband to respond. "Spices. We could put extra spices down there, like salt and garlic powder and onion powder. Oh, and that bullion powder that I use. I use that a lot."

"Okay, okay. I get it. So, is that a 'yes' to the totes?" He smiled. "You sound like you're getting excited about this."

"Yes. Get the totes. I *am* a little excited. This sounds like it could actually be fun."

And with that statement, Charles and Edna Michaels became preppers. That was two years ago and since that time, they had been working to better prepare themselves for emergencies. They would often speak to Paul about it and he would offer useful suggestions.

Last year, Charles decided he was going to improve the food storage situation in the house. He had taken out the back wall of the pantry. The spare bedroom lost its closet and some square footage, but the pantry had nearly tripled in size. Charles completely gutted the newly created room, even pulling out the drywall. While the studs were exposed, he ran the wires for better lighting and added a motion detector switch, so that the lights would come on as soon as someone opened the door. Rather than replace the drywall, he installed tongue in groove white cedar planks on all the walls and finished them with a clear polyurethane. However, at the back, he only built a wall that was three feet wide on the right side. In the remainder of the space on the back wall, he installed a set of double doors that were accessible from the spare bedroom.

In front of the doors, he built a set of shelves that were three feet deep and included low dividers that kept the rows of cans and jars in neat rows. When they wanted to add items to the shelves, they would take the supplies into the spare bedroom, open the double doors, and put the cans in from the back side of the shelving. This would push the older stuff forward, making it easy to continue with their habit of rotating the older stock.

On the three-foot section that was remaining on the back wall, Charles installed a full sized, upright freezer. On the front of the freezer, he put a hook with a strong magnet. This magnet held Edna's clipboard. She had a page for the store-bought food, a page for her canned foods, another page for the items in the freezer and finally, a page for anything that didn't fall neatly into the other categories.

The pantry was eight feet wide, and was now ten feet deep, six feet deeper than it had been originally. Edna joked that the project had gotten out of control, but she was very thankful for the added space and convenience. Along the left wall, Charles had added built-in beautiful poplar shelves. These shelves were about fourteen inches deep and held cooking oil and other bulky items like spare rolls of paper towels. He had built everything from scratch and had taken care to create a pantry that was not only functional, but beautiful.

The final touch was a set of cabinets on the right side. He built it as long as he could, without interfering with the opening of the freezer door at the back of the pantry. This cabinet was built like a traditional kitchen cabinet. The base cabinet had a countertop, like the one in the kitchen. Plus, there was an additional cabinet above that, mounted to the studs. This setup gave Edna some overflow for some things that she wanted to move out of her kitchen. She loaded it up with her larger pots, her canning supplies, and other kitchen tools that she didn't use all the time. The upper cabinets ended up being used for extra spices and other small items that didn't necessarily make sense in the big shelving unit.

The COVID hysteria had motivated Charles and Edna to work even harder on their preps. Now, the pantry was fully stocked and the bunker had a nice set of shelves. They weren't built of nice hardwood like the interior shelves were, but they were very functional. Charles had used two by fours and plywood to build a set of utilitarian shelves. There were several large plastic totes as well as cases of canned goods neatly arranged on the shelves. The front of the totes had a couple of strips of duct tape with handwritten lists of their contents. As Charles added or removed items, he would use a marker to cross out items or add more to the list. The marker hung from a piece of paracord tied to the front of the shelving unit.

Edna had focused primarily on the food preps. After all, she did all the cooking. At first, they hadn't used the term "preps." However, after numerous conversations with Paul, she had finally adopted the term, much like they adopted the term "bunker" for the cellar.

She wasn't as interested in the other aspects of prepping, but Charles was willing to give some of it a try.

During one of Paul's visits, Charles had engaged his son on the subject of communications. "So, I guess I don't really understand why you're recommending radios," Charles admitted to Paul.

"That's understandable Dad. But look at it this way: if the cell towers fail on you, your radios will still work. They don't need the towers. Plus, from the practical standpoint, Mama can use them to get ahold of you around the farm."

"Whoa, son. You had me until you added that part. I don't need your mama bothering me when I'm working," he replied with a grin.

"Okay, okay, Dad. Seriously though. What if you're out here on the farm and have an emergency? They're essentially souped-up walkie talkies."

Charles thought about it for a moment. "Look, I don't want to try to figure this out. I wouldn't even know what I was looking at. I'll get some, but I want you to just tell me what to buy. Fair enough?"

"Yessir. Fair enough. I'll write it down for you, but I use a radio called a Baofeng. They've been around for years, they work well, and they're cheap. For years they were only available up to five watts of power, but now they make a nice one that pushes eight watts. That's what my buddies and I are using right now." Paul replied.

"You just proved my point." Charles said. "I don't know what any of that means. I mean, I understand that eight watts are more powerful than five watts, but I'm gonna to need you to show me how to use them once they arrive."

"Of course, Dad. The model I use is called the BF-F8HP and it's not overly complicated. I have several of the older ones too, but I've relegated those to backups. But they work essentially the same. I'll make you a cheat sheet with instructions for setting the frequency and other things. I won't bore you with the details of it right now, but when they come in, I'll plan a visit and sit down with you and go over everything. You're going to want to go ahead and spring for the bigger batteries for it as well. They'll allow you to go longer between charges. But like I said, I'll write everything down for you."

"I have a better idea. How about you just order me what I'm gonna need, set them up, and tell me what it costs?" Charles said with a smile.

"That's fine, Dad. I'll take care of it," Paul said, smiling in surrender.

"Wait. About how much are we talking here?" Charles said, getting serious again.

"Don't worry, the radios are only about fifty bucks apiece. I can get you into everything for well under two hundred. That's two radios with spare batteries and everything. Each radio will come with its own charger, so you don't have to buy that separate. I do want to get you a car charger so you can charge them from the truck if you need to," Paul said.

"My side by side has one of those twelve-volt charger ports too," Charles added.

"That's great. I didn't know that," Paul said.

"Well, it didn't have one when I bought it. I added it because I wanted to be able to plug up my phone. They sell a little kit at AutoZone. I was in there buying the light bar for the side by side and saw it. It works great."

"Perfect," Paul replied. "Now, let's talk about your ammo supply."

"Boy, you just don't stop, do you?"

"Well, I figured while we're at it…" Paul said, smiling.

"Okay, okay, fine. Let's go look," Charles said, pushing back from the table.

Paul followed his father to the bedroom. Charles opened the closet, exposing a small black gun locker. He unlocked the locker and reached in, coming back out with his deer rifle. "I'm sure you remember this guy," he said as he opened the bolt on a Browning A-Bolt Hunter chambered in .270. He glanced into the chamber and handed the scoped rifle to his son.

"Of course, I remember this gun, Dad. I took my first deer with this rifle."

"Your brother took his first deer with it too." The pride was visible on Charles' face as he said it.

"You know, they don't make these anymore."

"I didn't know that," Charles responded. "That's too bad. That's a great rifle." He nodded his head toward the rifle in Paul's hand.

Paul looked inside the chamber, confirming it was empty. He flipped open the scope covers and turned away from his father. He threw the gun up to his shoulder and in smooth, practiced motion, pointed it toward the wall on other side of the room. He looked through the scope for a moment before bringing it back down. "This thing just feels right. That's even a classic scope, Dad."

"That thing has filled a lot of freezers, son."

"Yessir, it's hard telling how many deer you've taken with this thing over the years."

Charles turned back toward the gun locker and came back with another rifle. "This one too." He held a Marlin Model 336 chambered in 30-30 Winchester.

"Oh man, I haven't seen that one in a long time," Paul said as he placed the Browning on the bed.

Charles pushed the lever down and forward, opening the chamber. He repeated the motion of looking into the chamber to ensure it was clear and handed the little rifle to his elder son. "That thing's almost as old as you are. I never wanted to put a scope on that one. I like it just like it is."

"I love these lever guns," Paul said. He turned the gun on its side to quickly check the chamber. He closed the chamber and held the gun loose in front of him with the buttstock held on the inside of his right bicep. It was pointed at the floor in front on the closet. He slowly squeezed the trigger. The hammer released with an audible snap. Paul used his thumb to pull the hammer to the rear again. He dropped the hammer a second time. "That trigger's not too bad," he said, handing the gun back to his father. "How much 30-30 ammo do you have?"

Charles went back to the closet and sat the rifle back inside the gun locker. He looked at the shelf beside the locker. Paul could see him counting boxes. "Looks like I've got five full boxes, and one partial box. It's all 150 grain. That's what that gun likes."

Paul pursed his lips as if thinking, then asked, "What about .270?"

Charles turned and counted again. Without looking back from the closet, he said, "I have almost fifty rounds for the Browning, and before you ask," he was counting the other stacks on his ammunition shelf, "I have a few boxes of #6 for the shotgun, a partial box of double ought, a five-round box of 12-gauge slugs, two and a half bricks of .22, and almost two hundred rounds of .45 ACP for my pistol, plus the box of hollow points that you gave me."

"Is that everything?" Paul asked.

"More or less. I'm sure I have some more stashed is a drawer here or there, but yeah, that's the majority of it," Charles said. He picked up the Browning, closed the bolt, pointed it toward the outside wall, and pulled the trigger. He carefully closed the scope covers and placed the gun back in the locker, closing it and locking it.

"Okay, Dad. Well, it's good that you have that..." Paul paused.

"Buuuut..." Charles said, dragging out the word in anticipation of Paul's next sentence.

"Buuuut..." Paul said, mimicking his father. "I really think you should consider adding a little to your stockpile. You're in good shape as far as the guns are concerned. You have the two deer rifles, the Remington 870, a Ruger 10/22, and the 1911." He paused as he was thinking. "Didn't you have a .38 revolver too?"

"Oh yeah. The little Smith. I still have that," Charles replied.

"I didn't hear you say how much .38 Special you have."

"Yeah. I just have the one box. It's in the nightstand with the gun."

Paul reflexively looked toward the nightstand. *One box?* he thought to himself.

"Okay, well Dad, if you want, I can make some recommendations. They're going to reflect the recommendations on the document that I already sent y'all before, but I'll tailor the list to your guns. Obviously, you don't want to put yourself in a bind trying to buy ammo. It's expensive, so just add a little here and there when you can. What do you think?"

"Well, I think I have plenty of .270. Every year I check my zero at a hundred yards. As long as it's good, I hunt with it. I don't usually take more than three or four shots each year hunting, so I have several years' worth of ammo already," Charles said. He was not seeing this from the same perspective as Paul.

"I definitely see your point. I was just thinking that it would be nice to have a little extra in case you ever had to use it to defend the homestead for an extended period of time," Paul said, trying to find the right words to not sound too outrageous to his father. He immediately realized that he had failed to do so.

Charles chuckled. "You still think like a soldier, Paul. I appreciate your help. I'll get the radios, and I'll add a little ammo. But I can assure you that I will not be defending this place with my deer rifle. This is not Afghanistan and the

Russians ain't coming. If I need help, we'll call 911 and we'll have all the firepower that we need in just a few minutes. My .38 will hold us over long enough for the sheriff to arrive."

Paul thought of a saying that he had used in the past: "When seconds count, help is only minutes away."

"Yessir. On that note, we should go out behind the barn and do a little shooting before I have to leave tomorrow," Paul said in a rather cheery voice, trying to get the conversation back on track.

"I like that idea," Charles stated. "What pistol do you have with you?"

"I thought we might have a little time to shoot, so I brought my full-sized Kimber. That way we can both shoot 1911s. It'll be fun. I brought a couple hundred rounds of .45 ACP that I loaded. Lets' save your ammo. I loaded up some 230 grain solid lead bullets. Just the way that Saint John Moses Browning intended." He laughed as he delivered the line that he had used many times. Charles didn't get it. "We should break out your 10/22 while we're at it. I just so happen to have some .22 ammo with me too," Paul added, glancing over his shoulder.

Charles started toward the door and Paul turned to stay in front of him. Paul exited the room and a wonderful smell hit his nose. "Man, something smells good," Paul said as they walked into the kitchen.

"Yes, it does!" Charles added, turning toward his wife. "What's cookin', good lookin'?"

2

The Citizens Would Pay for It

Almost a year and a half earlier, January 20, 2021

White House, Washington, D.C.

Newly inaugurated United States President Joe Biden made his way toward the Oval Office surrounded by an entourage following the inauguration ceremony. The next task of the day was to sign a stack of seventeen documents that were already prepared and waiting for him. Among the orders was a document called the *Proclamation on the Termination of Emergency With Respect to the Southern Border of the United States and Redirection of Funds Diverted to Border Wall Construction.* Among other things, this document halted the construction of the border protection wall on the southern border of the United States that was initiated by then-President Trump.

The Democratic National Committee had mounted a huge, coordinated effort opposing the wall. The wall had been part of a larger initiative to reduce the flow of illegal immigrants into the United States from the south. Border security was a big part of Trump's campaign, and after he was elected, the Democrats had pulled out all the stops to interfere with the construction. The Democratic members of congress worked together to block every effort to secure the southern border. This was a favorite topic of discussion for talk radio. The conversation would typically go something like this:

> Host #1: "Why are members of Congress, who are sworn to uphold the Constitution and the laws of the country, trying so hard to prevent the law from being enforced? Immigration is governed by laws. I don't have a problem with immigrants. Hell, my grandmother was an immigrant. But she obeyed the law, worked hard and became an American citizen…in accordance with the law!"

> Host #2: "Look Tom, you just have to understand that there is an end game here. Where are most of these illegals going? I'll tell you where they're going. They're going to the liberal strongholds, especially Democratic run sanctuary cities."

> Host #1: "Okay, but how does that help the Democrats?"

And the conversation would go on with both hosts giving their opinions and offering up ideas for fixing the problem. They would cite statistics and point out that criminals were coming into the country. They would highlight the drug problem, the human trafficking problem, or the threat of terrorists using the southern border to gain access to the country. However, the conversation would typically return to the common question: Why?

On January 20th, 2021, President Joe Biden's second executive order was Presidential Executive Order 13986 *Ensuring a Lawful and Accurate Enumeration and Apportionment Pursuant to the Decennial Census*. With the stroke of a pen, the order required that non-citizens, both legal and illegal, be counted in the 2020 census. That number would be used in not just in calculating population, but also in determining congressional apportionment. That meant more seats in the House of Representatives for the Democratic areas. The conspiracy theorists and radio hosts who claimed that this was a goal were instantly proven correct.

Also included in the stack of executive orders was an agreement to rejoin the Paris climate accord. This was a legally binding agreement between numerous nations designed to reduce climate change by limiting the use of fossil fuels. Also included was EO 13992. This would give the President more power and flexibilities with his future executive order. His advisors had a stack of Trump administration executive orders that needed to be struck down and this was going to help him do so. The newly elected president didn't have the time or energy to look into these orders, but his advisors had assured him that this was necessary, so it must be true.

As he picked up the ceremonial ink pens and waited for the cameras to be ready, Mr. Biden turned to one of his numerous advisors and asked, "What does this one do?" LaShawnda Williams, an advisor who had been assigned to help guide the president when cameras were present, looked down at the waiting executive order and responded. "Sir, this is EO 13990, the one that I was telling you about that is going to help save the environment. Trump obviously didn't care about the damage being done to the earth and how it would affect our future generations. With your signature Sir, you will be directly responsible for saving the world."

"Great," responded the forty-sixth President of the United States. "I've been looking forward to signing this."

"Yessir," Ms. Williams said evenly. "Right there on that line Sir."

"Great. That's just great," the President mumbled and put the pen to the paper. With that signature, on his first day in office,

Joe Biden canceled the TransCanada Keystone XL Pipeline. TransCanada had already spent billions of dollars in the construction of a pipeline that would allow liquid petroleum to be moved safely across the border from Canada into the United States. The pipeline was nearing completion and was struck dead in the water by EO 13990, Section 6. The Executive Order stated that "...analysis further concluded that approval of the proposed pipeline would undermine U.S. climate leadership by undercutting the credibility and influence of the United States in urging other countries to take ambitious climate action." There it was in black and white. The new administration was happy to cut off a major avenue of oil to the U.S. just to look better in front of the international climate change community.

Estimates vary, but the cancellation of the Keystone pipeline likely resulted in the loss of thousands of U.S. jobs and billions of dollars in economic growth, not to mention the impact on American energy independence. TransCanada had begun the enormous construction project and had proceeded in good faith that the United States government would honor the agreements, licensing, and permits that were in place. The U.S. government did, until Joe Biden took office. Then it didn't, and TransCanada was left with a multibillion-dollar investment that would never earn them a penny in return.

However, the Keystone XL was just one aspect of the overt attack on fossil fuels. It was a lengthy Executive Order and did more than just stop one pipeline. It reversed more than 100 Trump administration actions on the environment. The resulting impact on fuel availability and the economy of the United States would follow almost immediately. Gasoline prices across the country varied state to state but were typically no more than two dollars a gallon at the time. Within two months those prices would begin to steadily climb as the market adjusted to the new restrictions. Additional actions would further exacerbate the fuel shortage, resulting in a corresponding increase in fuel prices across the country. By May of 2022, gas prices would be approximately double, and the average American citizen would regularly be paying more than four dollars a gallon for regular unleaded gasoline.

Likewise, diesel continued to climb in price. This increase in diesel fuel costs directly affected the delivery cost of nearly all consumer products in the country. Trucking companies were forced to increase the price of delivery in an effort to cover their increasing fuel costs. This additional cost was passed on to their customers, resulting in an overall increase in the cost of nearly every product in the United States.

The presidential advisers and handlers told the president that his actions would help reduce greenhouse gas emissions within the United States. However, in actuality, Americans continued to burn gasoline and diesel, but it was now being imported and cost more. The revenue that was formerly paying American companies, with American jobs was now going overseas, much of it to countries that viewed the United States as an enemy.

If there was any reduction in the use of gasoline, it was a direct result of the inability of Americans to afford the higher prices being imposed on them. They were forced to choose between gasoline and other products that they were accustomed to having in a flourishing society. The cost of living increased, and the quality of life began to decline. Lower income workers began to calculate what it would cost them to drive to work versus what they would make that day in wages. Some found that it was not worth the expense or effort to go to work. The country was already facing a labor shortage due to restrictions during the Covid-19 outbreak. The national economic situation began to steadily deteriorate.

In addition to fuel costs, Americans were about to be hit with runaway inflation. The government was "creating" U.S. Dollars at an unprecedented rate. These dollars were not backed by gold or silver, contrary to the U.S. Constitution, Article I, Section 10, Clause 1. The U.S. Dollar had become a fiat money. It was only valuable because the U.S. Government said it was valuable. Generally speaking, for many years, the other world governments agreed. However, as the U.S. government created more and more U.S. Dollars, this influx of currency diluted the value of the dollars already in circulations and other countries took note of this weakness. This resulted in numerous countries abandoning the use of the U.S. Dollar for international oil purchases. This fueled the growing concern for the stability of the U.S. Dollar.

In January 2021, when President Biden assumed control of the White House, the U.S. inflation rate was hovering around 1.4%. The new administration began to immediately implement new policies, and the American people began paying for it, quite literally. Within a year and a half, inflation would be over 9%. The White House Press Secretary would smile and tell everyone that everything was fine. The government would change the way it calculated inflation to downplay the negative effects of "Bidenomics." However, the citizens of the country could see the truth at the checkout counter, the gas pumps, and in their bank accounts. The number of Americans living below the poverty level would nearly double in Biden's first two years in office. The size of the middle class began to shrink.

The ultra rich were essentially unaffected by the inflation. Most of them rarely used or even needed cash. Their wealth was in assets, and therefore essentially protected from inflation. If they had a $1,000,000 home and the value of the dollar decreased by half, they now had a $1,500,000 home. However, the everyday citizen was not so lucky. The average American had a mortgage, at least one car payment, and countless other bills. Their money was not tied to assets. Their money was tied to a payday, and they were often counting down the days to the next one in order to pay a bill or buy something their child needed. Many Americans resorted to using credit cards every time they ran short of cash before payday. For some, this was every month and the credit card balances just kept climbing.

The resulting increase in credit card use, without an increase in income, made it nearly impossible for some families to reverse the cycle. Countless families lost their homes and there was a corresponding explosion in the homeless population. Some states with higher taxes saw a dramatic increase in homelessness. In numerous urban areas, homeless camps became the norm. By 2022, America had entered an irreversible economic tailspin. Just like many other governments before them, the U.S. government was abusing its power and the citizens would pay for it.

3

I Need Another Beer

May 19, 2022

Watson Property, Lawrence County, KY

Billy Watson was in a bad mood. He was getting sent home early today because there wasn't enough work at the shop. There was a time, only a couple of years ago, when Billy had felt like he had finally made it. He was working in the coal mines making good money. He had bought a new $60,000 Chevy Silverado and life was good. His wife, Jenny, had quit her job as a waitress at the Bluegrass Café because he was making so much money that she did not feel like she needed to work anymore. Besides, even working forty to fifty hours a week she wasn't bringing home enough money to make much of a difference in their lives. When people asked her what she did, she said she was a homemaker. That description was reasonably accurate. While Billy worked, she took care of their 2,200 square-foot rented home and dreamed of the day when they would start adding babies to the spare bedrooms.

The home was a beautiful single-story brick ranch with an attached one and a half car garage. When they had initially looked at the home, Billy had made a smart aleck comment about owning two vehicles, not one and a half. However, it worked out. After he added a 6" lift to his truck, it was too tall to go into the garage anyhow. The garage became a place to keep Jenny's car, a spare refrigerator, and overflow storage from the house. Jenny called the extra refrigerator the "beer 'fridge" since Billy usually kept it stocked with a variety of expensive craft beers.

All of that changed back in September of last year when Billy and all his buddies at the coal mine got a notification of a meeting to be held after work one Friday. The meeting was unusual for two reasons. First, it was being held on a Friday afternoon. They *never* held meetings on Friday afternoons. Secondly everyone was required to be there. *Everyone*. Everything in the mine had to shut down to allow for 100% of the employees to be there. This included heavy machine operators, the office staff, the miners, and even the safety staff, everyone. This was a first.

Jake "Buddy" Williams was standing on a loading dock of one of the main buildings of the compound. Billy was just pushing his way into the parking lot as he heard Buddy call for everyone to simmer down. All the vehicles had been removed the area to allow everyone to crowd around the loading dock. Buddy cleared his throat.

"Everybody, please quiet down and listen up. I know it's hot out here, so I'm going to keep this short and to the point. I've been in meetings for the last two days with all the bigwigs up at Appalachian Coal headquarters. There's a lot going on right now, and it ain't good. The federal government has placed new restrictions on the coal burning power plants regarding their emissions. The new restrictions demand a reduction of emissions that is unattainable based on the current configurations of the plants."

He paused, drawing in a deep breath. "The bottom line is that they could build a new plant for less money than it would take them to retrofit the existing power plants to meet the new government "green" requirements." Buddy used two fingers of each hand to make air quotes as he said the word "green" with a sarcastic tone.

The employees began talking in low tones amongst themselves as they immediately began to understand the implication of this meeting. Buddy paused again. He had a disposable bottle of water in his right hand that Billy hadn't noticed. Buddy took the lid off and took a quick sip before replacing the lid. It struck Billy that Buddy looked more uncomfortable than he had ever seen him. Buddy held the water bottle in front of his sternum with his left hand grasping the top of the bottle. It was an unconscious effort to protect himself as he prepared to pass information that he knew would not be well received.

He took another deep breath and continued. "Okay, okay. Listen up. I said I was going to keep this short, and I'm trying to do that. After an unknown amount of negotiations, dueling lawyers, threats, and promises, the Board of Directors up at Ohio Valley Electric have come to a decision. Two of the three power plants that we provide coal for will be shutting down within the next month. Essentially, this new environmental push from the government is regulating the power plants out of existence."

"So, who's going to take up the slack for the reduction in power?" yelled a man from the back of the crowd.

"Cut to the chase Buddy, what's this mean to us?" another man called out.

Buddy raised both his hands in the air with his palms facing toward the crowd and asked everyone to calm down, be quiet, and listen. His tone changed. As he began speaking again, he assumed a quieter, calmer voice, but still loud enough for those in the back to hear him. "Guys, there's no easy way to say this. The plants are shutting down in four weeks. They don't need our coal. This mine and three other mines controlled by

Appalachian Coal will be shutting down in two weeks. I'm sorry boys, but this is your two-week notice."

The crowd of men erupted in shouts of anger.

"How are we supposed to feed our families?" yelled one man.

"You can't do this!" yelled another.

Billy didn't yell. He just stood there in the hot September sun, stunned.

Now, just eight months after that meeting, the truck was gone, and they had gotten out of the lease for the big house. Jenny had gone back to the Bluegrass Café, where they were happy to have her. She was a good worker, and many businesses in the area were having difficulty keeping their staffs full. Although it wasn't a high-paying job, it was steady, and her boss wasn't terrible. Billy had taken up doing odd jobs in the area. He was mowing grass and helping maintain the fences and barn on a local horse farm.

A couple of months ago he saw a "Help Wanted" sign in the window of a local garage. They specialized in general maintenance such as oil changes and brake jobs, although they also did a few services that were more complex. He did not have formal training as a mechanic; however, he had maintained his own vehicles for years and was hired on at the garage for some of the simpler tasks. He learned how to use the tire balancing machine and had taken the lead conducting most of the tire balancing and rotation services. He could still be called upon for oil changes and other services as well, although he wasn't ready for the more complex jobs like alignments or *anything* to do with the computers. It seemed like you needed a computer programming degree to work on these new cars. To Billy, everything seemed unnecessarily complex on the newer cars. Even with a tire repair, one of the other guys had to take over after he fixed the tire to reprogram the Tire Pressure Monitoring System.

"People are stupid," he had said to Cameron, one of the younger guys working at the shop, not long after getting hired. Cameron was several years younger than Billy, but he had gone to Vo-Tech in high school to study auto maintenance.

"Why is that?" Cameron replied without looking up from the computer screen.

"How hard is it to just check your freakin' air pressure in your tires? People are so stupid now, that they have to have a computer to tell them what their tire pressure is," Billy said.

Cameron continued to work, but glanced up at Billy briefly. "Didn't that fancy truck that you sold have TPMS?"

Billy's face flushed red. "Of course it did!" He almost spat the words. "But not because I needed it! I know how to check my tire pressure. I'm not an idiot." Just the mention of the truck infuriated him.

Cameron didn't look up from the screen. He was looking at something Billy didn't understand. "Well," Cameron continued, speaking without looking at Billy, "not everyone out there is as smart as you are, Billy."

Billy felt a rush of heat behind his ears as the anger in him began to grow. "Oh, you're a smart ass now, Cameron?" Billy's hands began to slowly close into fists.

Cameron quickly recognized that his joke had not been well received. "No, Billy. I'm serious," he said, in an effort to calm Billy down. Cameron decided to go with it and not try to back pedal. He was pretty sure he could manipulate Billy into calming down.

"What are you talking about?" Billy asked. The aggressive tone was still very clear in his voice.

"Just what I said, Billy. Most people nowadays probably don't know how to check their own tire pressure. Most people don't know how to do *any* of the stuff that you do *every* day." Cameron decided to lay it on a little thicker rather than deal with Billy's attitude for the rest of the day. "How many nineteen-year-old kids do you think could change their own oil, let alone change a tire? And if they have to change that tire on the side of the road? No way."

Billy visibly relaxed. "Oh, I thought you were being a dick."

"No, I'm serious. I'm just saying that you're right Billy. How hard is it to check your tire pressure?" With that statement, Cameron knew he had disarmed Billy.

Billy suddenly thought that he had a new ally. "Right?" Billy said. "What a bunch of morons!"

"Hey," Cameron said in a friendly tone, to change the subject. "I'm going to finish up here. Would you mind grabbing the paperwork so we can get this car out of here. There's nobody else lined up right now, so we could grab some lunch. It's almost noon."

"Yeah, man." Billy turned to go grab the clipboard from the workbench nearby.

Cameron rolled his eyes as he turned back to the computer. *Idiot*, he thought as he shook his head slightly.

The next day, Billy showed up for work at 8:00 a.m. sharp, with a good attitude and ready to get some work done. Unfortunately, with the recent spike in fuel costs and the unprecedented inflation that was plaguing the country, the garage was beginning to see less work. People were driving less and pushing off that scheduled oil change for another thousand miles. The shop had a couple of jobs that morning, but they involved resetting some kind of collision avoidance sensor crap that Billy didn't understand. Cameron said that it was a one-man job, and he didn't need any help. What Cameron didn't say was that Billy would just be in the way.

Billy had sat around in the breakroom waiting for work until lunchtime when his boss came in. Billy did not initially react to his boss's presence. George stood there for a moment regarding Billy, wiping his hands on a dirty red shop towel. George McGuire was a somewhat soft-spoken man of sixty-two years. He had a full head of white hair and a bushy white mustache. George was 5'7" with a little extra weight around the middle. He wore the typical mechanics clothing of blue, Dickie work slacks and a blue, button-up shirt with an embroidered patch over the left breast pocket. The patch was the same dark blue as the shirt, but had a gray border. His first name was embroidered across the middle of the patch in gray script. He didn't speak at first, waiting on Billy to look up.

Billy was sitting back in a large, burnt orange, vinyl armchair that would have looked right at home in the 1970's. He was reading a two-year-old copy of Motor Trend Magazine. His feet were propped up on a small wooden coffee table that was covered with more car and mechanic magazines. His right foot was crossed over his left at the ankle. After a moment, he looked up to see George stuffing the shop towel into his back pocket. "What's up George, you goin' for lunch?"

George didn't answer the question. "Billy, it doesn't look like we have much work today, son. I'm gonna go ahead and cut you loose for the rest of the day."

Billy reacted instantly by sitting up straight and snatching his feet off the coffee table, planting them firmly on the floor. "Now George, that ain't fair. It ain't my fault that people don't need an oil change today. You had me on the schedule today and I need the hours."

"I hear what you're sayin' Billy, but I can't justify paying you to sit in here and drink coffee all day."

Billy reflexively looked down at the Styrofoam cup of coffee that he had placed on the table earlier. He had gotten lost in an article about a restored 1969 Dodge Charger and forgotten about the coffee. Now it was cold.

"I know I asked you to work today, but I have to be able to keep the doors open if you want to have a job tomorrow. Now I'm sorry, but I'll still pay you for the ½ day that you were here. Why don't you just go on home and enjoy a little unexpected time off. Hopefully we'll have more business tomorrow."

Billy slapped the magazine down onto the table without closing it and bolted to his feet. He stared at George for a couple of seconds before replying, "Fine, George." Billy walked over to the wall where there were several coat hooks, one of which held his lightweight camouflage jacket. He snatched the jacket off the hook and started for the door.

George spoke up. "Now Billy, there's no need to be mad about this. It ain't like I'm firing you, I just have to cut some hours around here."

Billy paused with his hand on the doorknob and looked back at George and scoffed. Then he walked out the door, swinging it open with a little more force than necessary, and stormed toward his car parked in the back parking lot. He was digging the keys out of his jacket pocket as he walked up to his 1999 Honda Civic when he noticed that the front left tire was almost completely flat. "Oh great. This is exactly what I need right now!" He spun around and headed back inside the shop. As he walked through the open garage door he called out to George. "Hey George! George!"

George had already returned to his office. He opened the door and leaned out the door to see what Billy needed. "What's up Billy?"

"Since you're not going to pay me for this afternoon, can I at least use the bay to fix my own freaking flat tire?"

It was hard to ruffle George's feathers, and that question, despite the tone it was asked in, was not enough to do so. He calmly replied "Of course son. You take care of you." With that, George disappeared back into his office. The door closed behind him with a light click.

Billy started back toward his car mumbling under his breath. "I guess I better. It ain't like nobody else is gonna do it."

As he walked back to his car, he had a look of disgust on his face. Just last year he had a nice four-wheel-drive Chevy with leather seats and a bad ass stereo. As Cameron had pointed out yesterday, the truck also had a tire pressure monitoring system, but Billy wasn't thinking about that. "And now I am reduced to this." Billy paused, took a deep breath and composed himself before undertaking the task of moving the car into the bay. "I'm definitely grabbing some beer on the way home," he mumbled under his breath.

Billy carefully pulled into the bay and got out of the car. As he closed the door, he looked over at Cameron to see if he was going to ask what he was doing. Cameron was sitting inside a customer's car with a computer in his lap. Cameron didn't acknowledge Billy's presence. He just kept doing whatever it was he always did on that computer. It was one of those little shock-resistant computers with the waterproof keyboard. It was plugged into a port under the steering wheel of the car and Cameron seemed engrossed in whatever was on the screen. In actuality, he just didn't want to deal with Billy's crap right now, so he was acting like he was busier than he actually was.

Billy waited a couple seconds, looking toward Cameron. When Cameron didn't respond, Billy just turned his attention to his own problem. He used the lift to raise the little car up. He walked over to the low tire and immediately saw the problem. There was a roofing nail firmly embedded in the tread. "At least it's not the side wall," he said with a sigh, then went to work. Billy could have just plugged the tire. That would have been faster. However, if he had this big shop at his disposal, why not take advantage of it? He took the wheel off and removed the tire from the rim. He carefully patched the tire, reinstalled it on the rim and aired it up until the gauge on the air compressor showed the appropriate air pressure. He replaced the tire on the hub and used an impact wrench to replace the lug nuts. *Jobs are a lot easier when you have the right tools*, he thought to himself. He grabbed a large tire gauge from the bench and double checked the air pressure. He never really trusted the gauge on the compressor. The air pressure was good. "See? How hard is that?" Billy said to himself and glanced over at Cameron again. He was still in the customer's car and still hadn't acknowledged Billy's activities.

Billy didn't bother speaking to Cameron or telling George that he was leaving after he finished the tire. He just got in his car, backed out of the bay, and left, heading straight toward the Exxon station. As he approached the station, he noted the cost of fuel on the large electronic display. $4.39 for regular gas. $4.99 for supreme. "You gotta be kidding me." He glanced down at his fuel gauge. He had nearly a half tank of gas. "Well, that's one good thing about this piece of crap. At least I'm getting good fuel mileage."

He parked the car in one of the three parking places in front of the store and killed the ignition. He walked in without acknowledging the store clerk and headed straight for the beer cooler. First, he walked over to the cooler with the Sam Adams, Shock Top, and other beers that he preferred. He looked down at the prices displayed below the six packs. "Sheesh," he mumbled under his breath. He stepped to his right to the next cooler and looked over the price tags in that cooler. "Looks like Natty Light for the win!" He pulled the door open and grabbed a 15-pack, tucked it under his arm, and headed up to the checkout counter. "Hey, can I grab a pack of Marlboro lights?"

The clerk did not respond to him but turned around and grabbed the cigarettes from the display behind her. She scanned the beer and cigarettes. "$15.67."

"Jeez! How much are the cigarettes?"

The clerk glanced at the screen on the cash register and replied "$5.78 before tax. You still want 'em?"

"Yeah fine. Whatever," he responded as he dug a $20 bill out of his pocket.

Billy had quit smoking a while back and the last time he remembered buying cigarettes they were around four dollars a pack. He had no intention of starting to smoke again, but right now he just wanted to calm his nerves, and a cigarette sounded like exactly what he needed.

He got back in his car, placed the case of beer in the passenger seat, and ripped open one of the flaps. He pulled out a can, opened it, and took a long drink of the beer before backing out of his parking spot. He passed the beer to his left hand and shifted the car into drive, then drove across the parking lot and turned right toward home.

By the time Billy got home, it was almost 2 p.m. and he was finishing up his third beer. He tucked his cigarettes into the pocket of his blue work shirt. His shirt didn't have an embroidered name tag like George's. He grabbed his beer, got out of the car, and shoved the car door closed with his foot. He started up the old, faded steps leading into their rented single-wide trailer. There was a trash bag on the front porch, partially blocking the front door. Jenny would often empty the kitchen trashcan and set the bags on the front porch for Billy to take to the outdoor trashcan. He kicked the trash bag out of the way, and the sounds of empty cans clanked as it came to rest against the rail on the small porch. He pulled open the spring-loaded screen door and let it rest against his back as he sorted through the key chain looking for the door key. He unlocked the door and left the keys hanging in the doorknob as he opened it.

As soon as the door began opening, Jenny's cat, Miss Priss, came bolting out the door and past his leg. The sudden appearance of the cat startled him, and he nearly spilled the beer cans from the open cardboard case that he held against his chest. "Stupid cat!" he yelled as the cat gracefully leapt from the porch into the front yard and began to walk away, not a care in the world. Billy watched the cat for a couple of seconds, her small metal tag jingling as it swung from her purple collar. He turned to go inside. Under his breath he once again mumbled the words, "Stupid cat." He didn't bother closing the door, although the screen door slammed shut behind him. Billy walked straight to the refrigerator and placed the case of beer inside, grabbing one more beer out of it, before nudging the door closed with his elbow.

He grabbed a lighter out of the junk drawer and headed back outside. He let the screen door slam again as he walked onto the front porch and flopped down in the plastic patio chair near the rail. He popped open the beer and took a drink before setting it on the 1x4 that he had nailed onto the porch rail to provide a place for this exact purpose. He pulled the cigarettes from his shirt pocket and packed the tobacco by tapping the pack into the palm of his left hand. Billy opened the pack and pulled out a cigarette, setting the opened pack on the 1x4 next to the beer. He looked at the cigarette for a moment, then said "Ah, screw it."

Placing the cigarette between his lips, he struck the red disposable lighter. He pulled the smoke into his lungs and held it for a moment before releasing it. "Oh, sweet mother." He looked down at the cigarette and paused. It had been a while. After a couple more drags on the cigarette, he dropped it onto the warped deck board in front of his foot and stepped on it. He sat back in his chair and thought about what George had said as he put the beer to his lips.

"You take care of you," George had told him. Billy felt the anger begin to swell again. *You take care of you*, he thought again. *He talks to me like I'm some kinda kid*, Billy thought to himself. *I ain't no kid.* He turned the beer up, finished it, crushed the empty can in his hand, and threw it at the bag of trash on the other side of the porch. He missed and the can went between the rails and into the yard. He stood up and turned toward the front door.

"I need another beer."

4

She Started to Laugh

Afternoon, May 19th, 2022

Office of the Speaker of the House, Washington, DC

The Speaker of the House hung up the phone and sat back in her chair contemplating the conversation she had just had with Adam Schiff. Schiff was also a California representative and they communicated reasonably often. Representative Schiff was essentially unknown to most Americans until his rise to fame during the Impeachment hearings of then-President Donald Trump. Of course, he was well known in certain circles in Washington, and in his home state of California. However, to most of the rest of the country, he was an unknown. During the impeachment process, his face was commonly seen on the news and many Americans began to refer of him as "that bug-eyed" guy. Nancy Pelosi was aware of this, but she had never mentioned it to him. She was sure that he knew too. He had called the Speaker to voice his opinion that it was the perfect time to try to push anti-gun legislation through Congress.

"Look Nancy, you and I both know that we have to strike while the iron's hot. We need to capitalize on the likelihood of emotional votes. We may be able to get votes now that we would have never gotten two years ago. We need to do this and do it now!" Schiff said in an overly excited and animated tone.

The country had been plagued for over a year with a steady rise in violent crimes. Much of it was in areas where local governments had discouraged, insulted, and even defunded the police. In some cities, the mayors had gone so far as to tell the police to stand down and not do their jobs. The police were later criticized for the increase in crime, especially violent crimes. But the crime was not limited to these areas. The violence was spreading to other parts of the country as well. No one could definitively identify the cause for the increase. However, there was a simultaneously noted increase in mental health illnesses across the country. Some cited the COVID quarantines and isolation of recent years as having a negative effect on the mental health of the American population. Other groups claimed that it was a generational problem, created by the current culture or violent video games. Others simply blamed Trump.

Regardless of the root cause, the Democratic leadership knew it was a fertile environment for pushing through anti-gun laws. "Adam, I know. You don't have to call me every single day to tell me. I'm going to talk to Joe and see what we can do with this," she replied. "I will let you know when I know something." Without waiting for a reply, she hung up the phone.

"He's such a little..." she began, but was interrupted by a light knock on the door. Maria Sanchez leaned her head into the door.

"Pardon me, Madam Speaker, it's time for your medication," Maria said politely, without entering.

"Please, come in. Come in. Close the door behind you."

Maria slipped into the door and pulled it closed behind her with her left hand. In her right hand she held a small silver tray containing two prescription bottles, a cloth napkin, and a crystal glass of water.

"Maria, what would I do without you?" began Speaker Pelosi. "Please, come on over."

Maria crossed the open space of the lavishly decorated office to the front of the desk. She walked with the smooth gait of a model.

Speaker Pelosi reached up and delicately plucked one of the bottles from the platter. "How many of this one?"

"Two of those ma'am, and one of these."

Speaker Pelosi attempted to take the lid off the bottle. It didn't budge. She repositioned her hands and tried again. "These damn childproof bottles. Here, you do it," she said reaching the bottle back toward Maria.

Maria carefully placed the tray onto the corner of the desk and took the bottle from the Speaker. She aligned the two arrows and deftly popped the top off the bottle. She retrieved the napkin from the platter and carefully shook out two pills onto the napkin, extending it toward her boss.

Speaker Pelosi snatched the two pills off the napkin with her right hand and reached for the water with her left. She quickly downed the medication with a couple of swallows. "And how many of these?"

"Just one of those ma'am, that's the one for pain," replied Maria.

"Hmm, maybe we'll just go ahead and go with two of those too," said Speaker Pelosi. "I anticipate another headache this afternoon." She looked up at Maria with a slight smile.

"Yes ma'am," replied Maria as she shook two of the pills from the second bottle onto the napkin. Once again with a quick swallow, the medication was gone. "Will there be anything else, ma'am?"

"Actually, yes. Call Joe's office and tell them that I need an appointment right away," she said.

"Yes, Madam Speaker."

"When you get the appointment, don't just put on my calendar. Come in here and tell me. If I'm not here, call me. Do you understand?"

Maria indicated that she understood.

"Maria, you speak Spanish, right?" Speaker Pelosi asked.

"No ma'am."

"But I thought you spoke Spanish. Wait. Have I asked you this before?" the speaker asked.

"Yes ma'am. We've spoken about it before," Maria answered. Her voice was smooth, measured, and professional with no indication of emotion.

"But you're from Mexico, right?"

"No ma'am. I'm from New Hampshire. My grandparents are from Mexico," responded Maria.

"Oh yeah. I think I remember something about that now. You said your parents couldn't speak English or something like that?" asked Speaker Pelosi. Maria detected a slur in the speech of the speaker.

"No ma'am. That's not it. After my grandparents immigrated to the United States, they encouraged my parents to embrace America. My grandfather said that if they were going to be Americans, they should learn English. So, they learned English, and growing up, my parents only spoke English to me. Looking back, I wish I had learned Spanish from them. I do understand quite a bit, but it would be an exaggeration to say that I speak

Spanish. Although my Russian is quite good. I took it in college for three years," explained Maria.

"Okay, I didn't really need a life history. On your way," the Speaker said, waving her hand toward the door. "And let me know when we get a call from Joe's office."

Maria nodded politely. "Of course, ma'am." She retrieved the silver platter with the two prescription bottles. The Speaker was still holding the napkin and the crystal glass. Maria did not ask for them. She turned and started toward the door.

From over her shoulder, she heard "Or should I say let me know when you hear from *El Presidente*?"

Maria paused as she was opening the door, looked back toward Speaker Pelosi, and smiled politely. "Yes ma'am, *El Presidente*." She turned and headed out the door.

As she was closing the door she heard, "I knew it! I knew you spoke Spanish!"

She pushed the door until the latch locked in place, rolled her eyes, and headed back to her desk.

Of course, the Speaker never saw Maria roll her eyes. She was focused on the bottle of liquor on the side table of her office. She got to her feet, pausing briefly to steady herself. With the crystal glass still in her hand, she walked directly toward the liquor that had been transferred into decorative decanters. Anytime you want to make your whiskey or vodka look more impressive, pour it into a $1,000 decanter.

Now sometimes, if it was an especially expensive bottle that she wanted people to know she had, she would leave it in the original bottle. For example, a few months ago, she received a $5,000 bottle of Pappy Van Winkle Family Reserve twenty-three-year-old Bourbon as a "gift" from a pro-abortion activist group, in exchange for consideration in future legislation. She left that one out where people could see it. But a few days after she received the bottle, the Catholic Archbishop of San Francisco, Archbishop Salvatore Cordileone, made it public that he would deny her Holy Communion if she did not rescind her support of abortion or stop speaking in public about her Catholic faith. "How dare that prick!" she had screamed as she read the announcement. She had already had some vodka and a Xanax that night, but she wanted something else. Something strong. So, she had opened the bottle of Pappy.

Now she held up the bottle and regarded it again. It was still about three quarters full. She removed the lid and smelled it, then sampled it right from the bottle. It wasn't bad, but she didn't really see what all the fuss was about. To her, it tasted like any of the other quality bourbons she'd had. Bourbon was not typically her first choice, but if she had it, it was going to be the good stuff. After all, she can have the finest booze, pills or whatever she wanted. She was accustomed to only the finest of everything. *Everything.*

She carried the bottle back to her desk. She reached for her "Diamond Forever" Chanel handbag. It was valued at over $261,000, but she had gotten a great deal on it for only $235,000. She was feeling the effects of the booze and oxycodone cocktail as she retrieved the handbag. She held open the handbag and began trying to stuff the bottle of bourbon into it. It wouldn't quite fit. "Fine," she said to herself, "I'll just carry it home. What are they going to do to me? Write me a ticket?" She chuckled a little at the thought of a D.C. cop trying to write her a ticket. With that thought, she started toward the door. It was already after 2:00 in the afternoon. It was time to call it a day. She picked up her phone and pressed the button for Maria.

Maria's voice came on the line almost immediately. "Yes, Madam Speaker?"

"Maria, tell my driver that I'll be leaving in five minutes."

"Yes ma'am," Maria replied in her typical, level, professional tone.

A few minutes later, she sat in the back seat of her Mercedes Premier Limousine and regarded the bottle of Pappy. She reached for a glass and poured a triple. The buzz of the narcotics was in full swing now. She noticed her phone was buzzing and looked down at the screen. 'Rep Adam Schiff' was displayed on the screen. "I don't think so," she said out loud as she hit the red button to decline the call. "Business hours are over."

Less than a half hour later, she was in front of her home on K Street. Her security supervisor opened her door. "Madam Speaker," he said by way of greeting.

"Frank," was all she said in reply. Frank offered his hand to help her out of the vehicle and she took it, pausing momentarily as she gained her balance. She released his hand with a curt "Thank you," and began to walk toward the front door. Frank passed her as they approached the door and opened it for her. He waited patiently to allow her to enter before closing the door behind her. He didn't follow her inside, as he had learned to only do that if she specifically told him to. As she entered her multi-million-dollar home in Georgetown, she said with a noticeable slur, *"You...know,"* not speaking to anyone in particular. *"On s-second thought, that's some pret-ty good whiskey."* The half empty bottle slipped from her hand and shattered at it struck the floor. Broken glass and liquor went in every direction around the foyer. She paused and looked down at the broken remnants of the bottle laying in the brown liquid on the polished white marble. Wavering in her power heels, she started to laugh.

5

Edna's Green Beans

Afternoon, May 19, 2022

Charles and Edna's farm, Lawrence County, KY

Edna Michaels turned on the television as she removed two chicken breasts from the freezer to begin thawing them for dinner this evening for herself and her husband Charles. The news was reporting on food processing plants that had been destroyed.

"The United States has seen an unusual number of mysterious fires in food processing plants in the last two years," began the reporter. "However, this trend has become even more alarming since the beginning of the year, as we have viewed an uptick in the number of incidents. We take you now to Salinas, California and our reporter on the ground José Fuentes. José, what's it like there in Salinas?"

Edna stopped and turned toward the television to watch.

"Thanks Jan. I'm here in front of the Taylor Farms plant. It has been over a month since a massive fire ravaged the 225,000 square-foot facility here in Salinas, California. Following the investigation, local firefighters have deemed the fire an accident, and not a result of arson. Nearly 3000 residents were evacuated from their homes at the time of the fire, while 35,000 more people were instructed to shelter in place. The plant contained a massive amount of ammonia and authorities were concerned about toxic smoke or even an explosion because of the ammonia stored on-site. Now, a month later, cleanup efforts continue. Officials tell us that no long-term effects have been identified in the immediate community, but for the employees of Taylor Farms, the work is just beginning. Back to you, Jan."

Roberta "Jan" Janson continued. "Thank you, José. Joining us now from Dufur, Oregon is Marcia Patterson." The screen split into three equal portions with Jan in the center, José on the left and a new picture on the right featuring Marcia Patterson.

"Good afternoon, Jan. I'm here in front of the Azure Standard Headquarters in Dufur, Oregon where an unexplained fire tore through the facility one month ago. If you haven't heard of Azure Standard, they are a producer of affordable, high-quality, organic, natural, and non-GMO products." As Marcia spoke, the screen changed to show a video of firefighters battling the blaze last month. "They are a family-owned business and have a dedicated following across the country. The company agreed to speak with us and has assured us that they are working diligently to move the production to another facility nearby. According to a company spokesperson they will strive to minimize interruptions to the supply chain following this horrendous tragedy. Jan."

"Thanks, Marcia. Thank you, José." As the two field reporters nodded their heads in acknowledgment, the center portion of the screen expanded and Jan's face once again filled the screen. "These fires are just two in a long string of fires that threaten food production in the United States. This includes several fires in fertilizer plants as well. We have an ongoing investigation following this potential crisis. However, we can tell you that fires have destroyed or damaged facets of the American food production across the country."

A list began to scroll up the screen showing some of the fire locations:

Taylor Farms, Salinas, CA

Azure Standard, Dufur, OR

Shearer's Food Plant, Hermiston, OR

Maricopa Food Pantry, Maricopa, AZ

East Conway Beef & Pork, Conway, NH

Wisconsin River Meats, Mauston, WI

Deli Star Meat processing plant, Fayetteville, IL

Walmart Fulfillment Center, Plainfield, IN

Nutrien Ag Solutions (Fertilizer Plant), Leoti, KS

Nutrien Ag Solutions (Fertilizer Plant), Sunnyside, WA

Cargill-Nutrena Feed Mill, Lecompte, LA

Nestle food plant, Jonesboro, AR

Louis Dreyfus Company soybean processing and biodiesel plant, Claypool, IN

Penobscot McCrum potato processing plant, Belfast, ME

Winston Weaver Co (Fertilizer Plant), Winston-Salem, NC

Rio Fresh produce warehouse, San Juan, TX

Jan Janson's face reappeared on the screen. She wore a solemn look on her face. "Not included on this list are two older but very significant fires. In 2019 there was a fire at the Tyson Foods meat processing plant in Holcomb, Kansas. At the time of that fire the plant was responsible for approximately 6% of beef on the US market. And more recently, in September of last year in Grand Island, Nebraska, the JBS USA beef processing plant suffered from yet another unexplained fire. That plant was estimated to be providing approximately 5% of the beef in the US market.

"Joining us now is Dr. Reginald Matthews from the US Department of Agriculture. Thank you for joining us Dr. Matthews." The screen once again split, with Dr. Matthews on the right side of the screen. He was a mildly obese black man with short, cropped hair and eyebrows that seemed too thick for him. He wore a thin mustache that had been trimmed into a neat, thin line across his lip.

"Thank you for having me today," replied Dr. Matthews. He spoke with an air of confidence, despite wearing a cheap looking-suit that may have fit him twenty pounds ago.

"I think the immediate question in everyone's mind is: Should we be worried about an interruption of the food supply chain in the United States?" asked Jan.

Dr. Matthews appeared very relaxed as he looked directly into the camera and responded. "Let me just say that this administration places the safety of all Americans first and foremost and we take any threat to the food supply chain of this country very seriously. However, at this point in time," he paused just long enough to grab a breath, "we do not assess that there is *any* threat to the average American citizen."

He dragged out the word "time" in a way that reminded Edna of a southern preacher.

Jan nodded slightly as she listened. "Okay, Doctor, but how would you respond to those who say that these fires are too numerous to be a simple coincidence?"

"It's quite apparent to me that the fires you have described have been an unfortunate string of unrelated events. The investigating authorities have been quite clear there is no connection between any of them. Each and every one of those fires has been proven to be from accidental causes."

Edna smiled as she pictured the man holding up a Bible in a Mississippi church.

"Sir, I believe that some of the fires are still under investigation," interrupted Jan.

"Well, I do not believe that these fires are related in any way and that they will all prove to be accidental in nature. And again, as I said before, the administration has already made an official statement and we do not believe there is any cause for alarm." His speech pattern was choppy and unnatural like someone who was trying to sound more educated than he was.

Jan turned the page of notes on her desk over. "Okay sir, then would you care to comment on the current baby formula shortage in United States?"

Dr. Matthews shifted in his seat and looked off camera at someone before returning his gaze to the camera. "Well, uh, that, uh was really more the FDA. Um, I'm not really prepared to answer for them at this juncture in time." Dr. Matthews now had droplets of sweat forming on his forehead and they were visible in the bright lights of the camera.

Jan smelled blood in the water. "Doctor, isn't it true that on May tenth, Senator Mitt Romney issued a letter to the FDA and USDA urging them to prioritize finding a solution to this critical problem?"

Dr. Matthews was getting visibly agitated. "Miss, I am certain that you do not understand the complexities of the inner workings of the FDA or the USDA. I *am* aware that the White

House has recently released a statement informing the public that we are working diligently to address this problem. In fact, we have had a team on it for several months now, and I am sure that we will be able to help provide the baby formula so desperately needed by young American families."

Jan smiled slightly before continuing. "I'm sure our listeners are happy to hear that, Doctor." There was a barely discernible note of sarcasm in her voice. "Can you tell me what exactly they are doing to address the problem?"

"Uh, not at this specific juncture in time, uh, no, I uh, don't have that specific, uh program with me." Dr. Matthews was fuming inside. This question was not on the read-ahead list.

"I see," said Jan, intentionally looking disappointed for the camera.

Edna turned away from the television and went back to the kitchen to continue getting dinner ready. She pulled out three potatoes, rinsed them off, and began peeling them, dropping the skins into a bucket that would later be added to the goat feed. She then cut the potatoes into 1-inch squares and dropped them into a sauce pan with some water and a little salt to be boiled and made into mashed potatoes later. She walked over to her pantry and reviewed the rows of Mason jars with neatly lettered descriptions on the lids. She chose a jar of green beans marked 2020. She carried the jar back to the counter to a waiting two-quart saucepan. She attempted to open the jar but the ring on the Mason jar wouldn't budge. She retrieved her trusty wooden spoon and tapped lightly on the ring as she rotated the jar. She placed the wooden spoon back on the counter and gave the lid a twist. It let go and she sat the ring to the side. She then picked up a tablespoon, and gently pried upward on the edge of the lid; it gave way with a satisfying pop.

Edna kept a small recipe box on the back of the counter. She retrieved the card that said "Mama's Green Beans" and placed it on top of the open box. She didn't need to do this. She knew the ingredients by heart. However, her mother always set out recipe cards as she was cooking, so as a young woman, Edna had adopted the practice, and she still did it now. The recipe card had everything listed along with measurements. However, she had stopped using measuring spoons for most things many years ago. She did everything by sight now. She poured the green beans into the saucepan and added some diced white onion, a little onion powder, garlic powder, black pepper, beef bouillon, ham seasoning, and some bacon bits.

Everyone loved Edna's green beans. Her son, Paul, used to say that he could make a meal from just his Mama's green beans. She sat them on the gas range and lit the flame. She placed the lid on the saucepan and then turned her attention to the chicken breasts. Charles was really going to like this meal. She didn't notice the sound of the 1999 Honda Civic driving by her house as her neighbor returned home early from work.

Charles didn't notice the sound of the car either. He was inside one of his high tunnel greenhouses. He wanted to adjust the placement of one of the hoses that comprised his irrigation system. Two of his greenhouses provided vegetables, while this one had nothing but flowers. He had a contract with two local florists to provide them with flowers. Mother's Day had just passed, and he had harvested nearly all the product from this greenhouse. The week leading up to Mother's Day was always his biggest sale of flowers every year. When a friend had suggested growing flowers a few years ago, Charles was initially skeptical. He had been pleasantly surprised at how much money he was able to make from this one greenhouse. Some of the larger operations had automatic, computer-controlled systems that managed the irrigation, but Charles was unwilling to spend the kind of money necessary to install an automated system. Instead, he was able to control the irrigation manually with a traditional faucet system, fed from a nearby well. He could manage the water two ways. The first was a set of hoses that ran along the base of the plants. These hoses had small holes along the length of them allowing the water to drip out directly into the soil. When he needed more water, he could also turn on an overhead sprinkler system, which was controlled by a different valve.

Next week, he planned to replant this greenhouse. However, he had been too busy with the other two greenhouses and the fields to do it yet. The other greenhouses were growing green beans, cucumbers, tomatoes, green peppers, hot peppers, squash, watermelons, and cantaloupe. His fields currently contained corn, cabbage, onions, and potatoes. Charles sold his produce to the local community in the form of a fresh vegetable delivery service. His friends and neighbors paid a flat fee and they would receive a box of fresh vegetables once a week. The local nursing home had a contract as well, but their delivery was significantly larger and was the bulk of his business. The box would be different each week depending on what was ready to be harvested, and the amount could be adjusted depending on the needs of the client. The nursing home purchased the majority of the tomatoes, green peppers, potatoes, onions, and cabbage. Every Saturday, Edna would take the old truck with the bed full of cardboard boxes and drive the delivery route. Sometimes Charles would accompany her, especially when delivering to the nursing home, as that was more strenuous. Additionally, any overflow produce could be sold at the local farmer's market. Of course, Edna always got first pick for her canning.

Charles exited the first greenhouse and walked to the next one in line. He checked the water content of the soil and plucked a small ripe tomato from the vine. He rinsed it off at the water spigot and left out the other end of the greenhouse, heading for the barn.

As he entered the barn, he stopped at the first stall, sat the tomato on the bench, and removed a clipboard that was hanging on a nail just inside the door. He flipped it to the page where he was tracking his fertilizer use. Charles frowned as he did some mental math while looking at the paperwork. At the beginning of last year's growing season, he had purchased enough fertilizer for the entire year's operation for a little over $6,000. This year, that same $6,000 had only gotten him about 60% of the fertilizer that he would need. He could have paid more and gotten all the fertilizer he needed, but he had chosen to wait until after he had sold his flowers to buy the rest of it. Essentially, the fertilizer that cost him $6,000 last year would end up costing him around $10,000 this year. Maybe it was time to start thinking about dialing back the farm and moving more in the direction of *actual* retirement. The way it was looking now, Charles was not even sure how much of a profit he would turn this year. However, just like he told his wife, he knew they wouldn't be going hungry.

Charles replaced the clipboard on the nail and looked around the first stall. He had numerous pallets along one wall stacked with bags of fertilizer. On the opposite wall was a homemade workbench about six feet long. The bench had a bench vice mounted on the left end. An old, dull hacksaw rested beside the vice, awaiting a new blade. Toward the back of the bench were a couple of yellow and black batteries sitting in a charger, ready for use in his cordless tools. Charles noted that the lights were solid red, indicating that the batteries were fully charged. When they were charging, the red light would blink. Mounted above the bench was a shelf running nearly the full length of the bench. The shelf contained several coffee cans full of loose nails, screws, nuts, and bolts, as well as a bowl with some old padlocks in it. The keys were stuck into the padlock keyways so they wouldn't get lost. At the end of the shelf, several nails were driven into the wooden frame. Several short, lightweight chains hung on the nails, waiting for a job.

Charles loved this barn. He didn't have a man cave in the house, but this barn always felt welcoming. It had originally been a wooden structure with wood siding and a red steel roof. Several years ago, he had sheathed the sides with gray steel siding and paid to have electricity run to it. That was a game changer. Now he had overhead lights, outlets for his tools and chargers, and a place to plug in his radio. For years he had used batteries in the radio; now it was plugged into the outlet next to the battery charger.

The barn was seventy-two feet long and forty feet wide, with a large door at each end. He could open one door and pull his tractor inside, and if needed, he could drive out the other end. Each side of the large central passage was divided into three stalls. He didn't have horses or cattle, so the stalls were used for other things, such as work areas and storage. One stall was dedicated almost completely to the storage of lumber. When he had a repair to do, he didn't want to have to go to the lumber yard to get a piece of wood, so he stocked up and built a set of sturdy shelves to keep the lumber elevated, flat, and organized. On one side of the shelves was an old plastic barrel with no lid. Whenever he was working on a project, if he had a piece of wood left over that still might be big enough to use for something, he would drop it into the barrel with the typical thought of "I might be able to use that one of these days."

His son, Paul, had asked to store some things here too, when he had been stationed at Fort Bragg. Charles had plenty of room in the barn, so he had dedicated the last stall on the left for his son to use. Paul had come home on leave and spent a week with his parents. He enclosed the stall with a sturdy wooden frame covered with steel siding. He added a steel door on heavy duty hinges and included a robust padlock. It was the circular type of padlock that was designed to make it more difficult to be cut. He also covered the entire floor with pea gravel before loading his things into the stall. Of course, Charles had a spare key to the lock, but he never felt the need to go into the stall. He didn't know what was in all the boxes Paul had stashed there, but he didn't mind sharing the space with his son. Most of what was there was stored in large black plastic cases. There was also an old red dirt bike and some empty fuel cans covered with a tarp. When Paul put the bike in there, he had drained the fuel and taken an afternoon to clean the carburetor. This was no small job. The seat and fuel tank had to be removed so that the rear sub-frame could be rotated up and out of the way to gain access to the carburetor. Charles had commented to his son about how much work was required to get the carburetor off. Paul had responded that it was better than having a carburetor that was ruined by old fuel the next time he wanted to use the bike. They were notoriously difficult to get running right again if you stored them with old fuel in them. He had taken the carburetor apart and meticulously cleaned the inside, before finally reassembling the machine. Before putting the fuel tank back on, he removed the fuel petcock and drained the last few drops of fuel. He checked the little "filter" on the fuel petcock for damage before reinserting it into the fuel tank and replacing the screws.

There was a wooden shelf on the wall over the motorcycle. Paul had stored motor oil, transmission fluid, air filters, oil filters, spare tires, inner tubes, and other miscellaneous parts and pieces for the bike. He also had a black and red toolbox with motorcycle-specific tools. The word "Bike" was scrawled on the lid of the toolbox, written in white paint marker.

Finally, he had a steel wall locker in the corner of the room. It was like a gym locker, but bigger, measuring about three feet across and about a foot and half deep. With the doors open, Paul had driven deck screws through the back of the wall locker and into the wooden framing, to stabilize the locker and prevent it from tipping over. The locker had an additional heavy padlock on it. It was a rectangular, silver padlock with the words "American Lock" on it and a depiction of a small American flag. "Michaels" was stenciled across the front of the locker in black letters. Charles had a spare key for this lock as well. He kept both keys on a keychain that he left in his nightstand drawer with his revolver.

After Paul retired from the Army, he had asked his father if he could keep the little storage area for "emergencies." Charles had replied, "I don't see why not. That stuff's been in there for a while now and it ain't eatin' hay. Keep it for as long as you need."

Charles checked his watch. It was getting close to dinnertime, so he grabbed the tomato from the bench, closed the barn door, latched the combination lock, and headed for the house. He was going to slice this tomato up as a side dish with dinner. As he approached the back door, the smell of Edna's green beans met him. He smiled and started up the steps.

6

The Green Berets

Twenty years earlier, Spring, 2002

Fort Bragg, NC

The United States Army is the only branch that has Special Forces. All branches have their own flavor of Special Operations, but the only one that is actually called Special Forces is the Green Berets of the Army. The Army has five active-duty Special Forces Groups, each responsible for a different part of the world. In addition to the active-duty Groups, the National Guard has two more Groups.

Anyone in the Army can try out for Special Forces. You could have a background in the infantry, or you could be a mechanic, or a cook, or literally any other job in the Army. Anyone who wants to try out for Special Forces can typically do so if they meet the minimum requirements.

In spring of 2002, the United States was only a few months into Operation Enduring Freedom, the war in Afghanistan. Specialist Paul C. Michaels had been in the 82nd Airborne Division at the time, in Fort Bragg, NC. Like the rest of the world, he was following the events as closely as he could. U.S. Special Forces was leading the way into this new war, and he wanted to be a part of it. Paul had gone to the Special Forces Recruiter's office on Fort Bragg and told the recruiter that he wanted to volunteer.

"You know there's a selection process, right, Specialist Michaels?" responded the Sergeant First Class sitting behind the desk. The man was a Green Beret who had formerly been a member of an ODA, an Operational Detachment-Alpha (sometimes called an A-Team). Now his job was to help find, recruit, and guide potential future applicants through the process of getting to Special Forces Assessment and Selection, commonly referred to as SFAS.

"Yes, Sergeant. I'm aware," Paul had replied. He reached forward and lay a manila folder on the desk in front of him. "Here's a copy of my physical, my APFT, and a printout of my ASVAB scores." The APFT was the Army Physical Fitness Test and an application to SFAS required a current test meeting a certain minimum requirement. The ASVAB was the Armed Services Vocational Aptitude Battery. Paul was a newly promoted Specialist, or as the old timers called it a "Spec 4." It was the fourth level of the enlisted ranks, an E-4, and still not considered a non-commissioned officer. The man sitting in front of him was a Sergeant First Class, or E-7, the seventh enlisted rank; he had already been in the Army for several years before Paul had enlisted. Paul looked at the man's uniform. On his left shoulder, above his unit patch, he had three tabs. The bottom one said "AIRBORNE", the middle one said "RANGER." The top one was bigger than the other two. It completed the trio with the words "SPECIAL FORCES." This configuration of tabs was commonly referred to as a "Triple Canopy."

On the right side of the man's chest there was a sewn name tape that read "Dorcinski." On the left side, above a tape that read "US Army", were three sewn-on cloth badges. The bottom badge was a winged helicopter, indicating that this man had attended the US Army Air Assault school. Paul had never been to Air Assault school, but most people in the Airborne made fun of it as being a "lesser" school than Airborne School. Paul secretly still thought it would be cool to do it. He heard that you get to rappel out of helicopters, and that sounded pretty darn cool.

Above the Air Assault wings was a winged parachute with a star on top of it. This patch indicated that the man was a senior rated jumpmaster. As a member of the 82nd Airborne Division and a paratrooper, Paul understood the significance of that badge very well. Everyone in the 82nd was required to maintain proficiency on airborne operations. That meant that at least once every three months, every soldier who was currently on jump status was required to complete an airborne jump, exiting an aircraft with a parachute. The Jumpmasters were the specially trained soldiers who made that happen. They organized the jump, lead the preparation, inspected the jumpers, and finally put them out the door of the aircraft. The vast majority of these were noncommissioned officers, or NCOs. In other words, sergeants. Officers would go to Jumpmaster school as well, but typically most jump master duties were handled by the NCOs. As you gained experience as a Jumpmaster and met certain requirements, you would be awarded a star on top of your airborne wings, indicating this additional experience. If you had this star on top of your jump wings, you were known as a "Senior Parachutist." The badge was commonly referred to as "Senior Wings." Sergeant Dorcinski was wearing those Senior Wings right now. There was another level above Senior Wings. That was referred to as a Master Parachutist or "Master Blaster," and with that qualification, the little star on top of the wings included a wreath around it. Sergeant Dorcinski didn't have that one yet. Above his wings was a long skinny patch with an embroidered Kentucky Long Rifle on it. This was the Expert Infantryman's Badge, or EIB. This was the only badge that the two soldiers had in common. Paul wore basic airborne wings and an EIB. He was quite proud of his EIB. It had been very difficult to earn. His Battalion has conducted a two-week cycle of training and testing soldiers for the EIB. Most of his peers had failed to achieve this coveted badge. It was not uncommon for soldiers to try for it numerous times before achieving it. However, Paul had been successful on his first attempt. There were others who were successful on their first try as well, but they were certainly in the minority.

"I know about SFAS. How quickly can I get a class date?" Paul was sitting forward in his chair. It was a typical, government-issued, steel framed chair with a slightly padded gray vinyl cushion. He was only using the front half of the seat.

The recruiter gave a light chuckle. "What's the big hurry, Airborne? Do you hate the 82nd that much?"

"Negative, Sergeant," replied Paul. "In fact, I love the 82nd. I love the infantry. I love being a paratrooper. I even love the jerks that I work with. Well, I'm not a big fan of the First Sergeant, but other than that, I'm happy there."

"Okay," replied the recruiter with a light chuckle. "It's just that you seem to be in an awful big hurry to leave."

Sergeant Dorcinski looked down at Paul's left hand that was now resting on the desk in front of him. "I see that you're married. What does your wife think of all this?"

Paul glanced down at the gold band on his left hand. He had met Sandy while he was in Fort Benning for Airborne School. After a short engagement, they had gotten married. She now embraced her new role as an "Army wife." "She's good with it. I told her what I wanted to do and she said she would support me in it. The bottom line is that I'm ready to move forward."

Sergeant Dorcinski stared at the intense young man for a few seconds, gauging him. He looked physically fit, and he was obviously motivated. "Okay. Let's take a look at your test scores, and I'll see what I can do." He opened the manila folder and shuffled through the paperwork. He raised his eyebrows. "126 GT score, huh?"

"Roger that, Sergeant," Paul replied without any other discernable reaction.

"That's pretty good."

Part of the ASVAB score was called the General Technical score, or GT score. At the time, applicants were required to have a minimum score of 110. Often soldiers would retake the ASVAB numerous times trying to get a high enough GT score to submit an SFAS packet.

"Okay, High Speed. That looks good. Your PT score looks great too. Is there anything in this physical that's going to be a problem?"

"Negative, Sergeant. I'm ready. I'll take the first available date."

Sergeant Dorcinski chuckled again. "You just told me that you love the 82nd. Why are you trying to leave something you love?"

Paul paused as if thinking about the question, then spoke. His tone was confident, and he looked the older man directly in the eye as he spoke. "Sergeant, I believe this is going to be a Special Forces war, and we don't know how long it's gonna last. It could be over in a year or two, and I don't want to miss out. So, when can I get a class date?"

The war would not be over in a year or two, and Paul C. Michaels would not miss it. In fact, he would go on to do three tours in Afghanistan and numerous other deployments to other places around the world over the coming years. This was the beginning of a new chapter in his life. And his life was about to go in a completely different direction because of it.

7

How to Hold a Grudge

Office of the Speaker of the House, Washington, DC

Maria Sanchez gently knocked on the door of the Speaker's office and waited for a response.

Nancy Pelosi quickly opened a drawer on her desk and placed her bottle in the drawer. She closed the drawer. "What is it, Maria?"

Maria opened the door and stepped inside. She held the door open slightly with her hand. "Ma'am, Representative Schiff is here to see you."

"What? I don't have him on my schedule," replied the Speaker.

"No ma'am. He just showed up and insists on speaking with you right away."

Adam Schiff pushed through the door, pulling it out of Maria's hand. "Nancy, we need to talk."

"Adam! This is not how we do things," Speaker Pelosi blurted out.

Adam Schiff turned to look up at Maria. At 5'10" and wearing 2-inch heels, Maria was taller than the representative. He stepped close to her, attempting to be intimidating. "I think that's all we need from you, miss." He spat out the word 'miss' with a sarcastic tone, intentionally trying to belittle the aide.

Maria, always the professional, looked at her boss for guidance.

"That will be all Maria. Thank you," Speaker Pelosi said with no inflection to her voice.

"Of course, Ma'am. If you need anything..." She let the sentence trail off and slipped out the door, gently closing it until it latched.

"What the hell, Adam?" began Speaker Pelosi as soon as the door closed.

Adam Schiff stormed across the office and tossed the folder, intentionally harder than necessary, for effect, onto the Speaker's desk. "Have you seen this?"

Speaker Pelosi looked down at the folder without opening it. The folder had a green stripe across the top and bottom. The word "UNCLASSIFIED" was printed in both green stripes. She responded in a measured, controlled tone. "I don't know, Adam. What exactly are you so upset about?"

"Freakin' Canada!" he responded in a raised voice. "Freaking Canada can get real gun control on the table! Trudeau just announced sweeping restrictions on handguns. They were able to outlaw hundreds of rifles, and now he's going after the pistols. This is embarrassing! How is it that we can have all this violence here and still not be able to pass some *real* gun control?" He was seething.

The Speaker waited until he paused. "Look Adam, I don't want Americans to have guns any more than you do. Believe me, nothing would make me happier than to take the guns away from every single citizen. But we need to play it smart. If we try to do it too quickly, it will fail."

Representative Schiff heard a pause in her speech and jumped in. "Well let's at least start with some executive orders. How about high-capacity magazine bans? Nothing in their *precious* second amendment says anything about magazine capacity. They don't need those stupid 30 round clips! I don't understand why these stupid rednecks love those damn black guns so much." He was still hovering at the front of her desk.

"Have a seat, and let's talk about this. I have an appointment with Joe tomorrow. Here are the things that we've been talking about." She pulled a folder from a drawer in her desk, opened it, and slid it across her desk to him.

He scanned the page before looking up. "This is the same stuff we tried to do before. Universal background checks? Don't they already have to pass a background check to buy a gun? Clearly *that* isn't working."

"They only have to pass a background check when they buy a gun from a *dealer*. Obviously, in California there are no private party transfers; citizens can't just run around selling guns to each other. The problem is, in many other states that's completely legal. We need to change this at the federal level."

"Yeah, yeah. So what? That still doesn't tell us anything because those records aren't maintained at the national level," he replied.

"Not officially," she said with a smile. "Keep in mind, Adam, that just because the law says we can't do something, doesn't necessarily mean that we don't do it."

"So, are you telling me there is a national list of firearm owners?" Adam asked.

"Not exactly," she began. "When a firearm dealer submits a background check, they must include what type of gun is being purchased, a pistol, rifle, or whatever. It doesn't have all the details on the gun, just a record of the background check. The actual paperwork that shows the specifics of the transaction are maintained at the local firearms dealer. The ATF can audit any firearms dealer in the country at any time for any reason, or for no reason at all. The way the law is written right now, they're not supposed to record any information regarding the details of the firearm or the person who bought it. They're only supposed to ensure that all purchases were done in accordance with all federal firearms regulations." She paused, letting that sink in.

"So, with that, we have an unofficial list of people who have at least passed the background check to purchase a gun. One of the first steps that I want to get in place is to move the information about every single purchase into a national database." She stood up and walked to her side table. She paused as she set out two Blade Runner whiskey glasses. Nancy really liked the glasses. They cost over $100 each, but what's a few hundred dollars when you want nice glasses to drink out of?

She reached into her cabinet and pulled out a bottle of Limited Edition Stolichnaya Elite Himalaya vodka. She poured them both two fingers of the $5000 per bottle liquor and returned to her desk. She set one glass in front of Adam and sat back down.

Representative Schiff looked at the glass, then his watch. "I guess we're starting early?"

Speaker Pelosi just glared at him for a couple of seconds and then continued. "We already have an operation going on behind the curtains," she began. "We've directed the ATF to accumulate as much information from the individual dealers across the country as possible. Now you understand that this must be done quietly, because it's obviously illegal." She took a sip from her glass. "However, we've started to consolidate this information into one list. We started this by creating a new automated system for conducting background checks. It made it easier for the firearms dealers because they would no longer have to call in every check on the telephone. Instead, they could simply type the information for the firearms purchase directly into the system and usually get a quick response. It was an easy sell. Now, we are simply stealing that information through a backdoor in the system." She took another sip of her expensive vodka, smiled, and leaned back in her chair.

Adam Schiff thought about this for a moment. "But if it's illegal, why is the ATF cooperating with it?"

Nancy looked at him as if he were small child asking why the sky was blue. "Adam, stop acting innocent. We've talked about this before. The ATF is in our pocket. Obviously, we don't use the word 'corrupt', but let's just say that the ATF is not concerned with 'Constitutional rights' any more than the FBI is. We have near total control of them. We've put *our* people in place, with *our* agendas. The ATF, the FBI, hell, even the IRS is being leveraged to support the big picture." She smiled again as she paused.

Representative Schiff did not smile. "So what? So you have a list of recent gun sales," he said, returning to the earlier point in the conversation.

Nancy Pelosi leaned forward slightly. "You're failing to see how this supports the final destination, Adam. This is just one step. One step toward registration. And registration is always the precursor to confiscation."

This time, Representative Schiff smiled too. "I'll drink to that." He picked up his vodka, smelled it and took a sip. "Well, that's how Hitler did it, right? He required registration, then he had a list of where to go to confiscate weapons."

"Precisely," Pelosi responded. "He said it was registration in the name of safety. It was to protect the *children*, and who's going to say that they don't want to protect little children? Only we won't just be going after Jews. We'll be going after *everyone.*"

"Okay," started Schiff, "let's not get ahead of ourselves. That's still only one step. How do we go from registration to confiscation? What's the next step look like?"

"Don't worry yourself about the details right now. When you need to know it, believe me, you'll know it. We have plans in place to ensure America's outrage toward guns. Especially that damned AR-15," she said.

"What do you mean you have plans in place?" inquired Schiff.

"Let's just say that if the crazies don't shoot up enough schools, we're going to make sure it happens," she responded coldly.

"Holy sh..." He let the word remain unfinished as he sipped his vodka. "You're talking false flags, aren't you? Was Las Vegas a false..."

The speaker cut him off. "Adam, you have no idea how many times we have used that tactic in this country. Let me paint you a hypothetical picture. Imagine this: You're down on your luck, maybe you're dying of cancer, maybe you're facing jail time. Whatever. Maybe you want to make sure that your family is taken care of. Then someone in a black suburban offers you the deal of a lifetime. Park this truck full of explosives in front of a certain building at a certain time. Or maybe you take this brand-new AR-15 with all this ammo and you go shoot up a certain place for me. All your problems can go away. Your family will be taken care of after you're gone, or your conviction will go away, or whatever it is that the desperate person needs. Easy."

She continued. "If you want to sculpt the political landscape of a nation this big, you must be willing to spill some blood. We *must* act to create the atmosphere necessary to pass the legislation that we want. If the court of public opinion is not in our favor, we simply create an event to swing things back to our side. It's that easy."

"Hmm," Schiff replied in a low voice. "That easy." He stared down at his glass in contemplation.

Pelosi began again. "Of course, Joe isn't helping us make any progress with public opinions right now, not with his ramblings. I swear he can't open his mouth without tripping on himself. How hard is it to just read the damn teleprompter? Lucky for us, the media is going to downplay his incompetence. Unfortunately, he's making that harder and harder to do."

"People know, Nancy. They know he's losing it."

"Of course they know! The whole world knows!" she spat. "We're just trying to keep him in the driver's seat for as long as possible. He's easy enough to manipulate and control. We just need to keep him from dying."

"What do you mean by control?" Schiff asked, his large eyes bugging out of his head just slightly.

"Adam, do you honestly believe that Joe is capable of making any decisions on his own right now? You've seen him. Jill should have put him in a home already, but *nooo*, she wanted to be First Lady," she dragged out the word no for effect. She looked down at the drink in her hand and then finished it off. "So now, instead of relaxing with some shuffleboard and a drink with a little umbrella in it, he thinks he's in charge of the free world. In charge! Ha!" she scoffed. "He hasn't had an original thought in years. He's told what his opinions will be and what policies he will pursue. We'll just have to wait and see how long he will continue to hold the office. As long as he remains useful, he'll remain President." She stood and crossed the office to the side table. She refilled her drink and held the bottle up to representative Schiff, asking if he wanted another.

"No thank you. That was enough for me," he responded. He waited for her to return to her seat with her refreshed drink. "What do you mean he'll remain President as long as he's useful. Who could change that? Are you talking about the Deep State?"

"Adam," she paused for effect. "I'm sorry, I'm afraid I don't know what you're talking about. Now you sound like one of those right-wing conspiracy theorists. No, I just mean his advisors."

"Okay, fine. But I assume Obama is part of this, right?" Schiff asked.

"Close the door on your way out, Adam," Speaker Pelosi said, as she looked over at her laptop, clicked her mouse, and began typing, completely dismissing Representative Adam Schiff.

Adam Schiff's face turned red with anger. He grabbed the glass of vodka and quickly downed the remainder. He turned abruptly and started toward the door, the glass still in his hand. He opened the door halfway and looked back toward the Speaker of the House. She didn't look up or acknowledge his departure. He turned and left, closing the door harder than necessary.

Maria stood to great him when she heard the door open.

Before she could speak, Representative Schiff stormed by her desk and threw the glass straight down into her steel trashcan. She jumped at the sound of the glass breaking. She quickly composed herself. "Have a good day, Representative Schiff. If you need anyth..."

He spun on his heels to face her. "Shut up! Who you think you are, talking to me? Do you who know I am?"

"Of course, sir. You're..." she began cooly.

"That's right, you know who I am! So, *you* do not speak to me, unless I speak to you first! Are we perfectly clear?" Spittle was forming at the edges of his mouth as he closed the distance between himself and the aide.

Maria looked down at the representative from California. She thought about how easy it would be to grab the stapler from her desk and knock that look off his face. She imagined pushing his giant eyes back into his head and stapling his eyelids closed.

She did not grab the stapler. Instead, she maintained a perfectly calm demeanor and replied, "Of course, sir." She turned to go back to her chair.

"Did I dismiss you?" Schiff started again.

Maria stopped. She paused for just a moment and then turned back to the raging man. In her head, she thought *Power trip much, Asshole?* However, that's not what came out of her mouth. Instead, she said, "No sir. You did not. Is there anything I can do for you?" She was careful to keep her tone perfectly professional and a neutral expression on her face as if she didn't even notice what an ass he was making of himself.

"No, there's nothing else you may *do* for me. *Now* you are dismissed." Adam Schiff glared at the pretty young woman with nothing but disdain and disgust on his face. He didn't know that she spoke two languages well and had a working knowledge of a third. He didn't know that she graduated at the top of her class in high school and finished her bachelor's degree in three years. He also didn't know that he had just created a new enemy.

"Of course, sir," Maria said politely, then gracefully walked back to her desk and sat down just as her phone buzzed. She answered it. "Yes, Madam Speaker?" She glanced back at

Representative Schiff who was still loitering by the door. "No ma'am. There's no problem." She glanced back over her shoulder a second time to see if he was still standing there. He was. "No ma'am." There was a slight pause as Maria received her instructions from the Speaker. "Of course, ma'am. Right away." She hung up the phone and looked back over her shoulder a third time. Representative Schiff was gone. She mumbled under her breath. "Creep." Then she stood and grabbed her purse. She carefully ran her hands down the front of her toned legs, pushing the wrinkles out of her skirt. It was time to get back to work and she had an errand to run. She was fuming inside. However, if anyone had been observing her, they wouldn't have seen any outward sign of her anger. She knew how to hide frustration and anger. Unfortunately for some people, Maria also knew how to hold a grudge.

8

Special Forces, and Beyond

Spring, 2003

U.S. Army Special Forces Training Facility, Camp Mackall, NC

Paul Michaels was in the first part of his training in the US Army Special Forces Qualification Course, commonly referred to as "The Q-Course." This portion was formally known as Small Unit Tactics. However, everyone just called it by its initials, S.U.T. Paul had enjoyed this phase so far and was thriving in it. As an infantryman, he was already well-versed in the tasks being taught in S.U.T. However, Special Forces recruits came from all parts of the Army and the course was designed to bring everyone up to the same level of training. This included planning, patrolling, ambushes, raids, and more. The terrain and vegetation were different from where he grew up, but he loved being in the woods, any woods. He had grown up running around in the steep terrain and hardwoods of the Appalachian Mountains.

The terrain in Camp Mackall, North Carolina was definitively different. It consisted of gently rolling hills intertwined with countless sandy roads and trails. The vegetation was mostly pine trees and thick brush. However, for Paul it still felt very comfortable, because he loved being out in the woods. The forest floor back home was typically covered with the shed leaves of poplar, oak, walnut, and other hardwood trees. The woods here had a thick covering of pine needles, which made it much easier to move quietly; it even felt somewhat soft underfoot.

However, that didn't mean that everything was easy. Streams were everywhere and the draws around them were surrounded by extremely thick vegetation. The vegetation was so difficult to pass through that the students collectively referred to that terrain as the "draw monster." Additionally, the undergrowth in the area was managed with periodic controlled burns. These burns would often cause the pine trees to be consumed all the way down into the ground, leaving behind small potholes that were just big enough to drop your foot into. Many students had sustained ankle and knee injuries over the years from stepping in these holes while patrolling, especially when they were wearing a heavy rucksack, a constant companion.

In addition to the streams, many areas contained legitimate swamps. The swamps just added to the difficulty in navigation because they were tough to negotiate and sometimes almost impossible to avoid. The instructors took advantage of these facts to place the objectives in locations that forced the students to deal with these difficulties. "The more you sweat in peace, the less you bleed in war." Paul had heard his instructor use that phrase more than once. He actually agreed with it. He had seen countless students fail out of SFAS, and now in S.U.T., he had teammates who were struggling to pass. He knew it was tough, but he felt like it *should* be tough. He recalled his father using the phrase, "If it was easy, everyone would be doing it." He thought about that statement often and understood the necessity of difficult training. He wanted to do more in his career. He wanted to face challenges and defeat them.

Sometimes, however, he felt the instructors were doing things that had no training value but were just designed to make it suck more. The worst part had been the sleep deprivation. The physical challenges were tough, but attainable. No matter how strong or tough you are though, you eventually need to sleep. His instructors had devised a plan where one would rest while the other ran the training. Then they would switch places and continue training, with no opportunity for the students to rest. Usually this was only for a night at a time. However, at the time of this patrol, they had been patrolling and conducting missions for two days already. The instructors had kept them going all day yesterday, through last night, and all day today. Now they were going into their second night with no sleep, and it was becoming increasingly difficult to think clearly.

During this phase of training, the students would take turns being in charge of missions. When it was their turn to be in charge, or be the "Patrol Leader", they would oversee planning the mission, using the entire team to complete the plan. Then the "P.L." would lead the mission and the cadre would evaluate him on his performance. The next mission, the cadre would put another student into the P.L. position so that he could be evaluated. Using this technique, the cadre would be able to observe and grade every member of the team.

On this mission, it was Larry Lawson's turn to be P.L. It was a pretty standard mission. They were to conduct an ambush on an unimproved dirt road four kilometers away at 0200hrs. The U.S. military uses the metric system to measure distance on the ground, and after you get used to it, it seems normal, but four kilometers is about two and half miles. They had to have this ambush emplaced by 2:00 a.m. For the uninitiated, two hours for a two-and-a-half-mile walk sounds like plenty of time. However, this patrol was moving "tactically." They moved carefully through the woods, at night, with no light. They needed to constantly watch for "enemy" soldiers during the movement. These "enemy" soldiers were collectively referred to as OPFOR, which stood for Opposing Forces. The students had to accomplish all this while simultaneously navigating without the use of roads, lights, or G.P.S. Any time they came to a road, or other "linear danger area," they would have to conduct a tactical road crossing. With all their gear, executing all their tasks, and navigating in the dark, it was slow movement. Additionally, once they got close to the objective area, they would have many tasks to complete in order to set the ambush up correctly. They were definitively behind schedule.

Night vision devices and G.P.S. units were commonplace in the military in 2003. However, when Paul and his team were going through S.U.T., the Special Warfare Center didn't allow them to use G.P.S. or night vision (commonly referred to as NODs, for Night Optical Device or NVGs for Night Vision Goggles. The two terms were interchangeable). The principle was that you should be able to conduct missions without the technology, concentrating on learning and perfecting the basics of small unit tactics. These men would have all that technology and more when and if they made to their teams. But for now, it was old school.

They were about halfway through the four-kilometer movement. Larry raised his hand to indicate the command of "halt." He wanted to conduct a map check. The team didn't need to be told to form a perimeter; they did it automatically, having established their Standard Operating Procedures (SOPs) earlier in this phase. Each member of the patrol took a knee behind a tree, faced outward and pulled security so that the leadership team could move into the center of the perimeter.

Captain Andrews was one of the other students on Larry's team and was assisting him. He quickly moved to the center of the group and linked up with Larry. Larry pointed to a spot on the ground that was generally free of vegetation. "Let's get a quick map check right there," he said.

The two men dropped down on a knee and they each slid an arm out of their rucksack strap, rotating their rucks to the opposite side, and lowering them to the ground. This was supposed to be quiet since they were in a tactical environment, but the heavy rucksacks both made a "thud" sound as they hit the forest floor. Larry pulled his poncho out of the outside, center pocket on his rucksack. The two men lay side by side on the ground with a Camp Mackall map spread out in front of them. They pulled the poncho over themselves, and Larry turned on his red-lensed flashlight to check the map. The poncho would dampen the red-light signature of the flashlight as they confirmed their position and made sure that they were adhering to the planned route. While this was going on, Paul and the rest of the team pulled security. After about five minutes, Paul looked back at his teammates. He could see their outline on the ground in the moonlight. There was no movement and no sound. Part of the poncho glowed slightly from the flashlight underneath, but the light was perfectly still.

Crap, Paul thought. *They're out*. He stood up and quietly moved in a crouch to check on them. Paul whispered the Patrol Leader's name.

"Larry." No response.

"Larry," he repeated. Still nothing. Paul was still wearing his rucksack. The weight of it made it difficult to lean over far enough to reach the poncho on the ground, so he dropped down to one knee, thankful that the pine needle floor was soft and that he hadn't dropped his knee down onto one of the numerous pine cones. He reached out and grasped the edge of the poncho and lifted the edge to look under it. The red lens flashlight was on the ground, illuminating Larry's face. Larry and the captain were out cold. Paul quickly looked around for the instructor. It was the middle of the night, but the moon was nearly full and provided a surprising amount of light. There was easily enough moonlight to see that there was no one within ten or fifteen meters. He looked at his watch. "I'll give them five minutes," he said to himself in a low voice and kept watch over his friends, watching out for their instructor. He stayed on his knee.

Paul didn't realize it when his eyes closed. He pitched forward as he drifted off to sleep and lost his balance. He threw his hands out and caught himself as he was about to hit the ground. He opened his eyes to see a pair of green-sided jungle boots in front of him. He looked up with a start. His instructor, Sergeant First Class LeFavor was looking down at him with a sadistic smile on his face. There was just enough moonlight for Paul to see it.

"If you aren't disciplined enough to pull security on a knee, then stand up," Sergeant LeFavor said in a low voice. Paul tried to stand up quickly, but his rucksack slowed him down and he nearly fell forward as he finally regained his balance and stood before the instructor. Had he actually just fallen asleep on a knee, while wearing an 80-pound ruck? Yes. Yes, he had. Then it hit him: Larry and Captain Andrews! He stole a look at his sleeping friends, but it was too late. "Don't make a sound," Sergeant LeFavor whispered. Paul complied. He just stood there silently and watched in horror as the instructor closed the distance to the sleeping men with three steps.

Sergeant LeFavor moved silently. His boots made no sound on the bed of pine needles as he moved with the practiced stealth of a man with years of experience moving in the woods. He stopped about a foot from the edge of the poncho and listened for at least thirty seconds. There were no whispers, but he could hear the slight rhythmic sound of breathing. He leaned over and slowly lifted the edge of the poncho and peered underneath at the two sleeping students. He wasn't wearing a rucksack and was much more agile than the heavily laden students. He smiled and gently replaced the poncho. *No problem,* he thought. He opened the ammunition pouch on his load bearing equipment, commonly referred to as an L.B.E., and removed a white cardboard tube about six inches long. He removed the metal safety clip, which released a small, round, plastic cap that was attached to a string leading back into the tube. He gave the string a sharp pull and threw the tube into the woods nearby. A few second later, the artillery simulator began to whistle loudly. This device was designed to simulate the sound of incoming artillery shells. Almost simultaneously, every student in the patrol began screaming "INCOMIIIIIING!" Paul and the other students dropped to the ground. This is the SOP to reduce the likelihood of getting hit by shrapnel from artillery shells. The correct way to do this is to flop flat on your belly and get as low as possible. However, in this training environment, the normal response was to drop onto your side because of the massive, heavy rucksack. The artillery simulator exploded with a blinding white flash. These artillery simulators were shockingly loud.

Larry and Captain Andrews bolted awake sometime during the whistling. Larry was laying on his stomach and rolled to the side, throwing the poncho off with a hard swing of his arm, just as the simulator exploded. The poncho wrapped around his arm from the effort.

Sergeant LeFavor glared down at them. He was standing with his hands on his hips, bent forward at the waist and as soon as Larry made eye contact with him, the instructor started screaming. "Whatcha doin', P.L.?! Were you taking a little nap while your fucking team pulled security for you? Huh? Why haven't you called out a direction and distance? Where's your rucksack? How many people did you just kill because you're too fucking undisciplined to run a simple patrol?" Sergeant LeFavor launched the questions at the stunned student rapid fire without pausing or giving him the opportunity to respond.

Captain Andrews tried to interrupt. "It was my fault, Sergeant. We were…"

The instructor didn't let him finish. "Oh, now you're going to try to act like a Captain? A minute ago, you were sleeping on a patrol like an undisciplined Private! Well right now, HE is the Patrol Leader, and YOU'RE just a squad member." He jabbed a finger at Larry as he stressed the word "HE."

 "Your counselling will reflect your lack of discipline and your inability to stay focused on the mission. But right now, I'm talking to the P.L. Are we clear?"

"Roger, Sergeant," the young captain replied and stepped back from the instructor.

For those who have not gone through Special Forces training, this situation would have seemed bizarre. This non-commissioned officer was in charge of training and evaluating this group of men, which included captains, who outranked him. But here, in this environment, the instructor had complete power over these men's lives. He could fail the captain just as easily as he could fail an E-4. In this world, the instructor outranked all of them, regardless of what rank they wore on their collar.

Sergeant LeFavor returned his gaze to Larry. "Well?"

Larry started moving. He quickly located his rucksack, while simultaneously turning off his flashlight and slipping it into his pocket with his left hand, since it wasn't entangled in the poncho. He then began stuffing his poncho into the outside pocket of his Army issued rucksack. The instructor was relentless. "Oh, *NOW* you wanna pack your stuff up! *NOW* you wanna do the right thing! I tell you what P.L., let's try this again." With that statement, he pulled the cord on another artillery simulator just as Larry was getting to his feet with his ruck slung over one shoulder. The second simulator began to whistle, and Larry instantly dropped back to the ground again, his rucksack pulling him to one side as he fell.

With the moon shining brightly overhead, Paul had seen the instructor throw the second artillery simulator. He was already on the ground before it even started whistling. A second thunderous explosion ripped through the North Carolina pines, tossing pine needles and pinecones in all directions. Sergeant LeFavor stomped over to Paul and kicked Paul's rucksack with just enough force for Paul to know it happened. "You! You're fucking dead! Stay down!"

Paul felt dread wash over his body. He knew what this meant, and he knew it was his fault for not waking his friends when he realized they had fallen asleep. At the time, he just wanted to help his friends with a couple of minutes of rest, but now the consequences of his decision were very clear. He had chosen not to do the right thing, and now it was biting his whole team in the ass.

The instructor bellowed. "How about now, P.L.? Are you gonna do something *now*? You better get some people over here and pick up this casualty!"

Larry sprang into action. He quickly got his rucksack up onto his back and yelled "Give me two!" The nearest two students came running up. One of them was Captain Andrews. Larry pointed at Paul on the ground. "We have a casualty. Let's get him up. We gotta GO!"

The first student pulled Paul's rucksack off while Paul continued to play dead. The student hoisted the rucksack up and threw it up on top of his own, grunting with the effort, the rucksack pushing against the back of his head. His knees nearly buckled under the weight, but he stabilized himself and looked back at Larry. Larry was helping get Paul up onto the captain's shoulder in an embarrassing attempt at a fireman's carry. This was almost impossible because the captain was wearing his rucksack and Paul was barely staying on his teammate's shoulder, doing his best to help by holding onto the captain's rucksack. Larry grabbed Paul's rifle from the ground and yelled "12 o'clock, 300 meters!" The team echoed the command and began moving into the woods at a slow shuffle. This was an extreme effort for the group. One man was carrying two rucksacks. Another was carrying Paul, who was all but sliding off his shoulder. Larry was shuffling in front of them, with two M4 carbines slung over his neck.

Sergeant LeFavor watched the chaos with muted amusement. As soon as the team started moving in the same direction as the P.L., he erupted again. "Oh! Is that 12 o'clock? Is *that* the direction you were going before you fell asleep? You don't know, do you P.L.? Now you've got a casualty *AND* you're fuckin' lost!"

 The team continued to move in the direction they were going, but Sergeant LeFavor wasn't having it. "*STOP!* Fucking *STOP!*" The team all stopped where they were. Sergeant LeFavor calmly walked up to Larry. "You don't know which direction 12 o'clock is. Your team is trying to help you out, because they saw you moving and followed your lead. Well, that's one point for teamwork and zero fucking points for *ANYTHING ELSE!*" He screamed the last two words.

Larry just stood there. He didn't know what to say, but he tried to salvage the situation. "Sergeant, I thought 12 o'clock was..."

Sergeant LeFavor cut him off. "*OH! OH!* You *THOUGHT* it was this way. Well, that makes it all better, doesn't it? I'll tell you what P.L., I'm gonna help you out. Do you see that?" He pointed off into the woods, significantly left of the direction the team had been moving. "Do you see where I'm pointing?"

Larry responded with a, "Roger, Sar'nt."

"Yeah. THAT is your 12 o'clock. Now how about we try this again?" Sergeant LeFavor just stared at the flustered student. "Well?"

Larry hesitantly looked back over his shoulder at his team. "Uh, 12 o'clock, 300 meters," he yelled unenthusiastically.

Again, the team echoed the command. "12 o'clock, 300 meters!" and collectively they began moving in the correct direction.

Sergeant LeFavor calmly walked behind them and watched them as they moved about fifty meters before Paul began sliding off Captain Andrews' shoulder. They were both trying to keep him up there, but it was no use, and he eventually slid off, reflexively twisting to land on his feet. Sergeant LeFavor reacted quickly and closed the distance on the two struggling soldiers. "What did I tell you?" He was looking right at Paul.

Paul looked back at him and initially didn't know what to say, but then responded. "You said I was dead, Sar'nt."

Sergeant LeFavor calmly responded. "That's right. I said you were dead. So how exactly are you standing up right now?"

Once again, the feeling of dread rushed over Paul. Without responding, he allowed his knees to buckle, and he fell to the ground in a heap.

"That's more like it. Now, where's the P.L.?"

Larry trotted up, the second rifle bouncing against his own as he did. "Here Sar'nt."

Sergeant LeFavor just stood there looking at him. He looked down at the soldier's feet and slowly back up to Larry's face. At first, he didn't say anything. He was intentionally increasing Larry's stress, by dragging out this interaction. Larry was breathing through his mouth. The moonlight was filtering through the pine treetops and falling on Sergeant LeFavor's face from above, casting shadows on his face. The two men were only about three feet apart and, in this moonlight, Larry thought that the shadows gave the instructor the appearance of a psycho in a horror movie. After an uncomfortably long pause, Sergeant LeFavor finally spoke in a calm, even voice. "Where did you come from, Lawson?"

Larry didn't know exactly how to respond, so he just replied with, "Sar'nt?"

"What unit, dipshit. What unit were you in before coming to the Q-Course?"

"Sergeant, I came from first of the seventy-fifth," Larry responded, indicated that he had come from 1st Battalion of the 75th Ranger Regiment.

Sergeant LeFavor already knew what unit Larry had come from. "And what's your rank?" he asked. He obviously knew this too.

"I'm an E-7, Sar'nt," Larry replied. Larry was actually the same rank as the instructor. It was uncommon for an E-7 to attend the Q-Course, but not unheard of. All the other enlisted students on the team were E-4s and E-5s with one E-6.

"And what exactly are you doing here?" the instructor asked forcefully.

Larry was completely frustrated. He'd been a successful member of the Ranger Regiment before he left to pursue a new career as a Green Beret. He was competent, driven, and professional, but no matter what he did, it didn't seem to be good enough. "I want to be Special Forces, Sar'nt."

"Oh, you want to be Special Forces? Well maybe you should have thought about that when you were a fucking E-5." Sergeant LeFavor glared at the man. "You're already a senior NCO, and *now* you decide you want to be a Green Beret? It's not looking good for you, stud." Again, Sergeant LeFavor paused and just stared at the student. "Now get your team out of here before I kill a couple more."

Larry didn't respond to Sergeant LeFavor. Instead, he spun on his heels and yelled, "Give me one more!" Another student ran over to him. "Help him get that casualty out of here!" he yelled, pointing toward Paul, who was still lying on the ground, watching the entire exchange.

Now there were two students to carry Paul. They hoisted him up, each pulling one of Paul's arms around his neck, and began moving.

"Let's go, let's go!" Larry yelled. The team resumed their trudge into the darkness.

Sergeant LeFavor looked down at his watch and hit the button on the side for the light. The watch displayed 2352. *Almost midnight*, he thought. *This is going to be a long night for the boys.* With that thought, he smiled and began to calmly walk into the night, following the team.

It wasn't difficult for him to keep up with the fifteen men moving through the pine trees. They were all carrying full rucks and a combat load of weapons, ammunition, radios, batteries, water, food, medical gear, inert Claymore mines, and everything else they needed to conduct mock combat operations in a training environment.

If they were successful, they would move through the night to a staging area to set up the ambush. That staging area is called an Objective Rally Point, or ORP. The patrol leader would take out a small group to conduct a leader's reconnaissance of the objective. They would identify all the positions they would need to conduct the ambush: left side security, right side security, the support by fire position, and the assault line. Then they would return to collect the team and place everyone in their assigned positions. They would emplace the M18 Claymore mine, then lie in wait for the OPFOR to pass in front of them so that they could initiate the ambush and kill them.

However, Sergeant LeFavor knew that wasn't going to happen. He hadn't coordinated for any OPFOR tonight. Tonight, the team would set up the ambush (probably late) and then try to stay awake and alert for the OPFOR that would never come. Sergeant LeFavor would observe the young men as they suffered and struggled, trying to stay awake. They would be lying on their bellies, looking at a dark road on a quiet night, while sleep deprived. There was no way they would all be able to stay awake. Eventually, he would pull out some more artillery simulators and wake everyone up. He would chastise them for not being disciplined enough to stay focused on the mission. Then he would force march them down the sandy road back to the Quonset hut squad bays where the other instructor would be waiting. He would tag out with the other instructor and go get some sleep.

The other instructor, another Sergeant First Class named Shane Ladd, would act as if he was frustrated with the performance of the men. He would tell them that they were the worse students in the history of the Special Forces Qualification Course. In an exasperated voice he would tell them, "Fine! Fine! You know what, go into the squad bay and go to sleep. I'll give you one hour! GO!" He would give the men just enough sleep to recharge and then push them hard for the rest of the day. Finally, the next night, the men would get a reasonably normal night's sleep. Then it would start over again. It was all part of the plan.

Paul would remember these times. Later in life, he would look back at his time in S.U.T. and recall both misery and satisfaction. But most of all, this phase of his training would help to reinforce his determination to push through adversity. He would always remember the night he chose not to do the right thing and wake up his teammates. He had chosen to offer them a moment of comfort rather than wake them up and push them to get back on task. He remembered his father's voice from when he was a teenager. His father was addressing him and his younger brother, Scott. "You're not always going to have someone taking care of you. It'll be up to you to choose your own path. Discipline is doing the right thing for the sake of doing the right thing, but self-discipline is doing the right thing when no one else can see it, or will ever know it." These were hard earned lessons that would serve him well later, because he still had a long way to go in the Q-Course, in Special Forces, and beyond.

9

Allahu Akbar

June 1, 2022

U.S./Mexican border near Eagle Pass, TX

Zamir Syed sat observing the group around him; there were people from all over the world. He could identify individuals from Central and South America, Africa, and Asia, as well as some other Arabic speaking nations. Most people were sticking together with others from their own country. As he scanned the group around him, he identified a group of Chinese men clustered together, whispering conspiratorially amongst themselves. Scattered in the group of nearly 600 people were twenty-nine more of his countrymen. Zamir had given them clear orders not to gather in groups of more than four men at any given time, unless he specifically told them to do so. He was trying to reduce the signature of his group by spreading them out among the large group.

They had been training and preparing for nearly two years for this mission. The recent changes to the U.S. immigration guidelines had paved the way for a successful infiltration into America. President Trump had made it one of his priorities to secure the southern border, but this new administration had flung the southern doors wide open, and the time was perfect to take advantage of it. It had already been a long trip and not without its discomforts. However, it would all be worth it when they finally got the chance to put all that training to work in the name of Allah.

Zamir was responsible for the thirty-man group. The youngest in the group was Omer Azam at seventeen years old. The oldest was Mohamed Tahir at thirty-one. Zamir was the second oldest in the group; he was thirty. They had received a significant amount of help getting them to this point. His superiors in Hezbollah had coordinated their passage from Lebanon to Libya, then the long trip across the Atlantic to Honduras. Finally, they had moved north through Guatemala and Mexico, walking and taking buses to arrive here. They were still in Mexico, but they were waiting their turn to enter the U.S., crossing the border into Texas. The Americans called this part of their country Texas. During their training, they had been told that Texas had cowboys, farms, and guns-lots of guns. That was good information.

Zamir thought back to when he and his group had linked up with their cartel contact in Honduras. The leader of the smugglers, a rough looking man named Manuel, had separated Zamir and his group from the others who were being smuggled. Manuel had a small man with him who spoke enough Arabic to pass instructions to Zamir. He told Zamir to take all his people, sit against a line of shipping containers, and wait. Zamir did as he was told. He gathered his men and watched the chaos as the AK-47 wielding cartel members separated the remainder of the people into several different groups.

All the girls, and any woman under the age of about forty were taken off to another area. Sometimes they were ripped from the arms of their husbands or children and forced toward a low building that Zamir thought looked like a warehouse of some kind. As the girls and women were marched away, the cartel members were laughing at the women and groping them as they walked past them. The women clutched their bags in front of them in a feeble attempt to protect their breasts from the hands of the men. One younger looking cartel member slapped an African woman on her round backside as she walked past him. The young woman spun around, put her finger in the face of the young man, and yelled something at him in a language that Zamir didn't understand. The young man was not expecting this reaction and recoiled from the verbal assault. Without warning, Manuel struck the woman in the lower back with a straight jab from the butt of his rifle. The young woman tumbled forward and landed at the feet of the younger man on her hands and knees. Manuel yelled at her in Spanish and pointed back at the line. The stunned woman staggered back to her feet and rejoined the other women as they moved in the indicated direction. She was holding her back, trying not to make eye contact with any more of the men.

Zamir watched the interaction that followed between Manuel and the younger man, who didn't look older than about sixteen or seventeen. Manuel cupped the back of the younger man's neck roughly. He was laughing at him and chastising him at the same time. Zamir couldn't understand the language, but he understood the dynamics of the relationship between these two men. Manuel pointed back in the general direction of the African woman as he spoke. Manuel was still smiling and clearly teasing him. The younger man was looking at the ground trying to avoid eye contact with Manuel. Manual put a finger under the younger man's chin and lifted his face up to look him in the eye. He continued to speak, and he roughly turned the boy toward the retreating women. Zamir recognized the body language. Even though Manuel was scolding this boy, it was clear that he was helping him, even mentoring him. Was this a little brother perhaps, who was trying to learn the ropes? Manuel motioned for the boy to follow the women, but the boy hesitated. Manuel gave the boy a firm push and the boy finally obeyed. When Manuel turned back around, Zamir could see that he was still chuckling.

Manuel went back to the task at hand. The men were separated into several groups. Zamir's group had a single guard who casually looked over at them from time to time, but they were generally being ignored as they sat with their backs against the shipping containers. One by one, the cartel members strip searched every person in the other groups. They dumped every bag and rifled through the contents, pocketing things at will.

Zamir watched the process for a couple of hours until, finally, they had searched and moved the last of the other groups. Throughout this process, Zamir could hear the cries of the women from the open door of the warehouse as they were being "processed" as well.

Zamir stood up when he saw Manuel look over at him and start toward him. His heart was racing as he thought of himself and his men being publicly strip searched. Manuel was joined by the small man that was acting as a translator as he closed the distance to Zamir. Zamir mentally prepared his argument against being strip searched as the two men closed the distance. As Manuel reached Zamir, he smiled and extended his hand. Zamir was initially surprised, but hesitantly took the offered hand in a firm handshake. Manuel spoke directly to Zamir in Spanish without looking at the interpreter and the interpreter did a reasonably good job of echoing Manuel's speech in poor, but understandable Arabic.

"You're Zamir Syed," the interpreter parroted.

"I am," replied Zamir.

"You have some wealthy friends, Zamir."

Zamir was very uncomfortable. He didn't like being at the mercy of this man. In an attempt to hide his nervousness, he didn't reply. Zamir simply returned the gaze of the man.

After a moment of awkward silence, Manuel suddenly started to smile and reached out and playfully slapped Zamir on the arm. "Listen, my friend. Your passage has been paid. I understand that you have quite a bit of money with you, among other things." Manuel looked past Zamir at one of the duffle bags on the ground behind him. The interpreter echoed his words as quickly as he could.

Once again, Zamir remained silent.

"Don't worry. I'm not going to take your money or anything else that you're carrying. Don't get me wrong, normally I would," Manuel laughed a genuine laugh. "However, apparently your organization has made a deal with my organization and you're getting..." The interpreter paused as he searched for the right way to say this in Arabic, "special treatment."

This didn't make Zamir any more comfortable. He didn't trust this man with the tattoos on his face and neck. He would use him to get to the U.S., but he would be happy when he could be free of this man and his organization.

"We have some trucks and buses coming in a couple of hours. I'll have my men get your men some food and some clean water. Please, walk with me. We have business to discuss."

Zamir turned to Mohamed, his second in charge and told him in Arabic to stay alert and that he would return soon. Zamir intentionally spoke quickly and used a slang phrase in an attempt to make it more difficult for the young interpreter to understand what was being said. He then turned to follow Manuel as he walked toward the warehouse.

Manuel continued, "As I was saying, I understand that you have money, some fake papers, credit cards, various tools of your trade, and some addresses that you need to get to in the United States." As the interpreter finished the sentence, the three men reached the open door of the warehouse and Zamir looked in.

Several of the women were sitting together crying. Many of them had had their clothing ripped. Zamir saw the young African woman who had yelled at the boy. She sat on the concrete, completely naked, clutching her knees to her chest and crying. She had her face pressed into her legs, but Zamir could see that her left eye was significantly swollen. Both of her knees were bleeding from abrasions.

Manuel saw her too. A smile crept across his face. "Pedro!" he called out. "Pedro, come here," he said in Spanish. Zamir watched the boy as he crossed the room toward his uncle. Manuel grabbed him in a one-armed embrace and pointed at the young African woman with his other hand. "Did you do that? Did you teach her to show some respect?"

The boy sheepishly nodded his head. "Yes, Tio." He looked toward the floor again. "The other guys beat her up a little and held her down for me," he replied with a sniffle.

"Hold your chin up, boy. If you're going to be a part of this organization, you'd better be a man! A real man! If a bitch talks back, you teach her some respect, Pedrito. Do you understand me?"

"Yes, Tio."

"Okay boy, back to work." Without any other response, Pedro turned and walked away.

This entire exchange took place in Spanish. Zamir didn't speak Spanish. He had only studied English as part of his training. As Manuel spoke to the teenager, Zamir simply stood stoically and observed the scenario.

Manuel turned back to Zamir. "You are the commander of this group, yes?"

Zamir did not reply verbally, but simply nodded his head slowly in response.

"Well, Commander, rank has its privileges. As a symbol of good will from one commander to another, please pick out a girl. You can have some fun while your men are fed." The interpreter was getting more comfortable and his translations were easier to understand.

Zamir did not respond. He understood, but he had no intention of raping one of these girls. Not that he had any problem with rape. In fact, as part of their preparation, they had been instructed that rape could be used at any time as a weapon of intimidation and humiliation, or even for just recreation. He knew the psychological effect it could have on a population. If you rape a girl in front of her father or her husband, you could mentally break the man. If you let the girl live after the rape, she would never be the same. Alternatively, you could rape her and then kill her in front of the men to further torture them. However, Zamir had no intention of putting himself in such a vulnerable position with these criminals.

"Sir," Zamir began, "thank you for your kind offer. However, I would like to return to my men."

Manuel smiled. "Oh, I'm sorry. How about a little boy, then?"

Zamir felt his anger building and the blood rush to his face. This man was toying with him and meant to insult him. "I will be returning to my men now." Zamir turned toward the door.

Manuel quickly pivoted and stepped to block the path back to the door. "Zamir, Zamir. I'm just trying to be a good host. You don't have to be angry." Manuel had the look on his face of a bully who was clearly accustomed to getting his way.

Zamir stopped, and with much effort, calmly responded. "Manuel, my organization has paid you for a service. I am but the first of many more who will follow. I hope to be able to report to my superiors that you upheld your end of the contract, and this should lead to many more lucrative dealings together."

The interpreter did not understand part of the statement. Zamir reworded it into simpler terms. A look of recognition washed over his face and he quickly turned to Manuel and spoke.

Manuel squinted slightly and leaned forward, closing the distance to Zamir, who was a little shorter than him. Zamir studied the man's serious face. His muscles were tense as he tried to read the situation. Mentally, he prepared to defend himself. Suddenly, Manuel burst into laughter again. It was a loud laugh and Zamir flinched at the surprise. Manuel turned to the interpreter, slapping him on the upper arm hard enough that the smaller man took a short step to maintain his balance. "He doesn't want a girl. He doesn't want a boy. He just wants his men." Manuel punctuated the statements with another obnoxious laugh. He addressed the interpreter directly this time and said, "Take this guy back to his men. He's no fun at all."

Without looking back to Zamir, Manuel turned and walked toward the group of girls. The interpreter spoke up. "Mister Zamir, please, this way." As he spoke, he motioned toward the door with his hand.

Zamir, slowly began moving in the direction of the door again. However, his eyes were still on Manuel. Manuel had walked over to a group of girls and women who were huddled together, crying. This group still had their clothes intact. He roughly grabbed a small Latina girl of about fourteen or fifteen and lifted her to her feet as an older woman clung to her arm, crying out, "No! No! Por favor! No!"

As Zamir neared the door, he saw Manuel backhand the older woman. She landed on her butt with an audible grunt as Manuel dragged the young girl toward the back of the building. Zamir paused at the door and looked at the group of women. He looked back at the interpreter who nodded with his head in the general direction of Zamir's men. Zamir turned and slowly walked back to his waiting group.

"Is everything okay, Commander?" Mohamed asked as Zamir walked up to the group.

"Yes, Mohamed," he replied. "I look forward to being rid of this group. They will try to distract us from the mission."

Mohamed did not reply but stroked his beard as he thought. "We will not be distracted, and we will not fail. Allahu Akbar."

Zamir looked back at the open door of the warehouse where new screams could be heard from a young female voice. "Allahu Akbar."

10

Robin Sage I, Preparation

Fall, 2003, Nearly twenty years earlier

U.S. Army Special Forces Training Facility, Camp Mackall, NC

A standard Special Forces Operational Detachment-Alpha, SFODA, or ODA for short, (also referred to as an "A-Team") consists of twelve me. The makeup of the team provides redundancies of the various Special Forces jobs within a small element. This allows the team to break into two six-man teams and still maintain the same capabilities.

Each detachment has a captain as a commander, His Military Occupational Specialty (MOS) is 18A, or simply an "Alpha". The 18 at the beginning indicates Special Forces. The commander is responsible for everything the team does or fails to do.

The Assistant Detachment Commander is a Special Forces Warrant Officer with an MOS of 180A. His job is to assist and advise the Detachment Commander, command half the team during split-team operations, or command the ODA in the absence of a captain. Often, they are simply referred to as "Chief," which is short for Chief Warrant Officer. These are former Special Forces non-commissioned officers (NCOs) who were selected to cross over to the officer ranks.

The NCOs on an Special Forces Detachment have various jobs. Each team has a Team Sergeant with an MOS of 18Z, commonly referred to as a "Zulu." He is the senior NCO on the team and runs the day-to-day activities. He works with the commander to ensure mission success.

Each ODA is authorized to have one Special Forces Intelligence Sergeant, MOS 18F, commonly referred to as a "Fox." The Fox is responsible for target development and other intelligence related tasks.

The remaining jobs on the team have two positions for each MOS. There are two Weapons Sergeants, MOS 18B, commonly referred to as "Bravos." In addition to weapons and ammunition, they're responsible for security, weapons training, and tactics.

The two Engineer Sergeants, MOS 18C, or "Charlies," handle all construction projects as well as explosives. They also manage the team logistics.

The two Medical Sergeants, MOS 18D, or "Deltas," act as the team medics and handle the administrative requirements for the team.

Two Communication Sergeants, MOS 18E, or "Echos," are responsible for the various radios of the team, including satellite communications. They are often tasked with other technical tasks related to the team computers.

In 2003, when Specialist Michaels and his team were going through the Q-Course, ODAs were identified by a three-digit number. For example, ODA 733 was a team in 7th Special Forces Group and ODA 512 was an ODA in 5th Special Forces Group. Specialist Michaels's team was ODA 919. The nine at the beginning indicated it was a training team in the Special Forces Qualification Course.

The final phase of the Q-Course is called "Robin Sage." During this phase, the Special Forces students learn how to conduct Unconventional Warfare (UW). Unconventional Warfare utilizes specially trained troops in denied or occupied territory to enable a resistance movement or insurgency. As part of the training, the students learn how to infiltrate a foreign country, link up with the resistance force, then equip, train, and lead that force in combat.

One example of this was in World War II when the Office of Strategic Services, the predecessor to modern Special Forces, dropped specialized troops behind enemy lines in Europe to organize, equip and lead the local population in combat against the Axis forces. Likewise, Green Berets worked with local Montagnards in Vietnam to fight the North Vietnamese. Robin Sage immerses the students in the fictitious country of Pineland where they train, equip, and lead local "Pinelanders" in a war to free their country from an occupying oppressor.

In fall of 2003, ODA 919 was in Camp Mackall preparing to "deploy" to Pineland. They had received their classes and were conducting the mission analysis prior to executing the mission.

D-2 (Two days before deployment)

Specialist Michaels was accumulating a list of all the equipment that the team would need to take with them on the mission. He saw Jimmy Roberts walk into the team room. "Jimmy, when do you want to check all the IFAKs?" An IFAK is an Individual First Aid Kit.

Between S.U.T. and Robin Sage every student had attended additional training in their specific MOS. Paul Michaels was an engineer. Jimmy Roberts was a medic.

"I've already got 'em done, man, they're good. I have them over in my area," Jimmy replied.

"Fifteen of 'em?" Paul asked

"Yeah man. Plus, I have the fifteen GFAKs." A GFAK is an unofficial acronym for Guerrilla First Aid Kit. These were additional kits that would be carried in to supply the guerrilla force, or G-Force.

"OK, I'm working out weights of everything so I can distribute the weight evenly for infil. I'll put the same weight for everyone for the IFAKs, since everyone will carry their own. But I need to know the weight of the GFAKs so I can figure out who can carry them," Paul added.

"Well, there's not much to the GFAKs, man. We don't have enough medical supplies to make a legitimate one, so each one will have an improvised tourniquet, improvised chest seal, one field dressing, and an improvised Needle D. We managed to come up with fifteen SAW pouches, so each one is in its own pouch. Plus, it has a carrying strap, so that's useful," Jimmy said. The SAW or Squad Automatic Weapon is a light machine gun that fires linked 5.56mm ammunition. The ammunition came in 200 round drums packaged in a lightweight bandoleer. Soldiers would often keep the bandoleers and repurpose them. The medics had done exactly that for the GFAKs.

"An improvised Needle D? How'd you improvise that?"

"I just took an old chemlight and wrote 'Needle D' on the side of it with a Sharpie," Jimmy replied with a slight grin.

"Needle D" is short for "Needle Decompression." It's a large hypodermic needle that can be used to relieve pressure from the chest cavity in the event of a tension pneumothorax. A tension pneumothorax can be created when a wound, such as a gunshot, allows air to accumulate between the lung and the chest wall, compressing the lung. After the entrance and exit wounds are sealed, the needle is inserted between the ribs, piercing the chest wall, and giving the air a path to escape, therefore relieving the pressure on the lung.

"Oh, gotcha. Well, a training environment is a training environment, I guess. You do what you can. What's everything weigh?" Paul asked.

"Do you want the individual weights or the total weight of all of them?" Jimmy asked.

Paul thought about this for a couple of seconds. "If they're all the same, just give me an individual weight. That way if I need to break up a few to different people, I can."

"Yeah man. That makes sense. I'll get it to you in a minute," Jimmy said. Jimmy was a skinny redhead from Iowa. He definitely didn't look like what most people think of when they think of a Green Beret. He was skinny with acne scars and he looked younger than his twenty-one years. He would be going to a National Guard unit when he finished the training, not to an active-duty Special Forces Group like the rest of the students.

"Thanks, man. I need the weight of your aid bag, and the other aid bags, if they aren't all the same." Paul added.

"They're not exactly the same. They're all pretty similar, but each medic packs his own bag, so there will be some differences. I'll get that for you, too."

"Cool," Paul replied and went back to his notebook. As one of the Charlies, he was responsible for distributing the weight so everyone was carrying approximately the same weight for the infiltration, or 'infil', as it was referred to. It was a complicated task.

The Bravos would be carrying things like machine guns and a mortar system with a base plate. The weight would add up quickly. The Charlies were responsible for both demolition (explosives) and construction. However, for this mission, the initial focus would concentrate on the demolition side, so they had simulated C-4, TNT, detonating cord (det cord), time fuse, fuse ignitors, blasting caps, and everything else they needed to blow things up. The Deltas had the medical gear and the Echos had all the radio stuff. Radio batteries also added weight quickly. The radio batteries were one of the items that would be distributed around the team to help even out the weight.

"Hey, Jeremy," Paul said as he approached Jeremy Burkhardt, one the Echos. "I need the weights of your radios, and all your MOS related gear, plus I need to know how many batteries are going, so I can break it up for infil."

"Oh yeah, I have that for you" Jeremy replied, pulling a piece of waterproof paper from his shirt pocket. "I'll be carrying the KYK-13 in a fanny pouch tied off around my waist," he added.

"Ok, got it," Paul replied. The KYK-13 (pronounced "Kick-thirteen") was a small electronic device that allowed for the electronic transfer of the cryptographic "fill" for the radios. This fill is what allowed the radios to transmit and receive in an encrypted manner. The KYK-13 being used in the Q-Course was the real deal. It was a legitimately classified and sensitive item that had to be kept tied off to a person at all times. Jeremy was that person. They would need the KYK-13 to fill the radios for the next two weeks to be able to communicate with higher headquarters and each other.

The captains didn't have much individual MOS-related gear, but one of them would carry one of the computers. Paul would round out the weight by having the captains carry part of the ammo and other necessities. Plus, it was supposed to be cold during the mission, so cold weather gear had to be taken into consideration. To make matters worse, all the rucksacks had to be waterproofed and packed in a way so that they could be rigged up to a parachute harness because the team would be jumping out of a C-47 aircraft. They would have to rig the rucksacks into a harness that would then be clipped to the front of their parachute harness. Then the aircraft would fly into Pineland and drop them into a farmer's field that was "behind enemy lines."

The C-47 was an ancient aircraft that was seldom used anymore. C-47s were used to drop paratroopers and tow gliders into Europe in WWII. When the team was told that the infil platform would be a C-47, one of the captains immediately responded with, "You mean a CH-47?" The CH-47 Chinook is a modern twin propeller cargo helicopter commonly used to drop Special Operations troops.

The cadre just laughed. "Did I say Chinook? No, I didn't. You'll be jumping fixed wing. A C-47."

After the cadre had left, Larry Lawson turned to Paul and said "A freakin' C-47? Are you kidding me? How old must that thing be?"

Paul replied, "I don't even know what that is."

Larry just laughed. "Dude! They used C-47s on D-Day!"

"Holy crap! I bet that thing is held together with bubble gum and positive thoughts!" Paul replied with a chuckle.

Larry just laughed. "Well, it is what it is. I guess we're jumping Grandpa's aircraft."

"I guess we are," Paul replied. Paul was close with Larry. He was the only person on this ODA that he had gone through S.U.T. with a few months back. Larry had gone to the 18B course to become a weapons sergeant. Paul really looked up to Larry. He'd been in the Ranger Regiment and had been in the army nine years already. But even though Larry was significantly more experienced in the army, they were now peers going through the Q-Course.

At five feet, eight inches, Larry was slightly shorter than Paul, but stocky. He was the only jumpmaster qualified student on the team and had already been to Ranger School. Larry was easy to get along with and was always ready to help those around him. One day during S.U.T., Larry made a statement to Paul that Paul would never forget. They were planning a patrol and Larry was supposed to be helping write one of the paragraphs for the Operations Order, or OPORD. Larry had completed that paragraph and helped with another paragraph. Paul asked which paragraph he was supposed to be helping with. Larry paused and turned to face the younger man. "Look Paul. OPORDs are easy for me. I'm a freakin' E-7. I've done more OPORDs than the rest of you clowns combined. If you're not working and one of your teammates is, you're wrong. If you ever find yourself using the phrase 'That's not my job,' you should reevaluate your vocation."

Paul didn't respond immediately, but just stood there, thinking about what Larry had just said to him. Larry continued. "Look man, I know you're from the infantry too, so you probably get it, but we're going to be working in twelve-man teams, not thirty-two-man platoons anymore. We need to be able to count on each other. When I got to First Batt, my squad leader told me something that changed the way I look at this business. He said, 'Be the type of teammate you wish you had on your team.' That really stuck with me. I've spent every day since that day trying to live up to that. You should too."

A smile crept across Paul's face. "You're a smart guy, Larry. I don't care what everyone else says about you."

"Shut up, Jackass," Larry said and playfully shoved Paul in the chest. "I'm just sayin' bro. It's a real thing. We're all gonna end up in a two-way live fire sooner or later and you need to know that you can count on those on your left and right. *Always strive to be the type of teammate that you would want to have on your team.*"

"Alright, man. Thanks."

Paul would remember that advice and he'd do his best to live up to it.

"Hey guys, listen up!" It was Captain Richard Tribiani, the current commander of the ODA. The team all called him "Joey" as a reference to the TV show "Friends." They paused what they were working on to look up at him. He was holding up a stack of papers. "I have three copies of the country study. I know everyone has already seen this, but I'm putting these up here on the table. Everyone needs to take some time to read through it again before the ISO test." The ISO test, or Isolation Examination was their last written exam before they would leave the team bay to head out into the field. It was called an Isolation Examination because they had been in Isolation for the planning portion of the mission. When a team went into Isolation, there was no outside contact to reduce the risk of an OPSEC (Operational Security) violation. They would live in the team room and concentrate on the mission, removing outside distractions. In the Q-Course, this was followed by a written test to evaluate the students on Unconventional Warfare and the specifics of the mission they were about to undertake.

Everyone was tired. At this point in the training, there was very little supervision by the training cadre. The team studied, prepared, practiced classes, and packed. They checked their gear and the gear of their teammates. There was no deliberate sleep deprivation, although there never seemed to be enough time to get everything done, so sleep was the natural place to steal more time to finish tasks.

D-1 (One day before deployment)

The next day, the cadre came into the team bay. "919, listen up!" he said as he burst into the room. Everyone stopped what they were doing. Those who were seated stood up. Everyone gave Sergeant Souby their attention. He held a single piece of paper in his hand.

"None of you idiots failed the ISO exam too bad. Good job. Now the real work begins. Medics, any new medical concerns?"

Jimmy spoke up. "Negative Sar'nt."

"Good. Team Sergeant?"

Staff Sergeant Billingsly, an 18B, was acting as the team sergeant for this phase. He spoke up from the other side of the room. "Here, Sar'nt"

"You're fuckin' fired. Specialist Michaels, you're the new Team Sergeant."

Paul felt a nervous knot form in his gut. "Roger Sar'nt."

"Captain Tribiani?"

"Here, Sergeant," Joey replied.

"You're fired too. Captain Wilkerson?"

Captain Jeremiah Wilkerson took a single step forward and replied. "Here Sar'nt."

"You're the new Commander. Here's your updated timeline for infil." He handed the paper to the new commander.

"Roger, Sergeant," Captain Wilkerson said as he took the paper and immediately looked down at it.

Sergeant Souby continued. "You'll see some updates on there. Pre-jump has been moved to 1700 hours tomorrow. Now listen boys. It's already been a long road to get to where you are. Don't lose focus and start thinking that somehow you're done, because you're not. Pay attention to your surroundings. Pay attention to what the locals are saying. You never know what useful information could be gained just by simply listening to people talk around you. Let me put it to you this way: If I want to know something about Texas, who do I ask?"

Several of the men responded simultaneously with a mix of "Texans" and "Someone from Texas."

"That's right. Well, this is the same thing. If you want to understand something about Pineland, what is your best source of information?"

"Pinelanders" was the universal response.

"That's right. Pinelanders. Listen to what your partner force is saying. You never know when you might hear something in a conversation that you can use later. Maybe you're in a truck with someone and they casually mention someone they know that owns a farm. What's the potential importance of that statement?" Sergeant Souby paused for the students to answer.

"Food," one person said.

"Maybe he has a truck we could use," someone else added.

"Yeah, maybe. Everything matters. Maintain situational awareness at all times. Don't try to game the system. Just do your job. If you go out there and just try to 'beat Robin Sage', you're doing yourself an injustice, and you're doing an injustice to your future team if you manage to pass. Just do the job you've been trained to do. Go out there and conduct Unconventional Warfare. Robin Sage will take care of itself. Am I clear?"

There was a chorus of "Yes, Sergeant" responses.

"Now, what are your questions?" Sergeant Souby looked around the room.

Everyone had questions. Everyone was nervous. No one spoke up.

"All right then. I'll check on you later. Get back to work." And with that, he turned and walked out the door.

The team went back to work. It felt like everything should be done by now, but somehow, they were still scrambling to get things done. Some things had to be packed and repacked. They would be receiving a resupply bundle later that would be dropped to them by parachute. That had to be inventoried and packed. At some point, everyone needed to get some sleep. However, by the time the flurry of activity died down and the team finally made it to their racks, most of them just stared at the ceiling. They were nervous, yet excited. This was it. They were about to begin the last stage to becoming a U.S. Army Green Beret.

Paul was lying back on his bunk with his hands behind his head, looking up at the darkness. He knew he needed to get some sleep. Wake up was at 0500, but he had his alarm set for 0445. Since he was the Team Sergeant now, one of his responsibilities was to make sure that the team was up on time. It was already around midnight. His mind raced as he tried to think if he had forgotten anything. Finally, he decided that it didn't matter. If he had forgotten something, he'd deal with it or figure it out later. He rolled onto his side, closed his eyes and was soon asleep.

11

Robin Sage II, Night Jump

Fall, 2003

U.S. Army Special Forces Training Facility, Camp Mackall, NC

D-Day (Deployment Day)

The next morning, Paul didn't have to wake anyone up. He got up with his alarm at 0445 as planned and two other men were already awake and moving around the team room. A few minutes later, one of them walked into the squad bay where the bunks were located and casually turned the lights on and walked back out. The team started coming to life.

They immediately launched into the tasks they wanted to get done before the cadre showed up at 0600. Larry walked up to Paul. "Good morning, Team Sergeant."

"Screw you, Larry," Paul responded with a laugh.

"So, I know you're not an engineer right now, but before you got promoted, did you finish up the ruck weights?" Larry asked, still ribbing Paul about being put into the Team Sergeant position.

"Yep," Paul said and pretended to be busy looking at an inventory sheet.

"Well?" Larry prodded.

"Well, what?" Paul acted like he didn't know what Larry wanted.

"Well, what's the weight per man come out to?" Larry asked.

"It's probably better if you don't know. You can carry it, just carry it. If I tell you how much it is, it will only make matters worse," Paul replied.

"Dude, I'm a big boy. What's the damage?" Larry asked again.

"Fine," Paul said and pulled a small green waterproof notepad from his pocket. He flipped through a couple of pages and stopped. "Rucksacks are 126 pounds, except for the machine gunners. The M60 gunner will have 112, the SAW Gunners will have 118-ish."

Larry's eyes widened at the report. "Are you screwing with me?"

"Nope," Paul replied. "Plus, we'll all have our LBEs with a basic load of 5.56, and two quarts of water. Of course, part of the ruck weight is that everyone will have two two-Quart canteens. That right there is over eight pounds. Plus for the jump, we'll be using M1950 weapons cases, so that's more weight, but we'll shed that once we get to the ground." The M1950 weapons case is a heavy canvas bag that is attached to a paratrooper's parachute harness during airborne operations to protect weapon systems, and sometimes other items as well.

"1950's? I thought we were jumping exposed weapons," Larry stated.

"Yeah, I thought that too, but Sergeant Souby said we weren't cool enough to jump exposed yet. He said something about stupid kids trying to run before they walk or some shit. I don't know. Anyhow, we're jumping 1950's."

Larry listened for a moment. "But we're still getting Dash One Bravos, right?" The MC1-1B was a steerable parachute and only certain units were authorized to use it. Special Forces was one of those units.

"Yeah man, we're getting Dash One Bravos. And it's a good thing. Did you see the size of that drop zone?" Paul asked.

"Yeah, I saw it on the imagery. That thing's gonna look like a postage stamp from the air," Larry said.

"Yep," Paul replied, "and in the dark," he added with a genuine laugh. "This is some cool shit, Larry."

"Oh, it's cool. Until you break your freakin' leg. It's *all* cool, right up until it isn't." Larry's age and experience was showing.

"Well, we won't be under canopy long," Paul added very seriously.

"Why is that?" Larry asked.

"Because, man. Do the math. Let's say the average dude here is two hundred pounds, and a few are more than that. Add on a 126lb ruck, a loaded down LBE, and a freakin' M1950 weapons case that's going to have various crap in it. Your reserve counts as suspended weight, unless you use it obviously. One dude, with all his crap is going to be close to four hundred pounds, give or take, suspended from the parachute. The more weight we put under the parachute, the faster we'll fall. So, like I said. We won't be in the air long. Drop altitude is 1,250' AGL." AGL is an acronym for 'Above Ground Level'.

Larry rubbed his freshly buzzed head and then just turned and walked toward the latrine. Paul heard him say "I'm getting too old for this shit."

To the men of ODA 919, the rest of the day seemed to fly by. Everyone was double and triple checking everything. Everyone was nervous. Paul barely remembered doing pre-jump. Pre-jump training was conducted before every jump. It was essentially a quick refresher of actions to be done during an airborne operation.

The team all helped each other get into their parachutes and attach their rucksacks and M1950 weapons cases. There were three jumpmaster qualified cadre members, including Sergeant Souby who conducted a JMPI (Jumpmaster Personnel Inspection) on all the jumpers. Once all the JMPIs were complete, the team began the long waddle out onto the airfield to load up the old aircraft.

Paul had jumped numerous aircraft in his time in the army. He had jumped from C-130s, C141s, UH-60 helicopters and even an old UH-1 Huey like they had during the Vietnam war. However, this aircraft was a different experience. For one thing, it felt small compared to the aircraft he had jumped in the 82nd -- really small. The men were jammed in very tightly. There were two jumpmasters on the aircraft who would be responsible to control the jump. One was called the "Safety" and he passed out little yellow foam earplugs to everyone as they got on. This aircraft was loud!

Within a few minutes, the old aircraft began moving. The pitch of the engines increased, and the team felt the aircraft lurch forward as the pilot released the brakes. They began turning to get lined up with the runway at the Camp Mackall Army Airfield. It was now dark outside, however, there were numerous small lights inside the aircraft. Once they got lined up, they felt the pilot reengage the brakes. The Safety was wearing a headlamp and Paul saw him moving around. The pitch of engines gently began to increase even more, and the aircraft pushed against the brakes that were holding it in place. The pilot suddenly released the brakes and the C47 quickly surged forward and began gaining speed down the runway. There was no question when they left the ground. The old aircraft swayed slightly left and right as the skilled pilot leveled it out and began the short trip west toward the drop zone.

Paul was packed in between Jimmy on his right and Larry on his left. They were all on the left, or port, side of the aircraft. The flight was only scheduled for about forty-five minutes. Within the training scenario, they were crossing from the unoccupied Southern Pineland Province into the occupied Northern Pineland Province. About thirty minutes into the flight, Larry nudged Paul and leaned over to say something. With the roar inside the aircraft and the ear plugs in, Paul could not make out what Larry had said. He leaned closer to Larry and yelled. "What?!"

Larry leaned closer to Paul as best he could with his giant rucksack sitting on his knees and pressing against Paul's rucksack. "I said," Larry yelled, "we should be over the English Channel about now!"

Paul paused for a second as he let the joke sink in. Suddenly, it was the funniest thing he'd ever heard and he began to laugh out loud. Larry immediately joined him, laughing at his own joke.

The jumpmaster stood up and positioned himself near the jump door of the aircraft. He gave the command, "Ten minutes!" Everyone echoed the command as they rocked back and forth to ensure that everyone to their left and right was awake. For those who have not lived the life of a soldier, it would probably be shocking to learn the places where soldiers can sleep. These men were wearing parachutes and helmets and had monstrous rucksacks sitting on their legs, but sure enough, a couple of the team had been lulled to sleep by the consistent hum of the engines.

The jumpmaster and safety went through their steps, checking the door and preparing to send the team out into the cold night air. When it came time for everyone to stand up, most of the men were unable to due to the tight conditions and the extreme weight of their equipment. The safety moved down the line helping everyone get to their feet. The jumpmaster told everyone to hook their static lines into the anchor line cable of the aircraft. "Hook Up!"

This static line would pull the parachute out of its pack tray as the jumper fell away from the aircraft. This was not a freefall jump, where the jumpers fall through the air and must manually deploy their parachutes. In a static line jump, the parachute is designed to begin deploying almost as soon as the paratrooper exits the aircraft.

The jumpmaster continued through the commands until he finally gave the command of "Standby!" The time came to exit and over the roar of the engines, Paul heard the jumpmaster screaming, "Green light, Go! Go! Go!"

The team began shuffling toward the door. Paul kept his eyes fixed on the Jumpmaster. His right hand covered the rip cord grip of his reserve parachute. His left hand held onto the yellow static line that dragged down the steel cable over his head as he moved. As he approached the door, he shifted his gaze from the Jumpmaster to the back of Jimmy's helmet. Suddenly, Jimmy pivoted, exited the door, and disappeared into the darkness outside the aircraft. Paul extended his left arm toward the Jumpmaster, who grabbed the static line from his hand and swept it toward the rear of the aircraft. With significant effort, Paul pivoted on his left foot and launched out the door of the aircraft into the night. He began counting: "One Thousand, Two Thousand, Three Thousand, Four...oooof."

The main parachute caught the air as it was designed to do and suddenly, it was quiet. Paul could still hear the aircraft, but it was growing quieter as it continued its flight into the night sky. Paul reached up and felt for his toggles that allowed him to steer the canopy. He quickly found them and looked down through the murky night. He was easily able to identify the drop zone below him, as it was illuminated by several small fires. They were arranged in the shape of the letter "L" on its side. He was over the central part of the field. The jumpmaster had put them out perfectly over the drop zone. Everyone in the airborne community had heard of instances when jumpers exited the aircraft in the wrong place. However, tonight, Paul was very happy with his position in the sky as he dropped toward the earth.

With the MC1-1B parachute, you want to hit the ground while facing into the wind. The parachute has a forward thrust, so if you land with the wind to your back, you could potentially be moving very fast when you hit the ground and you're more likely to get hurt. Paul rested his hands on his toggles briefly to see which way the wind was going to naturally take him. It was more difficult to judge the wind in the dark, but he could still see the fires, so he took note of the direction he was flying. Once he was sure of the wind direction, he looked over his right shoulder to ensure there were no jumpers there and pulled his right toggle all the way down to waist level. This caused the parachute to start turning to the right. He kept an eye on the fire to judge when he had completed a one hundred-eighty-degree turn. He could see that the ground was already getting close and with his left hand, he reached in front of himself and pulled the tab to release his rucksack. It fell away from him, and he felt the snap as it reached the end of the lowering line, allowing it to dangle below him for the final few seconds of the descent.

Judging the direction and feeling the wind in his face, Paul felt like he was facing directly into the wind. With his left hand, he pulled the quick release on the tie holding the M1950 weapons case against his side, then swept the release that kept it secured to his harness. It fell away from him as well and slide down the lowering line, impacting the suspended rucksack. Almost as soon as it hit the ruck, Paul heard the rucksack strike the ground. *Feet and knees together* went through his mind and a split second later he plowed into the ground slightly in front of his equipment.

Paratroopers are trained to conduct what is called a Parachute Landing Fall, or PLF. In practice, you should first impact with the balls of the feet, followed by the calf, buttocks and then the lats, or as the Army says, the "pull up muscle." However, in practice, it seldom works that way and so was the case tonight. Paul's feet hit and the next thing to hit was his left knee due to the forward motion of parachute. He maintained his elbows high and together in front of his face. The next thing to hit was his left elbow and then he was sprawled on his belly. Out of instinct, from countless times practicing the maneuver, he quickly reached up and pulled his canopy release assembly, cutting one side of the parachute away from the harness. *That hurt*. He lay in the field for a moment and rolled over onto his back, looking up into the night sky. He could hear several other impacts around him as the remainder of his team reached the earth. He heard a random voice in the night: "Son of a ...". Then all was quiet.

Paul did a quick assessment of himself. He moved both his legs and rotated his ankles. Everything was fine. His knee had struck the ground reasonably hard, but the ground was somewhat soft, and he didn't feel like he had any injuries. He got to his feet and began removing himself from the parachute harness. He quickly moved to his gear, unzipped the M1950 weapons case, and pulled out his M4 rifle. Without looking at it, he pulled the charging handle, chambering a blank round.

Each jumper had a parachute kit bag packed under the leg straps of their parachute harness so it would be readily accessible as soon as they hit the ground. Paul grabbed the bag and opened it. He stuffed his parachute harness into the bag.

He then moved to find the apex of the parachute and in a smooth, practiced motion, rolled the parachute as he moved back toward the bag and stuffed it inside. Next, he moved to his rucksack and pulled the quick release on the H-harness of his ruck. He pulled the harness off and stuffed it into the kit bag with the parachute and snapped it up.

Typically, on training jumps, paratroopers would all keep their own H-harness, but for this mission, they had been directed to stuff them into the kit bag with their parachutes to get rid of them. Now, he needed to get all his equipment and move to the assembly area. He had executed this task many times in the infantry and knew it would be easier to carry everything if he strapped the weapons case on top of his ruck. So he loosened the main straps of his modified A.L.I.C.E. pack and threaded the M1950 under them. He retightened the straps and then he was ready to move. However, the ruck was too heavy to just swing up onto one arm, so he spread the straps apart, sat down in front of the rucksack, and threaded his arms into the shoulder straps. He tightened the straps and then, with a significant amount of effort, rolled to one side so he could get his feet under him and stand up. He threw his rifle sling over his neck and moved back to the parachute kit bag. He grabbed it by the handles and spread his legs. Swinging the kit bag, now heavy with his parachute, between his legs to get momentum, he heaved it over his head. It landed on top of his ruck, pushing his head uncomfortably forward. He had everything; it was time to move out. He could see the blue chemlight in the tree line indicating the assembly area. With significant effort, he trudged through the night toward the little light.

Paul made it to the assembly area about the same time as two of his teammates. Paul could see a man with a blue chemlight hanging around his neck, so he headed directly toward this man. They had practiced the link up plan, and everyone knew the code words, or "bona fides" that they were to use to confirm that this was in fact the correct person. As Paul approached the man, he could see that one of his teammates was already walking up to him. Paul couldn't tell who it was. Then he heard Jimmy's voice as he asked "Hey man. Are you our ride?"

Paul was instantly furious. They had gone over the code words for the last three days and everyone was supposed to know exactly what to say, and that wasn't it. Then Paul heard the man respond, "I don't know what you're talking about, kid." Paul increased his speed to intercept the conversation before Jimmy could speak again.

"Sir. Sir!" Paul blurted out as he shuffled up to them.

The man turned to face Paul, who was breathing hard and struggling against the parachute kit bag that was pressed against the back of his head.

Paul stopped in front of the man, leaned forward, and shrugged the parachute over his head and onto the ground between them. It landed with an audible thud.

"Sir," Paul began again. "What my friend here *meant* to say is: Do you know of any good bass fishing around here?" Paul put some extra stress on the word 'meant' and glanced over at Jimmy as he said it.

Jimmy looked away, instantly realizing what he had done wrong.

"No, but we have plenty of turkey and deer," the older man replied. That was the correct response.

"Nice to meet you sir. I'm Paul." Paul extended his hand toward the man for a handshake. The man didn't seem to notice the proffered hand. Instead, he turned and looked toward the trees at the edge of the field.

"Ok buddy. Have everyone put their parachutes right there under that tree and camouflage them. We have someone coming in the morning to pick 'em up. I don't want any evidence of American paratroopers on my farm any longer than necessary. If the UPA finds those parachutes, they'll kill me and my family." The man was completely in role. He was worried about the "enemy," the UPA. In this scenario, the United Provinces of Atlantica, or the UPA, were the occupying force and the locals were afraid of them.

"You got it sir. What's your name?" Paul asked.

"You can just call me Jason," the man said in a curt response.

"Okay Jason, thanks."

"You can thank me later, after we get you out of here. Now get your team's shit put over there. Here's a camo tarp. Throw this over the parachutes and camouflage them. And hurry up, ib t's time to go!" Jason handed Paul a folded tarp.

Paul took the tarp and grabbed his kit bag from the ground. He didn't want to throw it over his head again, so he just picked it up in front of him and waddled over to the indicated tree, the bag bouncing off the front of his legs with every step. Once he got to the tree, he dropped the kit bag right at the base of the tree's trunk. He dropped the tarp on the ground next to it. He grabbed his knife and moved to the surrounding area and began cutting branches to put on top of the parachutes for camouflage. As he returned with the first armful of branches, a light rain began falling. The temperature was around forty degrees, and the rain was cold. *Great*, thought Paul. *That's just what we need right now*. The time was 11:15 p.m., or in Paul's brain, it was 2315hrs, military time.

The rest of the team was arriving one by one. Paul told Jimmy to keep harvesting branches for camouflage and took control of the team as they arrived, disseminating the information and urging everyone to hurry up. By the time they finished hiding all the parachutes, it was 2335 and Jason was growing visibly more agitated. "What on God's green earth is taking you guys so long? We have to go. Right now!"

Captain Wilkerson walked up. "Jason, I'm Jeremiah. I'm the commander of this team."

"Well, good for you, Captain. Get your shit and get in the trailer."

"Okay, what's the route that we're taking?" Jeremiah had his map in his hand. It was in a waterproof bag and the rain was dripping off the plastic.

"Look, Captain. I've already passed your little password test. You know who I am. Get in the trailer and I'm gonna take you where you're supposed to be. Now hurry up." He turned and walked toward the trailer, which was connected to a newer looking white Ford F-250. The trailer was a large, open-topped, cargo trailer that had wooden sides attached with ratchet straps. The sides of the trailer were only about four feet high. It didn't look like it was in very good shape to Jeremiah.

Jeremiah turned to Paul. "Crap. Okay. Get the guys loaded up."

"I'm on it," said Paul, and he moved to the team to pass out the instructions. Everyone began moving up the makeshift ramp onto the trailer. Once they were all in the trailer, Jason moved to the rear of the trailer and latched the plywood gate. He folded up the ramps and latched them to the rear of the trailer as well.

Jason climbed up onto the back of the trailer and leaned over the top, looking down at the Robin Sage students. "Keep your heads down. Don't make yourselves visible above the sides of the trailer. If we hit a checkpoint, I'll tap the brakes three times, so you know that there are bad guys. I expect you to kill everyone." He paused. "And don't shoot my damn truck." With that, he was gone. A few seconds later, the team heard the diesel engine fire up.

Sergeant Souby had watched the scene unfold from the trees, unnoticed by the students. As the truck and trailer pulled out, he moved to his government Dodge Ram and climbed in.

Water was beginning to pool up in the bed of the trailer and everyone was getting soaked. Jeremiah was trying to look at the map. He had his compass out and was attempting to figure out which way they were going as they began to move. He didn't like this at all. He was not in control of the situation and was completely at the mercy of this man they had just met. "Hey guys," Captain Wilkerson said, looking up from his map, "go ahead and get your NODs out and be ready to move as soon as we stop."

The current NODs being issued to active-duty teams was the PVS-14. The PVS-14 was a lightweight, single tube device that was worn over one eye. However, students in the Q-Course didn't get the most current gear and ODA 919 had the older, bulkier PVS-7 night vision. The PVS-7 also used a single night vision tube, but they projected the image into two lenses simultaneously. This had the effect of reducing the user's depth perception because both eyes were seeing the exact same image. To make matters worse, in this weather it was going to be hard to keep the NODs from fogging up. Regardless, they were still thankful to have them. They had completed the S.U.T. portion of the training without them.

Sergeant Souby trailed them in the rain as Jason drove around in an intentionally disorienting route for forty-five minutes. This route was designed to make it more difficult for the team to keep up with where they were. They knew where the next checkpoint was, and had he driven directly there, Jason could have gotten them to the drop off point in fifteen minutes.

However, forty-five minutes later, he pulled off the paved road onto a dirt road and stopped. He got out of the truck to open a gate. As Jason turned to get back into the truck, Jeremiah stole a look over the side of the trailer and Jason saw him. "What did I tell you?!" Jason barked. "Keep your head down!" The captain ducked back down inside the trailer.

"Dammit," Jeremiah muttered.

The truck door closed and they began to move again. After about 100 meters they stopped, and Jason turned the truck off. No one moved this time. They could hear the crunch of Jason's boots on the gravel as he moved to the rear of the trailer. The team listened as he put the ramps back in place and then they saw him as he stepped up onto the back of the trailer and unlatched the gate. "Ok. Get out," he barked.

Everyone began struggling back to their feet, pulling their rucksacks up with them, now even heavier because they were soaked from the rain. Captain Wilkerson led the men out of the trailer, slipping on the wet ramp and nearly falling. He caught himself and was greeted by a fit looking man about thirty years old. "You must be the American captain," the man said.

"Captain Jeremiah Wilkerson," Jeremiah said, and extended his hand.

The man took Jeremiah's hand in a firm handshake. "I'm your guide. Do you know where you are?"

Jeremiah hated to admit that he did not. "To be honest, it was hard to keep track of the route from the back of the trailer."

"No problem," the man said. "Do you have a map?"

Jeremiah produced the map from his cargo pocket and held it between himself and the man. "Okay, let's take a look," the man said. "Do you see that improved road right there?" the man asked, indicating a road on the map.

"Yes," Jeremiah replied.

"Yeah, that's the road you came in on. This dirt road right here is the road you're standing on. Do you understand where you are now?"

Jeremiah responded that he understood his position. It was the designated checkpoint where they were supposed to be. Jason had been true to his word.

"Okay, listen. We have a ways to go and we don't have a lot of time, so I'm going to need you to keep up. Are we clear?"

Jeremiah responded, "How far are we going?"

"We're going to keep going until we get there. Let your guys know. We leave in five," the man said without answering the question. He then grabbed a small civilian backpack from the ground and slung it up onto his shoulder. Jeremiah noted that the pack couldn't have weighed more that fifteen or twenty pounds by the way the man picked it up.

"What's your name, sir?" Jeremiah asked.

"My name's Rob. Now we leave in four. Do you have any other questions?"

Captain Wilkerson spun on his heels and headed over to the waiting team. "Hey guys, we have a guide. He won't say how far we're going, so let's just plan on moving in a Ranger file. Alpha team up front. I'm on point. Team Sergeant, count us out. You have trail."

Without responding directly to the captain, Paul immediately moved up beside him and said, "Alpha team on me." Without further directions, the men formed a line at Paul. "Cap, you're one." The men started filing past Paul, and as each man passed him, Paul slapped them on the shoulder and counted. "Two, three, four…" When everyone had passed him and he knew the count was good, he took up the trail position as they followed Rob into the night.

Robin Sage infil was something most Green Berets remember for the rest of their lives. It was meant to be difficult. This was one more step in the process of building the type of men who could be dropped off behind enemy lines with a mission and no supervision to accomplish the most difficult tasks the military had to offer. As the men started walking at just past midnight, they didn't know how far they were going, but they knew they had to do it. Every step hurt. The rucksack's weight was unforgiving, the straps biting into the men's shoulders. Vines were everywhere and seemed to have the uncanny ability to reach out and grab every possible piece of gear as the team moved. Several times, men would fall as their feet became entangled in the vines or slipped on the wet ground.

At one point, Larry's foot got caught on a vine and as he kicked his foot free, his other foot slipped in the wet leaves and he went down hard, bouncing his chin off the top of the M60 machine gun. The impact opened a one-inch gash across the underside of his chin. He was moving in the number two position, directly behind Captain Wilkerson. The captain stopped and helped pull him back to his feet. "Are you Okay, Larry?"

"I'm fine. Keep going, the scout is still moving."

Captain Wilkerson looked behind him to see that Rob was not waiting. Larry didn't bother pointing out that he was bleeding. It didn't matter. They didn't have time to stop.

"Dammit!" Captain Wilkerson said and turned to try to catch up with the scout who was moving downhill toward a creek.

As Captain Wilkerson caught up to Rob, the scout was wading out into a creek.

"Rob!" Captain Wilkerson called out.

Rob looked back over his shoulder, but didn't say anything.

"Rob, is the creek the best route?" the captain questioned.

"It's the only way to avoid the road. We have to go under the bridge up here. Tell your guys to keep up." Rob started moving slowly in the knee-deep water.

"Dammit," Captain Wilkerson muttered again. "Be careful guys, we have to go through some water," he said to Larry in a forced whisper.

One by one the men waded out into the creek. They were in the water for about 400 meters when they came to a bridge that passed over the creek. "Be careful through here," Rob said over his shoulder in a normal voice. "It gets a little deeper."

As the team passed under the bridge, the water *was* deeper. At the deepest point it was up to the men's rib cages. They continued in the water for another 200 meters and then came to a shallow area with a small sandy beach. They turned onto the beach and went back into the thick woods along a footpath.

At around 0300, Rob stopped at the edge of a pasture and took a knee, looking out across the field. Captain Wilkerson came up beside him and also dropped down on one knee. He looked at Rob through his NODs. He could clearly see that Rob was wearing the newer PVS-14 NODs. "What's up Rob?"

"You see that barn across the field there?" Rob asked.

Captain Wilkerson looked out into the darkness. Even with his NODs, it was difficult to see details, but he could tell that there was a large structure on the other side of the pasture. "Yeah, I see it."

"You have a package waiting in there." Rob stood up and stepped out into the field. Without saying another word, he turned to his right and ran off into the darkness down the tree line.

Captain Wilkerson called out in a forced whisper. "Rob!" Rob didn't slow down. "Rob!" the captain repeated. Then Rob disappeared behind some trees and was gone. "So that just happened," Captain Wilkerson said, shaking his head in disbelief.

"What's up?" asked Larry from behind the captain.

"Apparently, we need to go to that barn," replied Jeremiah.

"Okay, well this is an open danger area. How do you want to negotiate it?" Larry asked.

Captain Wilkerson was physically and mentally depleted. He knew what the right answer was. The right answer was to either skirt around the field and stay in the tree line, or at the very least to move half the team across at a time while the other half provided overwatch. He looked around. He couldn't see any cadre. "Let's just go. Tell the guys we're moving."

"Copy," replied Larry. He turned behind him and whispered to the man behind him. "Let's go. We're moving to that barn."

One by one, the team moved out into the field and crossed straight across in the most direct path to the barn. As they neared the barn, they crossed a road that led along the length of the pasture, with a driveway going to the front door of the barn. Captain Wilkerson turned around and saw the team all around him in no tactical formation whatsoever. "Dammit," he said under his breath. "Larry, pull security down the road."

"Roger that," replied Larry as he backtracked to the edge of the road with the big machine gun.

Captain Wilkerson grabbed the next two guys in line and sent one in each direction around the barn to find an entrance.

Thirty seconds later, he heard one of them calling out in a loud whisper, "I've got it. Over here!"

Captain Wilkerson directed the team to the open door on the side and the team moved into the old barn.

As soon as they were inside, Paul set up security. "Everyone, drop rucks. Let's get a SAW in each of those windows. Jeremy, do a quick radio check with us, then go link up with Larry. Set up an early warning OP, watching the road."

An observation post, or OP was typically just a couple of guys used to provide security or early warning for a larger group. This was also sometimes called an LP/OP for Listening Post/Observation Post.

"Got it," replied Jeremy. Jeremy walked over to a hay bale and sat down on it, leaning back and letting his rucksack drop onto the bale. "Oh, good Lord, that feels better. My freakin' shoulders are screaming." He slipped his arms out of the rucksack straps and unclipped his assault pack from the top of the ruck. He had a radio in the assault pack ready to go. He immediately started confirming comms with the other Echos.

Captain Wilkerson found another hay bale and mimicked the actions of Jeremy. He sat back and pulled his arms out of his ruck. "I need some Motrin," he said to no one in particular. He unclipped his NODs and let them hang around his neck from the dummy cord. He pulled out his red lens flashlight and began looking around the barn. He immediately spotted an Army-issue 5-gallon water jug in a corner. He went over to investigate. It had a tag on the handle with neatly written words: POTABLE WATER.

"Hey guys, top off your canteens, we have some water over here." On the floor beside the water jug was a small box. He grabbed the box and pulled the flaps open. Inside was a twelve pack of AA batteries. "What the hell?"

"What ya got, Cap?" It was Paul. He was looking over the captain's shoulder.

"They left us some freakin' batteries. Great. More weight," he said with a hint of disgust in his voice.

"Let me see that," Paul said, reaching for the package. He examined the package with his light. It was a cardboard package with a plastic front pinning the batteries in place. On close examination, Paul could see where the cardboard had been ripped and glued back together. "What's that? Right there," he asked the captain, pointing to the damage.

Captain Wilkerson reached for the package of batteries again. He pulled out his pocketknife and, using the point of the blade, peeled up the repair. The corner of a piece of white paper was visible under the glued down cardboard. He grabbed the piece of cardboard and carefully peeled it back, revealing the paper.

There were several things written on the paper. First, a grid coordinate, followed by a time, 0800. Finally, there was an additional set of bona fides.

"Well, I guess we know where our next checkpoint is," the captain said flatly.

"Let's see where that is," Paul said. "You got your map handy?"

"Yeah, I have it." They plotted the grid coordinates on the map. "Right there," said the captain. "A stream/trail intersection about four clicks from here." He used the military slang for kilometer.

"Okay, so we need to be at that location, four clicks from here in five hours. That's do-able," the captain stated.

"Yeah, that's four clicks straight line. But look at that terrain between here and there. Let's not underestimate that movement," Paul replied. "I vote that we move out as quickly as possible, get close and set up an ORP. Then we send out a scout element to get eyes on the linkup ahead of time."

"I like that," Captain Wilkerson replied, looking at his watch. "I've got 0343 right now. Let's plan on moving out at 0410."

"Sounds good," Paul replied, shrugging his shoulders repeatedly, fighting the soreness from the rucksack straps. Paul began moving around to the rest of the team, spreading the word of the plan. When he came to Jimmy, he was squirting some MRE cheese onto an MRE cracker. "Jimmy, how ya doin'?"

"I'm good man. My feet are chewed up from walking in wet boots. But there's no use in changing my socks, they'll just get soaked again, so screw it," Jimmy said as he stuffed part of the cracker in his mouth.

"I hear ya man. We're all in the same boat. We're moving out at 0410. Be ready to step, ok?"

"Yeah. I'll be ready," Jimmy replied unenthusiastically.

Paul moved over to the radio and grabbed the handset. "One nine OP, this is one nine Zulu, over."

"Go for OP," came the reply. Paul recognized Jeremy's voice.

"OP, this is Zulu. We're moving out at zero four ten. How are you guys on water? Over."

There was a pause and then, "Zulu this is OP, we both need water. Over."

"OP this is Zulu, standby, I'll take care of you. Zulu out." Paul signed off.

Paul finished his rounds, making sure everyone knew the new plan and was topped off on water. Then he ran the remainder of the water jug out to the OP, which was only about thirty-five meters away. When he got to Larry, he saw the blood on his chin. "Shit, Dude, what did you do?"

"It's no big deal," Larry replied. "You should see the other guy." He smiled broadly at his own joke.

"That's a pretty good cut man. Do you want me to get a Delta to take a look at it? "

"Yeah, tomorrow. I'm fine for now."

"You sure?" Paul asked again.

"I'm good man. I've had worse cuts shaving."

Paul just shook his head. "Then you're shaving wrong, you freakin' hard head."

Larry smiled back at him and in a poor attempt at a British accent added "It's merely a flesh wound."

"All right, but tomorrow you go see the medics, you hear me?" Paul spoke forcefully.

"Yeah, yeah. I hear ya. Quit making a big deal about this. We got STDs." That was a running joke in the team: STD stood for Shit To Do.

At 0405, Paul was moving around inside the barn giving everyone the five-minute warning. He moved back to his own rucksack and looked at it. With a sigh, he sat down, slipped his arms into the ruck, and tightened the straps. "Hey Cap, give me a hand?"

Captain Wilkerson reached down and crossed his hands so that both of them were grasping right hand to right hand and left hand to left hand. "Ready?"

"Yep," Captain Wilkerson leaned back and hauled Paul up to his feet.

"Thanks man. I'll help you next," Paul said.

At 0410 Paul counted everyone out the door. They were two men short because the OP was still out. As they formed back up into the order of movement, Larry and Jeremy came shuffling up and fell into their positions and the team started moving. Although they had been issued night vision, they still were not allowed to have GPS units, so the team began the movement while navigating with map and compass.

Sergeant Souby watched from a hidden position as the team moved out. He didn't reveal himself and the team never saw him. He had been in position watching the barn when they arrived. Now he would trail from a distance as they continued the next leg of the movement to the linkup with the partisan forces. If there was an emergency, he would make his presence known. If not, he would let this team of young men continue on their own. The less he interfered, the more immersed in the scenario they would be. This would help provide a better training environment. He wanted to give them the best training possible because he knew that their next war wouldn't be with blanks.

12

Robin Sage III, Linkup

Fall, 2003

Undisclosed Location, fictional country of Pineland

ODA 919 was moving at night, under extreme weight, in wet, slippery terrain, while simultaneously navigating and trying to move tactically. It was a slow movement, and they were forced to backtrack on two occasions when the terrain proved to be impassible. Finally, at 0720, they reached a paved road that indicated they were only about 400 meters from the linkup point.

The team was hidden in the woods. Captain Wilkerson was still up front. He called for the team sergeant to come up. It took Paul a couple of minutes to work his way up from the rear of the element. He took a knee beside the captain.

"Hey Paul. How ya doing?"

"I'm good Cap, you?"

"I'm alright. Check it out. If we cross here, we should be able to move into that cluster of trees over there and set up the ORP. That should only be about 200 meters from the link up," Captain Wilkerson stated.

"Well, the sun's up. How do you want to take this road?" Paul asked.

"Speed is security," Captain Wilkerson replied with a weak smile.

"You got it." Paul moved back to the team. He bypassed Larry, since he had the machine gun, and grabbed the next two men in line. Behind Larry was Brian Hansen, one of the other engineers. "Brian, you have left side security. Jeremy, right side."

Without responding, the two men moved into position. The correct procedure was to go up to the edge of the road and take a knee, facing your area of responsibility with your weapon at the low ready. However, due to fatigue, neither man dropped to a knee. They both knew they might not be able to get back up without assistance, so they simply stopped at the edge of the road. Since Jeremy had a tree at his position, he leaned his right shoulder against it and looked down the road. Brian simply stopped, facing left. Captain Wilkerson watched them move and once he was sure that they were both in position, he gave the hand signal to follow him. He started across the road and the team followed him, moving as quickly as they could, considering the weight they were carrying and the fact that they were utterly exhausted. It was little more than a slow shuffle.

When they got to the other side, the last two men took up the left and right positions on the far side, which allowed Brian and Jeremy to cross while the other two men maintained security. The team moved the last two hundred meters into some trees and set up the ORP with a circular defensive perimeter. Captain Wilkerson moved to the center of the circle along with Paul and Captain Tribiani. Captain Wilkerson and Paul both dropped their rucks in the center. "Okay, Joey, GOTWA," Captain Wilkerson said to Captain Tribiani.

A GOTWA is a mnemonic device to aid in briefing one group when another group is going to be temporarily separated. It stands for: Where I'm **G**oing, **O**thers I'm taking with me, **T**ime I'll be gone, **W**hat to do if I don't return, **A**ctions on contact.

Captain Wilkerson continued. "I'm going to recon the linkup. I'm taking Paul with me. I'll be back by 0745. If I don't return, send out a two-man element to find me. Actions if you make contact: defend in place, we'll return to you, and we'll withdraw together. Actions if we make contact, we'll break contact and move to you. Questions?"

Captain Tribiani listened as his friend spoke. "I got it man. See you in a few." Captain Tribiani held out his fist. Captain Wilkerson stood up and tapped it with his own fist. "One," said Captain Wilkerson. Paul followed suit and tapped his outstretched fist. "Two."

The two men moved stealthily, constantly scanning the area around them. They heard the creek before they saw it. The water rushing over the rocks in a short waterfall sounded clearly through the quiet woods. Paul was in the front so he identified the creek first. He held up the hand signal to halt and took a knee. The captain moved up and took a knee beside him.

Paul leaned over to whisper to the captain. "There's the intersection right there. I can see the stick by the creekbank." Their instructions were to identify a four-foot stick leaning against a tree at the linkup point and throw it into the creek as the initial step in the linkup.

"Ok, we're good. Let's go get the guys. We're short on time," the captain said.

The two men hurriedly moved back to the ORP and disseminated the information. Everyone had dropped his rucksack and was pulling security. As quickly as they could, the men were back on their feet, wearing their rucks and ready to move. Captain Wilkerson gave the hand and arm signal to move out.

Once again, Paul counted everyone out and took the rear position. They moved out in a Ranger file again and stopped at the last concealed position before the creek. Captain Wilkerson looked at his watch. It was 0758. He dropped his ruck as quietly as he could and stepped out of the woods onto the trail leading down to the creek. He scanned the area around the creek, but didn't see anyone. He checked his watch. It was exactly 0800. He casually walked over, plucked the stick from the tree, and tossed it into the creek.

Almost instantly, a bald man with a dark brown beard stood up from behind a rock in the middle of the creek! He was shirtless and had an AK-47 in his hand, the water running out of it as he stood there. The man had been squatted down in that freezing water! His sudden appearance had startled the captain, but he tried not to show it. *This guy must be nuts!* he thought to himself. He was so caught off guard that initially he simply said "Hi."

"Hi, yourself" The man replied flatly.

Captain Wilkerson recalled what was in the coordinating instructions for this linkup. Considering the situation, with this man just rising up out the water, he felt ridiculous as he asked "Uh, are there any good hiking trails around here?"

"Nothing but turkey farms around here," came the emotionless reply. It was the correct response. He had the right bona fides -- now what? The two men just stood there looking at each other. Neither speaking. Finally, the captain broke the silence.

"So, where do we need to go?" he asked the man.

"Follow me," the man said, and turned away from the captain.

"Hold on, let me get my men." Captain Wilkerson turned and motioned for the team. The first two guys came out carrying his rucksack between them. Each man had one shoulder strap. He trotted up to them and they quickly assisted him in getting the ruck up and onto his back. The man stood silently in the creek watching them as they waded into the frigid water. As the cold water hit Captain Wilkerson's legs, once again he thought *That crazy SOB was hiding in this water?!*

The man turned and began walking downstream. As they began following the man down the creek, Captain Wilkerson stole a glance back at Larry. Larry looked back at the captain with a look of "I don't know" on his face. If he hadn't been burdened with the weight of a medium machine gun and an infil ruck, he would have shrugged.

Captain Wilkerson spoke up. "Sir?"

No response.

"Sir?" he repeated.

The bald man turned to face him, and the captain said "Sir, maybe we should get out of the water."

The bald man sighed before responding. "You have a pretty big group. I'm sure you left a trail through the woods that a blind man could follow. We're going to move down the creek to throw off anyone who might be following you." It wasn't a question. It was a statement.

Dread washed over the captain. "Well sir, I think that…"

The bald man cut him off. "We're walking down the creek." Then he turned and resumed his slow walk downstream.

Over the next few minutes, two men tripped on submerged rocks and fell into the cold water. In both instances, their teammates were quick to help get them back up on their feet.

With the weight of the rucksacks coupled with the awkwardness of walking on unseen wet rocks, the captain was surprised that only two men fell. As they rounded a bend in the creek, Captain Wilkerson saw two more men standing on the creekbank about fifty meters downstream. One man held an AK-47 and the other held an old M16. Once again, Captain Wilkerson was startled. *Holy crap, man*, he thought to himself.

The bald man adjusted his path so that he was headed toward the two men on the creekbank. Captain Wilkerson wasn't directly behind the bald man, but he also started veering toward the bank. He noticed that this section of the creek was getting deeper. He felt his rucksack push up against his neck.

Everything in the team's rucksacks was waterproofed. The army issued a "waterproof bag," officially called a rucksack liner, but everyone just referred to it as a waterproof bag. Although they were designed to be waterproof, they were also notorious for developing holes and leaking. It was common practice to place the waterproof bag inside a trash bag to ensure that everything stayed waterproof. The logic behind the double bag was that the trash bag would provide an actual waterproof barrier, while the rucksack liner would prevent the items inside from damaging the fragile trash bag. The combination of the two bags worked well. This configuration was not only waterproof, but it was also airtight if sealed correctly. Each man had taken the top of the trash bag and twisted it, then folded it over and put a heavy rubber band around it to ensure that no water made its way to their clothes and gear. An interesting side effect was that trapped air in the bags would actually make heavy rucksacks somewhat buoyant. Captain Wilkerson's rucksack was over a hundred pounds, but he was about to learn that it would also float...kind of.

The water was a dark brown and the men couldn't see submerged hazards. As Captain Wilkerson pushed on, trying to keep up, he stepped into a hole hidden beneath the murky water. The current pushed him forward as he reached out with his foot trying to find the creek bottom. Suddenly, he found himself pitching head first into the water, the rucksack now acting as a floatation device on his back. It's not that the rucksack was floating on top of the water, but it wouldn't quite sink, either. It was staying just below the surface. This pushed his face downward into the water. Panic rushed over the young man as he flailed, trying to regain his footing. The next three seconds felt like an eternity as he attacked the water with his arms and legs, trying to right himself. Suddenly, he felt himself being pulled upright, and his foot struck something solid. He regained his footing and, as his head came up out of the water, he found himself standing face to face with the bald man. Captain Wilkerson gasped for air, despite only having been submerged for a few seconds. He locked eyes with the bald man.

"There are sinkholes in the creek bed. Don't drown." With that statement, he let go of the exasperated soldier, turned away, and resumed his trek toward the two men waiting on the bank.

"Shit!" Captain Wilkerson said, louder than he meant to. He turned to look at Larry behind him, who was shorter than he was. "Watch out, there's a hole right here, go left."

Larry acknowledged with a nod and began pushing left toward the creekbank. Less than a minute later, the bald man reached the two men who had been observing the scene without speaking or reacting to the captain's "near death" experience. As the bald man reached the bank, the two men both reached forward, each grabbing a hand, and pulled the bald man up onto the bank in one smooth movement. The three Pinelanders moved away from the bank about ten meters, turned around and observed as the team reached the bank one after another. They didn't offer to pull Captain Wilkerson up as they had the bald man, but rather watched silently as he struggled to drag himself up onto the bank on his belly. He was grabbing at a sapling as Larry came up behind him and pushed on his rucksack, helping him get his knee onto the slick bank and finally extract himself from the water.

Captain Wilkerson immediately turned to help Larry. Larry was lifting the machine gun sling over his neck and reaching the gun up to the captain. There was a defined trail that ran parallel to the creek. The captain turned and shoved the gun up onto the trail and then returned his attention to Larry. Together they worked to get Larry up onto the bank as well.

It took nearly another ten minutes to get the entire team up onto the bank and out of the water. The three Pinelanders observed without saying a word. They didn't even speak to each other. They just watched.

They weren't the only ones watching. A short distance away, Sergeant Souby observed. He sat in a concealed position on a small folding stool. At his feet lay a rope, three round rescue flotation devices, and a radio. Slightly downstream and on the other side of the creek, just out of view of the team, were two other cadre members sitting in a camouflage painted rescue boat, ready to fire up the engine and rush in, in the event of an emergency. The man sitting at the rear of the boat had nearly started the engine when he saw the student disappear beneath the water, but luckily, he had not. They didn't want to ruin the scenario. In the near future, these men could be working anywhere in the world, doing dangerous missions, with no rescue team nearby. The cadre didn't want to interfere with this training scenario unless there was a risk to life, limb, or eyesight.

Paul was the last man out of the water and as soon as he made it onto the bank, the bald man turned and started walking down the trail without hesitation. The two other men fell in behind him without speaking.

Captain Wilkerson motioned to the team to move out. They instinctively fell back into their earlier order of movement. The captain tried to close the distance to the Pinelanders, but they were moving too fast.

"Hey, sir! Excuse me, sir!" he called out to the bald man.

The man stopped and turned to face the young captain in an almost robotic manner. He didn't speak. He had an expressionless look on his face. He just stared back at the younger man. The two other men stepped to either side of the trail to allow the bald man to speak to the captain directly.

"Excuse me sir, but how far is it to your camp?"

The bald man replied in a flat voice. "We'll be there before noon." Without another word, he turned and took off, once again walking too fast for the team.

Shit, Captain Wilkerson thought. *Noon? I don't know if I have four more hours of this in me.*

Once again, he spoke up. "Sir, could you slow down? My men are carrying a lot of gear and you're moving too fast."

The bald man turned and looked at him once again. In an even tone, he replied. "Move faster."

He then turned once again and started down the trail with the other two close on his heels. However, after another thirty seconds of walking, he took a sharp left off the trail and walked into a flat open draw with sparse vegetation. They moved into the draw for about a hundred meters, then the three men turned right and started moving up the steep slope that formed the side of the draw. He and the other two men moved quickly up the hill, unladen by heavy packs or other equipment. They climbed all the way to the top without stopping. Once they reached the top of the hill, the bald man turned around and simply watched as the team struggled up the steep terrain. The two other men continued and disappeared from sight. The bald man was now easily seventy-five meters in front of the team. The hillside was covered with fallen leaves and pine needles; the footing was treacherous. Once again, several members of the team slipped and stumbled under the unwieldy backpacks.

About halfway up the slope, Captain Wilkerson came to a small band of shale rock that ran left to right across the hillside. He stepped over the small outcropping and, with significant effort, hoisted himself over the obstacle. He paused to ensure that he maintained his balance. Once he was sure of his footing, he turned and looked behind him at the string of men negotiating the slope. The team was getting spread out, with uneven gaps between them. No one was looking around or watching for threats. Everyone had shifted into survival mode, just trying to successfully negotiate their most immediate task. Right now, the most immediate task was this damned hill. Captain Wilkerson could feel the anxiety in his gut as he recognized the things that were going wrong. He made eye contact with Larry who was clearly struggling up the steep slope. The captain momentarily fixated on the swinging belt of ammunition hanging from the side of the machine gun.

During movement, machine gunners would break off a short belt of ammunition and carry that loaded into the machine gun. If they needed to shoot, another belt of ammunition could be snapped into the end of that smaller belt, known as a "starter belt." Captain Wilkerson stared at it for a moment as it swung left, right and left again with Larry's steps. Almost instantaneously, the young officer recognized what he needed to do. He reached down to offer his hand as Larry approached the rock outcropping. Larry took his hand and, with a quick pull from the captain, cleared the little obstacle.

"Thanks, Cap," Larry said in a genuine, although exhausted, voice. He then turned to help the man behind him over the hazard. Without direction, each man would automatically turn and help the man behind him over the rocks.

Captain Wilkerson once again began to slowly move up the hill. He could see the bald man just standing at the crest of the hill, watching them. To him, the man almost looked bored.

Everyone has heard the phrase, "Time flies when you're having fun." For Captain Wilkerson and the men of ODA 919, the last hundred feet of that hill were not fun. The time seemed to drag on and on. Each step seemed to him to be less and less productive. *Four more hours of this?* he thought to himself again. He hurt everywhere. His legs, feet and back were all screaming to escape this seemingly endless assault. However, his shoulders were the worst. Like most of the men on the team, Captain Wilkerson was reasonably lean. The rucksack straps had been straining against the tops of his shoulders now for most of the last eight hours, and pain had become a constant companion to the walking. He wasn't looking up toward the top of the hill. He was looking right in front of him, concentrating on the next step. He wanted to look behind him again, to check on his men, but the effort seemed like too much to ask of himself. *I'll check behind me when I get to the top of the hill*, he thought to himself. Left foot. *Right foot. Left foot. Right foot.*

What was that technique they taught us about ascending hills? The lock-step technique? He wasn't quite sure. He thought back to the class at Camp Mackall, trying to recall what the instructor from 10th Special Forces Group had told them.

"When ascending slopes, allow your forward knee to lock as you bring your trail foot forward. This will temporarily transfer your weight from your musculature to your skeleton, allowing your muscles a split second of rest. On a short climb, this will be inconsequential, but on a long climb those split seconds add up to seconds. If the climb is long enough, the seconds add up to minutes of rest for your muscles." He wished he had thought about it earlier. He concentrated and tried the technique. *Left, lock, right, lock, left lock.*

As he approached the top of the slope where the bald man stood waiting, he saw the man's feet first. He lifted his gaze from the ground to look the man in the eye, and prepared to tell the man that his team needed to stop for a security halt, which actually meant they needed to take a break. However, as he looked up, he immediately realized that behind the man were makeshift structures and tents. There were tarps strung up in the trees and men moving around. He saw a makeshift structure of saplings tied together into a frame with a tarp as a roof. Suddenly, he also registered the smell of a campfire.

"Is that your camp?" the captain asked the bald man incredulously.

He simply replied, "Yes," and stood there looking back at the young officer.

"I thought you said it was going to take us until noon to get to your camp," the captain said through gasps of air.

"That's not what I said. I said that we would be at the camp before noon. It's before noon. Gather your men here and wait for further instructions."

With that, he turned and walked away, leaving the captain confused, exhausted and frustrated.

13

Free Coffee

November 23, 2022

Louisa, KY

Billy Watson was drinking early today. It was Wednesday the twenty-third of November, the day before Thanksgiving, but Billy wasn't feeling very thankful. On Monday, his boss had told him he was reducing him to part time work. Billy had argued with the older man about it. "You're the one that put out the 'Help Wanted' sign!" Billy had said to George.

"Look Billy. I was expecting more work, but it just hasn't been as busy as I expected. You can still work a full day on Mondays and Tuesdays and I'll get you a half day later in the week," George had said, using his typical, even, professional tone.

"At least keep me at full time until after Christmas!" Billy had pleaded.

"I'm sorry Billy. This is how it has to be."

This morning, Jenny had left for work at 5:30 so she could be at the diner when they opened at 6:00. Her alarm had woken him up at 4:30, but he didn't say anything. He had rolled over and just went back to sleep as he felt her get out of the bed to get ready for work. He had woken up again briefly when he heard the front door shut an hour later. He stayed in bed until just after ten o'clock. Finally, his bladder left him no choice and he got up, heading straight to the bathroom.

A minute later, he left the bathroom and headed to the kitchen. He needed coffee. They had a nice Keurig coffee maker. It was a remnant of when he was making more money, and he loved the convenience of being able to make a single cup of coffee on demand. There was a medium sized bowl sitting on the counter beside the coffeemaker. The bowl had a half dozen of the little coffee pods for the machine. George had a Keurig coffeemaker in the breakroom at work too. Every day when he left work, Billy would grab one or two of the little pods and squirrel them away in a pocket. He was careful not to take too many at once, so George wouldn't notice.

George liked the dark roast. It wasn't Billy's favorite coffee, but he liked the price. He grabbed a dark roast and inserted it into the machine. He opened the cabinet above the machine and grabbed a white coffee cup with an inscription on the front. He sat it in the coffeemaker and hit the medium cup button. The machine began making a series of sounds as it prepared to deliver the brew. As the coffee began to dispense in a steady stream, Billy read the inscription on the front of the cup. "Only you can make your dreams come true. Caffeine helps." He scoffed. This was one of Jenny's cups. Her mother had gotten it for her on some vacation. Billy couldn't remember where the vacation was. He did know that he and Jenny wouldn't have a vacation anywhere in their near future.

After the machine finished dispensing the coffee, Billy retrieved the cup and sat it on the counter in front of the machine. He turned and opened the refrigerator door for some half and half. He looked around in the fridge and didn't see any.

"Great" he mumbled and grabbed the nearly empty jug of two percent milk, leaving the door hanging open. He twisted the top off and carefully poured some milk into the hot coffee. He saw a clump splash into the dark liquid. "What the...?" He looked at the top of the jug for the printed date. "Best by November 11, 2022. He took a quick sniff of the top of the open jug. "Damn it!" he said out loud as the smell of spoiled milk assaulted his nose. "Great! That's just great!" He grabbed the lid and twisted it back onto the jug. He turned and put the jug back in the fridge. "She can deal with that shit later," he said to himself and bumped the door closed.

He grabbed the coffee cup, moved to the sink, and poured out the ruined coffee. He quickly rinsed out the cup, shaking the excess water into the sink. Returning to the Keurig, he sat the coffee cup back in the machine and opened the top. He removed the spent pod and sat it on the counter. He grabbed another pod, leaving only four. *I need to make sure to grab a couple extra of those next time I work*, he thought. He placed the pod in the machine and closed the latch. He pushed the button again. Nothing happened. He stared at the machine for a couple long seconds, then noticed the little blue light illuminated beside the words "ADD WATER".

"Dammit!" He wanted to throw the machine across the kitchen. He didn't. He stood for a moment, just looking at the machine. He was clinching his teeth. "Is the world out to get me today?" He drew in a deep breath and grabbed the coffee cup again, taking it to the sink. He was going to add just enough water to make his cup of coffee. Apparently, he was drinking it black today.

Thirty minutes later, he was sitting on the front porch in the chair that had become his favorite retreat. The empty coffee cup sat on the shelf on the rail and he had just finished his second cigarette. He was wearing an old flannel shirt. The cotton was well worn and comfortable. The air was cool, but not cold. It smelled like fall. There were two large maple trees at the edge of their yard, near the road. The ground around them was covered in a blanket of maple leaves. Yesterday, Jenny had asked if he would rake the front yard while she was at work. "Why?" he had asked, "who are we trying to impress?"

Jenny had just sighed and walked off. Billy was looking at the leaves when movement caught his eye, and he looked up at the road to see a black Silverado coming from the left. He watched it pass the entrance to his gravel driveway and continue down the two-lane road. He continued to watch it until it drove out of sight. He sighed. He missed his truck. Yep, the world was definitely out to get him.

He needed food. He got up and dropped the cigarette onto the porch, not bothering to step on it, and moved to the door. The front door was open, but the screen door was closed. He pulled on the door and Miss Priss bolted out the opening as soon as the gap was large enough for her to fit. He jumped.

"Damn cat!" he yelled just as the cat turned and ran down the steps. He pulled the door open the rest of the way and headed to the kitchen. He pulled the cabinet door open and surveyed the selections of random boxes and cans. There wasn't much in the cabinet. However, they did have an open box of Frosted Mini Wheats. That sounded good. He grabbed the box but remembered the milk was bad. Annoyed, he started to put the box back, but he saw a package of chicken ramen at the back of the cabinet behind where the cereal box had been.

"Score!" he said out loud. He sat the box of cereal on the counter and grabbed the ramen. With a flick of his wrist, he closed the cabinet door with a slight bang. "The breakfast of champions," he said as he grabbed a bowl out of the drying rack.

Jenny would often leave the dishes in a drying rack after washing them. He was fine with that--he didn't have to get them out of the cabinet. The house they had lived in before Billy lost his job had a beautiful stainless-steel dishwasher. He didn't empty the dishwasher there and he sure wasn't going to put dishes away from the drying rack here.

Billy sat the bowl on the counter and ripped open the ramen. He poured the dry noodles out into the bowl and grabbed the little seasoning packet that had come out with them. He ripped the packet open and poured the seasoning into the bowl with the noodles. He grabbed the bowl and moved to the sink to add water. The trailer had a microwave that was built into the upper cabinet over the stove. He went over to the microwave, put the bowl inside and hit the "Add 30 seconds" button four times to start a two-minute cook cycle. As the microwave hummed, Billy walked back over to the sink and looked out the window above it. Jenny had a put a little plastic house plant on the windowsill. He didn't notice it.

His yard wasn't big, but his neighbor's yard was. He looked past the fence and across the yard at the single-story white house that was easily three hundred yards away. They had a big barn off to the side and some greenhouses behind the house. Billy knew that an older couple lived there, but he had never spoken to them. He didn't have a reason to. He studied the house for a minute. It looked neat and orderly. It had a gravel driveway like his place, but his gravel was thin and every time it rained, he had several mud holes that would develop. The neighbor's gravel was thicker and looked better. The barn looked good too. It had steel siding. *It's nice to have money*, he thought to himself. The microwave beeped two long beeps and snapped him out of his thoughts. He moved back to the microwave and opened the door. He saw that the water had boiled over and the bowl was sitting in some of the yellow broth from the soup.

"Of course," he said and sighed audibly. He grabbed a dishtowel that was hanging on the front of the stove and used it to grab the bowl. He knew from experience that the bowl was going to be hot. He turned and sat the bowl on the table, then closed the microwave and grabbed a spoon from the drying rack. He pulled one of the chairs out and sat down to his breakfast.

Around 3:30 that afternoon, Billy heard Jenny pull up outside. Sometimes her shift was eight hours, sometimes ten, and sometimes her boss would ask her to pull a twelve-hour shift. Billy looked at his watch. Apparently, she had only gotten an eight-hour shift today. He was sitting on the couch, watching TV. He had slid his feet into his boots that morning, never bothering to lace them up. Now, his feet were up on the coffee table next to three empty beer cans. A minute later, Jenny pulled the screen door open. The front door was already open. She had a paper grocery bag in one arm. He looked up as she came in, the screen door smacking shut behind her. "Hey," she said.

"Hey," he responded and returned his attention to the television. Jenny headed for the kitchen. "You get milk?" he asked without looking up from his show. He was watching alligator hunters in Louisiana.

"Yeah, I got milk," she responded as she sat the heavy bag on the table next to the empty bowl with remnants of ramen in it. She saw the bowl, sighed, picked it up, and sat it in the sink to be washed later.

"Good," he said. "I think we're getting low."

"I won't make that mistake again though. Don't ever go to the grocery store on the day before Thanksgiving. I would have been home a half hour earlier, but it was a freakin' madhouse in there," she said in an exasperated tone.

He didn't acknowledge the statement. "How was work?"

"It was fine. I don't have to work again until Friday. We're closed tomorrow for Thanksgiving."

"Ya'll ain't open for Thanksgiving?" He finally looked away from the show. "What if someone wants to eat out tomorrow?"

She looked at him, sarcasm apparent in her voice. "Well, I guess they'll just have to go somewhere else to eat out. I figured you'd be happy that I wasn't working on Thanksgiving."

"I mean, that's cool, but we're not doing anything, so I just figured you'd rather have the hours."

"No, what I'd *rather* have is a break!" Her voice had just gone up an octave.

Billy didn't feel like dealing with this right now. He looked back at the television and said, "Yeah, you're right. Whatcha making for dinner tonight?"

Jenny took in a sharp breath, but before she could answer, her cell phone rang. She let out the breath and pulled the phone out of her purse that was now hanging on the chair back. She didn't recognize the number, but it was a 606 area code, so it was Kentucky. She tapped the green icon to answer. "Hello?" She heard an unintentional remnant of frustration in her voice.

"Hello. Is this the owner of a sweet little cat named Miss Priss?" Jenny paused. She looked around the living room scanning for her cat.

"What? Uh, yes. Who is this?"

"Hi Sweetie, my name is Edna, and your sweet little girl ran into my house today when I was taking out the trash. I got your number from her tag. Don't worry, she's fine. I just wanted to make sure she got home safe."

"Oh my gosh. Thank you so much. Where are you? I'll come get her." Relief washed over her.

Billy turned the TV up a couple notches with the remote. Jenny was drowning out the guys on the show. This was the good part. They had a gator hooked and they were trying to get a clear shot at the head, but the beast wasn't cooperating. Jenny put a finger to the ear that didn't have a phone pressed against it. She turned away from the living room and took a couple of steps to distance herself from the sound.

When Edna gave her address, Jenny responded almost instantly. "Oh, wait. Are you the white house with the greenhouses in the yard?"

"Yes!" Edna replied, surprised that the young lady on the other end of the phone knew the description of her house just from the address. "How did you know that?"

Jenny chuckled. "We're actually your neighbors. We haven't been here long, but we live in the trailer next door."

"Oh, I know exactly where you are! I can see your place from the driveway."

"Yes ma'am. That's us. Thank you so much for calling. Would it be okay if I come over to get her right now?" Jenny asked.

"Of course. What's your name, Sweetie?"

"Oh, sorry. Yeah, I'm Jenny."

"Okay Jenny. I'll see you in a few minutes."

"Yes ma'am. Again, thank you so much. Bye-bye."

"Bye, Jenny," Edna replied and both women hung up.

"What was that all about?" Billy asked, still not looking up from his TV show.

"The lady next door has Miss Priss. I guess she ran into their house today. She was just calling me to let me know where she was so we can go get her."

"What do you mean 'we'?"

Why did he have to be such a jerk? "Come on. Just go over with me. You should introduce yourself to them too," she said.

"I have a better idea. How about we let her keep the stupid cat."

Jenny didn't respond. She crossed her arms and shifted all her weight onto her left leg, her hip sticking out, and she just stared back at Billy.

After a moment of silence, Billy looked up and saw her glaring at him. Billy drew in a deep breath and let it escape with an audible huff. "Fine," he replied unenthusiastically. He tossed the remote onto the couch beside him. "I need a smoke anyhow."

Jenny rolled her eyes. She hated that he had started smoking again. He always stunk of cigarettes now. At least he was smoking on the porch and not in the house. She was thankful for small victories. Billy left the TV going and went outside to smoke. Jenny took the time to put the groceries away. The local Kroger had started offering paper bags again as an optional alternative to plastic bags. She liked them. It didn't have anything to do with the environment, she just found the bags useful and stronger than the plastic ones. She pulled out a loaf of bread from the top of the bag and turned to place it on the counter. There sat a box of cereal and a used coffee pod. She shook her head. She sat the bread on the counter where they normally kept it and grabbed the cereal, placed it up in the cabinet, and threw the coffee pod in the trash can.

She then returned to her grocery bag and pulled out a box of hamburger helper that she planned on making for dinner and placed it next to the bread. There was no need to put that away, she'd be using it is a couple hours. Next was a pound of hamburger. She had never paid so much for a pound of hamburger before. She placed the burger in the refrigerator. Jenny had taken her tips and gone straight to Kroger after work to grab this stuff. She had planned on buying some eggs and bacon too, but when she saw the prices, she decided to wait until she got her regular paycheck for them. She had enough to get everything, but it would have taken nearly all the money she had, and she wanted to keep a little cash in her purse.

Next, she pulled the gallon of milk out and went back to the fridge. She pulled the old jug out and replaced it with the new one. She looked down at the date on the older jug. "Gross" she said under her breath. She took it to the sink and removed the top. She turned the cold water on, held the milk jug out at arm's length, and poured the disgusting, curdled mess into the running water. Once the jug was empty, she placed it under the running water and put some into the jug. Replacing the cap, she shook the jug to rinse out the inside and then poured that down the drain as well. Finally, she squeezed the jug to get some of the air out of it and replaced the cap so it would take up less space in the trash. She still caught a whiff of the spoiled milk even though she had her head turn away as she squeezed the jug. "Gross," she repeated. She dropped the jug into the nearly full trash can. She returned to the grocery bag and glanced into it, confirming it was empty. She folded it up and put it under the sink next to two more that were also neatly folded and awaiting their next job.

"Okay," she said, "let's go get Miss Priss." She grabbed her purse and headed for the door. She pulled the front door closed behind her as she walked out. She saw Billy just as he flicked his cigarette butt into the yard. "I really wish you wouldn't do that?"

"Do what, smoke?" he responded.

"Well, that too. Yes, I wish you wouldn't smoke. But if you're going to smoke, I wish you wouldn't throw your cigarette butts all over the place."

"Okay," he replied. "I'll start throwing them in the trash."

"No, don't bring them in the house, you'll make the whole place stink. Just put them in your beer cans or whatever and then put them in the trash when you take it out. That way you're not making a mess out here and you're not stinking up the house."

"You got it, hon," Billy replied with an artificial smile. "You ready?"

Jenny sighed. She knew that he wouldn't do either of those things, but she didn't want to talk about it anymore. Right now, she just wanted to go get her cat.

"Yeah, I'm ready." She started down the steps toward the car.

Next door, Edna Michaels was preparing dinner. She had recruited her son, Scott, to peel carrots. Scott had arrived earlier in the day and was planning on staying until Saturday. She loved having her kids home, and it was very seldom that she had both of them home at the same time. Paul and his girls would be arriving tomorrow, and she was excited about a family Thanksgiving dinner.

"Mom, what do you want me to do with these carrot scraps? I assume you're saving them for the chickens?"

"Yeah, just give me the carrots and go ahead and run everything else out to the chickens. They'll be tickled."

"Yes ma'am," he replied, standing up from the table. He scooped up the carrots and laid them on his mother's cutting board, then returned to the table and grabbed the bowl of peels. He headed out the door and walked to the chicken coop. The chickens saw him coming and several of the friendlier ones ran to the gate and waited for him. He smiled at the way they waddled as they ran.

"Hey girls!" he said to the chickens as a greeting. A couple were squawking at him. He opened the gate and pushed through them, careful not to let any get out. Now more were crowding around him as he walked toward the coop.

"Hey girls, I have a treat for you." He spoke to them in a regular voice as if he were talking to another person. Grabbing a small handful of the scraps from the bowl, he tossed it out among the birds. They dove on the orange scraps as if they were starving, even though they clearly were not. He scooped up everything else in the bowl and slung it out into the group of chickens in an arch. Some of the pieces landed on the backs of chickens and others immediately snatched the pieces up. Scott smiled as he watched the mild chaos created by the scraps.

Then he heard tires on the gravel. He turned to see an old Honda Civic turning into the driveway. He returned to the gate, exited, and latched it. He stood with his back to the gate and watched as the car came slowly down the driveway and stopped near the door. He started walking toward the car, just as two people got out. A man got out of the passenger side and woman got out of the driver side, which was closer to the house. These must be the people that his mother had called earlier about the cat.

Scott walked toward the car. The man saw him approaching and waited. "Hi," Scott said. "Are you the folks that lost the cat?"

"I wouldn't say we lost her," the guy replied. "We just live right there," he said, pointing to their trailer in the distance. "But yeah, that's my wife's cat. I'm just stuck with her."

Scott wasn't completely sure if this guy was being rude or if it was just a poor attempt at humor, but he decided to give the guy the benefit of the doubt, so he smiled.

"Yeah, I hear ya. I'm not much of a cat person myself, but that's a sweet cat. I'm Scott." He extended his hand as he got close enough to Billy for a handshake.

Billy took the hand in a quick shake. "Billy. This here's my wife Jenny. It's her cat."

"Hi Jenny, why don't y'all step inside. I'll introduce you to my mom and find the cat. She's running around the house somewhere." He started toward the door leading into the kitchen. As he came around the front of the car, Jenny was waiting and extended her hand as he approached. "Nice to meet you. Please, come on in," Scott said with a quick shake of her hand. Scott ascended the steps, pulled open the storm door, and called out to his mother. "Mom, the neighbors are here for their cat."

Edna walked out of the pantry, wiping her hands on a plain white dishtowel. She quickly flung the little towel onto her shoulder and walked across the kitchen toward them. "Hi! You must be Jenny. It's very nice to meet you." The two women shook hands. She turned toward Scott. "Scott, will you see if you can find their cat for them? She was sleeping in the living room a few minutes ago."

"Yes ma'am," he replied and headed out of the kitchen.

"Can I offer you two a glass of tea?" Edna asked.

"Oh, we don't want to be a bother, ma'am. I just can't tell you how much I appreciate you calling me. I'm so sorry she ran into your house. That's not like her at all."

"It's no bother, and please, call me Edna. Please have a seat. Are you sure I can't get you some tea?"

Billy spoke up. "Actually, if you're offering, sure. I'd love some tea." Jenny glanced over at him, but didn't say anything.

"Great!" Edna said with a clap of her hands. "Please have a seat."

Billy and Jenny sat down. Billy's back was to the door and Jenny's seat was facing away from the sink, but she turned her chair sideways and sat it to face Edna. Her back was now to Billy. They sat down just as Scott returned to the kitchen. He was holding Miss Priss against his chest, petting her. "I found her. She was curled up on the rug, living her best life." He was grinning. He actually did like cats; despite what he had told Billy earlier. Well, he like them when they were friendly like this one. They had a couple of barn cats when they were growing up. His father used to refer to them as his mousetraps.

Jenny bolted up out of her chair, reaching for the cat. "There you are! You've been such a bad girl!" She was speaking in the higher pitched voice people often use when speaking to a baby. Scott transferred the cat to Jenny, and she sat back down. "What were you thinking, running into Miss Edna's house?" She held the cat up so that she could touch the cat's nose against her own. Then she sat the cat down in her lap. Miss Priss immediately lay down in Jenny's lap and Jenny kept her hands on her to prevent her from jumping back down.

Edna returned to the table with two Mason jars of iced sweet tea and sat one in front of Jenny. She reached the other to Billy. "Thank you," both of them replied, almost in unison.

"So, Billy," Scott began. "Mom tells me that y'all haven't lived here long. Where ya from?"

"Oh, we're from here, but we used to live over closer to town in a subdivision. I got screwed over at my last job, so we had to move."

There it was again, Scott thought. This guy's tone was just on the edge of being rude. "Well, there's worse places to be. It's pretty nice out here. You're far enough out to feel like you're in the country, but you're not so far that it's inconvenient to get to town when you need to."

"I guess," Billy answered and took a sip of the tea.

Scott glanced at Jenny. She was still petting the cat, but she appeared to be a little uncomfortable. Scott heard footsteps on the gravel outside, just before the door opened. His father appeared in the doorway.

"Oh, I see we have company!" He was smiling broadly.

"Honey, these are our neighbors. They moved into Terry's old place up by the road." Edna referenced the prior inhabitant of the trailer where Billy and Jenny were now living.

"Oh, I was wondering who was there now. Nice to meet you, I'm Charles. He extended his hand toward Billy. Billy didn't stand up but took the hand in a quick shake. "And you must be Jenny. My Edna told me she spoke with you on the phone. Nice to meet you, young lady." His tone was warm and genuine.

Jenny smiled back at him. "Thanks again, Mr. Charles. We really appreciate you taking care of Miss Priss today. I'm sorry she ran into your house."

"Ah, think nothing of it."

Billy finished his tea. He exhaled with the last drink. "That tea is good," he said, looking at the empty jar.

"Would you like some more?" Edna asked.

"No. No we've been too much trouble already. We should be going," Jenny said. Her jar was still over half full. She stood up and pulled the cat to her chest so she could hold her with one hand. She reached over and plucked Billy's jar from the table. She started toward the sink. "Let me put this in the sink."

Edna intercepted her. "No, no. I've got it dear." She reached for the glass.

Jenny allowed Edna to take the glass with a quick, "Thank you," and turned to go back for her own. That's when she looked through the open door into the pantry. "Oh my God! What a beautiful pantry!" she exclaimed.

"Oh, thank you. Charles built it himself. Would you like to see it?"

"Yes! Yes, please!" She turned and took a couple of steps back toward Billy, thrusting the cat toward him. "Here, hold Miss Priss so she doesn't run off again."

Billy just sighed and accepted the cat. Jenny turned back to Edna and followed her to the pantry. "Oh wow! Look at all the storage! This is incredible. I don't think I've ever seen anything like this. The cabinets are beautiful too." Both the women were now inside the large pantry. Charles walked up and stood in the doorway.

"Thanks, the cabinets are red oak. I built them from scratch."

Jenny spun and looked at him incredulously. "Seriously? That's really amazing. I wouldn't even know where to begin building a cabinet. Billy's no carpenter. If the door hadn't been open, I would never have guessed this was even here. I would have just thought it was a regular closet." She paused and looked back toward the open door. "Billy! You have to see this. This is amazing!"

Billy sighed again and stood up. Charles stepped to the side to allow Billy to see where the women were standing. Scott stood off to the side, observing the scene. He saw Billy's eyes widen when he looked through the doorway.

"Holy shit!" said Billy.

Jenny's face immediately flushed red with embarrassment. "Billy! Language!"

"Oh, sorry. I mean holy crap. That's a ton of food. Why do you need so much food?" He looked at Edna, who was still standing beside Jenny.

"Oh, you know how it is. When you see something on sale, it's best to grab a few extra."

Scott felt the heat on his neck. He didn't like that his mother had shown this to these strangers. *We don't know them.*

Billy scoffed. "That's not a few extra. That's *years* of food!" He stressed the word 'years', dragging it out for effect.

Edna smiled. "No, sweetie, it's not years of food. But I don't like to run out of things."

"Yeah, I see that. Holy crap! That must be a thousand cans!"

"Oh, it's not that much, it's just..."

"Hey Mom?" Scott interrupted. "It looks like your carrots are starting to boil. Do you need to do anything to them?"

"Oh, I almost forgot that I have dinner on the stove. Thanks, baby," she still called her youngest son "baby." He would always be her baby, no matter how old he got. Edna started toward the door. Jenny followed her out and Scott stepped up to the door, bypassing his father to pull the door closed.

Edna moved to the stove and adjusted the flame on the carrots down to a simmer. Always the kind soul, she turned to Jenny and said "If you kids would like to stay for dinner, I can add a little bit to this and we'll have plenty."

Billy had noticed the smell of the food as it filled the kitchen. It smelled delicious. He was about to accept the offer. *Why turn down a free meal?* Jenny beat him to the punch.

"Oh gosh, no. We really appreciate the offer, but I already have dinner planned. We really should get out of your hair." She moved closer to Edna. "Thanks again, so much, for calling me."

"I promise, it was no bother at all. I'm just glad to help."

"Come on Billy, we need to get going." She started toward the door.

"Uh, ok. Uh, thanks for the tea." He looked at Charles. "Nice to meet you." He didn't acknowledge Scott who was across the room, still standing by the door to the pantry.

A minute later, Scott was standing at the door, watching the car pull away. "Mom," he said while watching the car pull out of the driveway and turn right onto the pavement. "I don't think you should have let them see your pantry."

"Well, I didn't mean to. She just saw it. Besides, she's a nice girl."

"I'm not talking about her. I'm talking about him." Scott stepped away from door, closing it behind him. "I'm not saying you were at fault. I mean, I brought them into the kitchen. Like you said it just happened. It's just that I got a bad vibe off that guy."

"I know son. You and your brother have been very clear that we shouldn't let people know what we have, but what are they going to do? Break in over some canned goods?"

"Most likely not." He paused as if he was thinking. "Maybe it was nothing." Not wanting to ruin the visit, he turned to look at the stove. "Okay. What else can I do to help with dinner?"

14

Robin Sage IV, Meet the G-Chief

Fall, 2003

Undisclosed location, fictional country of Pineland

Jeremiah Wilkerson, Paul Michaels, Larry Lawson and the rest of ODA 919 had finally made it into the camp where they would conduct the training making up the final phase of the Special Forces Qualification Course. They had received classes on how to conduct Unconventional Warfare. They had studied and participated in countless practice scenarios. They had memorized information about this fictitious country called Pineland such as the history, customs, culture, and climate. However, nothing truly prepared them for the real thing. That's a good thing. To be successful in the Unconventional Warfare environment, the training should not teach you the answers. Rather, it should teach you how to find the answers you need in any situation. In other words, the training shouldn't dictate what you think, but teach you to think on your own. The training isn't perfect, but after years of refining the process, Robin Sage is definitively the best Unconventional Warfare exercise on the planet. It's immersive. Every possible aspect of the exercise is designed to make the students feel like they are in a different country.

It's not only immersive for the students who are in the training, but the men who facilitate the training are immersed in the same environment. They live in the field with the students, day and night for two weeks at a time. There's no time off, no breaks. It's a twenty-four hour a day job. Robin Sage is one part training, one part evaluation, and the stakes are extremely high. The students must successfully negotiate this part of the training to complete the Special Forces Qualification Course and earn the coveted green beret and Special Forces tab.

If they fail to meet the standards, they could be sent back to the beginning of the phase to repeat the training. This is known as being recycled. That was a scary thought. On rare occasions if a student performs unusually poorly or shows that he is not competent in his MOS, he could even be given a "Day One Recycle." If that happens, they go all the way back to the beginning of the Q-Course and repeat *all* the phases again.

Finally, the worst possible scenario is a "Drop." These are not common, although they do happen on occasion. If a student's actions or performance is exceptionally poor, or they commit an especially grievous error, and the training cadre feel that the soldier should not be given any more attempts at passing the course, they can drop them from the course altogether and they go back to their old job in the Regular Army. They return to the job they did before they tried out for Special Forces. Drops are usually associated with a previously undetected character flaw, gross lack of judgement, incompetence, or behavior that has resulted in disciplinary action.

As the men filed into the camp, none of them was thinking about any of that. They were trying to gauge their environment. They were looking at the scene in front of them trying to make sense of it. The camp appeared to be full of civilians in a mixture of civilian clothing, hunting apparel, and pieces of military uniforms. Larry took note of the mixture of visible weapons as they were escorted to the center of the camp. By the time they stopped, he had identified an M4, M16s, two different variants of the AK-47 and some type of pistol that was difficult to identify because it was too far away and being worn in a holster.

"Drop your rucksacks here." The bald man was talking to the captain. Jeremiah had been looking around when the bald man spoke to him. He snapped his head around to look at the man.

"Um, okay. What are we doing?"

The bald man responded. "Drop your rucksacks here, then you and your team can go right over there and take a seat. The G-Chief will speak to you soon."

The captain looked in the direction indicated by the bald man and saw several rows of "seats." The seats were just pieces of tree trunks that had been cut into sections about two feet long and arranged in rows in front of a folding chair. The folding chair was one of those director style chairs and had a built-in shelf on one side with an integrated cup holder. "Alright, sir. And what's your name?"

"We'll get around to the introductions after you meet the colonel," he responded and then turned to whisper something to one of the men nearby.

"Team Sergeant!" Captain Wilkerson called out. Paul immediately came up. "Have the guys ground their rucks here, dress right dress." The captain dropped to one knee and loosened his left rucksack strap. He rotated the ruck off and made no attempt to control its drop to the earth. It hit the ground with an audible thud. "After you stage the rucks, we're going to go over there to meet the G-Chief."

"Got it, Cap," Paul responded. Then he directed the men to place their rucksacks on the ground in three rows of five. Several of the men had simply squatted down, fallen backwards onto their rucksacks and then pulled their arms out. This was not an unusual technique for escaping a heavy ruck.

The team began moving over to the stumps. Captain Wilkerson turned to Paul and said, "Place one man on rucksack security."

"Got it, Cap," Paul responded, then turned to Troy Billingsly. "Troy, stay here and keep an eye on the rucks."

Troy rolled his shoulders, enjoying the freedom from the weight of the ruck. He responded with a single word. "Cool." He held his M4 loose at waist level.

The bald man walked up and spoke to the captain, who had not yet sat down. "That won't be necessary. Your equipment is safe here, and you can see it from where you're sitting. The colonel would like for you to have all your men come and sit down."

"I'd feel more comfortable if I kept one man on the equipment. We have a lot of sensitive items in these rucks, and I need to make sure everything is safe," the captain replied.

"So, you're saying our camp isn't safe?"

"That's not what I'm saying. I'm just saying that I need to keep someone with our radios and other equipment." The frustration was creeping into his voice.

The bald man countered. "If my camp is safe, but you're still worried about your stuff, then you must be saying that you think my men are going to steal from you. Are you calling my men thieves?"

The young captain was incredulous. *What's this guy's problem?* he thought. But that's not what he said. Instead, he said "No, of course not. However, the Army has tasked me with the security of everything that we brought into Pineland, so I need to ensure its safety."

"Is that your final answer?" the bald man asked.

Captain Wilkerson regarded the older man. This was clearly a contest of wills. Would he look weak to the cadre if he gave in? Is this a trap designed to make him loose his equipment? Was he reading too much into this? He didn't know. He decided to dig in. "That's my final answer," he stated firmly.

"Okay," responded the bald man. "Leave your man on security and have a seat. Do you or your men need water?"

The captain didn't understand the shift from confrontation to hospitality, but he was going to take advantage of it. "Yes, actually. We could use some water. Thank you."

The bald man turned on his heels and called out. "Cake! Bring some water for the Americans!"

"I'm on it, Sergeant Major!" responded a tall, lean man in his late twenties. Less than a minute later, he came running up with a water jug. He went straight to the captain and poured water from the jug as the captain held his canteen. He ended up pouring water all over the captain's hands and boots as he tried to pour it into the small mouth of the canteen. Not that it mattered, the entire ODA was completely soaked. After filling the captain's canteen, he started down the line offering water to all the remaining seated men. He ignored Troy standing by the rucks.

The ODA sat there, sipping water. The camp was quiet. Two Pinelanders were off to the side of the ODA, pointing and whispering unheard secrets. One would whisper something and point at one of the team members. The other would laugh. They stayed just far enough away that the team couldn't hear the conversation.

Two others walked up and began looking at the collection of rucksacks. Troy pivoted to face the two men. One was an older gentleman with gray hair and a gray goatee. The other was notably younger, maybe late twenties. They discussed the gear.

"Look at that, Juice. I think that's a mortar strapped on top of that backpack," said the older man.

"No way," responded the younger man. "You mean like the tubes that the UPA uses to launch the bombs?"

"Yeah. I'm telling you. That's a mortar. I'm sure of it. I just thought they were bigger than that," the older man replied.

Juice immediately replied, "That's what she said." He began to laugh.

The older man was not amused. "Man, can't you ever be serious?"

"Chill out, Fatback. It was funny," Juice responded.

Troy did not think it was funny. In fact, he was getting uncomfortable at how close the men were to the team's gear. They had made no effort to touch anything, but they were very close. "Fatback? That's your name?" Troy said to the older man.

Fatback looked up at Troy. "Yeah. That's me. How ya doin? Hey, is that a mortar?"

Troy had both his hands on his M4, but was doing his best to not look like he was being aggressive toward to the two men. "Yeah. That's a 60mm mortar. Hey, listen, would you guys mind not bothering our gear?"

"We're not bothering anything," Fatback replied in a very matter of fact tone. "Hey, I thought those things were bigger."

Juice giggled beside him. Fatback just shot him a look. He looked back at Troy, waiting for an answer.

Troy was a Bravo and knew all about mortars. "Yeah, that's a small one, but we have bigger ones too."

"Cool!" exclaimed Fatback. "Are we getting one of the big ones, too?"

"Well, probably not," Troy replied.

"Why not?" asked Juice.

Captain Wilkerson could hear the exchange taking place at the rucksacks. He looked at his watch. They'd been sitting there for over five minutes. Where was the G-Chief? In the pre-mission training they had read the dossier on the commander of this camp, Lieutenant Colonel Owens. He was a retired infantry officer from the Republic of Pineland Army and had been pressed back into service as the commander of this guerilla force. He was the Guerilla Chief, or as everyone called him, the G-Chief. Where was he? He looked at his watch again. Six minutes. Seven minutes. Should he say something? Probably not. He didn't want to be rude, but at the same time, they had a mission to accomplish, and he was being evaluated on that mission. He looked around for the bald man. He didn't see him. He had heard the tall guy call him "Sergeant Major." That was good information.

 What was the tall guy's name? He had heard it. What was it? Cake? He had heard the Sergeant Major call him Cake. What kind of names were these? He'd heard Cake, Fatback and Juice. Are they using codenames? Eight minutes. He looked at his men seated around him. Everyone was doing the same thing. They were drinking water, looking around and occasionally checking their watches.

Captain Wilkerson stood up and turned around. He looked in every direction trying to identify the Sergeant Major. He didn't see him anywhere. He saw two men sitting around a fire in what was clearly an outdoor kitchen. They had a huge steel grate over a fire. The grate must have been five feet long and was sitting on neatly stacked rocks on each side of the fire.

There was a large stew pot sitting on the grate, but he still didn't see the bald man. He sat back down.

As he sat back down, he saw a young woman walking up the trail toward them from a cluster of tents. She was small, no more than five feet. She looked young, but it was hard to judge her age. She could have been sixteen just as easily as she could have been twenty-six. She wore no makeup, and she was walking like she had someplace to be. She had long black hair, falling to the small of her back and swinging back and forth as she walked. She had tanned skin and dark eyes. She was clearly Latina. This girl, or woman, wore green fatigue style pants, knee high rubber boots, and a black t-shirt. She had an AK-47 slung over her shoulder. She held the rifle in place with her right hand through the sling. The captain immediately thought she looked like the pictures he had seen of the women working in the narco-terrorist group in Colombia known as the FARC. He stepped out toward the trail and made eye contact with her. "Excuse me, ma'am?" he began.

She stopped and looked up at him without speaking. He was instantly uncomfortable. "Um, hi ma'am. Um, I'm uh, Captain Jeremiah Wilkerson." He extended his hand.

She didn't take it. She just responded with, "Uh huh."

He left his hand hanging out in space long enough for it to be awkward, then slowly retracted it. "Hi, uh, sorry to bother you, but have you seen the Sergeant Major?"

She responded with a quick, "No," turned, and walked away.

"Shit," he mumbled under his breath and looked at his watch again. Twelve minutes.

The men had started to talk amongst themselves in hushed tones. The captain turned and looked at Paul. He tapped his watch. Paul just shrugged. He looked calm. Paul always looked calm. Why wasn't he more stressed?

The team sat there until a half hour had passed. Finally, the captain saw the Sergeant Major leaving a large green tent. It wasn't an army tent. It was definitely a civilian tent. The fabric had dark green pine trees on a lighter green background. He wasn't looking toward the team. He was headed for the kitchen area. He was now wearing a shirt and appeared to have on dry pants as well. The captain sprang into action and headed out in a path to intercept the bald man. "Sergeant Major!" he called out.

The bald man turned to address him. "Yes, Captain?"

"Sergeant Major, I was just wondering when Colonel Owens would be joining us," the captain said in his best attempt to sound upbeat and hide his frustration.

"The colonel is waiting on *you,* captain," the Sergeant Major replied.

"What?" the captain said. He didn't understand. He looked back at the team waiting patiently on the tree stumps.

"I'm ready to meet him. *We're* ready to meet him. We've been waiting over half an hour." As soon as the words came out, the captain wished he had phrased it differently, but it was too late now.

The Sergeant Major looked past the captain at the assembled men. "That doesn't appear to be the case. Let me know when you're ready to meet my commander. I wouldn't wait too long, though. He's a busy man." He started turning to walk away.

That's when the young captain let his frustration get the best of him and he made a mistake. As the Sergeant Major turned to walk away, Captain Wilkerson reached out and grabbed him by the upper arm. "Hold on, Sergeant Major." It wasn't a violent or even a forceful grip, but it was enough to make the situation instantly uncomfortable.

The bald man froze and looked down at the captain's hand on his arm. It was at that moment that the captain noticed the cauliflower ears of the bald man. How had he missed that earlier? This man was a fighter. He had the scars and the self-confidence to confirm it. The captain snatched his hand back like he had touched the hot burner of a stove.

The Sergeant Major slowly rotated to face the young captain. The captain realized that he may have just committed a major cultural foul. "Uh, sorry Sergeant Major. I apologize for…"

The Sergeant Major cut him off. "What, exactly, do you want, Captain?"

"I apologize, Sergeant Major. I'm just wondering when we would be able to meet with the commander."

"What did I tell you?" asked the Sergeant Major. There was a slightly discernible edge to his voice now. Captain Wilkerson recognized that it was the first time he had seen any indication of emotion in this man.

"Uh, I don't understand." He was trying to sound cool and professional. It wasn't working.

"I told you that the colonel would like for you to have all your men come and sit down. You have yet to accomplish that task. Once you're able to accomplish that *obviously* challenging task, my commander would be happy to meet with you." The sarcastic tone stung as he referred to the task as "obviously challenging."

Captain Wilkerson was bewildered. He looked over his shoulder at the men seated together. Then he looked over at Troy, who was looking back at him. "Shit," he said under his breath. "Is this because I have one man on rucksack security?" he asked.

"Captain. I've just met you, but already I feel like we're struggling to communicate. Is English your first language?"

"Uh, yes. I'm from Kansas, uh, America," he responded. The question tripped him up. Of course, English was his first language.

"Okay, great. I know that we Pinelanders have a different accent than you Americans, but I'll try to be clear. The commander will see you once you have your men seated together."

The captain didn't respond to him, but instead turned to face Troy. "Thanks Troy. I think everything is safe here. Why don't you go join the team."

In Troy's typical west coast informality, he responded with "You got it, Cap." He turned and started toward the rest of the team that was only about twenty meters away, sitting on the stumps. There was one empty stump. He dropped onto it and looked at Jeremy on the adjacent stump. "'Sup?" Jeremy didn't respond. He just pushed his glasses up and looked back toward the captain to see what was going on.

"Thank you, Captain," the Sergeant Major said and headed back toward the green tent. Captain Wilkerson watched him walk away and disappear back into the tent. He sighed and returned to his stump in front of the director's chair.

Less than a minute later, the Sergeant Major came back out of the tent. He was immediately followed by another man. The second man appeared to be in his mid-forties. He was wearing a coonskin cap, an actual coonskin cap! He also had a thin walking stick in his left hand. It was more of a staff, really. It was about five feet long and well worn. He didn't appear to be using it for assistance in walking. Did it mean something? Was it a status symbol? The captain didn't know, but these things were going through his head as he watched the man moving in the general direction of the assembled ODA. Paul twisted on his stump to see what the captain was looking at. The two men sat in silence, watching this man as he began working his way across the camp toward them. The Sergeant Major had stepped to the side and was matching his pace, but walking slightly behind his commander.

This man, presumably the G-Chief, was clearly in no hurry. He hadn't even looked their way yet. He stopped to speak to every Pinelander who was near him. Paul closely watched the man's interaction with the others in the camp. They were too far away to hear their conversation, but the body language was apparent. As he spoke with one man, the man grasped his hands together in front of him in an overt show of respect. Lieutenant Colonel Owens reached out and put his hand on the man's shoulder as he spoke. The man nodded his head in what appeared to be a Thank you. He then spun on his heels and took off.

As he left, the young woman Captain Wilkerson had spoken to earlier approached the colonel. The interaction was noticeably different. The colonel hunkered down just slightly to reduce the height difference between them. He didn't reach out to touch the woman as he did the man. He just listened intently to her as she spoke, occasionally nodding his head. When the woman finished speaking, the colonel straightened back up and appeared to be thinking for a moment. He turned to the Sergeant Major and spoke. The Sergeant Major immediately pulled a pen and small notebook out of his shirt pocket and took a note. The commander was dictating something to the Sergeant Major who was writing as quickly as he could. As he spoke, he motioned toward the young woman. The Sergeant Major didn't look up, but nodded as he finished the note. The young woman reached out a small hand toward the colonel and they exchanged a short handshake. With a slight nod of her head, she turned and left in the same direction as the other man. Paul thought about what he had observed. Despite not hearing any of the conversation, it was apparent to him that these guerillas respected this man. He was very clearly in charge.

The G-Chief turned to face the Sergeant Major and the Sergeant Major began speaking. As he spoke, he gestured toward the ODA. LTC Owens glanced in the direction of the seated ODA but didn't make eye contact with the captain. He returned his attention to the Sergeant Major who had now stopped speaking. The two men turned together toward the ODA and began moving in their direction. They were walking slowly and leaned toward one another, speaking in a way to prevent others from hearing them. These two men were obviously comfortable working together.

As the two men approached the ODA, the captain suddenly stood to his feet, facing the approaching G-Chief. The ODA saw the captain and followed his lead. They all stood up as well. It wasn't quite the position of attention, but it was still a show of respect. As soon as the G-Chief was about three or four steps away, Captain Wilkerson snapped a salute and held it in place. "Good morning, sir. Captain Jeremiah Wilkerson, U.S. Army Special Forces."

LTC Owens stopped and regarded the man who was standing up straight and looking him in the eye. He held his salute perfectly and was making a good show of formalities. Good. LTC Owens returned the salute with less focus on perfection. "Good morning, Captain Jeremiah Wilkerson, U.S. Army Special Forces. Why don't you and your men have a seat?"

Captain Wilkerson dropped his salute and looked over his shoulder toward his men. "Go ahead and have a seat, guys." The team all settled back onto their tree stumps.

"Sir," Captain Wilkerson began. "First of all, thank you for the hospitality you and your men have shown us."

"What hospitality is that, Captain?" LTC Owens replied.

"Uh, well." With the first question, the G-Chief had tripped him up. The young captain could feel his men's stares drilling into the back of his head. "Well, I mean, your Sergeant Major guided us to your camp and gave us water."

"Ah, yes," the G-Chief replied. "And why are you here?"

"Sir, we're here to help you defend yourself against the invading UPA."

"No," corrected the G-Chief. "That's what you're planning to *do* here. The question is *why* are you here."

The captain was perplexed. He didn't understand the question. "Um sir, Pineland and the United States are allies and we are here to train, equip, advise, and assist you in your efforts to repel the UPA."

"Once again, Captain. That's what you're planning to *do*, but you're not answering the question. Why are you being evasive?" the G-Chief asked. His tone sounded neither angry nor perturbed. He was simply asking a question.

The captain, on the other hand, let his emotion slip into his voice. "Sir, I'm trying to tell you. I don't know what you want me to say."

"I want you to say the truth."

"I'm trying to tell you the truth."

"And yet, you've failed to do so," the G-Chief responded cooly.

Paul spoke up. "Sir, we are here because it's in America's best interest to push the UPA back out of Pineland and regain our ally."

The G-Chief looked over at Paul. "And who is this young man?"

Captain Wilkerson looked over at Paul. "Sir, this is my Team Sergeant, Specialist Michaels."

"Finally, someone who's willing to speak the truth. You're not here to defend democracy. You're not here because you stand with the people of Pineland. You're here because it serves your country's needs. I don't understand why you weren't willing to own up to the truth, commander," the G-Chief said. Captain Wilkerson detected just a hint of sarcasm in the last word.

"Sir, I apologize. I wasn't trying to be evasive. I just misunderstood."

The G-Chief didn't hesitate. "Captain, is English your first language?"

Before he could answer, the Sergeant Major spoke up. "I asked him the same thing sir. He claims that it is, but for some reason, he has difficulty communicating."

Captain Wilkerson could feel the heat in his ears and knew that his face must be flushing red. "Sir, maybe we could speak commander to commander."

"We *are* speaking commander to commander," the G-Chief responded flatly.

"I mean, maybe we could go talk privately, just the two of us." The captain was looking for an escape route. He wasn't going to find it.

"Why is that commander? Do you have something to say that's a secret from your men? Are you attempting to conceal something from my Sergeant Major?"

Crap! Captain Wilkerson thought. *What the hell is wrong with this guy?* Once again, he left his thoughts unspoken. "No sir. I just think that maybe we got off on the wrong foot and I'd like to talk to you about why we are here. Correction. I'd like to talk to you about how we can help you and what we bring to the table."

"Okay, captain. How can you help me? Because I'll be honest with you. We've been doing fine. However, I know that you Americans travel everywhere with backpacks full of cash, so how about we start off with that. Did you bring me money to finance this fight?" This guy was direct.

"Well, we did bring money. But that's not the most valuable thing that we brought." The captain felt good about that response. That was one of the questions he had anticipated and prepared for.

"Really? You brought something more valuable than money? And what's that?" the G-Chief asked. There was a conspiratorial tone to the question.

"Sir, I brought a Special Forces Detachment. We are experts in Unconventional Warfare, and we're prepared to train and equip your men to make you even more lethal than I'm sure you already are. I have weapons specialists, engineers, communication specialists, medical specialists, and an intelligence sergeant, in addition to my Assistant Detachment Commander and Team Sergeant." It sounded a little more rehearsed than he meant to, but it *was* rehearsed. He'd practiced that pitch for two days.

"Interesting," the G-Chief said and looked over at his Sergeant Major. "You hear that, Sergeant Major?"

"I did, sir," the Sergeant Major answered without emotion. He had his hands grasped in front of him. He looked like he was a bouncer at a night club.

"Sergeant Major, where's my coffee?"

"I'll check on it, sir." The Sergeant Major immediately turned and walked away. Before he made it two steps, Juice came quickly walking up with a French Press and a coffee cup.

"I have your coffee, sir," he announced as he walked straight up to the G-Chief. He sat the coffee cup on the side shelf of the chair and poured a small amount of coffee in it. Then he stepped back.

"Thank you, Juice," the G-Chief said and picked up the coffee cup.

Paul noticed that the front of the coffee cup was emblazoned with the phrase FREE PINELAND. *Wow,* Paul thought to himself. *That's some attention to detail.*

"So, you have communicators?" the G-Chief began, blowing lightly into the coffee cup. "And who is that?"

"Sir, I'd love to introduce the entire team to you, but I can start with the Echos."

"Echos?" the G-Chief asked.

"Oh, I'm sorry sir, that's what we call our Special Forces Communication Sergeants. Their MOS is 18 Echo, so we refer to them as Echos." The captain felt pretty good about that quick response.

"MOS?" the G-Chief asked.

Dammit! Captain Wilkerson thought. "Oh, sorry sir, that's another military acronym. That's a military occupational specialty. It just means that's their job in the army."

"Then why didn't you just say that? Listen, I know that you claim to speak English. Pinelanders speak English too, but right now, I feel like we're two countries separated by a common language. How about this--let's just use plain, common English to improve our communication. Can you agree to that?"

"Of course, sir. I apologize. It's just that we soldiers have our own language and it's a little difficult to turn that off. However, we'll make every effort to communicate to you and your men in plain English."

"Freedom fighters," the G-Chief responded.

"Sir?"

"Freedom fighters. You just said you would use plain English to communicate with me and my *men*. I have women fighting under my command as well."

"Oh, I see your point. Yessir. You and your freedom fighters." This was harder than Captain Wilkerson was expecting.

"As I was saying sir, I have communication specialists with me." He turned back toward the team and said "Echos, go ahead and stand up."

Three men immediately stood up.

The G-Chief pointed to the closest man. "You, what's your name?"

"Sir, I'm Sergeant Billy Murphy." Billy Murphy had already been in the army a few years and had achieved the rank of Sergeant.

"Murphy, Murphy. Did your ancestors come from Ireland?" the G-Chief asked.

"They did, sir." He didn't smile. He was doing his best to appear as a professional.

"Tell me something about your Echo job."

"Well sir, as the captain mentioned, we're the communication experts of the team. We brought numerous radio systems and are prepared to train your men on their use as well."

"Great!" The G-Chief said enthusiastically. "So, you're going to train my *Freedom Fighters* on radios. How many radios did you bring for me?"

Billy looked over at the captain. The captain knew what was coming.

"Uh, no sir...um, we didn't...uh. I mean we brought radios, but we don't have any for your men." Captain Wilkerson visibly flinched when Billy said 'men' again.

"No radios for my Freedom Fighters. I see. So, you can train us up on radios, but you don't have any radios for us. Then when you leave and take your radios with you, that training is useless."

"Um sir, we have other things we can teach you as well."

"That's enough, Sergeant Murphy. Go ahead and have a seat."

Sergeant Murphy sat back down feeling like he had just lost a fight.

"And you, what's your name?" The G-Chief pointed to the next man.

"Sir, I'm Sergeant Jeremy Burkhardt." He didn't wait to be asked what he could do. "Another skill that we're prepared to teach you and your men is the ability to use non-technical comms."

"Freedom fighters," the G-Chief responded.

Captain Wilkerson wanted to scream.

"Uh, yessir. That's what I meant. Your freedom fighters."

"And what exactly are non-technical comms?"

"Sir, we can teach your Freedom Fighters secure ways to communicate even when you don't have radios. To your point, we don't have extra radios, but radios are not the only option."

"Burkhardt, Burkhardt. German?" the G-Chief asked.

"Yessir, my great grandparents immigrated from Germany."

"Was your father in the military, Sergeant Burkhardt?"

"Yessir. I'm actually the third generation in a row to serve in the military."

"Interesting. Thank you, Sergeant Burkhardt. Go ahead and have a seat."

Sergeant Burkhardt quickly sat back down on his stump. He was glad to be out of the line of fire.

The G-Chief looked at the remaining man who was still standing. "And what's your name?"

"Sir, I'm Specialist Benjamin Horowitz. I'm the third communications specialist on the team."

"I see. Tell me something about your job that these two haven't already told me."

"Sir, in addition to the radios and non-technical comms that my teammates mentioned, we will work in conjunction with the Fox to help you develop an early warning network."

"The Fox?"

"Oh, yessir. Sorry, plain English. We have one man who specializes in intelligence, he's the Fox. We'll show you techniques you can use to help improve your security by utilizing early warning networks to give you advanced warning of enemy activity in the area that might put your freedom fighters or your camp at risk."

"Now that's interesting" the G-Chief began. "I can tell you that we've been trying to work on that exact thing. I'll be interested to hear what you have to offer."

Sergeant Horowitz felt like he had just hit a home run. *Freedom fighters, bitches!* He thought, suppressing a grin.

"Horowitz, Horowitz. Jewish?"

"Yessir," Sergeant Horowitz responded. "I'm from Massachusetts, but yessir, I'm Jewish."

The G-Chief appeared to be in deep thought. He put his coffee cup down. It was now empty. Juice immediately added a little more coffee to it. He picked his coffee cup back up and looked down into the cup as he gently swirled the dark liquid around.

"So, what you're saying is that *his* grandfather," he pointed to Sergeant Burkhardt, "tried to kill *your* grandfather."

Sergeant Horowitz froze. He had no idea how to respond to that. Sergeant Burkhardt couldn't contain himself and broke into a grin.

"Is that funny, Sergeant Burkhardt?"

Shit! thought Burkhardt. Then he got another idea. "Actually, yessir. That was pretty damn funny."

The group was dead silent. Captain Wilkerson felt like the air was getting thicker and harder to breath.

Suddenly, the G-Chief smiled. He looked over at the Sergeant Major. "That *was* some funny shit right there, wasn't it Sergeant Major?"

"It was, indeed, sir." The Sergeant Major suppressed a smile.

"Good, because I thought it was funny as hell."

The entire group let out a collective laugh.

The entire atmosphere of the meeting instantly shifted. "All right, Captain. Here's what we'll do. You introduce the rest of your men and then we'll plan a time for us to talk commander to commander. How does that sound?"

Captain Wilkerson breathed an audible sigh of relief. "I'd like that, sir."

"Great. Who's next?"

"Sir, I'll introduce the weapons guys, then the engineers, then the medics and we'll wrap up with my command team."

"Okay. Go ahead."

Juice poured more coffee.

It took another forty-five minutes, but the captain went through the rest of the team. The G-Chief asked them all various questions about their jobs and correctly guessed the country of origin of everyone's last name. Although, a couple of them, like Michaels and Roberts, he just said the "British Isles," which was technically correct.

15

Robin Sage V, Unconventional Warfare

Fall, 2003

Undisclosed location, fictional country of Pineland

Later that day, after the team had gotten settled into the area the Pinelanders had prepared for them, Captain Wilkerson, Paul, and Captain Tribiani came over to see the G-Chief. The Sergeant Major announced their arrival.

"Sir, the Americans are here to see you."

The G-Chief had a large brown tarp strung up in the trees, creating a good-sized working area under it that was protected from the sun and rain. He had two folding tables arranged in an "L" shape forming his working area. On the side table, there was a small, two-burner propane stove set up. The tree behind him had some nails driven into it. Hanging from the nails were a small pot and skillet. There was a map of the area spread out on the table with various markings on it. The folding chair from earlier was on his side of the table, and on the other side were several more cut stumps like the ones the team had used when they first arrived.

"Hello, sir, do you have some time to talk?" Captain Wilkerson said by way of a greeting.

"Of course, captain. Have a seat," he replied.

The three men pulled stumps up in front of the G-Chief's table. "Sir, I hope it's okay, but I brought Specialist Michaels, my Team Sergeant, and Captain Tribiani, my assistant detachment commander," he said as he settled down onto the stump he had just moved. He had a small camouflage backpack slung over one shoulder. He slipped it off and sat it on the ground at his feet. All three men carried M4 rifles. The two captains set them on the ground at their feet as well. Paul placed the butt of his rifle on the ground, with the barrel leaning against his leg.

"That's fine, captain. Did you get your team settled in okay?"

"Yessir. Everything is great. We can tell you cleared that area out for us to have a place to work and sleep and we appreciate the effort." *Show appreciation. Be respectful. Establish the relationship early.*

"Good, good. The Sergeant Major sent a few people over there yesterday to make sure you would have enough room to work. If you need to clear out more trees, let the Sergeant Major know and I'm sure he can help you."

"You clearly have a lot of trust in your Sergeant Major, sir. That's good. I try to maintain the same type of relationship with my Team Sergeant."

"That's good to hear. Now, what did you want to talk about?" The G-Chief opened a notebook and wrote the date and time at the top of the page. When he finished writing, he looked up at the captain without speaking.

"Well sir, I wanted to do a couple things in this first meeting. First, I wanted to give you a gift we brought for you." He reached down to the small backpack and unzipped it, pulling out three cigars. He extended two of the cigars across the table to the G-Chief. "Sir, I heard you like cigars, so I thought we could have a cigar together."

The G-Chief took the cigars, looking at the seal. "And how did you hear that I like cigars?"

"Sir, I was provided with a little information about you and your unit, and I read in the report that you like cigars. I brought you an extra one in case your Sergeant Major likes cigars too. We didn't have any information on him," the captain answered. He was feeling nervous, but he knew what he had to do, and he had a plan.

"Well, your report was correct. I do like cigars. I accept your gift. Thank you, captain." The G-Chief sat the cigars on the table beside the notebook.

The captain pulled out a lighter. "Sir, would you like to smoke now?"

"I appreciate the gift captain, but a cigar is a rare treat. How about we save them and enjoy them after our first combat mission together?" the G-Chief suggested.

Captain Wilkerson smiled. "I like that idea sir. I'll plan on it."

"And what was the second thing you wanted to do?"

"Well sir, I wanted to take this opportunity to discuss Unconventional Warfare with you. I'm not sure how familiar you are with it, but U.S. Special Forces specializes in Unconventional Warfare and the U.S. government feels like this is the best tool to use in your fight against the UPA." The captain reached down into the backpack again and pulled out his own notebook. His was a green pocket-sized notebook made by Rite in the Rain. The paper wouldn't get ruined if it got wet. Everyone on the team had at least one of these notebooks. The captains had two or three in different sizes for different things.

"I think I have an understanding of it, but I'd like to hear what you have to say."

Captain Wilkerson gave his rehearsed pitch, defining Unconventional Warfare. The idea was that the ODA would partner with LTC Owens's unit, the Sandhill Freedom Fighters. The Sandhill Freedom Fighters was just one of many guerilla bands (G-Bands) in the Pineland Resistance Force (PRF).

Captain Wilkerson explained that they would conduct the campaign in a series of phases. The three men explained the phases and stated that they assessed that the campaign was currently in the "Organizational Phase." He explained what it would take to move through the next phases, the Buildup Phase, the Employment Phase and finally the Transition Phase.

After explaining the phases, they started on the support networks that would be required to advance the campaign through the phases. "The Area Complex is a system of networks that support you and your unit, sir," Captain Tribiani said, offering Captain Wilkerson a break from the talking. "I know you used to be in the Pineland Army, and when you were in the army, you had entire units dedicated to support. Unfortunately, you don't have that now, so we need to develop various networks to provide the type of support that will facilitate your combat operations."

"I'll agree with that. We've been doing the best we can with support from the higher elements within the PRF, but I'll agree that it's not enough. What kind of support networks do you recommend?" the G-Chief asked, while constantly taking notes.

"Cap, can I jump in here?" Paul said to Captain Tribiani.

"Please. Go ahead," Captain Tribiani replied.

"Sir, every war runs on money. The first network is the Finance Network," Paul began.

"I'm not too worried about that," replied the G-Chief. "Now that you Americans are here, our financial concerns should be addressed."

"It's true that we do bring money to the fight, but ideally, we want to help you find ways to finance your own efforts, so you aren't completely reliant on the U.S. Government."

"Oh, I get it. You're pumping millions of dollars into Afghanistan right now, but *Pineland* is not as important." There was an accusatory tone to the G-Chief's statement.

"No sir, that's not the case." Paul didn't take the bait. "We just want to have additional revenue sources to help build redundancy into your efforts."

"Uh huh," the G-Chief murmured as he scribbled something down in his notebook. "We'll get into the details of each one of these networks, but first, just give me the list of all the networks so I can get a grasp on the bigger picture."

"Okay sir, that makes sense," Paul said. "There is Finance, Intelligence and Counterintelligence, Recruiting, Medical, Communications, Logistics, Information Operations, and Transportation."

"How is Information Operations different from Intelligence?" asked the G-Chief, without looking up from his writing.

Captain Wilkerson looked at Paul and nodded. Paul returned the nod and handed the conversation over to him.

"Sir, Information Operations is just what we call our messaging campaign. We want to get *our* message out to the people and counter the messaging that the UPA is pushing."

"Oh!" exclaimed the G-Chief. "You're talking about propaganda! You don't have to convince me of how important that is. I'm already on board. The whole world knows how good you Americans are at propaganda. You use it against your own people every day. It's impressive how well your government uses the media to push a false narrative on the public and Americans just eat it up! It's very impressive. I'm very excited to hear how we can use that American expertise to influence the fight here in Pineland. I mean honestly, your government's propaganda campaign against its own people is the most effective effort that the world has ever seen. Well, Joseph Goebbels probably has you beat, running the propaganda machine for Hitler. I actually remember a quote from him: 'Think of the press as a great keyboard on which the government can play.' I think I got that right."

The three men were taken aback by the 'compliment' which could just as easily have been interpreted as an insult. *Did he just compare the U.S. to Nazi Germany?* This guy was clearly a student of history. Captain Wilkerson tried to steer the conversation back in the intended direction. "Well, it's not exactly like that. For instance, we know that the UPA is already using the local papers to push out intentionally inaccurate information about their own activities. For example, a recent newspaper article described the population control checkpoints as aid distribution points. The radio stations are consistently referring to the PRF as terrorists. We want to be able to get our message out and tell people the truth. If the only information that they're getting is coming from the enemy, then they might start believing it."

"Repeat a lie often enough and it becomes the truth," the G-Chief said, looking directly at Captain Wilkerson.

"Goebbels again, sir?"

"Supposedly. Like I said, you don't have to sell me on propaganda. I know it works. I'll be interested to hear your ideas on how to actually employ it effectively in this environment."

"We're prepared to go over that with you in detail sir, but I'd like to have my intel guy with us when we do. He's taking the lead on that," Captain Wilkerson said.

"Yeah, I don't want to get too far down into the weeds on each one of these. For this meeting, let's just stick to the 10,000' foot view."

"Agreed, sir. That was my thought as well," Captain Wilkerson said and looked down at the notebook that he now had open. He leaned forward and placed the small green notebook on the edge of the table. The page was full of talking points for this meeting. "Do you mind if we go on to the next one?"

"Please."

"Sir, the next one I'd like to cover is Logistics. Keep in mind that I'm not giving you these in their order of importance. They're all equally important." He had planned to go in a certain order, but the flow of the conversation had pulled him in a different direction, so he was just going to go with it.

"Okay."

"Logistics is somewhat self-explanatory for a military man like yourself. It's the beans and bullets that allow us to continue with the war effort. We're talking food, a source of water, clothing, weapons, ammo, shelter, essentially everything you would have gotten through the supply system when you were in the army."

"Got it," replied the G-Chief. "That's already become an issue. We're low on food in the camp. And now I have fifteen more mouths to feed."

"Uh, yessir. About that...Captain Tribiani?"

Captain Tribiani was ready for the handoff. "Sir, if you had more money right now, would you be able to purchase food for the camp?"

"Yes, but it has to be done carefully," replied the G-Chief. "Any large purchases could attract the attention of the UPA. Most people are barely getting by right now and are buying just what they need. I have a guy that helps me, but he has to go to several different places and buy food in smaller quantities to prevent raising any red flags."

"I see," said Captain Tribiani, reaching into the cargo pocket of his uniform pants. "If we could provide some money to help get some food in the camp, do you think your contact would be able to do that for us?" He withdrew a Ziplock bag of currency from his pocket.

During the conduct of Robin Sage, the exercise uses a fake currency, called don, to represent the currency of Pineland. This currency exchange rate was two don to one dollar. Part of the responsibility of the ODA is to use this money as a tool to facilitate operations. They must manage the money, track it's use, and ensure that it's only used for authorized purchases. This is good training for the men going through the course, as they'll be required to do this in the future with real currency on real deployments. At the time, in Afghanistan, ODAs were doing exactly that, with U.S. currency.

"How much do you think you need sir?" Captain Tribiani asked. Paul immediately recognized the mistake in that question.

"I don't know," responded the G-Chief. "How much ya got?"

"Uh, well, I mean the money is for more than just food. We need to make it last. We may need it to buy weapons or information, or use it for bribes."

"You didn't answer the question. How much money did you carry into Pineland?" The G-Chief was staring intently at Captain Tribiani.

Captain Tribiani wasn't sure if he was allowed to reveal that information. He looked over at Captain Wilkerson. His face was a mixture of discomfort and confusion. He wasn't prepared for the question. Captain Wilkerson jumped in. "Sir, we came into Pineland with 125,000 don."

And there it was. One hundred twenty-five thousand don. The G-Chief rubbed the gray beard on his chin as if in thought. "Well, that's a good start, but I don't feel like that's very much money."

"Yessir," replied Captain Tribiani. "But we're going to help you set up a finance network, plus we'll be getting more money later."

Paul didn't overtly react to the Captain's statement, but in his head he said, *Damn, Joey. Don't you learn?*

"Really? How much?" inquired the G-Chief.

"Oh, uh, I'm not exactly sure. We'll need to see how long this money lasts and provide an estimate back to our higher command with the request."

"Hmm." The G-Chief was rubbing his chin again. "Well, let's see. We have thirty-two people in the camp right now. I estimate about thirty don per person, per day..." He started scribbling numbers on his notepad. "Let's see, that's almost a thousand a day, we'll just round that up." He wasn't speaking to the three men, more like just thinking out loud. "Let's say a week's worth of food. That's seven thousand. Plus, I'm going to have to pay my contact to drive around to different stores. He could encounter UPA checkpoints, so we'll need to factor bribes in so he can get through the checkpoints. Plus, of course we want to pay him for the risk he's taking so he'll continue to help us. That looks like about..." He dropped his pen on the table and picked the notebook up, as if examining the number. "I'd say about twenty-five thousand Don should get us started." The G-Chief looked up from his paper and regarded each man individually, looking for a reaction.

Paul tried not to flinch. *We walked into that one,* he thought, but he didn't speak.

Captain Tribiani didn't hide his surprise as well as Paul did. The look on his face gave him away and the G-Chief pounced. "What's wrong, Captain. That shouldn't be a problem, should it?"

"Um, I'll have to defer to my commander." He looked down the line to Captain Wilkerson. This was actually the right answer. The commander was ultimately responsible for everything the team did or failed to do.

This pause gave Captain Wilkerson just enough time to compose himself. "Well sir, that seems a bit high. That's twenty percent of our OPFUND and we haven't even been here a day yet."

"What's OPFUND?" the G-Chief asked.

"Oh, sorry sir, I said I was going to try to minimize the acronyms. That's our operating funds. That's what we call this money." He kept going, intentionally not giving this man a chance to trip him up again. "Do you think we could get four days' worth of food for ten thousand?"

"I don't know. I'll have to check with my guy and see what he can do. But I doubt it."

"Well sir, I'm prepared to give you ten thousand now. Would you be able to work with your contact and see what he could get for that?"

"I think twenty-five thousand would be better, but I'm not going to say no to ten. We'll see what happens."

Captain Tribiani sat the bag of money on the table in front of the G-Chief without taking any out and without counting anything. The G-Chief looked down at the unopened bag. "I guess you already knew how much you were going to offer, huh?"

Captain Wilkerson responded, "Well, sir, as I said we have to make this money last."

"Fair enough," replied the G-Chief. He reached for the money, removed it from the bag and began counting it. Captain Tribiani stole a look at Paul. Paul gave a slight shake of his head. Captain Tribiani looked away.

"Go ahead, captain. What's the next network?" He didn't look up from the currency but kept counting.

Before he could speak, one of the freedom fighters stepped up to the table. "Excuse me, sir."

The G-Chief looked up from the money. "Hey Lucky, what do you need?"

The man had a stocky build. He was wearing loose fitting green pants that looked perfectly suited for this environment. His shirt was a lightweight flannel in a combination of light brown and black. It hung loosely, untucked. His sleeves were rolled up exposing a full sleeve tattoo on his right arm and another smaller tattoo on his left wrist. Paul tried to see the tattoo on his wrist, but he couldn't make it out from this angle. His beard was cut short and had a noticeable hint of red in it. He held the French press in his both hands in front of him.

"Sir, I just wanted to see if I could offer you some coffee."

"Damn, Lucky! That sounds great." The G-Chief retrieved his coffee cup from the opposite side of the table and sat it on the table in front of Lucky. Lucky poured his commander a full cup.

"Captain, would you like some coffee?" the G-Chief asked Captain Wilkerson. He didn't offer coffee to the other two men.

"Uh, yes please, sir. Thank you."

"Do you have your canteen cup?" the G-Chief asked.

"Oh, uh, no sir. I don't have it with me," Captain Wilkerson replied.

"Hmm. That's unfortunate."

The G-Chief returned his attention to Lucky. "Anything else, Lucky?"

Captain Wilkerson looked over at Paul. *What just happened? Is this guy not going to find a cup for us so we can have some coffee?*

"Yessir, I was wondering what you wanted me to do about dinner tonight," Lucky answered.

"What do we have to work with?"

"Well sir, we have some white rice, a small bag of pinto beans and the roadkill squirrel that we got this morning. Viper and Rock just finished cleaning it," Lucky replied.

"It took two people to clean a squirrel?"

Lucky smiled a genuine smile. "No sir. But they wanted to argue about who could do it better or faster. I'm not sure who won the argument, but it's done."

"My money would have been on Rock," he said with a smile.

"You're probably right sir. Experience wins over enthusiasm," Lucky replied, still smiling.

"Okay. Let's save the beans so we can have some breakfast tomorrow. Boil the squirrel with some chicken bouillon, garlic powder, and black pepper, then strip all the meat off the bone. Once it's done, shred the meat and mix it into the rice so everyone gets a little meat. Use chicken bouillon in the rice when you're cooking it too. Do we still have some hot sauce?"

"Not much sir, but I'm sure we have enough for officer rations." Lucky still held the French press in both hands, holding it close to his body, in front of his chest like a waiter in a fancy restaurant.

"Good. Good. Thanks Lucky. Is that it?"

"Yessir. Thank you, sir." Lucky looked over at the three men sitting together. "Gentlemen," he said and turned away, leaving quickly.

The G-Chief took a sip of the coffee. "Rock is our resident hunting and skinning expert. He's been hunting since the 60s."

"Since the 1960s sir?" Captain Wilkerson responded with a sound of disbelief in his voice. "How old *is* Rock?"

"He's seventy-one years old, but he's still a helluva shot."

Captain Wilkerson's eyes widened. "You have someone in the camp that's seventy-one years old?"

"No," the G-Chief replied calmly. "I have *two* people in the camp who are seventy-one years old. Deacon and Rock are only a week apart in age."

"Seriously?" Captain Wilkerson was incredulous.

"Yes. Seriously. Look, you need to understand something captain. Our home has been invaded. Everyone wants to defend our home. Pinelanders are tough people. Those two men have life experience that you can't even fathom and if they want to fight for their country, I'm happy to have them."

Captain Tribiani weighed in on the statement. "That's impressive sir. I'm looking forward to meeting them."

"You will. Okay. Now, where were we? We were talking about these support networks, right Captain Tribiani?" The G-Chief had derailed the conversation, now he was helping it get back on track.

"Oh, yessir. Uh, okay. How about transportation?" Captain Tribiani asked.

Paul glanced over at him. Captain Tribiani caught the movement, made eye contact with Paul and looked down at his paper. They were planning on covering transportation last. Oh, well. Just go with it. "I wanted to thank you for the help getting here. Jason was very helpful and eliminated a lot of walking that we would have had to do. Do you have more trucks than just that one?"

The G-Chief picked the stack of money up and went back to counting as if the interruption had never happened. "Four thousand." He paused with bills in both hands. One hand had bills which had been counted. In the other were the bills that were yet to be counted. "I don't think you understand how this works. I don't have *any* trucks. That's not my truck. That's Jason's truck. He's a patriot and he wants to help, but he's not in a position to come out here in the woods and be a fighter. However, he has a truck, so he helps in his own way. But he's taking a risk every time he helps us. He's spending his own money, risking his truck, his trailer, and ultimately his life and the lives of his family if he gets caught. May I assume that you gave him some money for helping you?"

All three men looked at each other. "Uh, no sir," responded Captain Wilkerson. "I, uh, didn't realize that we were supposed to."

The G-Chief sighed and looked down at his hands. Paul instantly felt like he was talking to a disappointed dad. The G-Chief just sat there for a few seconds but didn't say anything. It was just long enough to make the group feel uncomfortable. He set the uncounted money aside and used both hands to tap the counted stack against the table, aligned all the edges. His movements were slow and deliberate. When he spoke again, he spoke in a quiet voice, as if he were talking to himself.

"You didn't realize you were supposed to."

He looked back up at Captain Wilkerson. "So, you just assumed everything was free."

It wasn't a question. It was a statement. "You're new here, so I'm going to chock that one up to a lack of experience and not understanding how life works. However, in the future, when someone risks their life for you, it would be appropriate to compensate them in one way or another."

"Of course, sir." Captain Wilkerson tried to sound professional, not like a kid in the principal's office.

Paul spoke up. "Sir, the next time we get a ride from Jason, we'll make sure to pay him for the ride that we've already received in addition to the cost of the next one. What's an appropriate amount?" Paul used the word "appropriate" mimicking the G-Chief's language.

"A hundred Don would keep him happy," the G-Chief replied, seeming satisfied with Paul's offer.

"Sounds good, sir. The next time we get a ride; we'll include an extra hundred."

"No, Team Sergeant. It's a hundred *per head*." Now the G-Chief was focused on Paul, gauging his response.

"Oh, I misunderstood, sir. We owe an additional fifteen hundred. Got it." He didn't show any emotional reaction to the number. He pulled his own notebook from his pocket and began writing with a Staedtler fine tip permanent marker. These were commonly referred to as "map markers" and if you wrote on a laminated surface, you could use the white Staedtler marker to erase it. Everyone carried the same markers, usually in two or three colors, plus the eraser marker.

Paul continued. "And sir, is there a possibility of getting additional vehicles?"

"I don't know right now." He again picked the uncounted stack of bills up and began counting. He paused as he added another thousand to the counted stack. "However, I don't want to get bogged down on one network. We can talk more about that soon." He held the remaining bills beside his notebook and looked down at it. "I see we're out of order on these networks, but that's fine. You said they're all of equal importance. Which one do you want to hit next?" He counted off another thousand don.

They spent the rest of this first hour trying to get through the remaining networks. Paul felt like the G-Chief kept taking them off on tangents and they weren't making very good progress. Plus, he was constantly writing and would pause as he added to his notes. They got through all the networks except for communications.

At the one-hour mark, the G-Chief looked at his watch and said, "All right gentleman, I'd like to take a break, if that's okay with you."

What could they say? Of course it was okay with them.

Captain Wilkerson responded. "Of course, sir. That sounds like a good idea. I should probably go check in on the team anyways. When would you like to get together again?"

"I'll make time for you, captain. When would *you* like to get together again?"

The captain looked down at his watch and did some mental calculations. "How about 1400?"

"1400 sounds fine. I'll see you then." The G-Chief picked up the money and started putting it back into the bag. The count had been correct. The two captains gathered their weapons and backpacks and turned to leave. Paul didn't move.

"Sir?" Paul began.

The G-Chief looked up.

"Sir, would I be able to meet with your sergeant major? I would like to talk to him about security and scheduling some training," Paul said.

Without warning, the G-Chief suddenly yelled, "Sergeant Major!"

Paul flinched from the sudden outburst. Then he heard every Pinelander in the camp echo the call. "Sergeant Major," they called out in a chorus of voices.

In the distance, Paul heard a lone voice reply. "Moving!" He looked in the direction of the voice and saw the sergeant major coming up the hill at a fast walk.

"There ya go," said the G-Chief and then returned to his work of gathering up the money, cigars, and notebook.

This is a crazy place, thought Paul as he watched the bald man approach. He smiled and put out his hand. "Sergeant major, I'm the team sergeant, Paul Michaels. Please, call me Paul.

16

Invasion

June, 2022

Texas desert

Zamir and four of his men followed the Mexican smuggler across the desert. He had chosen the four men, including Omer, based on their physical strength and endurance. It was dark and the men had to move slowly to negotiate the terrain. Several times, his men had fallen, but they quickly got back to their feet and continued their northern trek. Zamir wore the same backpack he had kept with him at all times since he left Lebanon almost two months ago. The other men with him were significantly more heavily laden. He had directed the rest of his unit to spread themselves out among the hundreds of other people and walk to the border. Their instructions were reasonably simple. Present yourself to the first U.S. official you encounter and claim to be seeking political asylum.

Zamir had personally overseen the inspection of the men. Everything that could potentially cause alarm was taken from them. They had all been provided with fake identification cards. They were from a variety of Arabic speaking countries, including Saudi Arabia, the UAE, Jordon, and Algeria. These stupid Americans wouldn't know the difference. No one carried more than two hundred fifty U.S. dollars, plus several of them had a little of the currency that matched their fake ID cards.

They all had cell phones. The phones themselves were not a problem as many of the immigrants seeking admission to the U.S. had cell phones.

Everything Zamir didn't want the border agents to see was now being carried by the four men with him. This included satellite phones, non-electric and electric blasting caps, knives, two pistols, ten M4 rifles, a little ammunition for the pistols, and several thumb drives. Zamir kept the money in his own pack. He also had his cell phone, the thumb drives, and one of the satellite phones. The blasting caps were packed in small containers specifically designed for the task. Zamir and his men could improvise explosives, but the blasting caps were considerably more difficult to produce. They weighed nearly nothing and having them would make his tasks much easier. Bringing the blasting caps was his idea. He was happy that his superiors had agreed to allow it.

They hadn't brought much ammunition for the pistols, and they hadn't brought any at all for the rifles. These weapons were not for the trip, they were for the destination. Ammunition was heavy. Too much ammunition would quickly make the packs unmanageable. Zamir and his superiors back home had conducted numerous planning meetings where they discussed and adjusted the equipment the men would be carrying into the country. There was no need to carry anything which could be easily acquired once they got to the United States. They knew that they could also get illegal guns from the cartel or through other illegal means in the United States, but automatic weapons were more difficult to get, and more expensive. They had chosen to bring the M4 rifles because these rifles had the option of a three-round burst. This wasn't as good as fully automatic, but it was preferable to the semi-automatic rifles that were legal for civilian ownership in the U.S. Of course, there was the added benefit of the symbolism--

using the weapons America had abandoned in Afghanistan to kill Americans.

The Hezbollah leadership that was working with the cartels to move the terrorists had made sure the cartel was well-compensated. The cartel would ensure that Zamir, his group, and the numerous other groups were taken care of. They would provide them with food and protection for the trip and would not confiscate their belongings. There were plenty of perks to be enjoyed by human traffickers. They had free reign to do whatever they wanted to the groups they moved. They would steal what they wanted and rape who they wanted. And if someone became too problematic, they could kill who they wanted.

Hezbollah understood this. However, they also knew they could develop a mutually beneficial relationship with the cartel. The key to this relationship was the appropriate application of money, and money was not really an issue. It was already common knowledge that Iran was funding Hezbollah, along with many other terrorist groups around the world. And Iran had money, lots of money. Under the Obama administration, the U.S., along with several European Union countries, had sent them literal planeloads of cash. The American public was mostly unaware of the exact amount of tax payer money that had been sent to the largest state sponsor of terrorism in the world, but estimates ranged from as low as $1.7 billion and as high as hundreds of billions. The official stance of the State Department was that the money would not be used for terrorist activities, but only for humanitarian aid. The problem with that was obvious. Once Iran had the money, they could do anything they wanted with it, including train Hezbollah terror cells and send them across the ocean to the American homeland.

The Mexican coyote had taken them through an uninhabited portion of the desert, avoiding the checkpoints. Zamir grudgingly admitted to himself that the coyotes were good.

They knew everything about the American "defenses." While still in Mexico, the smugglers had loaded the five men into the back of a pickup truck and driven them to an area just north of a little town in Mexico called Jimenez. The driver pulled over in an area that had no visible structures in either direction. The man tasked with transporting them spoke enough English that Zamir was able to communicate with him. The second man with them spoke no English at all. Just north of the town, their Mexican guides had ordered them out of the truck. The man who spoke English said something in Spanish to the other man and then turned to Zamir.

"We walk to the water."

Zamir looked warily back at the other man, still sitting in the cab of the old truck. "And him?" he asked.

"He stay with truck," the man said flatly. "We walk to water now."

The man wore an old straw hat that was missing part of the brim. It wasn't quite a sombrero but was too broad to be a traditional cowboy hat. It had a dark stain from countless days of sweating in it. Zamir thought the hat looked like it had gotten caught in a random piece of machinery, only to be saved at the last minute after a piece of it had been chewed off.

The man began walking northeast away from the road toward a fence that parallelled the road. He had a simple bag worn across his body. The bag had a long strap that was hung over the man's left shoulder, and it bounced on his right hip as he walked.

Zamir looked at the short fence posts. He had never seen fence posts like these. They were only about three feet tall and were made of concrete that had been painted white. The man had walked up to one of the fence posts and lifted the wire from it. It wasn't apparent from the road, but the fence had been cut and rigged back up in a way to essentially create a gate. He ushered the five men through the opening. They waited as he hooked the loop back over the post, erasing any indication that anyone had passed through it.

To their front was a two-track dirt unimproved road that was running roughly parallel to the road they had just driven on. Zamir had seen a sign on the paved road identifying it with a black number 2 on a white shield. He was certain that *this* road was unnamed.

The man turned to Zamir. "We go."

He walked to the dirt road and turned right onto it. It was sandy and difficult to walk on. Zamir now realized why they had chosen this specific location to unload. This was the site where the dirt road was the closest to the paved road. As soon as they started walking down the road, it veered to the left, away from the fence and the pavement beyond.

"How far to the water?" Zamir asked the man.

"Two kilometers," he replied without looking over at Zamir. The man's voice showed no indication of anger, but he was also not friendly. He was all business.

The sun was setting, but there was still sufficient light to see the trail. The area was covered with a thick growth of a low brown brush that looked like it was dead. The brush was punctuated by a spattering of trees, but they were small; few of them were more than twenty feet tall. The trees seemed to be faring better than the brush, as they had green leaves sprouting from them. The man followed the trail as it wove through the brush. He walked at an almost casual pace and continually looked over his shoulder to ensure that everyone was still close to him. At one point, one of Zamir's men, Amir, started falling behind. The man simply stopped and waited until the group was consolidated and then he began walking again, seemingly unperturbed.

They continued their movement toward the river for about twenty-five minutes, winding left and right through low, rolling sandhills. Suddenly Zamir detected the odor of manure. He looked back at his men and one of them scrunched up his nose, acknowledging the stench. It was now nearly dark, but in the moonlight, Zamir spotted a more significant road up ahead. The light-colored sand made it easy to identify, even in the low light. On the other side of the road, the trees were more substantial. The guide didn't pause at the road but crossed straight across to another trail that led into the trees. Beyond that it opened up into agricultural fields. That explained the smell.

The Mexican man didn't change his pace but continued along a dirt trail that separated two of the fields. As the group neared the far side of the planted fields, Zamir heard running water. His heart rate instantly sped up. *The famous Rio Grande,* he thought to himself. As they neared the water, the trees grew thicker, forming a light canopy over their heads. Then he saw it. The trail emptied onto a small, sandy clearing about twenty feet wide on the riverbank. The water was dirty, and it was moving faster than Zamir had pictured in his head. It reminded him of the rivers back home. It was water in the desert, the source of life. As in his home country, agriculture and homes followed the water in this dry environment. At that moment, Zamir missed his home. He knew that he would likely never see home again. He was okay with that. Allahu Akbar.

The guide looked down at his watch. "We wait," he said flatly and sat down, leaning back against one of the numerous trees bordering the sandy clearing. He fished a bottle of water from the bag on his side and begin sipping on it.

"How long?" Zamir asked.

The man looked at his watch a second time. "Fifteen minutes."

Zamir directed the men to put their packs down and find a place to sit. The next fifteen minutes felt more like an hour to Zamir. He looked at his watch every few minutes, willing it to speed up. His heart was still thumping hard in his chest. He looked over at their guide who looked like he was nearly ready to fall asleep. The water bottle was gone, presumably stashed back in the bag again. Then Zamir heard the sound of an engine. The guide heard it too. He stood up and pulled a small flashlight from his bag. He flashed it one time toward the river. The response was two flashes.

"You go," said the man. Without waiting for a response, he turned and walked back the way they had come.

Two minutes later, a boat pulled up and grounded on the little sandy beach. It was a long aluminum boat with an outboard motor. It had wooden boards for seats and room for about eight people. A man jumped out of the boat onto the beach. By this point all five men had their backpacks on and were ready to go. The man looked at the group. In the darkness, it was hard to see his face or who exactly he was looking at. "Who is Zamir?"

"I'm Zamir." He said as he stepped forward.

"Get in the boat. Vamos, vaaamos." The man drug the word out. He almost sounded like he was singing. He sounded happy, like he was having a good time.

As soon as they were all loaded, the happy man pushed off the shore and jumped into the boat. It was a bit of a tight fit with their packs, but the boat seemed to handle the weight well. It was surprisingly stable.

They turned left and continued on the water for less than a minute. Then the boat veered to the right into a small inlet that was barely wider than the boat. Vegetation hung over both sides and the bank was less than a foot away on the right. The bottom of the boat scraped on an unseen sandy bottom and they came to a stop.

The happy man spoke up again. "Vamos, vamos."

He motioned for them to follow and stepped off the side of the boat and onto soft, but dry land. He paused long enough to tie the boat off to a small tree. That hadn't taken long. This part of the Rio Grande was less than 100 yards wide. They immediately started into the green underbrush and within a minute were on a wide sand trail. About two hundred yards later, they came to what appeared to be a man-made canal. There was an old concrete bridge over the canal that was covered with the same green vegetation. They crossed over the bridge and met yet another sandy dirt road. The guide stopped. He turned and looked at Zamir. Zamir could see the man's toothy grin in the moonlight.

"Soy Carlos," he said. "Welcome to America!" His accent was strong, and he laughed out loud as he raised his arms out to his side, as if he were presenting the country as a gift. "Come, we go."

Zamir smiled to himself as he started walking north. Calling this border a defense was laughable. The massive area unprotected by the wall was essentially wide open and the coyotes had been navigating the border crossings for so long that they had every gap identified. This was unbelievably easy.

They headed generally northeast. It wasn't long until they came to a paved road. It was so straight that you would be able to see lights coming from a long way in either direction. Carlos stopped at the road and looked both ways, checking for headlights. When he saw none, he continued across the road. In the middle of the road, he spun around and walked backwards across the pavement, looking at Zamir. Carlos pointed down at the road beneath his feet.

"Two Seven Seven," he said.

Zamir didn't know exactly what he meant by that. Was that the name of the road? They continued across the road and began following another dirt road that led off into the desert. Even though there was brush all around them, Zamir felt exposed on the road. He felt the nervous knot in his gut returning. Would helicopters suddenly appear? Maybe military vehicles with mounted machine guns would come tearing across the desert to intercept them. Would they be caught? No, he didn't think so. Carlos was actually whistling now. Zamir tried to calm himself with deep breaths.

They zigzagged through the maze of jeep trails for nearly two more hours. Sometime during that walk, Zamir began to finally feel more relaxed and confident. He raised his hand to look at his watch and hit the button for the light. Then he held up his hand-held GPS device and hit a button on the side. The screen lit up in a gentle glow. He had adjusted the settings so that the light was as dim as possible while still being able to be read. It showed 1250 meters to go. They had a rendezvous to make in less than an hour. He liked the GPS on his phone better because the picture was much better. However, the man that had given them the ride in the truck in Mexico had instructed them to turn off all their cell phones and leave them off until they were told they could turn them back on. He had made them show him all the phones to confirm that they were off before allowing them to load the truck. The driver was concerned with the Americans tracking the cell phone signals. Zamir looked into the remote desert night and didn't believe that there were cell towers in this barren land.

Zamir was proud of how well he had been able to learn American style English in only two years. Actually, it wasn't really just two years. He had already studied English on and off for four years before that, but for the last two years, he had been studying in earnest. However, he hadn't gotten good at it until the last year or so. It had finally clicked. In addition to his studies with his English teacher, he would watch American TV shows and try to mimic their words, sometimes rewinding and practicing various phrases nine or ten times until he felt like he was saying it correctly. He spoke to Carlos. "Carlos, we need to be there in about fifty minutes."

Carlos didn't look over at Zamir. "I know this. We stop soon."

Zamir thought to himself. *We _will_ stop soon.* His English was better than this guy's.

They continued for another fifteen minutes until Carlos told everyone to stop. "You wait here. I check," he said.

Without waiting for Zamir to respond, Carlos trotted off into the darkness. Zamir was instantly furious. *This guy better not be trying to screw us over.* Then he smiled as he realized that he thought that in English, even using the slang he had learned.

He thought back to the training they had done in preparation for this glorious mission. Among other things, it had consisted of weapons training, training on the use of improvised explosives, communications classes, instructions of the American culture, and how to blend in. Then there was class after class on the American infrastructure and of course, English classes. He never admitted that he liked the language training. He would have been criticized. Instead, whenever anyone made a comment on how good his English was, he would respond with something like, "I must learn the language of the enemy, so I can kill the enemy. Allahu Akbar." His hard work had been rewarded four months ago when he found out that, not only would he be a part of this mission, but he had been chosen to lead it.

Suddenly, he saw Carlos coming back toward him. "Zamir, all good. All good." Carlos was smiling again and giving a thumbs up.

"Okay Carlos. What now?"

"You. All you, come now." He was waving for Zamir to follow him.

Zamir turned to his men. He spoke in Arabic. "Let's go brothers."

Without speaking, they all got back to their feet. Carlos began moving again, slowly, in the same direction he had gone earlier. After another five minutes, he stopped. He pulled a small flashlight out from his pocket and covered the lens with his hand. Zamir saw him turn it on. He uncovered and recovered the lens in a series of flashes. Zamir saw a response up ahead in the darkness. Carlos once again looked at Zamir, smiling and gave him another thumbs up. "We go. We go," Carlos said.

The group moved together for about five minutes until they came up on a two-laned paved road. They had hit the road at roughly a ninety-degree angle. There was a man standing there leaning on the post of a road sign. Zamir looked up at the sign. There was enough light to see the number 693 on a reflective background. Carlos said something in Spanish to the man, simultaneously motioning to the group of men. Zamir heard his own name in the speech.

The second man stepped forward and in perfect English with almost no discernible accent said "Zamir, I'm Javier." He didn't offer a handshake. "I'll be helping you on the next portion of your journey. All your debts have been paid. You owe me nothing, but you must do as I say. I will keep you safe. Are we agreed?"

Zamir looked at the man and then at Carlos. Carlos was still smiling. Javier was not. "Agreed."

Javier raised a small radio to his mouth and spoke. "All good."

Zamir heard two engines start up about a hundred yards away. Suddenly, headlights illuminated the space between them, throwing long shadows behind them. He glanced over at Javier. With the light from the vehicles, he got a better look at him. He was wearing jeans, cowboy boots, and a lightweight, button-up, tan, western-style shirt. He was not wearing a hat, showing his short black hair. Zamir looked back down at the boots. "Cowboy," he said under his breath. He had studied Texas. He knew this one state was nearly sixty-seven times larger than the entire country of Lebanon. He also knew that there were twenty-nine places in the United States called Lebanon. He found that piece of information more than a little amusing.

The vehicles began moving toward them. Zamir felt the familiar uneasy feeling creeping into his gut again. He tried to swallow, but his mouth was dry as well. He couldn't see what types of vehicles were approaching because the headlights of the lead vehicle were washing out his vision.

A moment later, a full-sized van stopped in front of them. The van was white with a logo for a home repair company on the side. Zamir tried to look at the logo and noticed two spots in his vision from looking into the headlights. A compact car of some type was behind it.

Carlos spoke up. "You go. You go." He happily motioned toward the van.

This guy was clearly enjoying his job. Zamir simply nodded at him. Carlos trotted past them, offering a casual wave as he did, and got into the passenger side of the small car. The car immediately passed the van on the empty road and sped off.

Javier spoke up again. "Get your men and get in the back of the van. There's a tarp back there. If I tell you to, cover yourselves with the tarp and don't move or make a sound. If we stop for anything, stay quiet unless I address you directly by name. I'll be with you the rest of the way and will take you to the rendezvous with your friends. Do you understand?"

Zamir nodded his understanding. "Do you have water?"

"Yes. There's water and food in the back. We have a long drive ahead of us. Load up."

Zamir passed the instructions to his men. They all spoke English, but no one's English rivaled Zamir's and he wanted to convey the instructions in their native tongue to ensure everyone understood. Javier opened the sliding door to the van and a dim interior light illuminated the space. Zamir looked up at the light. It had piece of silver duct tape covering most of it, only allowing a small amount of light to shine through. However, after walking in near darkness, the light was sufficient for the men to see into the cargo area, and they all got into the back of the van. Javier closed the door. The light went out. There was a divider between the front seats and the cargo area, but it had an open window. Zamir watched as Javier climbed into the passenger seat.

Zamir turned on his flashlight so they could see what they were doing. He noticed that the two windows in the rear door had been painted white, preventing anyone from seeing in. The cloth tarp, stained with various colors of paint, was in a heap on the floor toward the rear of the spacious cargo area. They all took their packs off and lined them up along the sides so they could sit on the ribbed metal floor and lean back on them. They scanned the floor for the food and water but didn't see anything. Omer lifted the edge of the tarp to peer under it. Zamir directed his little light in that direction. Under the tarp was a half case of bottled water and two McDonalds bags. Omer flopped into a seated position in the rear of the van near the tarp. He pulled the water into his lap, ripped the plastic holding the water bottles together, and passed a bottle to each man. There was enough for every man to have a second bottle. Next, they opened the bags of fast food. McDonalds had locations all over the world, including Lebanon. Everyone was familiar with it. There were ten hamburgers in the bag, no bacon. They distributed the cold burgers and men tore into the food hungrily.

They felt the van shift into gear, and they began to move. After the group of men ate their burgers and drank their water, it wasn't long until the hum of the tires on the road coupled with the dark environment lulled them to sleep. Zamir, however, did not sleep. He attempted to peer through the lone window, looking at the road ahead. Unfortunately, the view was limited, and he could make out very few details. He continued to watch, and he listened for the men to speak. They spoke very little and when they did, it was in Spanish. He would catch the occasional road sign, but he was looking for a specific one: San Antonio. He knew where they should be going. Every one of his men had it memorized. He strained to see any indication of their location.

After nearly two hours, he noticed a marked increase in traffic. He saw the headlights as they zipped past them in the opposite direction. He also saw houses and signs, lots more signs. He saw a sign that said Lackland Air Force Base and he knew they were close. Zamir woke the men. Omer didn't initially wake when Zamir shook him, so he kicked the young man in the foot, and he woke with a start.

The driver was careful not to speed or do anything else that would draw attention to their vehicle. He stayed on 90 until he came to the Interstate 37 on-ramp. He used his turn signal and very smoothly merged onto I-37. From there, the drove south to the 410 Loop. Once again, he was careful and deliberate with his driving. The intersection where 37 meets 410 is an impressive engineering feat. From the sky it looks like some type of tribal four-pointed star that could have been the inspiration for a tattoo just as easily as it was an intersection. The driver took the long bridge, curving to the left and turning them northeast. Five miles later, he used his turn signal and exited onto Rigsby Avenue, which is also Route 87. Zamir had seen the sign for the exit. They were almost there. He scooted up closer to the window to get a better view of his surroundings. They passed a gas station and a bank. He saw a sign advertising fireworks for sale. That was good information. He made a mental note to look for other fireworks stores in the future. They could prove to be a source of useful materials.

A few minutes later, the van began to slow. He heard the rhythmic click-clack, click-clack of the turn signal. He had learned when studying English that in the UK, they usually called the turn signal an indicator, but Americans often called it a blinker. He thought blinker was a stupid name, so he called it a turn signal.

The van turned into a parking lot and the men heard the distinct sound of the tires crunching on gravel. Zamir glanced back at his team. They were all looking at him. The driver stopped the van and killed the headlights, but left the engine running. Javier got out and opened the sliding door. The door was facing a concrete block building that looked like a warehouse of some sort. The building was old and had no illumination on the exterior. The driver had positioned the van so they exited directly in front of a set of double steel doors. Suddenly, one of the doors opened and Zamir smiled. Standing in the open doorway, illuminated by an interior light was Hassan Reza. He was smiling. He spoke in Arabic. "Welcome brothers! Come in, come in. Welcome, come in." The men got out as quickly as they could, bringing all their equipment with them.

Javier didn't speak. As soon as the last man exited, he climbed into the back of the van and swept a flashlight around the space, looking for any indication that the men had been there. He lifted the tarp to make sure there was nothing under it either. The empty water bottles and the fast-food trash were all he saw. He exited the van, closed the sliding door, and without saying a word, got back in the front seat. The van pulled away just as the steel door closed on the warehouse. If anyone had been nearby, they would have heard the sound of three separate locks slamming into place.

As the van pulled back out onto the pavement, the driver spoke first. His Spanish carried the accent of someone from rural northern Mexico. "Did you tell them they could turn their cell phones back on?"

Javier looked through the windshield as they picked up speed. "No, they can do what they want now. I don't care. I'm glad to be rid of them." He didn't look over at the driver. Javier's Spanish was more refined than the driver's. He was educated and had climbed the ladder of rank in the cartel. He didn't appreciate being sent on this delivery mission that should have been delegated to the grunts. However, his boss had told him that this group was to be treated with respect and he would be receiving a bonus following their safe delivery to the warehouse. That delivery was now complete.

As they drove into the night, he thought to himself, *Why is that group special?* Then he thought about the bonus he would receive for this simple task and smiled to himself. *Who cares?*

17

Robin Sage VI, Now We Wait

Fall, 2003

Undisclosed location, fictitious country of Pineland

The men of ODA 919 had been in the exercise for nearly two weeks now. They had settled into the routine of the training, but the nonstop nature of the scenario was wearing on them. Most had lost weight; everyone was tired, and they didn't know exactly when it would end.

Jeremy had been struggling more than anyone. During infil, he had kept his KYK-13 device tied off in a fanny pack. When they waded into water, he didn't think about it and the device had remained submerged for some time. The army called the device water resistant. This exercise proved, however, that there was a difference between water resistant and waterproof. The device had lost the cryptographic fill for the radios. Jeremy realized this the second day of the exercise when he tried to fill a radio. This was an exceptionally significant problem.

The U.S. radios can transmit in plain text, meaning unencrypted, but those unencrypted transmissions could be intercepted by an enemy force. To prevent this, all operations are conducted with encrypted transmissions. In theory, if you lose your cryptographic fill, another radio operator can send it to you over the airwaves. However, the three communication sergeants had tried this numerous times to no avail. This left morse code as the only option for communicating with the Special Operations Task Force (SOTF).

Communicating with morse code came with its own set of challenges. The radio transmission was still unencrypted, so the communication sergeants had to use a code book, called a one-time pad, to encrypt the morse code one letter at a time. Then they would travel at least a kilometer and one terrain feature away from the base and transmit the message. They would then have to return later to receive the response from the SOTF, which was also in morse code. Finally, they would return to the camp and decipher that message.

This had happened every day since day two. Jeremy had felt responsible, since he was the one who got the KYK-13 wet and he had done the majority of this work. It showed on his face and in his gait. He was beaten down.

However, Jeremy kept pushing, as did the rest of the team. They still had a mission to do. They had received intelligence about the route of an enemy resupply convoy, and they were going to ambush it. They knew what road they would be using and the approximate time the convoy would be passing through the area, 1700 hours.

They had planned through the night to prepare for briefing the OPORD this morning. It had been a team effort with numerous team members taking a part, but Paul was the patrol leader for this one, so he led the briefing.

Larry had built a terrain model of the ambush area. The terrain model was an area on the ground about 3' square that was a physical representation of the ambush site. The topography of the terrain was mimicked by adding dirt to create raised areas to imitate the hills of the target area. Larry had gone down near the creek and harvested some moss to use on the hills to make it look like they was covered in vegetation. He had used red yarn to carefully lay out the shape of the road. He used green plastic soldiers that they had carried in and arranged them on the terrain model showing the various positions. He also had two small plastic army trucks on the road representing the enemy vehicles. He had even taken the time to make small placards from cardboard salvaged from MREs that listed the names of everyone in each position.

They were in the employment phase of Unconventional Warfare. By this point in the exercise, the ODA had spent a tremendous amount of time training the Pinelanders and had accomplished numerous missions over the preceding days. The goal was to slowly reduce the PRF's dependency on the American forces and make them capable of conducting combat operations by themselves. As a result, they were trying to incorporate as many Pinelanders as possible, so the majority of them were on the mission. The remaining Pinelanders and members of the ODA had remained in the camp. They would be battle-tracking and planning for the next mission, as well as communicating with their higher headquarters.

Paul and his ambush force had been dropped off and moved through the hilly terrain to establish the ORP. Once in the ORP, Paul gathered the small group to conduct a Leader's Recon to positively identify every position they would need for the ambush.

He had taken Jeremy, Billy, Larry, and Cake with him. Jeremy was going to be on the right-side security with Fatback and Crash. Billy was going to be on the left-side security with Killer, the young Latina woman, and Rooster. Larry went with him because he was going to be in the support by fire position with Jimmy, the medic, and four Pinelanders: Bucky, Squib, Lucky, and Bubba. Paul and Cake would be on the assault line. During planning, he had originally planned on taking the G-Chief on the reconnaissance, but Cake had asked if he could do it and the G-Chief had allowed it.

Paul would be leading the assault element with the Sergeant Major and additional Pinelanders. Besides Cake, there would be several other Pinelanders: Deacon, Juice, Rock, Twain, Viper, Trigger, Chop and Freak.

The G-Chief had also insisted on being on the assault line. Paul had argued against it, stating that as the commander, he shouldn't be in such a vulnerable location. After a few minutes of debate, they reached a compromise. The G-Chief agreed to stay slightly behind the assault line, but would still assault with the main effort.

Departing for the reconnaissance, Paul was in the lead. They were on the reverse slope from the objective and were being careful to stay low and below the "military crest" of the small ridge. This made it unlikely that they would be seen from anyone else who happened to be in the area. The intel didn't suggest that the enemy would be in the area, but intel could be wrong. Plus, civilians were known to hunt and camp on these lands, so they would need to watch out for them as well. If they encountered civilians, they would need to make a decision. If the civilians appeared to just be passing through, they could stay hidden and let them move on. However, if the civilians appeared to be staying in the area, they would likely need to interact with them and move them away from the danger.

They were moving toward the area near the right side (the north), of the objective. Paul was in a crouch, his M4 rifle held comfortably by the slip ring, at the base of the barrel. He stopped and dropped down to one knee, spinning around to face the others. He spoke to the group just above a whisper.

"Billy, Larry, Cake." He made eye contact with each man as he said their names. "Hold here for a minute. Me and Jeremy are going to slip up and take a look at his position for right-side security. We won't be out of sight, so we don't need a GOTWA. We're just going right over there for a quick sneak and peek. I don't want to take any more people than necessary, especially since it's daylight. After we identify his spot, we'll come back here and then move out as a group. Good?"

The three men responded in the affirmative and Billy immediately flopped down on his ass with his back toward the direction that Paul would be moving.

"I guess you have rear security?" Larry asked, shaking his head.

"You know it, Boss," Billy replied without looking back at him.

Larry looked back at Paul. "You're good brother. See you in a few."

Paul nodded at him and looked over at Jeremy. "Let's go."

The two men moved in a low crouch until the terrain started to fall away, indicating the end of the ridgeline. Paul glanced back to see if he could still see Larry. He could. Without saying anything the two men dropped onto their bellies. They high-crawled the last few feet until they could see around the end of the ridge where it began sloping downhill to a creek that was visible below them and to their right. "What do you think, Jeremy?"

Jeremy examined his options for a moment, then he whispered, "Do you see right there where the point comes out into a little flat spot about halfway down to the creek?"

Paul was looking in the same direction as Jeremy and saw it. "Yeah. Got it."

"Those pine trees should provide cover and concealment from anything on the road. Plus, it's high enough that it'll be easy to get line of sight comms with you."

Jeremy was an Echo and was always thinking about communications. They would be communicating by radio during this mission and Jeremy chose a location that would allow him to do his job as right-side security, while simultaneously maintaining radio contact with Paul.

"Okay. Do you have everything you need?" Paul asked.

"Yeah man. I got this."

Paul gave a nod and the two men scooted backwards away from the ridgeline and back toward the others. Once they were far enough to do so without being seen, they stood up and moved quickly back to the group.

"Let's go guys," Paul said. He didn't need to tell them that they were going to recon the assault and support by fire positions next. They already knew that.

The group all stood up and began moving south, paralleling the ridgeline on the east side it. After about two hundred meters, there was a dip in the ridgeline. Paul held up his hand for the signal of "halt." Everyone moved close enough to hear him and stopped, dropping to a knee.

Paul began. "Jeremy, you and Billy stay here. GOTWA: We're going to recon the assault position and the support by fire positions. I'm taking Larry and Cake. We'll be back in..." Paul looked down at his watch. "...twenty-five minutes."

Jeremy looked at his watch as well.

"If we don't return, call us on the radio. If you can't get us on the radio, inform the ORP of the situation and move up to the ridgeline to identify our position. The slope is even here, so from the ridge, you should be able to see the entire objective area. Actions if you make contact: break contact toward the ORP, link up with the main body and defend in place unless it's an overwhelming force. If it is, break contact and move to ERP 1. We'll meet you there."

An ERP is an Emergency Rally Point. Two different ERPs had been identified during the Operations Order and everyone was supposed to know where they were and how to get to them day or night.

"If we get hit, we'll break contact back to you and we'll move together back to the main body for movement to the alternate exfil point. Contact prior to the ambush is abort criteria. What are your questions?"

Jeremy and Billy indicated that they didn't have any questions and then repeated the GOTWA back to Paul in their own words.

"Good. See you soon," Paul said. He made eye contact with Larry and Cake and with a nod of his head toward the direction they were going, they moved out.

In his best attempt at a British accent, Billy said, "God speed sir."

Paul just glanced back at Billy with a grin and started west toward the break in the ridgeline. The three men dropped onto their bellies as they neared the ridge. They observed the area to the west for about a minute before Paul lifted himself into a crouch and crossed through the low break in the ridge with the two other men close behind him. They quickly moved downhill to get below the military crest and then reduced their speed to a slow, careful walk. They were paying attention to the terrain and the vegetation around them as they crept forward to get a better look at the area they intended to use. Paul paused at a cluster of trees that provided them some concealment from the road. Larry and the Cake slipped up behind him and they all dropped down onto a knee.

"Larry, do you see that section where the trees are almost evenly spaced right there?" Paul indicated a line of trees that were about seventy-five meters from the road and running parallel to it.

"Yeah," he whispered back. "I got it."

"I'm thinking that's the assault line. I know the plan was to have the support by fire position to the south, but now that I can see the terrain, I think that high ground over there on the north has a better field of fire. What are your thoughts?"

"I was just thinking the same thing. Plus, it has that fallen tree we can use for cover and concealment. We should be able to set the guns up behind it and the barrels will still clear it. It looks good." Larry was looking toward the area that he was describing as he spoke.

"I'm good," Paul responded. "Do you have what you need?"

"Yep. I'm good too."

Paul looked over at Cake. "Do you understand the adjustment?"

"It makes sense to me. Let's do it."

Paul smiled when he looked back at Cake. The men had taken the time to paint their faces with camouflage face paint prior to leaving for this mission. The ODA used the traditional pattern typically used by the U.S. Army. The Pinelanders, however, had painted their faces however they wanted. Cake had painted his entire face with an even coat of light green and then written the word "KILL" across his face in black: "KI" on his right cheek, "LL" on his left. Paul thought it was hilarious.

Cake was all business and saw Paul smiling. "What?" He asked the question with complete sincerity.

"Nothing," Paul said. "Just happy to be here. Let's get back to the guys."

With that, they all started moving back toward the spot where Billy and Jeremy waited. As they moved, Paul keyed the mic on his radio. "Echo One, Echo One, this is Zulu, over."

The response was quick. "Go for Echo One."

"Echo One, this is Zulu. Moving to your location. Time now, over," Paul said while continuing to move.

"Copy that Zulu." Jeremy was using less formal responses which didn't include all the formalities of correct radio procedure.

"Zulu out." Paul ended the transmission. They were using their own internal radio frequency. No one else could hear them, not even Sergeant Souby, so they felt comfortable truncating the radio procedures in favor of brevity.

A few minutes later they were reunited with Billy and Jeremy and moving south again toward the left-side security position. They repeated the procedures they had used on the north end of the objective, but this time it was Paul and Billy who conducted the reconnaissance. After Paul and Billy had identified the location Billy would be occupying, they began the walk back to the ORP.

During this time, Jimmy had stayed back in the ORP with the remaining Pinelanders. He had overseen Deacon and Juice as they constructed a simplified terrain model in the center of the perimeter. The remainder of the team had been pulling security and doing final preparations for the ambush.

Jimmy's radio squawked to life. "Delta One, Delta One, this is Zulu, over."

Jimmy reached for the radio that was sitting beside him. "Zulu, go for Delta One, over."

Paul's voice came over the radio again. "Delta One, this is Zulu. Enroute to your location. ETA ten mikes, over."

Jimmy pushed the PTT, or Push To Talk button again. "Good copy Zulu. Ten mikes. Standing by, over."

Paul concluded the conversation as he had earlier. "Delta One, this is Zulu. Out."

Fifteen minutes later, Paul was at the terrain model with Larry. They made the adjustment to the new location of the support by fire position. He pulled Billy and Jeremy in around the terrain model as well. Jimmy was adjusting something in his aid bag and the Pinelanders were all pulling security. He quickly went over the adjusted plan with his teammates. Once everyone understood the updates, he passed additional instructions to the three men. "Pull your guys in, one element at a time and brief the changes. Right side, left-side, then support by fire. Larry, when you pull your guys in, leave the machine guns in place and I'll have guys from the assault element cover down on the guns while you brief. I'll brief the assault element last. Questions?" No one spoke up.

"Okay, we need to step off in forty minutes. Get your briefings done. Tell your guys to continue to hydrate. After I brief my guys, I'll take care of sterilizing the terrain model and we'll get into the order of movement. The order of movement will be right side, assault, support by fire, and left side bringing up the rear. We'll move up to the RP and then break off and you'll take your own element to your positions. I'm not going to emplace every element. Got it?"

Everyone responded in the affirmative. One way to emplace an ambush was for the patrol leader to lead every element to their positions and emplace them himself. However, Paul had taken the element leaders with him on the recon. They all knew where to go and Paul knew that they didn't need supervision to get into place. They would move as one group to the RP, or release point, and then break up into their individual elements and move to the appropriate locations. They would conduct this in the same practiced, deliberate, tactical movement that they always used when moving in enemy controlled areas.

The three men quickly took off to take care of the final brief. They had been working together for quite some time now. Their SOPs were second nature at this point. They all knew their jobs and were excited about this mission.

Time feels like it speeds up when you're trying to get multiple tasks done against the clock and that's how it felt to Paul. The next forty minutes seemed to fly by. As they got into their order of movement, Paul walked down the line double checking things. As he passed by Larry, Larry extended his fist toward Paul. Paul didn't stop, but he bumped his fist into his friend's. "You go this," Larry stated with a slight grin.

"Hell yeah," Paul replied. It wasn't an excited response. It was a statement of fact.

The men moved out and split apart at the RP as planned. Nothing was said. Right-side security split off to the right, assault and support by fire continued straight, while the left-side security split to the left. Assault and support by fire paused on the back side of the ridge to allow the security positions to get into place first. About ten minutes later, Paul got the first call. "Zulu, this is Echo One, over."

"Echo One, go for Zulu."

"Zulu, this is Echo One. Right side set, over." It was Jeremy's voice.

"Echo One, good copy. Right side set, over."

"Zulu, this is Echo One, out," Jeremy signed off.

It took another five minutes before Paul had the same confirmation from the left-side security to the south. He gave the hand and arm signal to move out and the remaining men resumed their trek.

The support by fire split off from the assault force later and Larry moved them straight to the position they had identified earlier. Lucky and Bubba to carried the two machine guns. The machine guns were heavy, so Lucky and Bubba had been chosen because they were two of the stronger Pinelanders in the camp. Lucky had the M249 machine gun chambered in 5.56mm NATO. He had shown exceptional proficiency running the gun and Larry was confident that he could deal with the malfunctions that often occurred when running blanks. Lucky was paired up with Bucky who would carry the extra ammunition. Plus, Bucky was also good on the M249 and could take over if Lucky became a casualty.

Bubba had the larger M240 machine gun chambered in 7.62x51mm NATO. Squib was carrying the extra ammo for that machine gun, and like Bucky, he was prepared to take over as gunner if necessary. Squib and Bubba had both argued to be the gunner, but in the end, Bubba was selected. Larry positioned himself between the two guns to control them. Larry placed Jimmy behind the firing line in reserve. Because Jimmy was a medic, Paul had chosen to put him behind the firing line so he could react if he needed to treat a casualty.

Typically speaking, military medics are considered non-combatants. They are only supposed to engage in combat to defend themselves or their patients. However, Special Forces medics carried a different classification under the Geneva Conventions. They were not a standard medic; they were also combatants. Paul hadn't put him behind the line because he wasn't a combatant. He put him behind the line because he was the only medic on this mission and he wanted him to be able to concentrate on his job as a medic if he was called upon to do so.

Paul and the G-Chief were finalizing the positions of the men on the assault line when Paul got a call on the radio from Larry telling him that the support by fire position was set. Paul started at one end of the assault line while the Sergeant Major started at the other end and they both moved toward the center. They checked to make sure that everyone had some type of cover from incoming fire. For most of the assault line, this was a pine tree. However, Trigger and Rock were in slight depressions that provided earthen cover to their front. They checked each man's camouflage and took the time to toss some pine needles over some of the men to better break up their outline. They also took the time to make sure that every person understood the left and right limits of their area of responsibility. This was important to ensure that every position's fire intersected with the adjacent positions. They instructed everyone to pull out a spare magazine and place it beside their rifles and finally, to stay awake. Once the two men were done, they met in the middle, at the G-Chief's position. "Everyone good on that side?" Paul asked.

"Yessir," responded the Sergeant Major. "All good."

Paul turned to the G-Chief. "Everything's set, sir."

The G-Chief nodded. "All right Team Sergeant. Do your thing."

Paul nodded back and turned to the Sergeant Major. "Okay, head back to your position and I'll see you on the other side."

"You got it, Team Sergeant," he replied. He turned and ran in a crouch back down the line to his position and settled in behind his own tree.

Paul moved over to his position and lay down on the soft bed of pine needles. He rolled partially onto his side and pulled an extra magazine from his magazine pouch. He positioned it on the ground next to his M4A1 rifle so that it would be easier to conduct his reload after the initial volley of fire. He looked at his watch. It was 1610. The plan had been to be in place by 1600. He knew that it was still acceptable. The intel had said that the enemy trucks should be passing through here around 1700, so they still had around fifty minutes before hit time.

That was assuming that the intel was correct and the truck was on time.

"Now we wait," he said under his breath.

18

Robin Sage VII, Ambush

Fall, 2003

Undisclosed location, fictitious country of Pineland

Paul glanced to his right. Deacon was positioned on a small flat spot with a significant pine tree in front of him for cover. He was right-handed, so his barrel was low and close to the ground on the right side of the tree. He had wrapped some brown burlap around the handguard of his M16 rifle for camouflage. He looked back at Paul and nodded. Paul was exceptionally fond of this seventy-one year old. Paul had learned that he had five children and several of grandchildren. He was the camp Chaplain, counselor, and confidant to the G-Chief. Everyone in the camp respected him and it was obvious. This included Paul.

He looked to his left. Cake was beside him on that side and Juice was beyond Cake. Juice had an AK-47 and his eyes were closed. His head was bobbing as he fought sleep. He was losing the fight. Paul just shook his head. *He'll wake up when the shooting starts*, he thought. He looked down at his watch. Time felt like it had slowed down. He was ready to get this thing started.

In an actual combat environment, Paul would have initiated an ambush with an M18 Claymore mine. They had those mines, but in this training environment, it was just a training aid and wouldn't make any noise, so it wouldn't work to signal the ambush. Instead, the plan for initiating the ambush was to open up with the two machine guns simultaneously. Several years earlier when Paul was attending Airborne School in Fort Benning, Georgia, he had gotten into a conversation with a Marine who was also attending the school. The Marine Corps didn't have an Airborne School, so the few Marines who got to go Airborne School attended the Army School. They were discussing differences in Army tactics and Marine Corps tactics. The Marine had pointed out that in the Marine Corps, they would never initiate an ambush with an open bolt weapon like a machine gun, because they are more prone to malfunction than a closed bolt weapon like an M4, M16 or AK-47.

In an open bolt weapon system, the bolt was locked to rear when it was prepared to fire. When you pull the trigger, the bolt would slam forward, strip a cartridge from the belt of ammunition, push it into the chamber, and fire. In a closed bolt weapon, the cartridge was already in the chamber and a pull of the trigger simply released the hammer, which would strike the firing pin and fire the cartridge.

"Any open bolt weapon is more prone to fail on the initial trigger pull than a closed bolt," the young Marine had said with a tone of confidence.

Paul had seen the logic in this argument, especially when using blank ammunition, so he had put a backup plan in place. He would call on the radio saying, "Initiate, initiate, initiate." Larry would slap both machine gunners simultaneously and they would open up. Then everyone else would open up as well. If he didn't immediately hear the machine guns fire, he would assume that either Larry didn't receive the transmission or the guns had both malfunctioned and he would fire his M4, initiating the ambush.

Fifteen minutes to go.

Ten minutes.

Paul looked up. The skyline was a seemingly endless line of tall pine trees. The ambush was facing west and the sun had dipped below the trees, shafts of light filtering through, connecting to the ground behind them. He thought about fall back home in the foothills of the Appalachian Mountains. He had grown up in mountains where the hardwoods ruled. At this time of the year, the trees would have already shed their leaves and built a thick blanket on the forest floor. When the dead leaves were dry, it was impossible to move quietly. Every step announced your presence with a crunch. It was so different here. The pine needles were quiet and soft. The woods even smelled different. Here, the pine forests dominated everything, but after nearly two weeks, he didn't notice the smell of pine anymore. He did however smell his rifle.

The army issues an oil called CLP. That stands for Cleaner, Lubricant, Protectant. In preparation for this mission, he and the team had cleaned their rifles. He had removed his bolt carrier group and disassembled it, taking the time to clean each component with an army issue cleaning brush that resembled a toothbrush. After scrubbing the parts with the cleaning brush, he had wiped everything down with a piece of an old T-shirt that was dedicated to that purpose. Prior to reassembling the bolt carrier group, he had lightly oiled each component with CLP. The rifle was old and well used. The parts were worn in and the bolt slid inside the bolt carrier as smoothly as silk. He had also cleaned the inside of the upper receiver and had taken quite a bit of time cleaning the chamber. Soldiers often referred to the chamber of an M4 as a "star chamber" because the shape of the locking lugs resembled a star. It was notoriously difficult to get clean and a dirty chamber could lead to malfunctions. They had been firing blank cartridges which dirtied up the rifles even more than standard ball ammunition. Now, as he lay on his belly with his rifle tucked against his shoulder, that distinctive smell of CLP tickled at his nose. It smelled sweet and he liked it.

Five minutes.

Paul's radio came to life. "Zulu, this is Echo One, over."

Paul hit the PTT and spoke softly. "Go for Zulu."

"Zulu, we can hear diesel engines, over."

"Copy," Paul replied, keeping the transmission short. Jeremy didn't acknowledge or sign off.

Paul turned back to look at the G-Chief who had an American radio. With a nod, he acknowledged that he had heard the transmissions. Next, Paul looked to his right at Deacon. Deacon was looking back at him. Paul pointed to the right up the road and tapped his right ear twice. Deacon acknowledged with a nod of his head and returned his focus to the road in front of him. Paul repeated the motion to Cake on his left. Cake nodded and looked to his left. Juice was out cold. His AK was flat on the ground and his head was laying on the buttstock. Cake looked around and spotted a pinecone that was within reach. He picked it up and gave it a hard toss, hitting Juice square on the chin. He woke up with a start, anger on his face. Cake had his finger to his lips telling him to stay quiet. He tapped his ear and Juice relaxed. He acknowledged as well.

Then Paul heard the engine. They were on time. He looked around. Everyone appeared to be ready.

Sergeant Souby had slipped around behind the assault line. He had been watching them for the last twenty minutes. He saw a guerrilla throw a pinecone. He smiled to himself. *These guys are funny*, he thought. In his right cargo pocket was a squirt bottle that was full of fake blood. There were going to be casualties. He wanted to evaluate Paul's plan for dealing with casualties as well as Jimmy Robert's ability to treat them. He heard the truck's engine.

Jeremy reported to Paul that he had eyes on the vehicles. The lead vehicle was a HMMWV. This stood for High Mobility Multi-Purpose Wheeled Vehicle, but most people just called it a "Hummer." That's what Jeremy reported, a Hummer. The second vehicle was a 5-ton cargo truck with a soft top over the bed.

Paul rotated the safety selector switch from safe to semi. Around him, he heard the click of safeties as the other men did the same. He held the radio microphone in his left hand, with his right hand on the pistol grip of his M4A1 carbine. His trigger finger was straight and off the trigger, resting on the side of the lower receiver.

Then he saw them. They were moving slowly, and he tracked them with his eyes, calculating the distance to the kill zone. He counted down in his head. "Five, Four, Three, Two." He pushed the PTT on his radio. "Initiate! Initiate! Initiate!" The third word was drowned out by the sound of automatic fire as the two machine guns opened up simultaneously. A split second later, the entire assault line joined in. The 7.62mm blanks from the AKs were definitively louder than the 5.56mm blanks from the M4s and M16s, but it all blended together. The smell of burning gunpowder replaced the smell of CLP in Paul's nose.

The trucks immediately stopped. Men poured out the back of the 5-ton, seeking cover to return fire. The driver of the Hummer opened his door and jumped out, He raised his rifle to fire and immediately crumpled to the ground after only firing a single shot. However, the remaining enemy fighters were on the other side of the vehicle firing back.

Sergeant Souby began moving forward. He withdrew the squirt bottle from his pocket. He headed straight to the man who had thrown the pinecone. As he passed the G-Chief's position, the two men exchanged a glance. No one else on the assault line saw him. He knelt beside Cake and Cake looked up with a jolt. Sergeant Souby began spraying Cake's right leg and right arm with a generous serving of the sticky red substance. He looked at Cake and said "You're hit." Cake immediately dropped his rifle and launched into a fit of screaming. He clawed at the two "wounds," doing his best to imitate someone who had just caught two rounds. The blood on his leg was on the outside of the thigh, just above the knee. On his arm, it was centered on his right forearm. Cake rolled onto his back as he screamed. Sergeant Souby casually walked away, moving down the line.

Deacon heard the screaming and glanced to his left. He saw what was going on and returned to his rifle sights. He continued to shoot but yelled "Medic" as loud as he could. The men echoed the call down the line.

Paul stayed focused on the men on the road. Everyone was shooting at them. One by one they fell. One man took off running south down the road, trying to get away from the volume of fire. The left side security began firing with all three. The man suddenly stopped, dropped to his knees and then softly fell to the ground, indicating that he was "dead." He was an older gentleman. Not as old as Deacon and Rock, but too old to throw himself onto the ground in some theatrical version of a death scene. He was the last OPFOR to fall. There was no more enemy fire.

Suddenly someone else started screaming. "Viper's hit! Viper's hit!" It was Freak's voice, and the words were laced with panic. Viper wasn't yelling, but he was gasping for air. He had a large bloody stain spreading just below his right collarbone and a matching one at the top of his right shoulder blade. Sergeant Souby stepped back and observed the chaos. He slid the bottle of fake blood back into his pocket but didn't say a thing.

"Cease fire! Cease fire! Cease fire!" The command echoed down the line. Cake's screams still punctuated what would have been a sudden silence in the woods. Paul was trying to assess the target to see if anyone was still alive. The idea was to watch and listen. If any sign of life was detected, the team would reinitiate fire to remove all threats before they broke from their cover to cross the objective. Cake was moaning loudly. Paul looked at the fallen OPFOR in the road. None were moving. He rose up onto a knee in a fluid motion and yelled, "Assault!"

Nearly everyone on the assault line jumped up and ran toward the road. Juice jumped to his feet but paused. He looked down at his fallen teammate. He quickly pulled the tourniquet that was sticking out of one of Cake's ammunition pouches. As fast as he could, he applied the tourniquet to Cake's leg. Cake howled. Juice turned to follow Paul down to the road. Cake cried out to him. "Juice! Juice! Don't leave me!" Juice dropped back down to his knees by Cake's right side. Cake's acting was as good as any Hollywood production. Better than most.

As the assault force ran forward, Jimmy jumped up from the support by fire position and ran directly toward Cake, his aid bag bouncing as he ran. He had it slung over his left shoulder, holding it in place with his left hand. He had his M4 in his right hand, holding it around the slip ring. Jimmy ran right past Viper, who wasn't moving and wasn't yelling. He appeared unconscious. Freak had run down to the road on the assault. Viper was alone with a simulated chest wound. Sergeant Souby pulled a notepad from his shirt pocket and scribbled down some notes.

Jimmy kept running until he reached Cake and Juice. As he arrived, he dropped down onto his knees by Cake's left side, opposite from Juice, sending a small wave of pine needles into the air. He dropped his rifle beside him on his right side and slung the aid bag around, planting it on the ground beside his left knee. He launched into his casualty assessment. Cake was not making it easy as he writhed on the ground. Jimmy looked him in the face and spoke quickly as he began checking him. "Cake! You're gonna to be alright buddy. I'm going to take care of you." Jimmy saw the tourniquet on Cake's right thigh. It was about four inches above the simulated wound.

Mentally, he started going through his assessment checklist: *I know his airway and breathing are good because he's screaming*, he thought. In the stress of the moment, Jimmy didn't think to put on his surgical gloves. He began speaking out loud to himself as he continued his assessment. "Next is circulation. Check for major trauma." He thrust his hands over Cake's shoulders and under his back. He raked his hands back out and then quickly looked at both his hands, inspecting for blood. His hands were clean. He shoved his hands into Cake's armpits and forced his way under his back a second time. Still clean. He repeated the maneuver again, this time in the small of Cake's back. Still clean. He checked behind the pelvis. Same answer.

Next, he moved to the arms. He saw the blood on Cakes right forearm, but he still started in the armpit and worked his way down to the wound, looking for additional injuries. He found no other indications of injury. He assessed the apparent wound. He spoke out loud to himself as he worked. "No apparent arterial bleed. I'll come back to it."

Cake howled in pain as Jimmy moved the wounded appendage. Jimmy concentrated, trying to block out the incessant screaming. He moved to the left arm and found no injuries.

Cake continued to wail. He appeared to be crying now, actually crying! This guy was simulating being wounded, but he was screaming and writhing and now he was crying? Cake was putting everything he had into this performance.

Jimmy hopped on his knees to reposition himself where he could better reach Cake's legs. He looked down at the tourniquet.

Juice spoke up. "I put the tourniquet on. Is he going to be okay?"

Jimmy didn't respond to Juice. He stayed focused on Cake. He quickly checked the tourniquet to see if it was on correctly. During the classes they had conducted with the guerillas, he and the other medics had taught them to place the tourniquet two to four inches above the wound, but not on a joint and to tighten the tourniquet until the bright red bleeding stopped. At the time Jimmy was going through the Q-Course, the Army was in the process of changing those procedures based on experiences from combat in Afghanistan. However, in 2004, this was still the method being taught.

From the direction of the road, someone yelled "LOA." The rest of the assault force echoed the command. "LOA, LOA." This indicated that the assault force had reached their Limit of Advance on the other side of the road.

Juice looked toward the road. He was supposed to go with them, but it was too late now. He heard Paul's voice. "ACE report!" ACE stood for Ammunition, Casualty & Equipment. An ACE report was a quick report given by each man to tell the PL the status of his ammunition, report any wounds or injuries (casualty) and state if they had lost any equipment.

Juice heard various voices calling out. "Green. Up. Up." Green indicated that they still had sufficient ammunition. The first "Up" meant they were not wounded and the second "Up" meant they still had all their equipment.

After checking to see that the tourniquet was placed correctly, Jimmy moved up to Cake's groin. He elbowed Cake's left leg out the way to see if there were any additional wounds higher on the leg. He pushed his right hand between Cake's legs, high in the groin and his left hand on the outside of Cake's right leg. He pushed his hands together until fingers touched under Cake's leg and slightly curled his fingers to put pressure against the leg as he quickly withdrew his hands. That's when he noticed that his right hand was wet, but it wasn't the fake blood. It was just wet. He stared at his hand for a moment, not understanding why his hand was wet. Then he looked down at Cake's pants. There was a growing dark circle spreading out from his zipper. "Are you fucking kidding me?!" He yelled. "Did you just piss yourself?!" Out of reflex, he sniffed his hand and the unmistakable smell of urine hit him like a slap. He looked up at Cake who was still fully committed to the show.

"I'm sorry! I'm sorry!" he spat through the sobs.

Jimmy was furious. This asshole just pissed on himself! What the hell was wrong with this guy?! Jimmy quickly wiped his hand on Cake's shirt out of spite and went back to work, starting below the wet spot and inspecting the rest of the leg. He gritted his teeth in anger as he completed the initial assessment. He reached over to his aid bag. There were two tourniquets attached to the outside of the bag with heavy rubber bands. He snatched one of them off, snapping the rubber bands. One of them flew off into the pine needles. He quickly slipped the tourniquet up Cake's arm just above the elbow and began tightening it. He was still angry. He could still smell the urine, although he wasn't sure if it was real or in his head. He tightened the tourniquet a little tighter than he needed to in a training environment, eliciting a real pain response from Cake. He raked his finger through the fake blood on Cake's arm and used it to quickly scrawl the letter "T" on Cake's forehead.

Meanwhile, down on the road, the assault force was conducting a search of the enemy bodies and vehicles.

Jimmy called out. "I need the litter!"

The assault force continued to work. Various members of the group had spare weapons slung across their back and two men were pulling cases of MREs out of the back of the cargo truck.

Paul called out again. "Aid and litter!" Trigger and Twain had been designated during the planning to be the primary team to assist the medic with carrying any casualties, so Trigger had a collapsible litter strapped to the top of his small backpack. The lightweight litter was called a SKEDCO and it was minimalist, but it worked.

When he heard Paul yell the command, Jimmy looked up and yelled at the aid and litter team. "I need the litter up here!"

Trigger immediately took off back up the slope toward Jimmy. Twain was hot on his heels. As soon as they got close, Jimmy started screaming commands. "Get that litter out! Now! Hurry up! Hurry up!"

Trigger stopped and fell to his knees. He dropped his AK-47 onto the ground and wiggled out of his backpack. The SKEDCO litter was a rolled up green plastic model and was attached to the pack with two bunji cords, pulled tightly to minimize movement while walking. He began untangling the mess. Twain spoke up in his unique southern drawl. "What do you need me to do, Doc?"

Cake's voice was overwhelming Jimmy. "Please! Please! I don't wanna die!"

Jimmy was frustrated, angry, and getting impatient. "Get me the damn litter!"

Twain immediately began trying to help Trigger. The bunji cords had gotten tangled and had somehow formed a knot, preventing the litter from being released from the pack. Trigger said, "Ah screw it," and yanked hard, attempting to snap the cord. It didn't break.

Twain reached to his belt and pulled out a classic-styled hunting knife. "I got this." With a smooth motion, he dragged the blade across the bunji cord and the litter fell free."

Paul was down on the line trying to get accountability of the team. "We're still down one! Team leaders who are you missing?"

The G-Chief called out to Paul. "Team Sergeant! We need accountability! Who are you missing?" He already knew the answer.

Freak spoke up. "Viper was hit! He's still on the assault line."

To anyone watching, the scene would have appeared simply chaotic. However, in reality, it was somewhat controlled chaos. Paul reacted. "Alternate aid and litter! Go find Viper!"

Chop and Juice were the alternate aid and litter. Chop reacted, running back to the assault line. He called out to Juice. "Juice, let's go!"

Juice looked up from Cake and identified Chop yelling at him. He grabbed his rifle and took off toward Chop as the remaining three men tried to get Cake onto the SKEDCO. That was when Juice slipped on the pine needles and went down. His rifle went flying and he threw his hands out in front of him to protect himself as he hit the ground with an audible thump. His chest and chin impacted the ground, and both his feet went up in the air, his legs bending toward his back. Chop saw the whole thing. He changed his course and angled toward Juice. "Damn Juice! You just did a scorpion! Are you okay?"

Juice was fine, but he was pissed. He bounced back up to his feet and took two big steps, snatching his rifle up from the forest floor. "Yeah, I'm good, I'm good. Come on."

With that statement, they both began to trot over toward Viper. Sergeant Souby was already standing there.

As they arrived at Viper's unmoving body, Sergeant Souby spoke to them in a quiet voice. "He's dead."

Without any more prompting Chop and Juice immediately began screaming. "He's not breathing!" yelled Chop.

"Mediiiiiic!" Juice followed up, screaming as loudly as he could muster. "Help us!"

Jimmy looked up at the sound of the two men calling him. He looked back at Trigger.

"Finish securing him to the litter and move him down to the road for exfil."

He scooped up his aid bag and took off toward where Juice and Chop were emphatically waiving to him. *Shit!* he thought. *I saw that guy earlier.*

Seconds later, he came flying in and repeated the maneuver he had performed earlier, slamming down onto his knees beside Viper. He didn't see the tree root that was hidden just under the heavy blanket of pine needles. His right knee struck the root and he instinctively jerked his knee back from the pain, causing him to lose his balance and fall forward onto Viper's chest. His rifle bounced off Viper's boot and slid on the pine needles for a foot.

"Shit!" he cried out. He reached down for his knee.

"Are you okay?" Juice's eyes were wide open.

Jimmy struggled back up onto his knees, but he kept all his weight on his left knee, with his right knee just barely touching the ground for balance.

"Viper! Viper! Talk to me buddy." He launched into his procedures. He leaned his face down in front of Viper's to check for breathing.

Suddenly Sergeant Souby's voice sounded behind him, startling him. "No breath sounds."

Jimmy put his hand on Viper's neck, checking for a pulse.

"No pulse." Sergeant Souby's voice was calm and even.

Jimmy heard the G-Chief's voice from the road. "Hurry up, Team Sergeant! We've been on this objective too long!"

Jimmy felt the stress in the pit of his stomach. He sat back up and looked down at Viper's unmoving form in front of him. He felt Sergeant Souby's gaze watching him. He turned and looked at Juice and Chop who were looking back at him, eyes wide.

"I'm sorry guys, he's expectant. We have to get him out down to the road for exfil." Exhaustion was apparent in Jimmy's voice.

Juice immediately responded. "What's that mean? Why aren't you working on him?" His voice was shrill, an octave higher than normal.

"He's not going to make it guys. I need you to work with me. We have to move him, and we need to go. Now!" He emphasized the last word.

"I got this," Chop said getting to his feet. "Juice, snap out of it and give me a hand."

The two men worked together to get Viper up onto Chop's shoulder. Chop wasn't wearing a large rucksack, just a small assault pack. The fireman's carry actually worked. He paused for a moment to make sure he had his balance. "Okay, I got him. Just grab his stuff and my gun."

He didn't wait for a response and started slowly moving down the gentle slope toward the road as Juice gathered up the equipment and rifles. He checked his steps carefully to avoid stepping in any holes or slipping on the ever-present pine needles.

Jimmy gathered his own gear and took off down the hill. Juice was right behind carrying three rifles and Viper's pack. By the time he reached the road, he had caught up to Chop. "Chop, let me know if you need a break."

Chop was breathing hard. "No, it'll be more work to switch. Let's just keep going."

Paul and the other members of the assault force had finished checking the bodies, taking all weapons and equipment and searching for anything of intelligence value.

"Fire in the hole one!" Paul called out. He repeated the order into his radio. The right-side security broke down and moved down to the road upon hearing the command. The pickup point was at the left-side security position and Paul could see their truck pulling in about four hundred meters down the straight road. He made a decision. Pressing the button on his mic, he said "Echo Three, Echo Three, this is Zulu, over."

There was a short pause before Billy answered. "Go for Echo Three."

"Echo Three, do you have the exfil platform at your location?"

"Roger that Zulu. He's here."

Paul didn't hesitate. "Echo Three, tell the driver to drive right down the objective road to pick us up. We have casualties."

"Copy that Zulu. Standby." There was a pause of about thirty seconds, then Billy came back on the radio. "Zulu, driver says he can't do that because he won't be able to turn around with the trailer on the road. It's too narrow."

Paul cursed under his breath and looked around. Everyone was still moving toward the waiting vehicle. He looked at the sides of the road. *Crap. He's right. I should have seen that. Stick to the plan.*

Paul spoke into the radio again. "Echo Three, this is Zulu. He's right, go ahead and get the trailer open, but keep security down the road until we get there."

Billy gave a succinct, "Copy all."

By this point there were still nearly three hundred meters to go to the truck. Paul had two enemy rifles slung over his back and a case of rations in one hand, with his rifle in the other hand. He looked around, trying to evaluate the situation to see if he could do anything that would make this more efficient. Then he saw Chop toward the rear of the formation. He was carrying someone over his shoulder. It must be Viper. Chop was moving at a slow walk.

Paul sat the box of rations on the ground and quickly unslung the two enemy rifles and put them on the ground beside the box. Then he took off at a moderate run, directly toward Chop, who was about a hundred meters back. He held the pace as he passed those going in the other direction.

As he passed a group of Pinelanders that were not overly laden he called out to them. "Grab that crap I left up in the road when you get to it."

A couple of voices answered, "I'll get it." Paul couldn't tell who had responded.

Twain and Trigger had gotten Cake down to the road and had unfurled a strap that was attached to the SKEDCO litter. Trigger and Freak were now dragging Cake down the road on his back as fast as they could pull him. Cake had his chin tucked down against his chest to protect his head from the bouncing assault of the uneven road surface. Freak was covered in sweat but showed no sign of slowing down. Twain was beside them, ready to switch out as soon as someone needed a break. He had Cake's pack and rifle in addition to his own.

As soon as Paul got close enough to Chop to speak to him, he called out. "Chop, trade out with me!"

Sweat ran down Chop's face. "I'm good," he replied through gritted teeth.

"That wasn't a request. Give him to me."

Paul saw the right-side security. They were the only ones behind them. They were staying close, but still watching behind them down the road.

Chop stopped and slowly squatted down until Viper's feet touched the dirt road. Paul pushed in between Viper and Chop.

"Give him a boost," Paul said and Chop helped push Viper up onto Paul's shoulders. Viper was now laying across the back of Paul's neck. His left leg and left arm were in front of Paul's chest. Paul passed his left arm in front of Viper's leg, trapping it against his chest and grabbed Viper's wrist. He still held his rifle in his right hand. He shrugged Viper up a little higher, until he was sure he was in a stable position. Then he took off. Running! He ran back down the road. Viper was trying to act like he was dead, but the position was a full assault on his abdomen. Every time Paul's foot struck the ground, it forced the air out of Viper's lungs. He tensed up, trying to absorb the force of the impacts. Paul didn't stop. When he passed the spot where he had left the gear earlier, he saw that it was gone.

Jeremy called out from behind him. "Paul, do you need to switch out?"

"No!" He kept running. His thighs burned and his throat was dry, but he kept up the pace. He didn't slow down until the last ten meters.

Cake was already loaded on the trailer and the Sergeant Major was getting accountability of the Pinelanders. The G-Chief was there as well. He had his M-4 slung across his back and an enemy machine gun in his hands. He was watching Paul.

The driver had backed the trailer into a small jeep trail that was going off into the woods to the east. Paul turned toward the back of the trailer and called out, "Left side, are you up?"

Billy answered immediately. "We're up!" This let Paul know that the left side security had accountability of all men, weapons, and equipment.

"Right-side?"

Jeremy was right behind him. "We're up, Paul."

Paul rounded the end of the trailer and stopped. Trigger and Freak were waiting for him. He turned around so that Viper was toward them and stepped backward until the back of his legs touched the trailer. They wrestled Viper off Paul's shoulders.

"Support by fire!" Paul yelled, feeling the relief as the weight was taken from him.

Larry popped up from the open trailer. "Support is up!"

"Sergeant Major, how we looking?"

The Sergeant Major was not yelling, but he was talking quickly. "You're the last one. All weapons and equipment are accounted for. Cake's stable. I don't know about Viper yet."

Paul knew the answer, but this was not the time. They had to get out of here. "Okay, right side, get in, we gotta go!"

19

Death to America

June, 2022

San Antonio, Texas

The Hezbollah cell was happy that it was cool in the warehouse. It also had running water, cots, food, and boxes of numerous other supplies. Zamir looked down at the bottled water in his hand. It was from an American big box store. He noticed the droplets of water forming on the outside of the bottle. It was cold. He pulled the bottle across his forehead allowing it to linger to enjoy the cooling effect of it.

He thought back to the beginning of this journey as they were preparing to leave Lebanon for this glorious mission. He remembered the speeches given in the private conference room. He remembered the pride he felt in his chest as the commanders stood in front of them, flanked on both sides by the yellow Hezbollah flag. They had spoken of other missions that would support this mission and how this was all part of a larger plan to praise Allah.

Is that what this mission was, a praise for Allah? Zamir pushed the thoughts from his mind. Of course it was. Everything was for the glory of Allah. But he also felt a personal motivation. That was okay, wasn't it? Allah would be happy with him if he did something that he wanted to do on a personal level, as long as it glorified Allah.

Zamir knew that America was evil. He had always known it. He had learned it as a child. As he grew up, he watched as the Americans killed Muslims in Iraq and Afghanistan. He would avenge every Muslim who had ever died at the hands of an American. Allah would approve of his actions.

He took another drink from the water bottle. As he turned the bottle up, he noticed the ceiling. He capped the bottle, but continued to look at the ceiling. The building had once been used for some type of industrial use, he was sure of that. The rafters were steel I-beams. They tied into the wall with huge flat steel plates mounted in concrete block walls. Just below the steel plates, there was a line of windows that looked like a grid running nearly the entire length of the structure. Long florescent light fixtures hung from the rafters every sixteen feet, providing a soft light to the space.

Along the back wall was a line of numerous aluminum tables. What was the word Americans used for these tables? Tic-Tac? No that wasn't it. Pick-pack? No, that wasn't it either. Frustration began creeping its way into his mind as he struggled for the word. Picnic. That's it. Picnic tables. Beyond the tables was a large open doorway with the door propped open. He saw two men moving around with bowls. He could smell food cooking. It was a kitchen.

A voice greeted him from behind him. "Zamir, brother."

He spun around to see the man approaching him. It was Hassan. He greeted him in Arabic with a broad smile highlighting a missing tooth on his left side.

"Hassan. You've done well, finding this place. It's perfect for our needs." He smiled back as he swung his arm around, indicating the structure.

Hassan wore blue jeans and a gray shirt emblazed with the word "Texans" across the chest. Beside the word was the depiction of a bull's head, half blue, half red. The blue side had a star where the eye should have been. He and his men had already been here for some time preparing for the arrival of Zamir's team. Their instructions were to try to blend in. Zamir thought Hassan looked ridiculous in the American clothing. It looked like a costume. However, Hassan was doing exactly what he was supposed to be doing.

"I can't take all the credit. I had help," Hassan responded. "For years, we've been sending families here to America as legal immigrants, entire families. They have a system here to provide refuge for people seeking political asylum. We had the foresight to create "refugees" who were accepted into the American system. Their instructions were quite simple: Go, go to America, learn the language, the culture, the people. Complete all the steps to become an American citizen. Learn to act like an American, follow the rules and laws, but never forget who you are or what your mission is. Some of those we sent here had children after arriving. Those children are now native-born American citizens, but in their heart, they know they are Lebanese. Some are in the universities now. Right here in Texas in a city called Austin, numerous universities in California, Columbia University in New York, Yale, Virginia, and even in a school called George Washington University. I find that one both ironic and amusing."

"I'm aware of the program. So these families were able to help you?" Zamir continued to nurse the water.

"Yes, one is a real estate agent here in San Antonio. He's been here for years. His English is quite good. Once we explained to him what we needed, he went to work. He actually found three different possible locations. I chose this one out of the three options. One was too small and the other was in the heart of the city. It was a good structure, but there was no privacy. This was the third place he showed me and I knew it would work for our purposes as soon as I saw it."

"It's a good structure. There will be plenty of room for everyone else once they arrive. Actually, I need to check in on everyone else. Do you have the cell phones?"

"Yes, yes of course. Please follow me. I have converted one of the offices into a living space for myself, and a second one for you. I have the phones in yours."

Hassan turned and walked across the open space. Zamir retrieved his pack that was sitting on the floor by his feet and followed. The concrete floor wore a tangle of cracks that looked like a road map. There was a light layer of dust covering everything. Their shoes left tracks as the two men moved together toward the other end of the building.

"Here you go," Hassan said as they arrived at a steel door. The door had a glass window in it with a grid of reinforcing wire embedded in the glass. He pulled the heavy steel door open and flipped the light switch just inside the door. The light inside the room was brighter than the rest of the building and Zamir squinted briefly as his eyes adjusted. The room was about twelve feet from the door to the back wall. An old steel desk faced the door. Atop the desk were stacks of small cardboard boxes. Zamir looked to the right and saw that the room was longer than it was deep, maybe eighteen feet. There was a mattress on the floor, plus an additional small table and chair.

A laptop computer sat in the middle of the small table. A cord running down the back was plugged into the wall. Zamir walked over to the table. Hassan motioned to the laptop. "Yes, the laptop you required."

Zamir opened the top and the screen lit up to show a desktop background of a lush green coastline. The ocean was blue with small waves clearly visible toward the sand beach. The picture appeared to have been taken from a porch or balcony, as a railing was visible near the bottom of the screen. A short wooden flagpole was mounted to a railing, displaying the red and white flag of Lebanon. The green tree depicted in the center of the flag had a fold across it, as it flapped in the wind. It made it appear as if the tree had been poorly cut and pasted back together. There was no prompt for a password.

Hassan spoke up again. "You and your men have all kept their cellphones turned off, yes?"

"Yes," Zamir responded. He looked at the numerous white boxes on the desk. "Are these our new phones?"

"Yes, yes. All these phones have been purchased locally and they have no way of tracking who owns them. If you would collect up your old phones, I'll take those off your hands. We may have a use for them later, but we don't want to turn them on here and create an electronic signature that could connect foreign phones to this location."

"I know how it works Hassan." There was a slight hint of annoyance in Zamir's voice when he spoke. This was all part of the plan. He didn't need to be reminded. He was tired and didn't have much patience at the moment.

"Of course," Hassan replied. If he noticed Zamir's tone, he gave no indication of it. "And the weapons? Those are in the bags?"

"They are."

"May I see them?" Hassan asked. He grasped his hands in front of his chest. It reminded Zamir of the swindlers in the bazaars back home when they were trying to ingratiate themselves to you before attempting to sell you a trinket.

"Now?" The hint of annoyance was there again, slightly stronger than before.

Zamir looked at Hassan. He didn't initially answer the question. Hassan still held his hands in front of him. The look on his face reminded Zamir of a child waiting for a piece of candy. Zamir sighed. He didn't want to question the commanders, but he wasn't sure that Hassan was the best choice to lead the support cell. He was intelligent, of that there was no doubt, but Zamir was unsure of his maturity.

"Sure Hassan. Come on," he replied with a sigh.

Zamir dropped his pack onto the mattress and turned toward the door. He pushed against the heavy door and let it go as he passed it. Hassan caught it with his hand, holding it briefly as he exited the room. He let the door slide from his hand and a top mounted hydraulic cylinder hissed and closed it until the doorknob latched with an audible click. The two men walked across the open room again. The florescent lights buzzed overhead. The conversation of the other men drifted out the door of the kitchen. Their steps kicked up tiny specks of dust. They could be seen floating in the air, made visible by the artificial light.

The equipment that the men had carried across the border was lined up by the wall near the door, still sitting where they dropped it. They hadn't carried it far when they unloaded the van, happy to be rid of the weight. Zamir walked directly to the first bag and grasped it by one of the straps. He planted his feet and slid the bag away from the wall. Bending over at the waist, he unzipped the bag, reached in, and withdrew a rifle. It was wrapped in a simple cloth to keep it from rattling against the other two rifles in the bag as it was carried. The cloth was held in place by three short sections of string. Zamir untied the strings, one by one, then threw the cloth open to reveal the prize to Hassan. Hassan rubbed his hands together in anticipation.

Grasping the rifle, Zamir stood upright and handed it to Hassan. Hassan reached both hands out and received it as if it were a fragile piece of art. He turned the gun over in his hands, looking at it from every angle. Silvery gray metal peaked out from beneath the black finish showing scratches and other obvious signs of wear on the lightweight rifle. Along the side of the lower receiver, the words "Property of U.S. Government" were visible above the model designation and serial number.

Hassan looked up from admiring the rifle. "It's lighter than I expected." He was smiling.

Zamir nearly rolled his eyes, but he didn't want to be overtly disrespectful. He needed this man, regardless of his opinion of him. "Yes, they're light. It's poetic that the United States used these weapons to kill Muslims and now we will use the same weapons to kill Americans."

Hassan put the weapon to his shoulder and looked through the sights. He dropped it back down, allowing it to hang loosely in his hand, then suddenly threw it back to his shoulder again as if he were reacting to the sudden appearance of a target. He lowered it a second time.

"I can't believe they just left these behind," he said, his eyes were wide like a child receiving a gift.

Zamir reached for the rifle and Hassan surrendered his hold. Zamir held the gun by the lower receiver with his left hand under it. His thumb rested on the bolt catch. With his right hand, he gave the charging handle a quick, smooth pull, then shoved it forward until it locked back in place. It was a familiar, practiced move. This locked the bolt carrier group to the rear, exposing the empty chamber. "This is nothing compared to the number of weapons, vehicles, ammunition, aircraft, and other equipment the Americans abandoned when they ran from Afghanistan like defeated dogs. There were even pallets of U.S. dollars abandoned like rubbish."

"Nothing but cowards!" cried Hassan. His smile was gone and his eyebrows were pressed slightly toward one another in a mild scowl.

Nearly a year earlier, the United States had executed a hasty withdrawal from Afghanistan. After nearly twenty years in Afghanistan, Americans had grown weary of America's longest war. President Trump had initiated the end of the war and established a timeline for its implementation. However, by the time President Biden took office in January of 2021, the American senior military leadership had failed to implement a timeline for the departure. Biden asked the Taliban to extend the timeline. This was potentially a good thing as it allowed more time for the Pentagon to organize an orderly removal of equipment and personnel. Unfortunately, that is not what happened. After nearly two decades in the country, the amount of equipment was astronomical. As the deadline approached, President Biden once again went to the Taliban and asked for an extension. The Taliban refused and Biden buckled to their demands. He gave the order to evacuate Afghanistan as is, surrendering billions of dollars of military hardware to the enemy. The departing Americans absorbed a parting blow as they pulled back into the Kabul airport. A suicide bomber detonated his bomb near one of the gates killing thirteen Americans and an estimated 170 Afghan civilians.

The U.S. servicemembers remaining had plenty of fight left in them, but they were given no choice by their leadership. They were ordered to retreat, in accordance with the Commander in Chief's orders. They obeyed.

The Taliban wasted no time, swooping in and gathering up the abandoned treasure. Overnight, the Taliban had an air force, weapons, money, and untold amounts of ammunition. Ten of those weapons were now in a warehouse in San Antonio, Texas.

Iran had negotiated with the Taliban for these weapons. This was no simple task. The Taliban is a primarily Suuni Muslim movement. By contrast, Iran and Hezbollah are Shi'ite Muslims. However, there are numerous examples in history when the two sects of Islam cooperated, often to face a common enemy. The fact that Iran sponsors Hamas, a Suuni movement, is an example of this. Iran also has an embassy in Kabul, Afghanistan and the two nations maintain an open line of communication. Iran leveraged their ambassador to obtain the American weapons. He had been necessarily vague, only explaining that the weapons were required for "jihadists." The Taliban representative had finally acquiesced when the Iranian ambassador agreed to pay a generous price for the weapons.

During the planning of the mission to America, there had been numerous debates about bringing any weapons at all. Some argued that the cell should not carry anything with them that could give away their intent. Others argued that they should bring weapons, but it should be AK-47s. However, the idea that won was killing Americans with their own weapons. Zamir had finally gotten onboard with the idea when the conversation turned to ammunition. "I think the American rifle is inferior to the Kalashnikov," he had stated.

Muhammed Bari, one of the men responsible for the planning of the mission had responded. "We don't disagree with you, Commander Zamir. However, in the United States, it will be easier to find magazines and ammunition for these American guns."

That was a good argument. Their contacts in the U.S. had pointed out that it was easy to get those things in America. They would only carry some 9mm ammunition for the pistols with them across the border, but that was for emergencies.

The conversation had gone back and forth for several days. Finally, Zamir had conceded and their training began on the

M4. After weeks of training with it, Zamir had grown to appreciate the accuracy and relative light weight of the firearm, although he would never admit that to anyone. One thing everyone did like was the placement of the safety on the M4 versus the safety on the AK. It took no more than a flick of the thumb to put the M4 on fire. By contrast the AK-47 had a large lever on the right side that had to be pushed down. The round fired by the AK-47 carried more punch, but the M4 was easier and faster to use. It was also easier to add an optic to the M4, if they decided to do that later.

Zamir placed the rifle back into the bag. He didn't bother rewrapping it in the cloth. He just stuffed the cloth in beside the gun and zipped the bag, then turned to face Hassan.

"Hassan, back to the phones. I need my phone set up so I can monitor the progress of our other brothers. Once they send their emails, letting me know they've made it across the border, they'll turn their phones back off and leave them off while travelling here."

"Of course, of course Commander." It was the first time Hassan had used Zamir's title. "My men are preparing a meal for you and your men. After we get you set up with your phone we will eat and celebrate the beginning of our glorious mission."

"That will be fine, Hassan."

Following the meal, Zamir and his men slept. They were all exhausted from the trip and as the adrenaline from the reunion worn off, they all felt the pull of sleep.

Zamir retired to his private space with a full belly. He lay down on the mattress and used the provided blanket to cover up. He stared up at the ceiling. The lights were off in the room, but enough light snuck through the glass on the door that he could vaguely make out the designs on the ceiling. He stared for a moment, tracing the grid pattern with his eyes.

He was finally here. He would finally get to do what he had been born to do. He turned his head and stared at the window on the door. He could still hear men talking outside his room. He closed his eyes and tried to will himself to sleep. With his eyes closed, he could still see the residual shape of the window as a white square in his vision.

He started thinking about tomorrow. How many of his men would arrive tomorrow? Would *any* of them make it tomorrow? Surely, they would. The planners had said it could take several days for everyone to make it to the rendezvous, but surely someone would make it tomorrow. He was anxious to begin.

He needed sleep. He took a deep breath and let the air escape slowly, willing the tension to release in his shoulders. When he was under a lot of stress, his shoulders would get tense and would sometimes stay that way for days. He rolled his head to one side, then the other, stretching the muscles. He adjusted the blanket and after a few minutes, finally, he slept.

Zamir woke to the sound of voices. He had been dreaming. It was a good dream. Almost as soon as he rose from the bed, the memory of the dream escaped him. It *was* a good dream, wasn't it? It felt like it was a good dream, but he couldn't recall the details. Something about an ocean? Or maybe it was a river. It didn't matter. It was time to get up and focus on the mission. There was much to do today. He quickly dressed and headed to the bathroom to relieve the pressure in his bladder.

When he returned, he used his new phone to create a hotspot for the computer. There was no internet set up in the building, but the phone would be fine for this. He entered in his login data for his email account. Seventeen new messages. That's promising. He clicked on the inbox icon and the screen changed to reveal a list of emails. Four of the emails were from the same sender. He clicked on the first one.

Brother,

I've been detained for additional questioning. Don't worry. I know what to say. I will send another message after they release me.

Abu-bakr

Zamir cursed under his breath. Abu-bakr Waheed was twenty-one years old and known for his quick temper. However, he was also intelligent and if he relied on his training, he should be fine. Zamir skipped over the next couple email to check the next one from Abu-bakr.

They have moved me to another area, into a tent. They provided me with food and water, but still have not questioned me.

Abu-bakr

He cursed again. Next message.

Brother Zamir,

I pretended not to speak English, as I was instructed, but they brought in an interpreter, so I had to talk with them. They asked me about my country of origin. They said that there was an irregularity on my identification. They asked me questions about Saudi Arabia. I did the best that I could, but the interpreter told them in English that he didn't believe I was from Saudi Arabia. He spoke in English and didn't think I understood him.

Zamir moved to his backpack and retrieved a thumb drive. He returned to the computer and plugged it in. It was password protected. He entered the password then opened the file with the information on his men. He scrolled down to the section on Abu-bakr. It showed his fake credentials and the background story that he was to memorize. His eyes darted across the screen as he read the information.

Abu-bakr Waheed.

Name to be used: Muhammed Raad

Saudi Arabian

Birthdate: 3 Jan, 2001

Occupation: Carpenter

Following the information was a short background describing why he had fled from Saudi Arabia and was seeking a better life in America.

Zamir absently rubbed at his dark beard, thinking. He returned to the computer and selected the last message from Abu-bakr.

Brother Zamir,

The Americans released me. They asked me where I was going, and I told them California, as instructed. They gave me a date to go to a court for a judge to hear my case. The date is in four years! I am on my way brother. Peace be with you.

Zamir released a sigh of relief. So far, all their intelligence on the border had been more or less accurate. It was essentially an open door. It was an open door that he and his cell were happy to use. They were issuing court dates and releasing them into America. Four years! That was unbelievable. He knew that most immigrants probably wouldn't even show up for the hearings; his men certainly wouldn't. But the fact that they were giving dates that were years away highlighted the vast numbers that must have passed over these borders in recent years. He leaned back in his chair and smiled to himself. He knew that many of those who had passed over the porous boundary were his allies and America would learn that soon enough as well. He leaned forward, returning his attention to the computer and opened the next email.

Over the next few days, the remainder of the Zamir's men filtered into the warehouse. Every one of them had stories about their adventures travelling from the border checkpoint and they wanted to share them with their comrades. After crossing, most of them had linked up with others and traveled in small groups. They had enough money to eat and secure transportation. Every one of them laughed at how easy it had been. Everyone had been nervous, including Zamir, although he would never admit it. However, with the exception of Abubakr, it had essentially been without incident.

Zamir had taken that time to study the maps. The paper maps here were incredibly accurate and useful. Of course, he also had detailed satellite imagery of essentially every inch of every possible target with Google Earth. The initial targets had been identified during the planning phase, but he would send teams to do a detailed reconnaissance of each site prior to the mission. Even with maps, imagery, and all the information available on the internet, nothing was better than physically going to look at a target. They had complete freedom of movement here. There was no military presence, and the police presence was minimal. His teams would be able to walk right up to the targets in broad daylight and take pictures and pace off distances. It almost seemed too easy.

The one piece of the puzzle that he didn't have was the timeline. His instructions were clear: Prepare, rehearse, practice, train, and wait. He didn't know when he would be able to execute the mission. His commander, Ebrahim Assaf, had been quite clear about it when he explained.

"Commander Zamir. You will need discipline, patience, and trust. The discipline to continue training and be ready. The patience to wait until you are given the order to proceed. Most importantly, you need to trust us when we say that this is all part of a larger plan with many moving parts. You are but one of those parts. However, I can openly share with you that it is a very important part. In fact, I would say that if you fail, the entire mission could fail. I offer you my trust as well."

"Thank you, Commander." Zamir sat in a straight-backed chair beneath a slowly turning ceiling fan at a small facility, several miles from Beirut.

"I will tell you the truth, Commander Zamir. I am jealous of you."

Zamir failed to hide his surprise at the statement. "Oh, um, why could *you* be jealous of *me*?"

Ebrahim smiled a kind smile. His expression looked like he was a parent answering a child's simple question. "Commander Zamir, if I were younger, I would be leading this mission myself. However, Allah has other plans for me. I will stay here. I will provide you guidance and support. I will still be a part of the mission, but your part will be glorious."

Now, sitting in his room in a San Antonio warehouse Zamir felt proud of himself. He *would* lead the glorious mission. He vowed to stay focused on the tasks ahead. The training would not end. He would live up to his Commander's expectations. No, he would exceed his expectations. For the glory of Allah, he would be patient. When the time came, Zamir Syed would bring death to America.

20

Robin Sage VIII, ENDEX

Fall, 2003

Undisclosed Training Location, Rural North Carolina

The U.S. Army John F. Kennedy Special Warfare Center and School conducts several Robin Sage exercises every year. Paul's class was to be the last class of 2003. They were at the end of the exercise, and everyone was exhausted. Not just the ODA, but everyone involved in the exercise, from the training cadre to the Pinelanders to the back side support that kept things running behind the scenes.

The end of the exercise is known as ENDEX and it was a tremendous accomplishment for the men who were now standing around the campfire in the middle of the camp. All eyes were facing the G-Chief. However, he was no longer in that role. He introduced himself with his real name and gave his true background as a retired Green Beret. Of course, Paul and his team already knew that.

The fire crackled and occasionally sent sparks into the cool air. All the students were on one side of the fire and the "Pinelanders" were across from them. "Listen up guys," the G-Chief said. "We still have a lot of work to do today, but let's take a moment to catch our breath. I want you to think back to the beginning when you first arrived here in the camp. It seems like a long time ago now, doesn't it?" There was a chorus of agreement.

Jeremy spoke up with, "Hell yeah, it does." This elicited a few chuckles from the group.

"In the beginning, how difficult was it to build rapport with the Freedom Fighters? It was tough, wasn't it?"

A few nodded in response to the question.

"You were foreigners here. That's a real thing. Don't think that everywhere you go, people are going to be happy to see you just because you have the stars and stripes on your shoulder. If you want to be able to work with others, you have to earn their trust, their respect, and build a personal relationship with them. For some of you--I'm looking at you, Troy--it just comes natural."

The group gave out a collective laugh as Troy smiled. Billy lightly punched Troy on the arm.

"For others, you have to work at it. That's up to you. At first, every time you spoke to one of my Pinelanders, you sounded like robots who were forcing the words. But eventually, it got easier, didn't it?"

Paul thought back to the beginning of the exercise. *He's right,* he thought to himself.

"Learn your partner force. Identify their strengths and weaknesses and use those strengths to your advantage while compensating for the weaknesses."

He paused to look across the group.

"Sympathy can go a long way. How upset were the Pinelanders when Viper got killed?"

He paused again to allow for a response. There was a muttering as everyone acknowledged the point.

"We were very upset. That was our brother. Your commander came to me and told me that he was sorry for my loss and offered his support for whatever I needed. Sympathy can be real, or it can be faked. Maybe you don't give a crap that a local fighter just took one to the chest, but never let your partner force know that. If they think you don't care about them, then they aren't going to give one rat's ass about you. However, I want to clarify something about your relationship with your partner forces. Never, ever trust them completely. You should be able to make them think you trust them, but trust your team, not foreigners.

"Let me tell you something. Men join Special Forces thinking it's all going to badass shit, kicking in doors, and shooting people in the face. Sure, that's part of it, and when you get to do that, it'll be great, and you'll tell lies about it for the rest of your life."

The group chuckled.

"But I'll give you some truth right now. A larger part of your job is going to be managing humans."

He looked over at Jeremiah Wilkerson. "Captain Wilkerson, what's my definition of leadership?"

Captain Wilkerson didn't hesitate. He had heard this numerous times over the last two weeks.

"Sir, your definition of leadership is getting other people to want to do what you need them to do."

"That's right. Getting other people to *want* to do what you need them to do. Notice that I didn't just say getting them to do it. You need to make them *want* to do it." He stressed the word *want*. "You need to influence them, mold them, manipulate them. You may need to be a used car salesman to get someone

279

else on board with a plan, and that's a supporting effort for shooting bad guys in the face.

"I have a question for you. Can you lie to the host nation?" He looked over at the ODA, but no one immediately spoke. "That wasn't rhetorical. Can you lie to the host nation force?"

Paul spoke up. "Yes sir."

"Hell yeah, you can lie. But don't get caught. If you need to lie to accomplish the mission, so be it. There's nothing that says you can't. But if you get caught, you're going to destroy all rapport that you've built, so pick your lies like you pick your battles."

He moved on to his next point. "Captains!"

He looked over at the captains who were standing together. "Command!" he said forcefully. "You were already captains when you got here. Now you want to be Detachment Commanders. If so, then you need to Command. You are responsible for everything that team does or fails to do, and the burden of leadership is real. Every one of you was a platoon leader at one time, correct?"

The captains responded almost in unison. "Yes sir."

"So, you've felt the burden of leadership before. At least you should have, if you were doing it right. But this is different. You'll be commanding a Special Forces Operational Detachment Alpha, one of the deadliest tools in this country's arsenal. And you'll probably be doing so with little to no supervision, and very likely in a combat zone."

The captains looked solemn.

"However, understand this: you have a tool at your disposal that has never existed in the history of warfare. Do you know what it is?" The G-Chief stared intently at the captains. They looked at each other, not sure what to say. The silence was only broken by the crackling of the camp fire.

"I'll tell you what it is. You have the smartest, most educated group of non-commissioned officers in the history of the world. NCOs, raise your hand if you have education higher than a high school diploma."

Half of the non-commissioned officers raised their hands.

"Look at that! Half of the enlisted men have been to college. Go ahead and put your hands down guys." They obliged. "And I'll tell you something else, the other half are still smarter than most of their peers. They're smart, tough and they have drive. If they didn't, they wouldn't be standing here today. Use them. Let them do their jobs. *Enable* them to do their jobs and then get the hell outta the way. If you try to do everything yourself, there is a one hundred percent chance that you'll fail. Your NCOs have knowledge, experience, and ideas, just like you do. If you don't take advantage of that, you're setting yourself and your team up for failure."

He shifted his gaze to the group of enlisted men. "Now, NCOs, I just called you smart, so don't screw this up!"

The entire group laughed out loud. Even the Pinelanders laughed along with them.

"Continue to seek self-improvement. Educate yourselves. Are the officers better versed in Unconventional Warfare than you are?" He didn't wait for a response. "Of course they are! They got introduced to it in their MOS training and then got it again here in Sage. Who cares? Everyone here should be able to give an elevator pitch explaining Unconventional Warfare and how the insurgency support networks work. If you can't, then you need to dive back into the books and close that gap in your knowledge. Think about this, this exercise was in English! The next time you do this, it will most likely be in a two-way live fire zone and it sure as hell won't be in English. It's going to be through an interpreter or," he paused for emphasis, "through your target language."

A few of the men shifted on their feet as they considered this. Every Special Forces soldier is trained in a foreign language that is consistent with the part of the world where their group has responsibility. For example, 1st Special Forces Group is responsible for Asia, so they study languages spoken in Asia. 7th Special Forces Group is responsible for Central and South America, so they study Spanish, and sometimes Portuguese. However, when the United States is at war, those areas of responsibility go out the window and all the Groups are eligible to go to the combat zone. So even if a Green Beret knows his target language, he could still go into a combat zone in another area and need an interpreter.

Everyone was listening intently.

"NCOs, another thing. If you're just doing your job, then you're only doing half your job. What do I mean by that? If you're a Delta and all you're doing is 'Delta-ing', you're messing up." He slowed as he pronounced the made-up word. "The second half of your job is keeping the commander informed on all medic related issues. The same thing for all the rest of you. Sergeant First Class Lawson, I have a question for you."

Larry perked up at the mention of his name.

"Arc thc officers as good at being an 18 Bravo as you are?"

Larry looked over at the collection of officers who were looking back at him. He smiled.

"No way, sir."

Everyone laughed. Captain Tribiani spoke up too. "Definitely not."

The laughter increased slightly at the comment.

The G-Chief gave it a couple seconds, allowing the noise to die back down. "No, they aren't. So, you need to make sure that your command team is informed on 18 Bravo stuff. Look, your Detachment Commanders are *always* going to try to make the best decision they can, based on the information that they have. It's your responsibility, NCOs, to make sure they have the most information possible so they can make an informed decision. Does that make sense?"

There were nods all around.

"Okay, a show of hands, who here has heard the term 'Look for work'?"

Everyone in the group raised a hand.

"Of course you have. We hear it all the time. I'm here to tell you that it's a real thing. Not just in Robin Sage, but in the regiment. How many of you, at one time or another in this course, have felt yourselves getting overwhelmed?"

Once again, every single man raised a hand.

"If one of your teammates is working and you're sitting around with nothing to do, you're wrong. Get off your ass and go help. It doesn't matter if they are a different MOS, you don't have to know their job to assist them. I'll give you an example: 18 Deltas and 18 Deltas only, Echos don't say a word. 18 Deltas, what does FM stand for?"

The medics looked at each other.

Finally, Jimmy spoke up. "Um, Field Manual?"

The group broke out into the loudest laughter yet. Billy laughed so hard, that he dropped his hands onto his knees as he shook his head laughing.

The G-Chief laughed along this time. "Well, you're not wrong," he said. "But in relation to radios, it stands for something else."

The laughter fired up again.

"I'll tell you what is stands for: it's fuckin' magic, because nobody really understands how those damn radios work."

Jeremy feigned insult. "Come on, sir. It's Frequency Modulation. We know how it works."

"No, you don't," said the G-Chief springing the trap of the joke. "You just have a theory, an antenna theory."

The laughter was raucous at this point. They all got the joke. When the 18 Echos were in the MOS phase of the training, they studied 'Antenna Theory' as part of that training.

"Okay guys, okay." The G-Chief extended his hands toward the group with his palms facing down toward the ground. He moved his hands in an up and down motion, signaling everyone to calm down. "Listen, it's good to laugh. After what you just went through, you've certainly earned it. But I want to get serious again before we wrap this up.

"I'm also going to let y'all in on a little secret. In Special Forces, you're going to get shoehorned into one of two groups. You're either going to be labelled as a good dude, or a shitbag, and there ain't a whole lot of gray area in between. Whether you realize it or not, you've already started to develop your reputation. That reputation will follow you from the Q-Course to your ODA and beyond. And if you stay tied into the Regiment like we have," he paused to motion to the other retired Green Berets who were there in support of the exercise, "that reputation will follow you for the rest of your life. Now understand this. If you've started down the road to the wrong camp, it's not too late to untangle yourself and get going down the right path."

He had everyone's attention. Paul was listening intently.

"You need to wrap your head around the fact that Special Forces is a small community, and an ODA is even smaller. Your reputation is going to mean a lot. You need to learn to trust those on your left and right and you should strive to earn their trust in return. You should be able to trust your teammates with your life or your money or your wife."

That last comment elicited a few smiles from around the circle.

"The bottom-line is don't be a dick. Be a good teammate. Look out for each other and make the others on your team glad that you're their teammate."

Paul felt a tinge of recognition in that last statement. Where had he heard that before? He looked over at Larry who was looking back at him. That's it! Larry had told Paul to be the type of teammate you would want to have on your team. Paul gave Larry a quick nod and Larry acknowledged it with his own. They both returned their attention to the G-Chief.

"I understand that everyone's Robin Sage experience is different, and that's a good thing, but one thing remained constant throughout the exercise." Once again, he motioned to the group of men behind him that ran the exercise and made the training possible. "We, all of us, were rooting for you. We want you to be successful. We've already fought our wars, and guess what? Fuckin' Tag! You're it!"

Not a person in the group moved. They all knew that once they finished with the training, they could be on the next thing smoking to Afghanistan. This was a serious moment, and the air even seemed to stop moving, if only for a moment.

"The United States is a warring nation. If you count up the years of peace in this nation and the years that we were in a war or some other type of armed conflict, which one do you think wins?"

Once again, the question was rhetorical, and he didn't wait for a response.

"War! By a long shot. The rest of the world can be divided into two groups: those who want to be like America and those that want to kill us, and I can guarantee that the group that wants to kill us is a helluva lot larger."

Around the group, various men absently nodded in agreement. They all understood the point of that statement.

"I know y'all are smart. Hell, you know it too. Take advantage of that. Seek out training. Compete for schools. Don't get lazy. Never overlook the opportunity to become more educated on the profession of killing. Regardless of the type of mission you're charged with, at the end of the day it's your job to kill the enemies of this country."

For the final time, he motioned to the gathered group of retired Green Berets.

"We view you, rightly so, as the protectors of our children and our grandchildren, and we wish you success." He paused as he let that sink in. It was the strongest of compliments and he wanted to give it an extra moment for emphasis.

"On that note, gentlemen, I'm going to stop. I wish you all the best."

Several of the men started clapping and after a second, the rest of the team joined in. The team that had been playing the part of the Pinelanders joined in the applause that only lasted a few seconds.

The group began to disperse, and the majority of the ODA worked their way toward their now former G-Chief. One after another, they thanked him and several took the time to point out a specific time in the exercise when his actions or counsel had been helpful to them personally. The former Freedom Fighters drifted over and began talking and laughing with the team as well.

Paul waited patiently. He didn't go talk to the other group yet, he waited as the men in front of him filed by to shake the hand of the man who had run the camp for the last two weeks. The captains took the most time, but eventually they too broke away. Paul walked up to the older man. As he approached, the G-Chief smiled at him.

"Specialist Michaels."

"Sir," Paul replied.

"I had my eye on you. You did a helluva job out here. It was a pleasure to work with you." He extended his hand toward Paul.

Paul accepted the offer, and the two men exchanged a handshake. They released the handshake and Paul grasped his hands in front of him, his left hand hooked around the outside of his right wrist.

Paul smiled back. "Thank you, sir. I learned a lot. I just wanted to tell you myself that I appreciate everything."

The retired Green Beret regarded the younger man. "You know, you remind me a lot of myself when I was your age."

Paul smiled at the compliment.

"I'll tell you something that's not a popular opinion. The army says that leaders aren't born, they're made. Well, I disagree. I think that leaders *can* be made. However, I also believe that some people are just born with natural leadership qualities. Others gravitate toward them and listen to them. I've watched you with your team. You're one of those people. Generally speaking, that's a good thing, but you need to understand this: sooner or later, your decisions are going to have life or death consequences. If you're going to be in this line of work, you need to know that making the best decision doesn't always mean that everybody's coming out of it on the other side."

21

Attack on Israel

October 7, 2023

Eastern Michigan

Zamir and his men crowded around the two televisions in the large living room. One was a flat screen TV mounted on the wall above the fireplace and everyone was jockeying for a position where they could best see. Not everyone could squeeze into the living room and some were standing in chairs in the dining room for a better view. The news anchors were dutifully conveying the information as fast as they could get it. The screens changed to show an image of a Hamas militant in a paraglider and the room burst into a roaring approval. Men slapped each other on the back, several applauded.

Zamir's seat was in front of one of the televisions. As the commander, he had the best seat in the house. Mohamed Tahir, his second in command sat beside him on his left side. They both wore camouflage pants obtained from an Army-Navy surplus store. They were of the old-style woodland camouflage used by the U.S. military in the twentieth century. They both also wore tan-colored suede military-style boots and black t-shirts. Zamir was not cheering, but rather studying the television, listening to every word and attempting to analyze every image. He was sitting in a stackable chair, the kind often found in community centers or churches. He sat back in the chair. His left arm was crossed in front of his chest, with his left hand trapped in place by his right elbow. His right hand was at his mouth, fingers loose. His right pointer finger was slightly curled and resting against his lips. If anyone had been paying attention, it would have been obvious that he was deep in thought about what he was observing on the screen.

The crowd was unruly, however, celebrating with each detail of the attack on Israel. Everyone was caught up in the excitement of the moment.

On the screen, a solemn man in a blue Kevlar helmet held a microphone in front of his mouth. He wore a matching blue Kevlar vest with the word 'PRESS' across the front in bold white letters.

"Initial reports are indicating that perhaps upward of one thousand people have been killed. Numerous others are missing and reports have come in indicating that at least some of these missing people have been taken hostage by the terrorists." This elicited another response from the crowd.

Zamir didn't move. He stared at the screen, as still as a statue.

The reporter's jaw was covered with a dark shadow of stubble. A coiled wire ran up the side of his neck to an earpiece tucked into his right ear. People could be seen running behind him in the frame.

"The eye witness accounts are, quite frankly, hard to imagine. Survivors are telling stories of murder, kidnapping, and rape. Peter, let me reiterate that these stories are, as of yet, unconfirmed, but my sources are saying that the terrorists killed children in front of their parents, and Peter, they, they…"

The reporter hesitated and looked at someone off to his left, not visible to the viewer. He nodded in acknowledgement to the unseen coworker.

"I'm sorry, Peter, reports say that they raped wives and daughters in front of their families." The man's voice wavered as he said the word daughters.

The man was trying, mostly successfully, to maintain his professionalism and report the story. Zamir wondered about this man. He caught the deviation in his speech at the mention of the daughters. Perhaps this man had a daughter. Perhaps she was here in the U.S. His accent certainly sounded American. Perhaps his daughter would die at the hands of Zamir and his men. For the first time since he began watching the newscast, he smiled, ever so slightly.

The reason Zamir was not happier was simple. He was jealous. As he watched the images unfold on his screen, he was jealous that Hamas was undertaking a glorious mission against Israel. He had now been in the United States for well over a year. He had maintained his focus on preparing for his mission, but he hadn't been allowed to *do* anything beyond training. He had heard of grumblings among his men. He knew they were getting impatient as well. However, he had handled it and managed to keep tight control of the group. When he had become aware, a few months earlier, he had discussed the situation with his second in command, Mohamed Tahir.

"Mohamed," Zamir began, "I understand the men are disappointed that we haven't received the order to attack yet."

"Yes, Commander. But they are loyal and dedicated. There's nothing to be concerned about. The reconnaissance missions and training do a lot to help them stay occupied and focused on the upcoming tasks. However," he paused, "we *have* been here for a year and we don't have any indication of when we'll be able to execute our mission. Perhaps you could speak to them to ease their concerns."

"I speak to them every day, Mohamed."

"I know you do, but maybe you could speak to them about patience and share some of the information you have received from Commander Assaf. You've told everyone that you check in often, but you never share information about those conversations." Mohamed was choosing his words carefully, trying not to appear demanding or disrespectful to his commander.

It almost worked. Zamir didn't *need* to tell them any more information. In fact, he was intentionally limiting their knowledge of the higher workings of the mission. He wasn't quite angry, but he was definitely annoyed. He felt the tension building in his neck and shoulders as he pictured the men whispering behind his back.

"Gather the men up after training is completed today. I will talk with them. Have them gather at the barn." He looked down at his watch and appeared to be doing mental calculations. "Tell them 6:00. I will speak to them before dinner."

Zamir attempted to mask the anger in his voice, but Mohamed heard it, so he simply responded with "Yes, Commander," and politely excused himself from the conversation. As he left the room, he closed the door gently and then quickly walked away. He would go out and check on the training and make sure everyone knew that they would be assembling for the commander later.

Mohamed walked over to one of the vehicles, a Toyota Tacoma that was a few years old. He liked this truck. He had been driving it a lot lately, so he had the key in his pocket; one of the perks to being the second in command. The Toyota was painted tan with numerous small dents and scratches, but it was reliable. It was similar to the Toyota Hi-Lux pickup trucks that Hezbollah had in Lebanon. This truck was a little bigger and had an automatic transmission; it was nicer and more comfortable to drive. The Hi-Lux trucks they had back home had manual transmissions with a peppy little four-cylinder diesel engine.

He stopped with his hand on the door handle and looked into the bed of the truck. Some of the Hi-Luxes were equipped with gun mounts in the bed for machine guns. He wished they had those machine guns here. *A PKM would look great right there.* He pictured the PKM Machine Gun. It fired a 7.62x54R linked ammunition and he loved it. A good PKM gunner could do some major damage. He returned his attention to the truck and got in. He started the truck and drove away, pushing the machine gun out of his thoughts.

Most of the men were at the range today. They were very fortunate to get access to this rural area with a field that was suitable for constructing a range. One of the contacts they'd been given before coming to the United States was a Lebanese-born doctor. He worked a couple of hours south from this location in the city of Dearborn, Michigan. He had purchased this farm several years back and when they contacted him, he had simply said that "The training base is ready."

The older two-story farmhouse there was used as a headquarters and housing for Zamir, Mohamed, Haig, and Ahmad. The unit was divided into four groups: The Command Cell and three additional cells, differentiated by colors: green, blue and yellow. Mohamed was the second in command, but he was also the Green Cell leader. Haig El Knoury was the blue cell leader and Ahmad Abufaysal was the yellow cell leader. There were four bedrooms in the house, so Zamir had decided that the cell leaders would stay in the house with him.

The property also had some outbuildings and a large, modern barn. The barn had been converted to billeting for the men. The fields had formerly been used for agriculture. Now, one of those fields had been converted into a rifle range.

Mohamed pulled up behind three men. One man was lying on the ground with a rifle. Another man was sitting beside him looking through a large scope mounted on a tripod. The third man stood behind the two, observing. He placed the truck in park, reached into the glove compartment, and extracted a set of earmuff-style hearing protection. He slipped them over his head and centered them on his ears. Just as he opened his door, a shot cracked. A second later, the man sitting beside the shooter, looking through the scope called out in Arabic. "Hit, but low and right. Come up about fifteen centimeters and left about ten centimeters."

Mohamed looked out in the field. He could see the target. It was a large black and white bullseye style target mounted on a wooden stand. The target appeared to be about 150 meters away.

The shooter echoed the command and he cycled the bolt on the bolt action rifle. "Up fifteen, left ten." He pushed the bolt down, locking it in place and about two seconds later, the rifle barked again and jumped against the man's shoulder.

The man on the scope called out a second time. "Hit! Almost in the center!"

Mohamed spoke to the man who was standing behind the other two. "Hello Ahmad."

"Hello Mohamed. I didn't expect to see you out here today. I thought green cell was shooting tomorrow."

"New target!" announced the man behind the scope. "Look to the right of that one and a little further in the field."

"I see it," announced the shooter.

"Two hundred meters."

The shooter echoed the distance. "Two hundred meters," and cycled the bolt.

Mohamed responded. "Yes, Ahmad, you're correct, my cell will be shooting tomorrow. How is Yellow Cell doing?"

Ahmad had his arms crossed across his chest, but motioned to the man behind the gun with his chin.

"Nour had been doing very well with his marksmanship."

He motioned toward four more men lounging off to the side under the shade of a tree, its leaves were a deep green and the tightly woven branches provided ample shade for the group.

"Faheem over there is the only other designated shooter I have right now. He's doing okay too, but he's not as consistent as Nour."

Mohamed crossed his arms, absently mirroring Ahmad's stance. "I see. How's the rifle?"

The rifle cracked and the spotter communicated a correction.

"It's good. It's accurate, but I wish all the rifles matched. The guns all function similarly, although the safeties are not in the same places on the different brands. Also, I wish we had been able to get them in all the same caliber. Using multiple types of ammunition creates unnecessary complications with our logistics."

Ahmad turned to face him as he spoke, speaking loudly so that he could be heard with the hearing protection that they both wore. Ahmad had little yellow foam earplugs visible in his ears.

"I understand and I agree with you, but you know how we got these rifles, so I'm just glad we've been able to find some that meet our needs."

Ahmad nodded. "Yes, yes, of course."

Everyone who was going to be using one of the captured military M4s was already trained and they continued to train occasionally with the rifles to prevent the skills from fading.

The terror cell training in Michigan had acquired several other rifles over the preceding few months. They had primarily been obtained by their contacts who had immigrated to the United States and had obtained their U.S. Citizenship, thus allowing them to buy guns. They hadn't bought any new guns, but rather had opted for buying used guns that already had scopes mounted. One of the shortcomings of their training in Lebanon had been the lack of precision rifles. It was built into the plan that they would find the guns once they got to the U.S. and train on them then.

A couple of the rifles, like the one currently being shot by Nour Hallal, were stolen. They didn't steal anything here in Michigan, as they didn't want to garner any attention to the area. However, on the long trip from Texas to Michigan, they had taken the time to break into numerous houses along the way, specifically looking for guns, ammunition, or any other items they could use. It amazed Mohamed how many U.S. houses were empty during the day. Here, it was not only common for the men to work outside the home, but the women too. The group would watch a house to see if everyone left in the morning and then break in, searching it as quickly as they could. Several times, they had found large safes in homes. When they encountered these, they would destroy other items in the room as a punishment to the homeowner for locking the guns up. Mohamed had learned that these safes were literally called gun safes and it was a testament to the wealth of these Americans. It disgusted him.

The gun that Nour was shooting right now was found in a home in eastern Tennessee. They had raided a house just outside of a subdivision, near a city called Johnson City. They had found two rifles and two shotguns displayed in a wooden gun cabinet in a room that also had a pool table, a miniature refrigerator, and a dartboard on the wall, among other things. The cabinet had two small doors at the base. When they opened the doors, they found several boxes of ammunition, so they took all of that as well. Mohamed remembered the home. The occupants were obviously very wealthy. He had used his knife to cut the green fabric of the pool table just for good measure.

He had also grabbed the small refrigerator and carried it out. When he picked it up, the door had come open and numerous bottles of beer had spilled out into the floor. He snatched the plug out of the wall and as he headed for the door. He had kicked one of the bottles across the room, expecting it to break. It hadn't. It hit the wall, leaving evidence of the impact imprinted in the drywall, but had fallen undamaged to the floor.

After they were back on the road, they inspected their haul. One of the rifles was a Winchester Model 70 Featherweight. They were sure of that because it was printed on the right side of the barrel. It was chambered in an American cartridge called 30-06. That was printed on the left side of the barrel. The rifle had a nice wooden stock and a nylon sling. Mohamed had since learned that the Americans pronounced the name of the cartridge: "Thirty aught six." He didn't understand that, but that's what they called it.

Three of the boxes of ammunition were green and yellow boxes with '30-06 Springfield 180 GR. CORE-LOKT SP' printed on the flaps of the boxes. The rifled already had a scope mounted on it and although Mohamed was not familiar with the American scopes, this one had proven to be excellent. On the side of the scope was a logo of a set of crosshairs and the capital letter "L" in the middle of the crosshairs. It held its zero and appeared to be well made. *Probably expensive*, Mohamed had thought at the time.

The other rifle was smaller. It was chambered in a small cartridge called .22 long rifle. Although Mohamed didn't expect the little rifle to be of much use for their combat mission, Zamir had pointed out that it would be useful for training. They had also stolen nearly two hundred rounds of ammunition for it, and the ammo had proven to be easy to find and inexpensive. It had a simple scope and wooden stock. On the side of the receiver, it said: "10/22" followed by "22 LR." Under that was the manufacturer's name and city: "Ruger, Newport, NH, USA." Mohamed had gotten to shoot the gun several times and he enjoyed it. He saw the value in it, using it for marksmanship training as Zamir had suggested.

Finally, there had been two nearly identical shotguns. They were both Remington 870 shotguns with laminated stocks. However, one was chambered in 12 gauge, and the other was in 20 gauge. They had found miscellaneous shotguns shells in the cabinet in both chamberings. Someone had suggested that the larger one, the 12 gauge, was probably for the husband, while the smaller 20 gauge could be for the wife. Mohamed recalled thinking how odd it was for women to be shooting.

Zamir and Mohamed had discussed the haul as they were driving later. "Zamir, that was a nice find. That was a lot of guns in one house. We should consider looking in more houses here."

Zamir didn't look over at Mohamed. He continued to look forward, through the windshield.

"No, Mohamed. We'll keep moving. We'll continue to look, but in other towns. Multiple homes in one town will bring a different kind of interest from the police. Always remember that we must keep our presence a secret until Allah wishes us to reveal ourselves. And when that time comes, all of America will know we are here." He paused as if thinking about what he wanted to say next . "And then they will cry for mercy."

Mohamed was thinking about that conversation when the report of the rifle brought him back to the present. He looked over at Ahmad. "Ahmad, the reason I came out here today was to deliver a message. Zamir would like for us to assemble after training today. He said to be at the barn at 6:00."

Ahmad's brow wrinkled. "Why? What's wrong?"

"Nothing is wrong brother. I would tell you if it were. I believe he wants to talk about the mission."

Ahmad was skeptical, but would do as he was told. "Okay. I'll have my cell there. Thank you."

"Of course, of course. Now, please excuse me, I need to go speak with blue cell."

Mohamed left the makeshift rifle range and informed everyone else of the plan, then headed back to the farmhouse to let Zamir know that everything was set up. He also stopped by the kitchen to speak to the two cooks, letting them know about the meeting.

At 6:00 everyone was assembled. Everyone, except Zamir. The men spoke in small groups, mostly talking about their day. One of the men in Yellow Cell praised Nour for his marksmanship. He smiled and held the Winchester up in the air by one hand, the muzzle pointed toward the sky. A couple of men slapped him on the back in admiration. Mohamed observed the group without interacting. He hoped that this went well. He saw one of the men looking toward him. But he wasn't looking at him. He was looking *past* him.

He casually turned to see Zamir approaching. His steps were deliberate. He wore his camouflage pants and tan boots that he favored. However, what stood out was that he was wearing his red headband usually reserved for public displays. The Arabic writing across the front was in a bold yellow. The headband was tied over a yellow keffiyeh.

Everyone stopped talking as he approached. Nour slung the rifle over his shoulder and turned slightly to face the approaching Zamir.

Zamir walked past Mohamed and right up to the group. Mohamed quickly moved past him and joined the rest of the crowd. Zamir looked to the man on the far left of the group and then slowly panned across the group, making eye contact with everyone there, one at a time. The action took nearly a minute and the group was completely silent.

Mohamed realized that his heart was thumping in his chest. How was this going to go? Was Zamir about to chastise the group? Punish the group?

Zamir began to speak. "Brothers! Today I speak to you not only as your Commander, but as the representative of my Commander, Ebrahim Assaf. I spoke with him today and told him of your great progress, preparing for the holy mission that Allah has granted us. I spoke with great pride as I told him of your unwavering loyalty to our cause. Commander Assaf was very pleased with your dedication and assured me that our time is coming."

Mohamed looked away from Zamir and looked into the faces of the assembled men. He could see the expressions of pride on their faces.

Zamir continued. "He said that he was giving us time to ensure we were fully prepared and trained for the mission. I told him that we were grateful to have been chosen for this mission. I vowed to him that we would continue to stay focused, as we have this first year, and when the time comes for us to bring death to America, we will be ready to strike!" He delivered the last word with emphasis, and one side of his mouth crept upward in a slight smile.

The group erupted in a chorus of, "Allahu Akbar! Allahu Akbar! Allahu Akbar!"

Zamir waded into the group and slapped men on top of the shoulders. He joined them in the chant. "Allahu Akbar! Allahu Akbar!"

Mohamed joined in as well, but he was no longer observing the group. He was staring intently at Zamir, watching his every move. He watched the expression on his face and how he interacted with the men.

Later that night, after dinner, he joined Zamir at the kitchen table in the farmhouse. Zamir had papers and maps spread out on the table and he was looking at the screen of his laptop. There was no one else in the house at the time.

"Zamir, the gathering today was exactly what the men needed."

He pulled a chair out and sat diagonally across from Zamir so the laptop screen would not be between them.

Zamir looked up from his work but didn't speak.

"It made the men feel important that you spoke on their behalf to Commander Assaf. I thought you might chastise them for their lack of discipline, but instead, you reinvigorated them."

Zamir sat back in the chair and crossed his arms over his chest. He took a deep breath and slowly let it out before speaking in an even, controlled tone.

"I haven't spoken to Commander Assaf in over two weeks."

Mohamed had a visible reaction of shock to the words. "What? But I thought..."

Zamir cut him off. "Mohamed, do you think I'm an idiot?"

Mohamed recoiled from the question. "No Commander. Of course not, it's just that..."

Once again, Zamir didn't let him finish. "If I had spoken to Commander Assaf and gave any indication of the men's impatience, I would look like a weak leader. I'm not a weak leader. Instead, I evaluated the situation and came up with a solution. The men need to be reminded of their faith. They need to be reminded that it is a great honor to have been chosen for this mission. Praise from Commander Assaf was exactly what they needed, so that's what I gave them."

Mohamed regarded the man in front of him. Zamir was about a year younger than Mohamed, yet he was in command. In that moment, Mohamed understood why.

Four months after that conversation, the two men sat side by side, watching the events unfold halfway around the world as Hamas attacked one of their common enemies. Zamir knew things that Mohamed didn't. Mohamed was okay with that, but he had to ask himself. Did Zamir know that Hamas was going to attack? No, surely not. He seemed just as surprised as everyone else when they found out.

However, their common sponsor, Iran surely knew about it. Hamas was getting a constant flow of money from Iran, just like Hezbollah. *Maybe that's who's painting the big picture that Commander Assaf talks about.* Mohamed wasn't sure. However, he didn't need to ask Zamir if this was the start of something bigger. He was already sure of it. Neither man realized just how big that something was.

22

Mutiny Metals

October 7, 2023

Kentucky

Paul Michaels sat in a black Chevy Suburban, watching an empty parking lot and listening to a satellite radio news channel. All day, the only thing on the news had been the attacks in Israel. Since he had retired from the army after twenty-three years of service, Paul had been doing military contracting and security work. His military career had taken him all over the world. He had seen plenty of combat on multiple tours in Afghanistan. He had worked in the jungles of Central and South America. He had gotten some of the best training at the best military schools in the world. As it turned out, all that had made a pretty good-looking resume. Now he worked for several different companies doing a variety of jobs. Most of the jobs had been in support of the U.S. military. However, there were gaps between those contracts. This work in Kentucky was steady, reasonably low risk, and he liked the other guys who worked for the company. Tri Point Solutions was a security and executive protection agency operating primarily in Kentucky, with services all over the east coast. A couple of years ago, Paul had done a military contract, supporting the Marine Corps Special Operations Command (MARSOC) and had met McCoy McMaster, the co-owner of Tri Point, which had eventually led to this job.

303

When the two had met, they hit it off pretty quickly and it didn't take Paul long to make a comment on McCoy's unusual name. "So, Mack, your parents couldn't squeeze one more 'Mc' into your name? They could have given you the middle name of McDonald, just to top of off."

"Close," Mack said without hesitation. "It's McDugal."

"Seriously?" Paul exclaimed.

"No, not seriously."

Paul just stared at him for a second as he processed the joke. They both busted out laughing. "Pretty funny, bro."

"I get it all the time man. Everyone makes a comment on it. I've heard them all: 'McCoy? Is that your first name or your last?' When I was a kid, the other kids would call me Mc-Mc-McCoy." He said it mimicking the sound of a chicken. "You're not going to come up with anything that I haven't heard before."

Paul just smiled. "Okay, I've got it out of my system. So do you do anything else besides contracting?"

"Actually, I rarely do contracts. My day job is security. I own a security company. Well, I'm *one* of the owners. We primarily do corporate security and executive protection stuff."

"Executive protection?" Paul asked. "Like bodyguards?"

"Well, yes, but there's more to it than just standing next to someone and protecting them. We take site security into consideration, route security, cyber security, we do threat vulnerability assessments on their homes, sometimes their workplace, their vehicles, all kinds of stuff. There's a lot more to it than people realize, but if we're doing our job right, no one even knows we're doing it."

Mack reached into his shirt pocket and pulled out a small tin. It was about five inches square and about a half inch thick. The word ACID was visible on the front of the tin as Mack opened it up and reached it toward Paul.

"Cigar?"

Paul looked down at the little cigars. "Um, sure. Thank you." He withdrew one of the little stogies from the tin.

Mack produced a cigar cutter from his pocket and smoothly snipped his cigar, offering the cutter to Paul.

Paul accepted it. "You just keep a cigar cutter in your pocket all the time?" He cut the tip off his own cigar and returned the cutter to Mack.

Mack smiled as he slipped the cutter back into his pocket. "There's no need to carry cigars if you're not going to carry a cutter. I'm not going to rip the end off with my teeth like a savage."

Paul laughed again. He liked this guy. He had some swagger, but it just came across as confidence.

"So why are you doing this contract if you have a security company?"

"Honestly man, this is a break for me. It's hectic at work and I make time for one or two contracts a year to get out of the office and remember my roots." Mack lit the cigar.

Paul motioned to the tattoo of the Eagle, Globe, and Anchor on Mack's arm. It was the emblem for the U.S. Marine Corps. "I see you were in the Marines, so this probably feels right at home for you."

"Well, I wasn't in MARSOC, but I *was* in the Marine Corps, so yeah, I'm comfortable around these guys. How about you. I don't see any tattoos giving away your history."

"Army, retired," Paul said, lighting his own cigar.

"Ok, that was vague. What did you do in the Army?"

Paul pulled on the cigar, and held the smoke for a couple seconds, then he tilted his head back and slowly let the smoke escape. "I was Special Forces. Hey, this cigar's pretty good."

"Yeah, they're good." Mack replied quickly almost dismissing the compliment. "So, what did you do in Special Forces?"

"Sorry bro. I'm not allowed to talk about that stuff," Paul replied evenly.

"Oh. Yeah man, uh sorry."

Paul held it for about three more seconds before breaking out laughing again. "I'm just messing with you Mack. What do you want to know?"

"Damn man, you had me going for a second. Okay, okay, fair is fair. So, what group were you with."

"Seventh Group. I started off as a Special Forces Engineer Sergeant, construction and demolition. Then I became a Special Forces Intelligence Sergeant. I ended up crossing over and becoming a Warrant Officer." Paul took another pull on the cigar.

"An officer! I knew it. You talk like an officer." Mack had a slight grin on his face as he said it.

"To be fair, I was an NCO first. I always put in the effort to remember where I came from. Like you said, you gotta remember your roots."

"I hear ya. What did you do before Special Forces?"

"I came from the infantry. I was a paratrooper in the 82nd Airborne at Fort Bragg," Paul responded.

The two stood under a stand of trees near a creek in the training area. Their conversation was punctuated by the chirping of birds, the croaking of frogs, and the gentle gurgling of a creek flowing over rocks nearby.

Paul motioned to some folding camp chairs arranged in a circle around the remnants of last night's campfire.

"You want to sit down? We don't have to be anywhere for a little over an hour. I have some water in the cooler."

"Yeah, sounds good. Bourbon would be better, but water will have to do."

The two settled into the chairs near the creek and smoked their cigars as they talked about various subjects. They really did have a lot in common. They were both former military and enjoyed guns, they had read some of the same books, and as it turned out, they were both preppers, or as Mack called it; preparedness enthusiasts.

Paul explained. "I've introduced my parents to prepping, but they live on a farm, so many of the things they do in their everyday life are already considered prepping, even though they just think of it as another Tuesday."

"Yeah, I went through the same thing. My dad's on board and my mom just rolls her eyes, but doesn't try to stop us." Mack puffed the cigar.

Paul continued. "I wrote up a document for my folks as a cheat sheet to get going, plus I make recommendations for them. But they're not into it like I am. I've been at it in one form or another for probably twenty years now."

Mack responded. "Wow, I haven't been at it that long, but I feel like I'm doing pretty well."

As the conversation progressed, they compared notes and ideas and Paul promised to send Mack a copy of the document he had produced.

Paul asked, "What do you feel like the most likely SHTF scenario is?"

Mack looked out toward the creek as he answered. "I'm preparing for an EMP."

"Okay, I hear ya," Paul replied.

Mack looked over at him. "I take it you don't agree?"

"Well," Paul said, "I'm not saying it isn't possible. I'm just looking at the direction the country is going, especially the economy and I'm feeling more like economic instability leading to social unrest." He paused as he took a drink of water. "However, to be fair, if you're ready for an EMP attack, you're ready for about anything."

"Yeah, that was my thought. No one can be prepared for everything." He paused as he reconsidered that statement. "Unless you're a billionaire, like all the ones building super bunkers right now. So, you gotta choose what you want to focus on and try to keep your preparations as broad as possible." Mack paused and then his face lit up as if he had just thought of something. "Hey, if you're thinking economic collapse, are you into precious metals?"

"I am," Paul replied. "Although most of my metal is silver. Well, to be fair, most of my precious metals are actually lead, brass and copper." He smiled as he looked over at Mack. "Ammo never depreciates."

Mack chuckled lightly. "Truth."

"Seriously though, I usually buy silver. I've bought gold too, but I prefer the silver. When I first retired, I did a few contracting jobs overseas and I was bringing in some pretty good bank, so I took advantage of it while it lasted and plussed up my supply of metals, among other things. I got into it years ago, mostly going to pawn shops, flea markets, and gun shows looking for junk silver. That eventually evolved into bullion. I like one ounce silver, although I have silver in all kinds of different sizes; one tenth ounce, half ounce, and larger ones like two-, five- and ten-ounce pieces. The gold is cool, and if nothing bad ever happens, it's a great investment for later in life. However, if things go sideways and I need to use my metal for barter, a two-thousand-dollar gold coin would be difficult to use."

Mack stood up and reached into his pocket, coming out with a one-ounce silver South African Krugerrand. He held it up in front of his face, smiling. He didn't say anything.

Paul focused on the coin. "Damn man, you have a cigar cutter *and* silver bullion in your pocket?"

"I love silver, man. I like the way if feels. I like the way it looks. I just like it." He held it out toward Paul.

Paul leaned over so he could grab the coin without getting out of his seat. He looked closely at the coin. "Ah, the Krugerrand. I like these. I have a few myself."

Mack reached out and accepted the coin as Paul offered it back. "Yeah, the same amount of silver as an American Silver Eagle, but cheaper."

"Yeah," Paul added. "I have some Canadian Maple Leaf bullion, the Swiss Philharmonic, and a bunch of silver rounds from different mints."

"Funny you say that," Mack said. "Hold that thought for a sec." He got up and went back to where they had been standing earlier and retrieved his backpack. He opened the pack and unzipped an inner pocket, coming out with another piece of silver. He passed it to Paul.

Paul laughed again. "You just have silver stashed everywhere!"

"You have no idea," Mack replied.

Paul examined the small silver rectangle. On the front was the Tri Point Solutions triangular logo. He flipped it over. On the back, stamped into the silver was:

> MUTINY METALS
> 2 OZT .999 FS

"You had these made? Dude. That's legit!" Paul was impressed by the piece.

"Yeah man. Mutiny Metals is a cool company out in Idaho. I sent them our logo and they make them for us. I get them made in one-ounce, two-ounce and five-ounce pieces. It's all poured silver, so it looks rustic...and I love it."

"Okay," Paul began. "I'm going to go out on a limb here and say that you're probably more into silver than I am. I didn't even know this was a thing. All my silver is in coins, common rounds, and bars."

"I'm glad you differentiated between coins and rounds," Mack said. "It drives me crazy when people call every round piece of silver a coin. I guess you know that to be considered a coin, the silver must be produced by a government and be legal tender in the country of origin."

"Yeah," Paul replied. "But to be fair, I only learned that a few years ago. A lot of the private mints intentionally produce rounds that look almost just like a coin. That probably throws some people off. But from what I've seen, rounds are typically a little cheaper than coins even though they have the same amount of silver in them."

"You're speaking my language, man," Mack said with a grin.

They eventually made it onto the subject of firearms. "What kind of pistol do you like?" Mack asked.

"That's not a simple question for me. I love my 1911s..."

Mack interrupted him. "Of course you do old man." He continued, trying his best to sound like an old man. "Freakin' .45 ACP, you can sink battleships with that round!"

Paul laughed. "Well, I don't know if you could sink a battleship, but there is a documented incident in WWII of a guy shooting down a Japanese Zero with a 1911."

"What?" Mack said skeptically. "Shut up!"

"No, seriously. It was in Burma. There was an American pilot that had to bail out over Burma and was floating down under his parachute when a Japanese Zero flew by him. He had his 1911 in his hand and shot the Japanese pilot in the head as he flew by," Paul said in a matter-of-fact tone.

"Okay," said Mack. "I'm going to have to look that one up."

"Be my guest. I wish I could remember the guy's name. I used to know it, but I can't remember it now. I just remember the story, because that's pretty badass."

"Yeah, I'll give you that one. That *is* pretty badass. But why did you say that the pistol you like is not a simple question? It sounds like you like the 1911."

"Well, I carried a 1911 for years. Back when I was shooting competitively, I used a 1911 for that too. I just loved it, I still do. But a few years back, I saw a video of some protestors tearing down some statue that they found offensive." He rolled his eyes as he said it.

"About two blocks away, a lone guy was standing on the street corner waiving an American flag. Suddenly, one of the protestors saw him and said something to the crowd. The next thing you know, there are like fifty of these masked nutcases running down the street toward this guy with ball bats and pipes and all kinds of makeshift weapons. At first, he didn't react, he just kept waiving his flag. Then once they got closer, he suddenly panicked. He dropped the flag and pulled out a pistol. He got off one or two shots before the crowd swarmed him and had him on the ground kicking him and hitting him with crap.

I thought about it for a while. When I carried a 1911, I carried an eight-round magazine and a spare mag. That's sixteen rounds. Seventeen if I top off the magazine after loading. I don't expect to be facing a crowd of fifty people, but neither did that guy. Now, in theory, if he would have pulled his gun faster and smoked the first couple of people, the rest of the crowd would likely have stopped. Likely. Then I thought, well what if I needed more ammo?"

He paused to swipe a mosquito away that was buzzing in his ear. "So, yes, I prefer the .45 ACP, but I also acknowledge that 9mm is a more than capable round. About fifteen years ago, I picked up a Gen 3 Glock 19, but I never really cared for it."

Mack interrupted again. "How the hell do you not like Glocks? That's the most common handgun around."

"I know, I know," said Paul. "I shot the crap out of it. I even tried using it a couple of times in competition shooting. I know it's a good gun, and I *wanted* to like it more. Unfortunately, there's just something about it that's not a great fit for me. I don't really have bad things to say about it. It's reliable. Hell, the magazines are probably the most reliable pistol mag out there and the aftermarket for the Glock is unparalleled. Not to mention, in an SHTF scenario, you could probably find mags for it everywhere because it's so common. It's just not the gun that I prefer."

"Okay, so what 9mm *do* you prefer?" Mack asked.

"I like the CZ P10C. It's essentially the same size as the Glock 19, but for me it's a better fit."

"Oh, God. You're a CZ guy! I hate to say it, but I may have just lost some respect for you," Mack said with a grin.

"Yeah, yeah. I know," Paul said, smiling now too. "CZ versus Glock, .45 versus 9mm, Ford versus Chevy."

"Chevy. All day long," Mack cut in, still smiling.

"Anyhow," Paul continued, "I know I like the grip angle better. It's not quite a 1911 grip angle, but it's comfortable. I have a couple of them. I have one with iron sights that was my daily carry for a couple of years. Then I wanted to try a pistol optic, so I got an optics-ready one and mounted a Trijicon SRO red dot on it. That's my EDC now. It has a few other upgrades as well, and I'm really happy with it. It has a 17-round magazine. Plus, I have a single and a double mag carrier that I keep 21-round mags in. For normal day to day stuff, I usually just carry one spare mag. If I know I'm going somewhere where things might get spicy, I use the double mag carrier. They're 21-round mags are for the P10F, the full size, so they stick out a little, but I figure if I've gotten into a situation that requires me to reload, I won't give a crap about that, I'll just want ammo. It's essentially like slapping a Glock 17 magazine into a Glock 19. It's bigger, but it still works. So, with that setup, I went from sixteen rounds of .45 to fifty-nine rounds of 9mm. Sixty if I top off the mag. I like those numbers."

"I think I'll stick to my Glock," Mack said after the explanation.

Paul smiled. "Of course. That's what you're comfortable with, so that's what you should do. I have people ask me all the time what the best concealed carry gun is."

Mack jumped in. "Let me guess, you tell them the CZ and how it's *way* better than the Glock."

Paul rolled his eyes. "No, I always tell them the same thing. You have to figure that out for yourself. What's good for one person may not be a good fit for the next person."

"Okay, what about for your rifle?" Mack asked, shifting gears.

"Actually, I build my own," Paul replied.

"You build your own?" Mack leaned forward as he spoke. "Okay, now you have my attention."

Paul looked down at his watch. They needed to meet the rest of the group soon for the next part of the training. "We'll have to get into that one next time brother, we're running out of time."

Mack looked down at his watch as well. "Yeah, you're right. But one quick question: AR or AK?"

"Seriously, dude? We definitely need to talk about this later."

The two rose and started across the grass. After a few steps, Mack spoke up. "Dude. I can't believe you don't own a Glock."

Paul smiled as he answered. "I said I don't carry it. I didn't say I got rid of it."

That conversation was two years ago. Paul and Mack had become good friends following that trip and now, on the seventh of October, 2023 as Paul listened to the radio, he was working for Tri Point Solutions, or as everyone called it, TPS.

The radio broadcast infuriated him. He listened to the details as they came out. The number of dead, wounded and missing was unclear at this point, but there was enough information to know that this was bad. Very bad. Paul had never been to Isreal, but he had done three combat tours in Afghanistan and numerous other deployments around the world. As he listened to the reports roll in, he thought back to his second tour in Afghanistan...

His ODA was conducting a dismounted patrol and stopped at a small cluster of structures on the patrol route. They knew the dwellings were there because they had seen them on the satellite imagery when planning the route, but they had never stopped to talk to the inhabitants. As they approached the largest of the structures, the women scattered and disappeared into the buildings, out of sight. An older man walked out to the front of the central one and waited for them as they approached. He had a white beard and wore the typical loose-fitting clothing worn by essentially every male in the country. He also wore a neatly wrapped light gray turban and was leaning slightly on a long walking stick. His face was solemn as the group approached. The captain moved toward the front of the group with one of the two interpreters.

Using the interpreter, the captain exchanged greetings with the older man. The man was cordial, but didn't smile. After the initial exchange, the man asked the captain if he would like some chai. In the Afghan culture, it was the normal thing to do--offer your guests some chai, a mild green tea. Most of the team spread out and assumed defensive positions around the "village" as the captain, Paul, and the interpreter sat down with the man. There was no table, no chairs. There was a blanket on the hardpacked ground and the man sat down with his legs crossed and motioned for the Americans to join him on the ground. They did.

In typical American fashion, the captain got right to business. He immediately began to explain to the man that the team was there to assess the security in the area and asked if the man had seen any Taliban recently. The man looked at the interpreter, but didn't immediately respond. He sighed softly and looked back toward the doorway of his home.

A young boy came out with a little teapot. A smaller boy followed him with four small glass teacups and spread them around on the ground, with one in front of each person in the group. Once the teacups were distributed, the older boy immediately began pouring chai into each one. When he finished, he stepped back and attempted to stay. He wanted to listen to the conversation. The elder wasn't having it and sent the boy scurrying with a quick burst of harsh sounding words. The boy sat the teapot down and quickly retreated inside.

"As I was saying," the captain continued. "Have you seen any Taliban in the area?"

The old man waited for the interpreter to finish his translation and then pointed a single bony finger at the captain as he responded. "You are not the first American to ask me these questions. I've seen other American soldiers before you. They came to my home without an invitation, just as you have. They asked me about the Taliban. I gave them honest answers. They gave my grandson a ball to play with and then left. After they were gone, the Taliban punished me for talking with Americans. They hit my grandson and took the ball. They shot the ball with their rifles as my grandson cried." He paused to allow the interpreter to catch up, then continued.

"I did not ask you to come here, but I will speak to you with respect. I will offer you chai, even though I have very little. Then you will leave and the Taliban will punish me again. I will not give you any more information about the Taliban. This is not because I am loyal to them. It is because I fear them. I do not fear you."

The captain looked back at Paul, somewhat in disbelief of the candor. Most Afghans did not speak so directly. Most village elders talked in circles, avoiding questions and diverting blame to anyone but themselves. This man spoke clearly and to the point.

Paul spoke up to the captain. "Cap, I think we should let this man be and move on. I think he's being straight with us. Let's not make this any worse on him."

The captain just nodded and looked back toward the old man. "Can we give you anything for you time? Bottled water for the children perhaps?"

The old man looked toward the interpreter as he began to translate the captain's question. Anger flashed on the man's face. "I've been very truthful with you and you haven't heard my words. If you give water to the children, the Taliban with beat the children for accepting it. This is why you will not win this war. You don't understand your enemy."

In three tours in Afghanistan, Paul never heard another Afghan speak so bluntly. The man was defeated. He told it straight because he was resigned to the fact that he would be beaten for something that was not his fault. He might as well just tell them the truth and get them to leave as quickly as possible. The man just wanted to be left alone, but he was caught in the middle and had no way out. He understood the savagery of the Taliban. Paul understood it too.

Now he thought of the Taliban as he listened to the atrocities being inflicted by Hamas on the people of Israel. He knew they were different, but he also knew that in some ways they were the same...exactly the same.

Paul's phone rang, pulling him back to the present. Damn, he needed to turn that ringer down a little bit. He looked at the screen. It was Mack. He hit the green icon to accept the call.

"What's up Mack?"

"Not too much man, I'm just calling to check in with you. How's it lookin' out there?"

"All quiet on the western front." Paul grabbed a clipboard from the passenger seat and looked down at the paper. It was the activity log for his shift. "I've been doing the standard patrols. NSTR."

NSTR was an acronym for "Nothing Serious to Report." Paul hadn't had any trouble this shift.

"Good deal man. You been listening to the radio?"

"Oh yeah. That's some ugly business going on over there right now." He tossed the clipboard back into the passenger seat.

The line was quiet for a moment as Mack thought about Paul's words... "over there." After a few seconds, he spoke. "I'll bet you're already working on an analysis of this situation, aren't you?"

Paul smiled. "You know me so well." Paul paused as he thought about how to respond to Mack.

"Here's the thing, Mack. This attack was a surprise, but it's not actually *surprising*. Hamas has been pretty straight forward about their desire to wipe Isreal off the face of the earth. Now they're just doing what they've always said they want to do. The U.S. just freed up a few billion dollars for Iran and Iran is sponsoring them, so they're feeling pretty confident."

"Yeah man. After your shift, let's talk. I'd like to hear your take on how this might affect us."

"I have a couple things I've been considering. I'll put some more thought into it and bounce them off you later," Paul said, scanning the fence again of the facility they were protecting.

"Sounds good buddy. If you need anything, give me a holler."

"You know it. Later," Paul said.

"Later man," Mack replied and both men hung up.

23

Contingencies

Easter, 2024

Charles and Edna's Farm, Lawrence County, Kentucky

Paul and Scott Michaels sat at the kitchen table of their parent's home. The brothers had made the trip to spend Easter together as a family. Both of them had arrived on Saturday, Paul had his wife and daughter in tow. The entire family had gone to the Easter Sunrise service at the church that morning. It was a rare treat for Charles and Edna to have both their boys, their daughter-in-law, and their granddaughter in church with them at the same time, since both of their sons lived in different states now.

Paul's daughter, McKinley was now sixteen years old. Sandy had gotten pregnant with her right before one of Paul's deployments to Afghanistan. Sandy and McKinley were now kicked back in the living room watching reruns of a sitcom. It had been a chore to get a sixteen-year-old girl to church at 6:00 a.m. and now she acted like she was totally exhausted from the effort.

Charles walked into the kitchen and sat down with his sons, letting out a groan as he lowered himself into the chair, followed by an audible sigh as he settled into his seat.

"Boys, I'll tell ya. This getting old ain't for the weak," he said with a smile.

"No sir," Paul replied. "But it's better than the alternative."

Scott chuckled, but didn't say anything.

"No truer words, son. No truer words. What're you two boys talking about?"

"Scott was telling me about some of the crazy stuff he sees at work," Paul offered.

Scott had taken a job working as a Paramedic in South Carolina. Paul was always interested in the stories Scott came up with.

"Oh yeah?" Charles asked. "What's the latest?"

Paul and Charles both looked at Scott expectantly.

"Okay, let's see. What happened last week? Well, Monday I went on a call into the city to pull a needle out of a druggy's arm and hit him with Narcan. Then Tuesday, let's see." He took a drink of his tea and looked up at the ceiling as if he was trying to recall. "Then Tuesday, same thing, except the guy tried to fight me for ruining his high. Then on Wednesday, oh yeah. Same thing. It's the same thing every day, Dad." His voice was dripping in disgust. "I became a paramedic because I liked the idea of helping people. But I thought I'd be, you know, helping at car wrecks and helping an old lady who fell down her stairs, that kind of thing. Don't get me wrong, sometimes I get to do that, but most of my days are just reacting to overdoses."

"That's terrible, son."

"Dad, the drug epidemic in this country is out of control, and I can't see any possible solution for it. The stuff is flowing into the country across an open border and it's everywhere. Everywhere!" He sighed and sat back in his chair, falling silent.

Paul leaned forward. "I saw a reporter on the news the other day and he was down in southern California. There was a line of illegal immigrants as far as you could see in the picture. He was walking down the line and asking people where they were from. Most of them answered him. The answers were all over the place, but some common ones were China, Syria, Turkey, Russia, and Iran with a few more mixed in from Central America. The bottom line is that most of the answers were from countries that consider us their enemy. He must have talked to at least thirty people in the clip and only one was a woman. All of them were young men."

The two other men were listening intently as Paul continued. "I'll tell you what I'm thinking. First of all, there is a one hundred percent chance that drugs are flowing freely across that border, supporting what you said, Scott. However, in addition to that, I'm also sure that there are enemies of this country crossing right along with the drugs."

Charles spoke up. "I guess I don't understand why the left is so opposed to protecting our borders, son. I mean they fought Trump tooth and nail as he tried to build the wall, and eventually, they stopped him altogether, right? Why would they even do that? It doesn't make sense."

Before Paul could answer, Scott jumped in. "Oh, come on Dad. Don't you watch the news?" Scott was always very direct with his father.

Charles faked insult. "Why Scott, why hadn't I thought of that?" he responded with smiling sarcasm. "You mean that new-fangled machine with the picture tube?"

Scott didn't take the bait. "No, seriously Dad. They passed a law to count the illegals in the census. Most of the illegals flock to the urban areas, which are primarily Democratic strongholds. If you count them, it increases the number of seats in the House of Representatives for the left."

Charles was no longer smiling. "Seriously? That's not right. They aren't Americans, so why would they be represented in Congress?"

Paul jumped in. "Now you're seeing it, Dad. They're using the illegal immigrants for political gain regardless of the damage it does to America. What Scott said is just one way they're using the illegals. Some states even allow them to vote in certain elections because they expect them to vote Democrat. The left feigns outrage about foreign election interference while simultaneously facilitating foreigners voting. That's the epitome of foreign election interference."

Edna caught everyone off guard when she jumped in. She had been moving around the kitchen doing her thing, but listening to the conversation. "You boys always end up talking about politics every time you get in the same room. I have a question for you. Why would they do that, knowing that it was not the best thing for the country?"

Paul answered before anyone else had a chance. "Mama, have you ever heard the phrase: An evil man will burn his own nation to the ground to rule over the ashes?"

She just stared at him for a moment. "Well...no."

"It's a perfect description of what's going on right now. There are politicians who support policies that they absolutely know are bad for the country, but will keep them in power. Personally, I consider that to be evil."

She paused as she wiped her hands on a dish towel. All three men were looking at her. "That may be so Honey, but what can we do about it?"

"That's the right question to ask. What *can* we do about it? There are two things." Paul scooted his chair out a little and turned to face his mother. "First, we vote for the best candidates."

Scott interrupted with a scoff. "Dude, that doesn't matter. There is no way the powers that be are not rigging the elections."

Paul looked over at his brother. "Okay. There's actually a lot of evidence supporting that. However, let's assume that they can't fix *every* election. We should still vote for what we want."

Edna spoke up. "We're already doing that. What's the second thing we can do?"

"We take measures to protect ourselves and our loved ones," Paul replied. "We prepare ourselves for whatever we think we might face. That's why I've been preaching about this for years. We need to get things set up now, while we can."

Edna slung the towel over her shoulder. "Ah, there it is! You found a way to slip prepping into the conversation." She suppressed a smile.

"Mama, that's because I'm practicing what I'm preaching. I've spent years building my preparations, but I said that we should take care of ourselves *and* the people we love. I do what I can. I just want y'all to do the same." Paul sat back, yielding the conversation to whoever wanted to take it up.

Initially, no one spoke. After a short, awkward silence, Edna walked over to the table and pulled out the fourth chair, sitting down. She snatched the towel off her shoulder and tossed it into the middle of the table.

"Okay son. I'll get more on board with this plan. You've been pitching your ideas to us for years and We've adopted some of your suggestions. I haven't really objected to any of the ideas.

However, to be fair, I wasn't actively trying to do them either, except for the food. I'll say it right now in front of all of you boys. I think you're right. I think something is coming, I just don't know what. Let's work this out as a family. What's next?"

Paul didn't miss a beat. "Approaching this from the perspective of a family effort, the immediate problem we face is geography. Y'all are here in Kentucky. Scott's in South Carolina and I'm in West Virginia. Obviously, I'm a lot closer to you than Scott, but it could still be problematic. So, we need to come up with a plan of mutual support if things go sideways. I've put a lot of effort into building a homestead that's stocked with everything I could think of. We have contingencies in place for the things that I consider critical. However, obviously, I don't have the kind of food production that y'all have here. Assuming we still have freedom of movement, I could use the things I have to help you and your farm could support all of us with sustainable food." He paused and looked over at Scott. "And *you* need an exit strategy."

"An *exit strategy*? What's that supposed to mean?" Scott asked incredulously.

Paul continued. "Let's just say that you needed to make it back here, like immediately. What would you do?"

"I'd jump in my Jeep and hit the road."

"Yes, you would," Paul said. "Unless you couldn't. What if the roads are closed? What if an EMP knocks out vehicles? What if there's an interruption to the fuel supply? Do you keep enough fuel on hand at your place to take off and get here without a gas station? How about if GPS goes down and you can't use your normal route? Do you have paper maps? Could you walk it? Is your Bug Out Bag packed to support that? That's what I'm talking about: contingencies. And everyone has to know what the contingencies are in case comms go down."

"Comms?" Edna asked.

"Sorry Mama. Communications. What if the phones don't work? Everyone needs to know the plan and what the others in the family are going to do."

"Okay, Paul. If you have to get from your place to here, what's *your* plan?" Scott raised one eyebrow as he asked the question.

"My primary plan is not to bug out. My primary plan is to bug in. As I said, I intend to use our homestead as our castle. However, if we had to leave, I have a plan. Like you said, the first one is to load up the truck with the trailer and the SUV and drive here. I'll drive the truck. Sandy drives the SUV. But..."

Scott cut in. "Oh, yeah? What if the roads are closed? What if an EMP knocks out your vehicles? What if...what if...those other things you said happen?" Scott had a playful, sarcastic tone in his voice. Nobody can mess with someone better than their brother.

Paul chuckled. "Exactly. What if? I have plans for various scenarios. No one can foresee every possible one, so I picked a few plans that will fit most scenarios. For example, closed roads or an EMP both eliminate the vehicles, so I have a plan for that. If it's just a fuel problem, but the roads are open and the vehicles are working, I have that covered with the fuel I keep on hand. I rotate it to keep it from getting too old. I don't need GPS to get here, but I promise you that there are side roads between here and my place that I don't know. For that, I keep a U.S. atlas and maps for every state on the east coast in both vehicles. The state maps have better detail for the small backroads. I also have planned locations between there and here to resupply. In addition to that..."

Scott interrupted again. "What do you mean locations to resupply?"

"My old army buddy, Dangle, lives in Wayne County, not too far from the Kentucky line. I have stuff stashed there. And, he has stuff stashed at my house."

"Oh, yeah, Ol' Dangle," Charles said, dragging out the name. "That guy's hilarious. How's he doin', by the way?"

Paul looked over at his father. "Oh, you know how he is. Loving the single life. He's been doing some contracting with me, so we've spent quite a bit of time together lately. He's doing great. I just built him another gun."

"Stop getting off the subject," Scott said. "You said locations, plural. Where are your other resupply points?"

"There's just one more. There's a self-storage place down in Fort Gay. They rent traditional storage units, but you can also store things there like RVs, boats or trailers. When I got the new enclosed trailer, I loaded some stuff into my old five by eight trailer and stored it down there. For a trailer that small, it's super cheap. Of course it's not climate controlled, so I had to pick and choose what I put in the trailer. But it's there and it's reasonably secure in a fenced-in area. Dangle has the code for the place and the trailer too, in case he needs it."

Scott conceded. "Wow, you really have put some effort into this. What kind of stuff do you have in the trailer?"

"I tried to picture the scenario that would lead me to needing to resupply there on the way here so I packed it with stuff I thought would help, whether I had a vehicle or not. There's food, water purification, warm and cold weather clothing for the whole family, including broken-in boots. There are some basic tools, a tent, three of my older sleeping bags, and other camping supplies. I've been camping so long that I had older stuff that wasn't getting used anymore, but I didn't want to throw it away. That ended up being the perfect place for it. There's a first aid kit and a bunch of other stuff. I have an inventory at home. I can't remember everything off the top of my head, but you'd be surprised how much you can pack into an eight foot trailer."

Scott grinned. "Of course you have an inventory. Are you sure you're not secretly still in the army?"

Edna responded. "Oh, Paul will always be a soldier. Yesterday, he told me he'd have his girls at church by Zero Six for sunrise service."

"Old habits," Paul said with a grin. "To be fair, I corrected myself immediately and said six o'clock."

"You did, Honey. You did." Edna slid her chair back from the table and stood up. "Well, this lunch isn't going to fix itself. I'd better get back to it."

"I'll help," Paul and Scott said at the same time.

Edna smiled at her husband. "Look at these two. We did *something* right."

After lunch, Paul asked his father if he and Scott could borrow the side by side to take a ride around the farm.

"Yes, you may," replied Charles, and while you're out there, check on the animals, move the tractor back to the side of the barn and top off the fuel on both the side by side and the tractor. You know where the fuel is."

Paul looked at his brother. "Looks like we have chores to do."

"Looks that way. Don't forget to grab the key to the tractor."

The two men headed out the door. After moving the tractor, Paul jumped into the passenger seat of the side by side.

Scott slipped the machine into drive and started moving. "You been following this stuff about Trump?"

"Oh, the trial? Yeah. Man, talk about blatant lawfare."

"Yeah, they're not even trying to hide it at this point," Scott replied, reaching into his back pocket and coming out with a stainless-steel flask. He offered it to Paul without looking.

"Thanks," Paul said, taking the flask. "Don't mind if I do."

The two brothers rode around for a while, catching up and having the type of relaxed conversation that brothers have. Eventually, they ended up at the back of the property, which was bordered by a small creek. Scott put the side by side in park and killed the engine. "You got your gun on you?"

"I'm awake, aren't I?" Paul patted the pistol on his right side, concealed beneath his loose-fitting shirt.

"Good. Let's shoot that can over there." Scott motioned toward a can on the far side of the creek, half buried in the sandy bank.

"Good call," Paul said, getting out of the machine. "You know you can't beat me."

"Whatever, Rambo. Let's do this."

An hour later, the two men walked back into the house. The side by side was full of gas and the tractor was full of diesel. Everyone else was in the living room, watching a show about some ghost chasers. Clearly, they had given control of the remote to McKinley.

"Did you boys have fun?" Edna asked.

"Yes ma'am," Scott replied. "I outshot Paul with my pistol."

"Whatever," Paul answered, rolling his eyes and bumping his brother's shoulder with his own.

Sandy spoke up, smiling. "Damn Hon, you getting rusty?"

"Yeah, clearly I need to practice more," Paul said, the sarcasm apparent in his voice.

Sandy looked over at her mother-in-law. "These men. You put them together and all of a sudden, they act like kids again."

"Don't I know it." Edna glanced back at her sons as she spoke, smiling.

"Come on Scott, we don't have to take this abuse," Paul said, turning to go back through the kitchen.

Scott turned to follow him and everyone in the room let out a collective laugh.

As they walked back out the door, Scott retrieved his flask again, took a sip, and passed it to Paul. He looked across the driveway to the fire ring in the back yard. "We should have a fire tonight."

Before Paul could answer, they both heard yelling from the neighbor's place. They both turned toward the sound of the voices. They could see two figures on the front porch of the trailer across from the house, a man and a woman.

"What did I tell you?!" the man yelled.

"What are you talking about?" the woman screeched in response. "Just go back in the house! You're drunk!"

"Don't you tell me what to do! I'll go when I'm ready to go!" he yelled back at her.

Even at this distance, Paul and Scott could see that the man had his hands balled into fists.

"That's those people who came over to get their cat that time," Scott said calmly, still observing the scene as the two continued to scream at each other.

"Yeah. That guy's an ass," Paul replied flatly.

The woman's voice again. "Fine! Stay out here and smoke your stinkin' cigarettes!" The woman turned, stomped away, and disappeared from view, presumably going back inside.

"Yeah. That relationship's gonna last," Scott said sarcastically and turned back to face Paul. "So, anyhow. As I was saying, we should have a fire tonight."

"I'm on board. Let's grab some wood from the wood shed. Hey, is there anything left in that flask?"

"No, but I have the bottle in the Jeep. I'll grab it. They both walked over to the back of the Jeep Cherokee and Scott opened it. As the hatch opened up, Paul saw a tan backpack sitting there. "Is that your Go-bag?"

Scott looked at the bag. "Yeah, that's it."

"Let's have a drink and check it out." Paul reached for the backpack.

Scott swatted his hand away. "Hey! That's mine. Get your own!"

"I do have mine. It's in the back of the Durango."

Scott grabbed the bottle in one hand and the bag in the other. "Okay, let's compare notes. Go grab yours and I'll meet you at the kitchen table."

A couple of minutes later, Paul walked into the house carrying a full-sized military-style rucksack. Scott was already sitting at the kitchen table. His bag was unzipped, and he had a Mason jar in his hand. He looked at Paul's large ruck.

"Damn dude! That's not a go-bag. That's an expedition pack! Sit that beast down, let me see what it weighs."

Paul lowered the ruck to the floor as Scott sat his whiskey on the table, ice cubes clinking against the glass as he did. Scott quickly reached down for one of the shoulder straps and gave it a pull.

"No way man. That's way too heavy! You're not walking with that thing!"

Paul moved to the cabinet and grabbed a Mason jar, then to the freezer for some ice.

"I have backups to some of the more important items. The idea is to have plenty of everything, so that if I have a vehicle, I'm better off. I definitely went heavy on tools. If I have to walk with it, I can shed weight by getting rid of the non-essentials or duplicates. Plus, I like that it's not completely full. If I'm able to do a resupply while I'm moving, there's space in there to stash more stuff as I get it." He grabbed Scott's bag from the table, testing the weight. "Not bad. It's not too heavy. Is it comfortable?"

Scott looked at the bag. "Yeah, not bad. I have water filtration and purification, a good fire-starter kit, the Mora Companion that you gave me, and a folding saw." He opened the bag and looked in. "Let's see. What else? I have..."

"Which saw did you go with?" Paul cut in.

"Oh, I have a Bahco. It's Swedish, I think."

"Oh yeah. I know it. I have one of those too, the Laplander. I'm not carrying it anymore because I changed to a Silky saw, but I used the Bahco for a while. It's a solid choice. I put my Bahco in Sandy's pack when I built her get home bag."

Scott was digging around in his backpack. "Oh, I have my Leatherman, a small tarp, some paracord and some bunji cords."

"Yep. Good stuff. I know you like Victorinox Swiss Army knives like I do. You should check out their multitool. It's called the SwissTool. It's legit." As he spoke, Paul reached over and unzipped the top pocket of his ruck and retrieved a small black leather case, offering it to his brother.

"Man, I've seen this. You've shown it to me before. And you're right. That thing's nice." He handed it back without taking it out of the case and returned his attention to his own backpack. "Oh, here's my cooking setup." He withdrew a nylon bag and held it up briefly. "This has a cookpot and a stove stand so you can cook over a small fire. There's some additional stuff in the pot too like a spoon and a scrubber pad for cleaning the pot."

Paul looked toward the bag. "You're a paramedic. Where's your first aid kit?"

"Oh, that's separate. It's still in the Jeep, but I can strap it onto this pack. I like to keep it separate while I'm travelling in case I need it for something."

"That makes sense. I use this setup." Paul motioned to a green pouch attached to the outside of his ruck. It had a small Velcro patch on it in the shape of a red cross. "You attach this Velcro panel to your pack with MOLLE straps and the first aid kit sticks to the Velcro. Then there's this strap that goes over it to make sure it can't come off the Velcro unless you release it. My thought was that if I needed the first aid kit fast, and I didn't want to have to take the whole pack, I could unclip it and take the kit to the problem." Paul demonstrated how to quickly release the strap.

"That first aid kit's pretty small," Scott noticed.

"Yeah, I know. I put some thought into narrowing it down to just the essentials. It's not bad, but more medical gear is always better. I keep a non-emergency kit in both our vehicles with band-aids and over-the-counter meds and stuff in them.

McKinley calls it the 'Boo-boo kit'. If I had to abandon the vehicle, I'd go through that kit and cross-load most of it into this bag. Plus, I have freakin' Motrin stashed everywhere. We lived off that stuff in the Army. We used to call it vitamin M." Paul was smiling as he said it. "Now it helps me deal with the aches and pains of my earlier life choices."

"I hear that." Scott took a sip of his whiskey. "This helps too. Cowboy medicine."

Paul chuckled. "Truth." He nodded toward his pack. "I just built one for McKinley's car too. I don't know if I told you, but I stumbled on a great deal on a little Honda for her, so I started setting her car up with its own set of stuff. Obviously, I had to cater it to her needs and what she can actually use. Plus, I left out some things that I would have liked her to have because she's driving it to school and I don't want to have anything in the car that she could get in trouble for on school grounds."

Scott chuckled. "Oh, I can hear that conversation now: Uh, Mr. Michaels. This is the police. We'd like to talk to you about why your daughter has two knives, a ghillie suit and an AR-15 in the trunk of her car at school." Scott changed his voice as if mimicking his brother. "Well, officer, obviously, if we get hit with an EMP while she's in class, she might have to fight her way home." Scott laughed out loud.

Paul was laughing too. "Yeah, I'm going to avoid *that* conversation!" He laughed again. "It's a small car, so I'm trying to keep the kit small too. She has some space around her spare tire where I can put some small items, but for her, I just made sure the car is reliable and that she has the traditional emergency items. You know, the Boo-boo kit, a tire plug kit, and mini-air compressor, jumper cables, maps..."

Scott interrupted him. "Maps?! She's sixteen. Does she even know how to *use* a paper map?"

"I've taught her, but she's never had to do it in an emergency. She's not going to be driving very far by herself yet, so I'll keep working on that. From the survival standpoint, I kept it pretty simple for her. There's a multitool in her spare tire compartment, a couple of lighters, and some fire starter. I'm sure the Leatherman is against the rules, but I figured it would be fine. It's hidden and she knows not to take it out of there unless its an emergency. I was also able to get a small tarp to fit over the spare tire and still put the cover back in place. She always has her fancy water bottle, so I put some water purification tablets in there too. I got her a little plain-looking school backpack and put everything in there that I couldn't hide around the spare tire. Then I wrapped it with a bunji cord to make it as small and unobtrusive as possible and attached it to the tie-down point in the back so it doesn't slide around while she's driving. If she does have to walk, it has enough room to put the other items in it, so she doesn't have to leave anything behind."

"That's not too bad. What about food?" Scott asked.

"Oh yeah. The backpack has some granola bars and other ready-to-eat stuff. Plus, I put a hundred in there in small bills. I didn't tell her it was there though. However, if she ever has an emergency and has to use that pack, she'll see it. If I told her it was in there now, she'd have to have an 'emergency' coffee or something and then the next thing you know the money would be gone."

Scott did his best impersonation of a teenage girl voice, which was terrible. "But Daaaaaad. It was an emeeeeeergency! I totally needed a soy café macchiato with two squirts of sugar free, sustainably harvested caramel."

Paul was laughing at Scott's antics. Suddenly from the other room, McKinley yelled. "Uncle Scott, I do NOT sound like that!"

Both men burst into a raucous laugh. After a moment, Paul leaned in toward his brother and lowered his voice. "I hope she didn't hear me talking about the money!"

"Oh, yeah Dude," Scott said. "That money's going to be gone as soon as she gets back to her car."

24

Building Guns

May 11, 2024

Paul and Sandy's Farm, Lincoln County, West Virginia

Paul had spent the day at home working on things around the house and the property. Chores and "Honey Do" lists would build up when he was working, so there was always stuff to do when he got home.

He also had things that he wanted to get done for himself. Yesterday, he had cooked some food to freeze dry. He had scrambled up three dozen fresh eggs from his chickens and sauteed some diced bell peppers, onions, jalapenos and ham to add to it. In a separate pan, he fried up some potatoes. After mixing it all together, he divided it equally into the freeze dryer trays and topped it off with some shredded Colby Jack cheese before putting the trays in the freezer. Paul called this mixture "Western Breakfast Scramble." When he got up this morning, he had put the trays into the freeze dryer and started the machine. He knew it would take more than twenty-four hours to freeze dry, so he went on about his day, getting things done.

By noon, he had done the monthly maintenance on both the generators, cleaned out the chicken coop, repaired a wobbly cabinet door, replaced a light bulb in the laundry room and hung two picture that Sandy had bought for the den. The goal was to get everything done early so he would have some time to run up to his shooting range before dinner. So far so good.

As Paul removed the small level from the top of the second picture, Sandy walked into the room.

"That looks good," she said with an approving smile and walked over to give him a quick kiss. "I knew I married you for something." She turned and walked away, looking over her shoulder and offering a wink.

"Oh, yeah," Paul replied. "I forgot that I had 'live-in carpenter and general handyman' on my marriage résumé."

"And I'm glad you did!" she called out, no longer looking over her shoulder.

Paul looked at his watch. It was just after 12:00. Dinner was in five hours. He did some quick math on the remaining things he was trying to finish and decided that he could be done by 2:30, be up at the range a few minutes after that, and still get home in time for dinner.

The range was just up the mountain from the house and by 3:15, he had the side-by-side parked at the range and was squaring up with one of his AR-15s to do some drills. Paul didn't have much flat ground on his property. It *was* West Virginia after all. However, there was a nice, gently sloping, uphill portion that made a decent range location. The targets got higher in elevation the further they got from the shooting line. Paul had numerous steel targets that he had accumulated over the years and now most of them were on this range. The closest ones were eight-inch squares, no closer than twenty-five meters. Beyond that, starting at fifty meters and scattered up the hill were additional steel target in the shape of a traditional army silhouette target, known as 'E-Type Silhouettes.' Finally, there were several randomly shaped targets at miscellaneous distances throughout the range.

Paul considered this to be his pistol and carbine range. In addition to the steel, he had built a handful of wooden target stands for hanging paper targets. He typically used these to train for pistol accuracy or for zeroing optics. Right now, the target stands were still sitting in the simple range shed and Paul was focused on the steel in front of him.

He mentally plotted the course of fire in his head: "Alpha, Charlie, Square 1, Square 3." The silhouettes had letters painted on them, A through E. However, the letters were not in order. The first target was A, then as they got farther away, they were D, B, E, and finally C, or Charlie, near the ridgeline. The smaller square, diamond, and round targets had numbers on them. He mentally pictured his movements. Alpha was near the right side of the range at about fifty meters from his position. Charlie was just left of center and at one hundred eighty meters. Then transition to Square 1 the left side of the range at twenty-five meters, ending on Square 3, at thirty-five meters and the right boundary of the range. This would be with a red dot non-magnified optic.

"Alpha, Charlie, Square 1, Square 3."

Then he turned his back to the targets. His gun hung on the sling casually and comfortably across his body. He had his Walker earbuds tucked into his ears as hearing protection. His AR-15 was fitted with a SureFire suppressor, but the 5.56mm ammunition would still produce a notable 'crack.' He pressed the button on the shot timer clipped to his belt...and waited.

The shot timer announced the beginning of the time with a loud beep. Paul rotated to his left, assuming his shooting stance as he did, feet roughly shoulder width apart, left foot forward. As the first target came into view, he focused on it, bringing the optic up to his eye, his right thumb sweeping the safety down as he did. He positioned the red dot at the center of the target and squeezed off his first round of the day. As soon as he felt the mild recoil of the 5.56mm round, he was already transitioning to his next target at the top of the ridgeline.

Ding!

The first round rang off the silhouette.

He placed the red dot in the upper part of the chest of the far target. He slowed just slightly for the longer shot.

Crack...Ding! As the second round impacted Paul was already dialing into the small square target with a number one painted on it.

Ding!

Then once again. Ding! as he hit the fourth target.

He was having fun. He decided to keep going. He released the AR-15 and it fell naturally across his chest as he drew his pistol and engaged Square 3 again, then Square 1, and the Alpha silhouette. He returned the pistol to the holster and removed the shot timer from his belt to check his time.

First shot was at 1.42 seconds. Paul considered this. He'd had faster times, but this was a cold start, not having practiced much lately. He checked his other times. *Not terrible*, he thought, but not his fastest time either. He turned his back to the targets. *Let's go again*, he thought to himself. *I can go faster than that.*

Beep!

Paul continued to shoot for an hour and a half. He switched up various shooting scenarios between his AR and his pistol, and by the time he was getting into the side-by-side to drive back down the mountain, he was feeling much more relaxed. Shooting was his happy place.

A month earlier, Paul's former teammate, Randy "Dangle" Taylor, had been there and they had gone up to the range together. Of course, it immediately turned into a competition with lots of trash talk. It reminded Paul of something his father had told him when he was young: "As iron sharpens iron, so does one man sharpen another." It wasn't an exact quote, but rather a paraphrase of a Bible verse. When two people compete against each other, both people get better. Paul had definitely found that to be true.

Now, as he started back toward his house, he made a mental note to give Dangle a call soon. They needed to get together and do some more shooting. Paul had built two AR-15s for Dangle and Dangle was rough on his guns. The first one he had built was a carbine with a sixteen-inch barrel, a nice trigger, and an aggressive muzzle brake. Paul had installed a low powered variable optic (LPVO) on that one. The second one had been an AR pistol with a seven and a half-inch barrel. Paul recalled the conversation that led to the construction of that gun.

Dangle had brought it up one evening as the two were sitting around a campfire on Paul's property. "Hey man, I'm thinking I want a shorty AR. Would you be interested in building it for me?"

Paul took a sip of his beer. "Sure. How short are we talking?"

"I was thinking like a seven point five inch. What do you think?" Dangle offered.

"Well," Paul began. "I've built seven point fives before, but I usually recommend a ten five. They tend to be more reliable."

Dangle smiled. "Oh, so you're saying if you build me a seven five, you can't make it run? I see how it is."

"I didn't say that, dick. It's just with a seven point five, it will be a pistol length gas system. With a ten point five, it will be a carbine length gas system. The advantage is...you know what? You don't care. You want a seven five, no problem."

Dangle started laughing and pointed at Paul over the fire. "There he is. I knew you'd do it."

"Screw you man." Paul was chuckling now too. "Okay, what else do you want in it?"

"Like what?"

Paul shook his head. "What do you mean 'like what?' Like what receivers, what trigger, what type of brace. It has to be a brace and not a stock because of the barrel length. What kind of hand guard do you want? Do you want a fixed front sight post? That kind of 'like what.'"

Dangle looked into the fire for a few seconds as if considering the questions. "I have an idea. How about you tell me what you think I'll like, and I'll tell you if you're right." Dangle looked sideways at Paul and maintained eye contact as he took a sip of his beer and grinned.

"Man, you sound like an amateur. You're a freakin' shooter, man."

Dangle was amused by the whole line of questioning. "Yeah, I use a laptop too, but I can't tell you how it works. It's like when we were in the army, they gave us guns and they just worked."

"Except my Beretta," Paul interrupted.

"Oh yeah, that's right. Except for your Beretta," Dangle acknowledged.

"The locking block broke on me," Paul added. "But to be fair to that gun, it's hard telling how many thousands of rounds had been put through it."

Dangle continued, "So anyhow, you know all this fancy crap about gas systems and this buffer weight versus that buffer weight. Man, I don't study that crap, and I don't need to. That's why I have you." He was smiling broadly. "Now if you want to talk about Glocks, I can talk about Glocks."

"Oh yeah, your Glock." Paul used air quotes as he said Glock. "Are there any Glock parts left on that thing?"

Dangle feigned insult. "Yes, I'll have you know. As a matter of fact, there are Glock parts on it still. And that's a good gun."

"I know, I know. I shoot against you. It does great. Let's get back on track here. So, you just want a solidly built seven point five inch AR..." Paul paused. "I didn't ask, but I'm assuming five five six?"

"Oh yeah. I might get into 300 Blackout later, but yes. For this one, five five six. Oh, and none of that expensive designer crap you like. I'm not made of money. I know you like your Noveske barrels and all that. What can you do that's reliable, but affordable? Just something straight forward. I'm not trying to drop two grand on this thing."

"Okay, here's what I'd say man. Keep in mind, this is just off the cuff. I'll put it on paper, and we can look at it before I start ordering parts. How about an Aero Precision M4E1 receiver set, with a Ballistic Advantage Barrel and Bolt Carrier Group. That's good for the money." Paul looked up as he thought. "Do you want a skinny handguard like the one I have on my ten point five?"

"Oh yeah. I like that thing."

"Okay, that's an Aero Precision S-One. With that barrel, we'll have to go with like a seven-inch handguard. I'll need to look at the Aero Precision and Ballistic Advantage websites. I'm pretty sure Aero is making the BA handguards anyhow, but the two websites have different lengths available. Whatever, I'll find you a handguard that's the right length. Since I'm using a Ballistic Advantage barrel, I'll go with their gas block too." Paul paused again. "You know, if you went with a little longer barrel, we could use a BA Hanson barrel from Ballistic Advantage with a pinned gas block. Those things are bullet proof."

Dangle didn't hesitate, he just yelled, "Seven five!" and took a drink of his beer.

"Okay, I'm just saying. I don't have the setup for drilling a barrel for a pinned gas block, so we'll have to go with a set-screw gas block," Paul said. "Which is fine for what you're wanting. For the brace, I'll recommend an SB Tactical brace. I'll show you the options on those so you can pick the one you want."

"Wait, I didn't even think about that. Are those things legal again?" Dangle asked.

"Ha!" Paul forced a sarcastic sounding laugh. "Yeah, the powers-that-be got overruled by the courts. They're legal 'again'." Paul used air quotes as he said again. "The written law never changed. The ATF just decided they were going to *reinterpret* the exact same words differently than they had in the past. So, they tried to artificially manufacture millions of felons by saying 'We know we said this was legal. We know that millions of Americans bought this item in good faith, because we said it was legal, but you know what? We changed our minds. Now destroy them or you're all felons!'"

Dangle shook his head. "That's ridiculous."

Paul pointed at Dangle. "Yes. Yes, it is. And the courts agreed with you. They struck it down. So yes, they're legal again. Anyhow, there are a bunch of options. I'll walk you through it." He paused again, thinking for a moment for asking, "What are we missing?" He looked up into the night sky as he thought about it. "Oh yeah, what trigger?"

"What's in my sixteen inch?"

"Seriously? You don't know?"

Dangle just shrugged.

Paul shook his head slightly. "That's a Geissele SSP, Single Stage Precision, but we don't have to do that for this build."

"Why not?" asked Dangle.

"Well, that's a great single stage trigger. That's what I use in my twenty-inch AR precision rifle and my AR-10, the 308. Hell, I use that in several of my guns. However, some people like a nice two-stage. In the past, I liked a two-stage trigger in my shorter guns. Now I'm going the way of single stage in everything. There's no science behind it. It's all about personal preference. The M4s we had in the Army were a two-stage trigger. Do you remember that ever bothering you?"

Dangle thought about that for a second before replying. "I don't really remember it one way or the other."

"Exactly," Paul said. "Once you get used to it, it just feels natural. However, I'm not recommending a Mil-Spec trigger. If you want a two-stage trigger, I'd say either the Geissele SSA-E or the LaRue Tactical MBT-2S."

"What's the difference?" Dangle asked.

"To start with, about a hundred thirty dollars."

"What?! A hundred thirty dollars difference? Just for the trigger? Which one is more?" Dangle asked, surprised.

"The Geissele is more, but the LaRue is similar. Not the same, but similar."

"Oh, and let me guess, you prefer the Geissele?"

"Actually, I like them both; it depends on the application. Some guys want the exact same trigger in everything, and I get that. Muscle memory and all, but I don't do that. I prefer one trigger in some setups, but a different trigger in other setups. Besides, it's not like we're running across the desert in Afghanistan anymore. Most of my shooting is right here on the farm. They're my guns and I enjoy shooting them, so I set them up however I want, depending on what I want to do with that gun. I own plenty of guns that I enjoy shooting, but I wouldn't want to take into combat."

Dangle nodded at this last statement. "I know that's right. We shoot the hell out of some .22s."

"Exactly. I love my .22s, but I also don't plan on betting my life on them. Now, about that trigger. I tell you what, I built McKinley an AR with a LaRue trigger in it. She likes it. I'll bring it out along with one of mine with the Geissele. You can try them both and then decide."

"Deal!" Dangle said enthusiastically. "You bring the ammo!"

"Whatever man." Paul rolled his eyes at his friend.

"O.P.A., baby. O.P.A."

"Yeah, yeah. Other People's Ammo." He shook his head.

"I will say this about the LaRue, though. I've put several of those triggers in at the shop and I've never had anyone complain about them. It's a good trigger, but at the end of the day, it comes down to your personal preference and how much you're willing to spend. There's a bunch of other good triggers out there too, like the Hyperfire or the Timney, but I'm just trying to keep this simple."

Paul had taken a side job working at a local gun store a few years earlier and had been building AR-15s, AR-10s, and AR-9s ever since. Many people didn't realize there are different types of Federal Firearms Licenses. The shop where Paul worked allowed them to buy, sell, or build most guns, including the AR-15. Actually, saying he 'worked' there was a bit of a stretch. He would just do jobs for the shop when they needed him. That worked out well with his contracting because he could work on guns between contracting jobs.

He also offered a repair service for ARs. Sometimes, people had tried to build guns themselves and after they got into it, realized they needed a little help. Sometimes he would just install parts that someone didn't know how to install or didn't have the correct tools to do so. Other times, he would repair factory-built guns. Many people didn't want the hassle of sending a gun back to a manufacturer for repairs, even if that repair was free. Sometimes it was just easier to have it done locally and pay for it. Paul was happy to oblige. He got requests to fix all kinds of different guns, but he was quick to point out that he was not a gunsmith. "I'm just an AR mechanic," he would say. It was little more than a hobby, but he enjoyed it and he was good at it. He had spent countless hours studying the AR platform and learning the ins and outs of it, or as he called it, 'AR Science.' The side effect had been that he also worked on all his buddies' ARs too, and, as in this case, would build their guns for them.

"Alright, here's what you do. Go down to the gun store and buy the lower receiver. Then I'll help you get everything else, and we'll get this done," Paul offered.

"Cool, how long will it take?"

"That depends on you," Paul said, a grin creeping onto his face again. "How long until you get off your ass and go buy the lower?"

"Fine, I'll go down there Monday," Dangle said with a tone of finality.

"All right. After you try the triggers, if you decide on the LaRue trigger, you can get that at the shop too. They usually have them in stock. If you want a Geissele or something else, we'll have to order it; they don't carry those."

Dangle slapped his hands together and rubbed them back and forth in anticipation. "This is going to be great."

"Yep," Paul said. "Now what optic do you want?"

"Crap. What red dot do you recommend?"

"You're ridiculous, Dangle."

25

Tactical Operations Center

May 13, 2024, Two Days Later

Paul and Sandy's Farm, Lincoln County, West Virginia

Paul had a few more days before his next contract, so he continued to work on things around the house and on the property. Grass mowing season had begun, so he had taken the tractor down to the pasture and used the brush hog to mow everything down. He didn't have any livestock, so he just needed to mow it once a month to keep it from looking too unruly. He would still have to come back and run the weed eater around the edges, but that was a job for tomorrow. Now, it was close to lunch time. As he walked into the house, Sandy greeted him from the kitchen. "You get the pasture done?"

"Yeah, except for the trimming. What are you working on?"

"Oh, I'm just thawing out meat for dinner."

"What are we having?" Paul asked as he closed the distance, looking at the package in her hands.

"I thought I would do that chicken you like with the bacon bits on it."

"Oh, that sounds great. I'm going to grab a sandwich and head out to the shop. Dinner at five?"

"Yep," she replied and went back to what she was doing.

Paul's shop was a two-story affair, the size of a three-car garage. It had one garage door and a standard three foot steel exterior door. The bottom floor was set up with a wood shop area on one end and a storage area in the middle. He kept the area inside the garage door clear. He would store the tractor there sometimes when he didn't want to take it all the way to the barn. He also used this area for working on his vehicles and equipment. Besides the tractor, he had two side by sides. Add in two weed eaters, a few chainsaws, his generator, and other miscellaneous tools that are required to keep up a large piece of land and a maintenance bay was a good idea. They also had a whole-house generator, but it was permanently mounted on a concrete slab by the house and fed by a natural gas line. That one obviously got its maintenance done in place.

The storage area included the typical items one might expect to find in a garage such as holiday decorations and recreational items like fishing poles and tents. Additionally, Paul had a portion of it dedicated to the preps he wasn't concerned about keeping in a climate-controlled area. This included things like toilet paper, paper towels, paper plates, cleaning supplies, and most hygiene items.

The top floor ended up having a little bit of everything. When he had designed the building, he knew he wanted a climate-controlled area that could have multiple uses. He jokingly referred to it as the TOC, which stood for Tactical Operations Center, a throwback to his days in the army. The space had evolved over the last couple of years after building it. His house wasn't large, and he wanted to have a comfortable place for people to stay when they came over. He had sold the idea to Sandy as a "mother-in-law" suite.

To support this idea, Paul had built a simple kitchen and bathroom. To simplify the plumbing, he had put both of these on the same end of the structure. The kitchen had a basic stove he had picked up at a scratch and dent sale, plus a small refrigerator/freezer and a microwave. The refrigerator had been salvaged from an old RV and would run on either electricity or propane. Paul had added an inexpensive coffee pot to round out the appliances. The simple sink had a small counter on each side. The setup was completed with a simple set of cabinets Paul had built himself. They weren't fancy, but they were sturdy and functional.

They hadn't spent very much money outfitting the kitchen. Sandy already had more cookware than she could use, and the extra pieces found a new home in the TOC kitchen. Likewise, the dishes and other kitchen utensils were duplicates from Sandy's kitchen, or scavenged from boxes stored in the barn. The glasses were Mason jars and the coffee cups were random souvenir cups picked up over the years.

Just outside the kitchen, Paul had put a simple farmhouse-style table. The table had six chairs of mixed origins. This had become a general-purpose workspace used for everything from eating to cleaning guns.

The bathroom was not fancy, but it had everything you would need; toilet, sink and, a shower. It also doubled as the utility room, so it included a water heater and the old washer and dryer that had since been replaced by a newer set in the house.

Running water to the structure had been simple. Paul had done that himself by running a line off the house main supply line. The trickiest part of the addition had been tying it into the existing septic system. Paul didn't even attempt this part. He brought in professionals for that part of the project. By the time it was done, everything worked as designed.

Paul moved his reloading station from the cramped spare bedroom in the house out to the TOC. He also built a set of robust storage shelves for the bulk of their food storage. The idea of the shelving was to make everything as accessible as possible. Sandy never complained because she liked the convenience of having a consistent food supply, especially considering it was a half hour drive to the nearest grocery store. Storing the extra food preps out here had the additional advantage of being in a climate-controlled environment without taking up precious cabinet space in the house.

Paul put a tremendous amount of effort into organizing the food preps. He took a page out of his father's playbook and built the shelves with a gap behind them so that they could be loaded from the rear. The food was divided into four sections. One section was dry goods such as rice, beans, and pasta. Another section was canned goods, both store-bought and home-canned. The third section was dedicated to freeze dried food. The final section held military MREs.

The freeze-dried food was great when camping or at home, because most of it required rehydration to eat. The rehydration worked best with hot water, so you needed a heat source. It would still rehydrate with cold water, but it took longer and you didn't get a hot meal out of the deal. The MREs weren't Paul's favorite, but they definitely had their place. To be fair, the current MREs were dramatically better than the ones Paul received when he first joined the army. MREs could be heated with the included chemical heater, or simply eaten cold. They didn't have the extreme shelf life of the freeze-dried food, but were still shelf stable for years. The military claimed a shelf life of a minimum of seven years, although Paul had gotten MREs older than that when he was still in the army and they were fine. Paul still considered this an option when he was out doing something and knew that he wouldn't want to take the time to stop and rehydrate one of the freeze-dried meals.

He had also chosen to keep the bulk of his ammunition storage in the TOC because of the extra climate-controlled space. He always kept some in the house for easy access, but the majority of it was out here. He knew that the ammunition didn't need to be in a climate-controlled space, but he preferred it and he had the space, so why not? As he loaded ammunition on his reloading bench, he would label everything and move it straight into the ammo stores in a shallow closet built for just that purpose. He chose the dimensions of the closet based on the size of the military ammo cans he preferred for storing ammunition. He built the shelves large enough to load them two cans deep and four cans wide. Like the food shelves, he had used two by fours for the shelf supports so they could handle the weight.

Inside the door was a list of the ammo with totals. He actually tracked the ammo count on a spreadsheet on his computer, but he would make notes on this list when he took ammo or added ammo to the closet. Periodically, he would print a new copy with the updated numbers. The ammunition was primarily manufactured ammo, although he augmented it with the stuff he loaded himself.

Generally speaking, he only loaded .45 ACP, 9mm, .38 Special, .308 Winchester, .300 Blackout, and occasionally .300 Winchester Magnum. He had the reloading dies to do various other calibers, but seldom did. However, he considered the ability to load the additional calibers to be an appropriate preparation. To support this idea, he was also able to load 5.56 NATO, .223 Remington, 9mm Parabellum, 45-70 Government, 30-30 Winchester, and 7.62 x 39. The problem with that is different calibers use different powders and specific primers for reloading the shell casing. So, his approach was to stock enough to do a little of everything. Unfortunately, during the COVID scare, reloading components had gotten more difficult to find and the prices had gone up dramatically. Reloading ammunition had always been cheaper than buying ammunition. But the new prices on reloading supplies closed that gap considerably.

Last year, Mack and Paul had gotten into a conversation about stocking up on ammunition. Mack explained his approach.

"I try to keep most of my guns in only three calibers so I don't have to stock ammo for so many different calibers. Pretty much everything I have is in 5.56, 9mm, and 7.62 x 39. Of course, I have a few others, but I'm not worried about them as much. If shit goes sideways, the guns I'm reaching for are in those three calibers," Mack stated.

"I get that," Paul replied. "For my primary stuff, I'm in the same calibers. However, let's keep it real here. I love collecting guns. I've been collecting them my entire life. Hell, I got my first .410 shotgun at eight years old. I actually still have that gun. It's an old Harrington & Richardson single shot. Anyways, I've accumulated guns in numerous calibers, so I have some ammo for all of them. For pistols alone, I have, let's see…" He stopped to think about it. "Five different calibers. Oh, no, I also have a single action army in .45 Long Colt, so six. Anyhow, I only stock the 9mm and .45 heavily. Well, that's not true. I stock the crap out of some .22, but that's because I also have a collection of .22 rifles. For .380 and .38, I don't keep much on hand, although I do have a box of 500 lead bullets for the .38 ready to be loaded if I need more. I have two or three thousand .45 caliber lead bullets as well."

"Like legit lead bullets? Not full metal jacket?" Mack inquired.

"Yep. I get them in bulk from a company called Missouri Bullet Company. Just plain lead bullets. I've been using them for years. I've had really good luck with their bullets."

"Do your guns have any problems with those?"

"Nope. If you think about it, the M1911 was patented in…" He paused for effect. "You guessed it, 1911. It was designed for lead bullets. The 1911 and lead bullets go together like beer and pretzels," Paul responded with a grin.

"Hmm, I'd never thought about that. What about rifle bullets?"

"I take a different approach with my rifles. You can load some rifle ammo with lead bullets, but the only one I load with lead is .45-70. For everything else, I buy factory made jacketed bullets."

Mack nodded as he listened to the explanation. "I've always wanted to get into reloading but I just never got around to it. I just buy the crap out of ammo instead. You can never have too much ammo."

"Unless you're swimming or on fire," Paul corrected, laughing at his own joke before continuing.

Mack was taking a drink from his beer bottle when Paul made the joke and he nearly spit it out laughing. "I never thought about that, but yeah. There are exceptions to the rule." He shook his head.

"Reloading's definitely not for everyone. I just find it very satisfying to start with this pile of components and finish up with this beautiful little thing that's also functional. I enjoy it. I think it's therapeutic. That's probably the same reason I like carpentry. I start with a pile of wood and create something that's useful."

"Yeah, I get that," Mack said.

Paul started grinning. "Fun fact: the patent for the M1911 pistol was approved on February fourteenth, 1911. You know what that means?"

"What's that?" Mack asked.

"That means the 1911 is the perfect Valentine's Day gift," Paul said, once again laughing at his own joke.

"You and that dang 1911. You don't even carry one anymore."

"Hey, she was my first love and always will be. I still have a few and I actually *do* still carry one sometimes, thank you very much. Besides that, I just love shooting them."

"How many's a few?" asked Mack, raising his eyebrows.

"Well, let's see." Paul looked up as he thought about it. He resorted to counting on his fingers again. "I have the two five-inch models in .45…"

Mack interrupted. "Never mind, if you have to sit there and go through your mental inventory, it's safe to say several."

Paul dropped his hands back onto the arm rests of his folding chair. "Yeah. Let's go with several."

With that approach in mind, Paul had stocked the ammo closet in the TOC with numerous green ammo cans of various calibers. It had everything from .22 long rifle all the way up to .300 WinMag and 45-70 Government. The bottom shelf also had a collection of shotgun shells in .410, 20 gauge, and 12 gauge. And yes, it had plenty of .45 ACP for Paul's 1911 collection.

The space had clearly taken on the appearance of a 'man-cave.' The vaulted ceilings displayed various flags. One side had an American flag and a U.S. Army flag. The other side had a solid red flag with the Special Forces Crest on it. The red signified 7th Special Forces Group, the group Paul had served in. Beside it was the flag of the Pineland Resistance Forces, the fictitious unit central to the Unconventional Warfare training of the U.S. Army Green Berets. The American flag was the one given to

Paul by the army upon his retirement. It had just been sitting in his closet since his retirement and he decided that he wanted to display it. He had never flown it outside because he didn't want it ruined by the sun, wind, and rain, but in here it would be protected.

Along the wall outside the bathroom was a final set of shelves. Here he kept his medical supplies and other miscellaneous supplies and equipment. He put curtains on the front of the shelves keep the area looking neat without having to build more doors.

On this warm day in May, Paul was down in the wood shop building a new shelf. He wanted to mount his six-bay radio charger on the wall in the TOC, but he didn't have a good place to put it. That gave him an excuse for a new woodworking project. He had his earbuds in, listening to the news on his satellite radio app on his phone. He was putting the finishing touches on the shelf when the conversation on the radio turned to the border.

Honestly, he was tired of hearing about the border. It was the same thing every time. There's an open border. Bad people are coming in. Drugs are flowing freely. Human traffickers are working unopposed. He knew all this and the fact that he could do nothing about it just made him angry. He pulled his phone out and switched to a different news station.

A man with a Boston accent was speaking. "How are American citizens supposed to deal with this? This administration is denying how bad inflation is, but they can't hide that from hard working families who are just trying to feed their kids."

A woman responded. She was clearly *not* from Boston. She had the flat accent common with television personalities. "James, don't you think that's a bit of an exaggeration? Americans are not starving. They can still feed their kids. The country certainly has inflation, but we've always had inflation. It's part of the normal economic cycle."

This statement instantly angered the man and he raised his voice as he replied. "Are you blind? You think *this* is normal? Have you heard of the explosion in the homeless population? Have you heard of the..."

Paul closed the app and pulled his earbuds out, putting them back in their case. He didn't want to hear this either. He looked at his watch. He had time for a shower before dinner. He'd had enough news for the day. This crap is depressing. They were already doing everything they could do to prepare for emergencies, whether it was an economic crisis or a simple power outage. He didn't need to listen to people argue about how bad it was getting. He was well aware.

An hour later, he walked into the kitchen, wearing clean clothes and ready for dinner. Sandy had her back to him finishing up a dish on the kitchen bar. He walked up behind her and leaned around to kiss her cheek. "That smells great."

"Thanks, now quit before you make me spill something. Can you get the plates out?"

"Yes ma'am." She didn't see him smiling as he moved to the cabinet, retrieved three plates, and placed them on the counter.

"Did you finish up whatever you were working on out there?" she asked.

"Yeah. More or less. I was making a shelf for the TOC. I still have to put a clear coat on it, but other than that, it's done." He turned and faced the other end of the house, calling out toward McKinley's room. "Mic! Dinner's ready!"

"I was just about to do that."

McKinley came padding through the house in her typical pajama pants, T-shirt, and house shoes. "Man, I'm starving."

"Good," Sandy replied. "Come make your plate."

A few minutes later, the trio was sitting at the table. Paul had asked the blessing over the meal and everyone was eating. He paused between bites.

"I was listening to the news when I was out in the shop and they can't find one single good thing to talk about. It's violence in the cities and drugs at the border and blah, blah, blah. I swear, I'm about to just stop listening to the news."

"Ha, yeah right," Sandy responded. "We both know that's not going to happen. You're always listening to the news, or reading it. Besides, if you stop listening, who's going to tell me all the exciting news stories?"

Paul just rolled his eyes and continued to chew.

It was McKinley's turn to jump into the conversation. "Seriously, I don't know how you listen to it anyways. It's so boring."

Paul looked over at his daughter. "The news is boring, huh? This coming from a girl who literally watches a show of some British dude playing video games."

"Hey! He's funny."

"Yeah, I don't get it," Paul said, returning his focus to his plate. "I'll tell you this though: I've never felt more like something bad is going to happen. Besides all the stuff that's going on inside the country, I feel like we're about to get dragged back into another war. That's *exactly* what we need." His sarcasm was not lost on the women.

"They can't pull you back onto active duty, can they Dad?" McKinley looked concerned.

"Well, technically, yes. But don't worry. I'm certain that won't happen. The best thing we can do as a family is to just continue doing what we've been doing. We take care of ourselves. We take care of the animals and our garden, our home. We just do what we do." He started to speak and then stopped himself.

Sandy noticed. "What is it, Hon?"

"I've put a lot of work into this place. *We've* put a lot of work into this place. Our backups have backups."

"The PACE plan," McKinley chimed in.

"Exactly, Honey." He smiled at his daughter.

She grinned as teenagers do when they are proud of themselves for getting the right answer.

Paul had adopted the acronym from his time in the army. PACE stood for Primary, Alternate, Contingency, and Emergency. He taught his family that everything they considered to be essential should have four options. Backups to the backups. When they moved out here to the country, they had intentionally built the homestead with that in mind. Now, sitting around the kitchen table enjoying a nice meal with his family, he immediately began wondering if he had done enough.

Epilogue

Same Day, May 11, 2024

The other side of the country. Secure Communication Room, Nancy Pelosi's Private Residence

San Francisco, California

Nancy Pelosi, former Speaker of the House, entered her four-digit personal identification number into a keypad beside the door to her private communication room. She then looked down at her "other" phone and read the six-digit RSA SecureID OTP credential, which changed every sixty seconds. She entered the six-digit RSA code into the keypad and hit the "Enter" key. The screen changed from red to orange and requested a fingerprint on the small biometric reader below the keypad. She obliged and placed her left ring finger on the pad. The screen changed from orange to yellow and prompted her to look into the portal at face level for a retina scan. Once again, she obliged and the screen changed from yellow to green. The four locks made four audible 'thunks' as they withdrew from the bottom, left, top, and right sides of the door in quick succession.

When she was having the room secretly constructed, she was instructed by the security advisor to not use her right index finger for the biometric scanner. "If someone were to try to force you to open the door, most people assume that you will use your right index finger. Use your left ring finger. It's not a natural movement to try to extend your ring finger, so no would expect you to do so. No one would be suspicious if you use your right index finger," the technical expert advised. "Your right index finger will automatically force a secure lockdown of the room and disable all electronics inside."

She had nodded as she listened to the advisor, who had flown in from Switzerland in 2019 to oversee the construction and setup of the facility. He had been back five times in five years for updates and checkups on the system.

Now, with authentication complete, the heavy door automatically swung silently inward on hidden hinges. As she walked through the door, she heard it close and lock back in place with four more 'thunks.' The room was dark, save a small light in the back of the room illuminating the back of a small but comfortable leather chair in the center of the room. A computer console was centered in front of the chair. On the wall in front of the console was a large screen, nearly five feet wide. She moved to the chair and sat down. She looked down at the phone in her hand and checked the time. After waiting a few seconds, she placed her hand on the biometric scanner that quickly scanned her palm with a visible flash of light. The screen instantly lit up and a message appeared.

--ESTABISHING SECURE SATELLITE LINK—

A moment later, the screen was divided into six equal-sized boxes. Four of the boxes had the silhouettes of other members of The Collective. Two of the boxes were empty. However, within five seconds, both the empty boxes came online to show the remaining participants in the meeting. No one's face was clear. Like her setup, everyone was backlit by a small light, leaving their faces shrouded in darkness. She didn't need to see their faces. She knew everyone who was to be in attendance for this meeting. She was one of two women. The remaining five were men.

Five of the people in the meeting were in the United States. Besides Pelosi, there was another in California; Del Mar,

California to be exact. The only other woman was in Washington D.C. Of the two final attendees in the U.S., one was in New York City and the other, the chairman, was in Massachusetts. Of the two men outside the United States, one was in Germany and the other in Switzerland. Of course, this was not all the members of The Collective, but this group included some of the most influential, and the wealthiest.

The chairman began to speak. The bottom of his screen read '—Martha Vin.—'.

"I see that everyone is here. Before we begin, as always, I'll ask if anyone has any immediate security concerns."

No one spoke. No one moved. Any answer meant that something was wrong and the meeting would automatically be shut down.

After a five second pause, the chairman continued. "Good. Let's continue. As usual, the first order of business will be finances..."

The next forty-five minutes was taken up with the discussion of the multitude of funding sources and updates on the distribution of the billions of dollars at their disposal. Everyone is the group was being enriched by the coalition and they all preferred to discuss this aspect first. The attendee from Del Mar discussed the instructions to the Federal Reserve along with some adjustments to the short-term and long-term plans being implemented through them. This tied into the updates related to the International Monetary Fund. The representative in Germany was a controlling member of the IMF and he took the lead on that part of the discussion. The man in Switzerland gave updates from the World Economic Forum. After a very brief discussion, he yielded the conversation back to the chairman. They were not discussing new ideas, just providing updates.

The chairman acknowledged everyone's contribution, then quickly moved to the next subject. "I want to briefly touch on the border situation. We don't need to spend much time here, as very little has changed. However, the latest estimates are in and the number of future Democratic voters is looking great. Vice President Harris has done a tremendous job as the Border Czar." The joke elicited a collective, although restrained laugh from all in the group except for the man in Switzerland. He didn't entertain jokes in business meetings.

"Nancy, would you please share your findings with the group?" the chairman asked.

Nancy cleared her throat. She was not typically self-conscious about her voice, but compared to the chairman, she was aware that she sounded old. She sounded weak. She pushed the thought from her mind.

"The situation in Texas has forced the migrants west to enter the country through California, Arizona, and New Mexico. That caused a temporary slowdown."

She heard the waiver in her voice. She cleared her throat again. "However, our numbers are still holding and our people in ICE and the DHS have assured me that we *will* hit our 2024 goal." Despite not being able to see their faces, Nancy could make out the approving nods of the group.

Quick and to the point. She didn't want to speak any more than absolutely necessary. *Finish strong.*

"If there are any significant updates or changes, I'll notify the group immediately." She saw the chairman nod again.

"Thanks Nancy. Does anyone have anything to add?"

The screen marked '—NYC—' lit up. "Do we have a breakdown by nation of origin of the number of immigrants making it into the country?"

Nancy wasn't expecting any questions. "Oh, uh, yes, uh. I don't have that report with me, but uh, I'll...I'll get it...uh, for everyone."

If the screens had not been blacked out, the group would have seen Nancy flush with anger and embarrassment. She fumed. Soros knew she wouldn't be able to respond to that question off the cuff and he did that just to ambush her.

He spoke again. "That's fine, but may I assume that there are still plenty of people arriving from our ally countries?" he asked. He was referring to allies of The Collective, not allies of the United States. The two groups rarely overlapped.

Nancy saw her opportunity to recover. She knew the answer to this without consulting the document.

"Yes, tremendous numbers from China and Pakistan, with smaller numbers from Iran and various other countries," she stated with as much authority as she could muster.

"Of course, Latin American immigrants continue to pour in as well, which includes our Venezuelan friends," she added.

The chairman spoke up. He was ready to continue with the meeting. He had a tee time at an indoor driving range later. Warm weather was coming soon and he was looking forward to enjoying some time on the golf course.

"Good, Good. Thanks again Nancy." He said it with a tone of finality.

"Now, let's move on to Joe. Everyone should be up to date on the current situation. The handlers we have in place are doing everything they can to keep him upright. Unfortunately, they are reporting a rapid decline in his ability to continue the charade. His condition is quite obvious to everyone now. Our people in the news networks are still doing their jobs, downplaying his condition and calling it right-wing propaganda. Unfortunately, it doesn't appear to be working as well as we would like. Even some of our hard-core zealots are losing faith.

"In accordance with our last meeting, I have moved an additional medical asset in place to assist with his medication and monitoring, but let's just say that the situation is not ideal. I've spent enough time with him to know that he's fading fast. There will be no way to hide it in the upcoming debate. The docs are going to dose him with the cocktail we've been using to keep him going. However, it usually only works for about thirty to forty minutes at best. Ninety minutes is a pipe dream. If he somehow manages to stumble through the debate and emerge intact on the other side, great. However, it doesn't matter. He's going to crash and burn soon, and we're going to let him," he said, letting the words hang in the air for a moment.

The Washington screen lit up. "What are you saying, exactly?"

The chairman sighed and looked down at his watch. "I'm saying that we are going to throw Joe Biden to the wolves. We need to cut our losses and move on."

Nancy spoke up. "Are you talking about the nuclear option?"

The chairman paused. "No. At least not yet. I'm saying that if he doesn't agree to step down, we need to consider forcing the exit strategy. As you know, I've been meeting with him regularly. I've already breached the subject, probing to see what kind of response I would get. He's resisting. More accurately, *Jill* is resisting." He paused as he took a drink of water.

"The bottom line is that he simply will not be the Democratic candidate in November. One way or another, he will leave the race, he just doesn't know it yet. Jill has convinced him that he's going to run and win. We will convince him otherwise," the chairman stated in a very matter of fact tone.

"The Collective will determine who his replacement will be to run against the Republican candidate, and that will be that. Obviously, the existing political climate will require a more robust effort to influence the results of the election than we've used in the past. We don't want a repeat of 2016 when we didn't do enough. We underestimated the right-wing vote. Obviously, we didn't make that mistake in 2020, nor will we make that mistake this year."

The woman in Washington D.C. scoffed at the mention of the 2016 election. Then she realized what the chairman had said. "Wait, what do you mean *the Republican candidate*? You mean Trump, right?"

"For the time being. We'll continue our multifaceted attacks on Trump, and we'll make our final decision after the trial. For now, the trial is going according to plan, However, obviously it's creating a less than desirable reaction from the American public. They're beginning to view him as the victim and his popularity is actually increasing," the chairman responded. Disgust was obvious in his voice.

The woman's screen lit up again. "And the judge?"

The chairman responded. "As I've said before, the judge is bought and paid for. There's no need to worry about him. He's being very well compensated, plus he's a true believer. He'll do his part."

There was a brief moment of silence as everyone considered the last statement. Then the Washington screen lit up again. "If the trial doesn't get him out of the race, the nuclear option is still on the table though, correct?"

"You've made your preference very clear. We already know what your vote is," the chairman answered. He resisted shaking his head as he thought of the number of people who had died because they had crossed paths with that woman. She and her husband had left a trail of bodies in their wake. Not that the chairman had a problem killing people to protect his secrets or eliminate problems, but at least he was discreet.

"To answer your question, yes, the nuclear option is still on the table. In fact, one of our associates in the FBI is already developing an asset as we speak. Donald Trump thinks he's untouchable. He runs around in public like he's bulletproof. I promise you that he's not," the chairman responded, his voice cold and deliberate.

Switzerland's screen lit up. The man's voice had a notable German accent. "And the Secret Service? How will this *asset* get past the agents?"

The chairman chuckled. "Trust me Klaus, the Secret Service won't be a problem. I've taken care of that part personally." He flashed his signature smile that had charmed so many millions of people in the past, although no one in the group could see it.

"For now, we need to show some patience. There are a multitude of variables that have nothing to do with Trump which must be taken into consideration to ensure we maintain our position of power in the U.S. Government."

He temporarily slipped back into politician mode as he used one of his well-known phrases. "Let me be clear. We'll eliminate Trump with the pen or the sword. Once he's out of the way, it will be back to business as usual."

The screen in Germany lit up. "Thank you, Mr. Chairman. Might we move on to Ukraine and Israel?" He was all business. There was no emotion in his voice.

The chairman was thankful. He was tired of talking about Donald Trump.

"Of course. Please, go ahead."

"As you all know, Ukraine is going according to plan. However, the Israelis are not being completely cooperative. I'm sure you are all aware of the discontent this is creating with our Muslim allies," he said. Once again, this was a reference to allies of The Collective, not allies of the United States. This group held no loyalties to any country. They were loyal to power and money, not to nations.

"Yes, everyone is aware," responded the chairman.

The man in Germany continued. "However, we are still able to capitalize on the situation. It's bolstering our efforts to further divide the population. We are ramping up our activities to fund and organize the protests. Mr. Soros has taken the lead on that, as usual."

"Obviously we also have numerous District Attorneys on the payroll," the chairman added, even though everyone there already knew that.

The chairman continued, "If our protesters continue to get arrested, we'll just have our DAs release them without charges, or at least with very minimal charges. This will embolden them and make them feel like they're untouchable. The next time we use them, we can escalate our tactics and they'll go with it, assuming that nothing will happen to them. These protesters may be naïve, but they're useful. I'll admit that it's been somewhat entertaining to watch them. They're so certain they're holding some arbitrary moral high ground, but really all they're doing is helping to galvanize the national division we've worked so hard to build."

"Of course, it's also helpful that they're keeping public attention off our other efforts. Every headline is about the protests and the occupied campuses," the chairman added.

A slight chuckle escaped as he thought of the protestors. He viewed them as nothing more than a disposable asset to be used until it was depleted. They were the cannon fodder that The Collective would use in future wars and it still amazed him how easy they were to manipulate and transform into progressive zealots. Propaganda is a beautiful thing.

Washington spoke up again. "But there are divisions in our own party as well!" She spoke in an octave higher than normal, ruining the mood that the chairman was working to establish.

That tone of voice was maddening to the chairman. He had spent countless hours with her and her husband in the public eye and he had grown tired of hiding his disdain for her. He took a breath and responded calmly.

"We'll address those individuals one at a time. We'll allow them to continue to be pro-Israel, but we will encourage them to be pro-Israel *quietly*. They are a minor inconvenience. The Ukrainian situation will continue to be our primary effort for the immediate future. It's the most lucrative. I'm sure you're all pleased with your latest bonus from the Ukrainian aid package." He was intentionally redirecting the conversation.

Everyone was silent, despite the fact that the nearly million-dollar bonus was little more than pocket change to many members of The Collective. They had each received a gold bar, commonly referred to as a "Good Delivery" bar. These bars weigh roughly four hundred Troy ounces.

"That's what I thought. Everyone loves gold. Now, let's not lose focus on the big picture here. Regardless of which one of our options plays out, at the end of the day when the smoke clears, we *will* be on top. The plan is complex. That's why we have contingencies."

He continued, his tone shifting into politician mode once again.

"Now, I'm going to conclude this meeting. I'm sure we all have someplace to be. We will meet again as scheduled. However, I'll leave you with this: We're at a pivotal time in history. Our actions over the next few months will determine the extent of our success. We all know that in one way or another, America is going to suffer. That doesn't mean that we will. We'll continue to thrive, just like we're thriving now. We'll continue our efforts to fundamentally change America in ways that benefit us and our organization."

He paused as a smile spread across his face, unseen in the dark.

"And if America resists, we'll just have to push harder."

About the Author

Charlie Mike Adkins was born and raised in West Virginia, although he graduated High School from Millersburg Military Institute in Millersburg, Kentucky. He took an early interest in wilderness survival and the military, deciding at a young age that he wanted to pursue a career in the military, specifically Special Forces.

He served as an infantry paratrooper in the 1/509th Parachute Infantry Regiment (Fort Polk, LA) and the 3/505th Parachute Infantry Regiment of the 82nd Airborne Division (Fort Bragg, NC) before being selected for Special Forces and being assigned to the 7th Special Forces Group (Fort Bragg, NC and Eglin AFB, FL). His military service includes numerous overseas deployments including three combat tours in Afghanistan as a member of a Special Forces Operational Detachment-Alpha, or ODA. He also did extensive work in Central and South America including Venezuela, Honduras, Colombia, Bolivia, Suriname, and Guyana. He retired in 2013 after twenty-three years of active-duty service.

After retirement, he worked as a private security contractor in the U.S. and overseas. Additionally, he taught Human Behavior Pattern Recognition & Analysis (Terrorist Profiling) to various military and law enforcement units including the US Army Sniper School, Colombian Special Forces, and the US Secret Service, but primarily to units from the United States Special Operations Command (USSOCOM).

Charlie Mike also ran various other training courses including military land navigation, wilderness survival, children's survival, pistol and rifle marksmanship, kidnapping awareness and escape, lock-picking, and more.

Additionally, he worked for several years as a G-Chief/Unconventional Warfare (UW) Coach/Instructor for the

US Army Special Forces, the US Marine Corps Special Operations Command and the Canadian Special Forces.

His higher education includes both the United States Military Academy at West Point and Campbell University in Fort Bragg, NC. He now works in the private sector and lives on his own piece of Almost Heaven in West Virginia with his wife and two daughters.

Connect with Blacksmith Publishing

www.thepinelander.com

www.ingramcontent.com/pod-product-compliance
Lightning Source LLC
Chambersburg PA
CBHW021233190726
48289CB00005B/1306